Secrets of the Sewing Bee

Kate Thompson is a journalist with twenty years' experience as a writer for the broadsheets and women's weekly magazines. She is now freelance, and as well as writing for newspapers, she's a seasoned ghostwriter. *Secrets of the Sewing Bee* is her second novel, following the *Sunday Times* bestseller *Secrets of the Singer Girls*.

Praise for *Secrets of the Singer Girls*

'Poignant and moving'
Val Wood

'The way Kate Thompson writes . . . made me feel that I was reading about old friends. I just *had* to keep the pages turning. I am sure that before long her readers will be clamouring for more'
Pam Weaver

'Marvellous, full of gutsy characters I immediately empathised with'
Margaret Pemberton

'Kate Thompson is a brilliant author, who pulls her readers in to her novel and has them believing they are a part of it'
Mary Wood

Secrets

of the

Sewing Bee

Kate Thompson

PAN BOOKS

First published 2016 by Pan Books
an imprint of Pan Macmillan
20 New Wharf Road, London N1 9RR
Associated companies throughout the world
www.panmacmillan.com

ISBN   978-1-4472-8088-0

1 3 5 7 9 8 6 4 2

A CIP catalogue record for this book is available from the British Library.

Typeset by Palimpsest Book Production Limited, Falkirk, Stirlingshire
Printed and bound by CPI Group (UK) Ltd, Croydon, CR0 4YY

Visit **www.panmacmillan.com** to read more about all our books
and to buy them. You will also find features, author interviews and
news of any author events, and you can sign up for e-newsletters
so that you're always first to hear about our new releases.

In loving memory of my grandparents Joyce and Alan, Monica and Neilson, who lived and fought their way through the Second World War, in the factory, the RAF, at home and in the Royal Navy. Never forgotten.

Dedication

To all the women who stayed in the towns and cities of Britain during the Blitz and attempted to continue their day-to-day lives, working and raising children, as the bombs rained down around them. Over an intense eight-month period of nightly bombing raids, women found their streets transformed from the Home Front to a battlefront.

The Blitz was Hitler's attempt to bring Britain to heel. He believed it would have such a devastating effect on civilian morale that the government would be forced to negotiate peace terms. He underestimated the British character and overlooked their secret weapon – British women!

Life became a cherished gift, and living to see the dawn of a new day was far from a certainty. No one went to bed on a row or took a solitary moment of their life for granted. Or, as sparky eighty-nine-year-old Pat from St Hilda's East Community Centre in Club Row, East London, told me she used to say when she bade her fellow factory workers goodbye at the end of a shift, 'Goodnight, God bless, see you in the morning, PG [please God].'

Thank you, Pat, Dolly, Vera, Kathy, Sally, Vi, Emily, Nell, Peggy, Gladys, Minksy, Dot, Mags, Glad, Babs, Pat S. and Iris . . . mothers, machinists and East End Blitz survivors. God bless you all.

Prologue

As dawn broke, a pale winter light filtered through the high windows, seeping into the white-tiled sanatorium. Every part of her felt as if it was on fire, and her limbs, jerky and uncoordinated, twitched violently beneath the leather constraints that bound her to the rusty iron bed.

The slightest touch left the girl in agony; even the weight of the bed sheets against her skin was a pain that could not be borne, so much so that her physician had ordered that they be suspended over her body in a bed cradle. Six weeks she had lain like this, unable even to move her head without volts of hot pain slicing through her, day following torturous night . . . Apart from her mother's fortnightly visits, she had scarcely seen a soul, her loneliness sharpening her suffering. Soaked in sweat, at the height of her fever she had even begun to hallucinate, sworn she had seen the mythical Blind Beggar of Bethnal Green, cap in hand, pleading at the end of her bed.

The door swung open and the nurse entered to perform her morning treatment, clutching a white enamel dish in her hand. The patient followed the nurse with her eyes, her pupils dilating in horror as she realized it wasn't the usual lady on duty. The younger nurse with the soft, wavy hair and delicate hands always performed her treatments slowly, gently and rhythmically, so as to impose minimum suffering, and took time to carefully feed her spiced barley water and beef tea afterwards. The sour-faced nurse marching towards her now with a heavy step and florid cheeks possessed neither her deftness nor her compassion.

'Now, then, young lady, don't start with the trembling lip,' she ordered. With that, she cast aside the bed cradle, pulled out a brush and began to paint her limbs roughly with oil of wintergreen. The pain was exquisite, every touch like being brushed with shards of glass, and the girl wept hot tears of pain and fear.

'Well, whatever did you expect?' the nurse admonished briskly, when she had finished. 'It's the very nature of the beast. Licks the joints and bites the heart.'

The girl closed her eyes. When she opened them again, the nurse was gone. She didn't need her bitter sermonizing: she was all too familiar with her disease. This was her third attack in three years, each episode irrevocably damaging her body that bit more. She was deeply grateful to the guardians of the Poor Law, who sanctioned her stays, but the fear of the future was riveting, casting an even darker shadow over her adolescence. She was only ten, after all, a girl whose body was already giving up on her.

One

Never underestimate the power of a smile, thought Dolly Doolaney, daughter, sister, tea lady and all-round darling of the East End. Pausing outside the doors to the fifth floor of Trout's garment factory in Bethnal Green, she gripped the handles of her tea trolley, took a deep breath and plastered on a smile. She had been away from the factory for a little over a week now and it was vital no one guessed the truth about where she had really been.

For a second, her reflection sparkled back at her from the vast stainless-steel tea urn. Dolly took a moment to regard herself. The image was a pleasing one. Thirty-six years old, but her looks had not diminished over time. Cornflower-blue eyes, blonde curls peeking out under a red polka-dot turban and soft, dimpled cheeks.

Dolly may only have been five foot nothing, but the diminutive tea lady was a gently curving powerhouse, with a generous bosom and nipped-in waist, all wrapped up in a white pinafore.

Reaching into the pocket of her pinny, she fished out a tube of pillarbox-red Coty lipstick and, using the tea urn as a mirror, painted on a slick of colour. Smacking her lips together, her smile now dazzled that bit brighter. There, now. That was better. There was nothing in her reflection to betray her secret.

For a second, that practised smile quivered on her lips as she recalled the turbulent meeting she had just come from, at the end of which her mother's words still ricocheted through her brain: *Isn't it time you told them?*

Get a grip, Dolly Doolaney, she scolded, shaking herself to banish the image of her mother's face. The show must go on.

'All right, everybody, let's be having yer! I'm back now and I know how much you've missed me,' she hollered, using her tea trolley like a battering ram to push open the door to the factory floor. 'It's eleven o'clock. Shut them machines down and gather round. It's time for a nice cup of Rosie Lee.'

The vulnerability of moments earlier dissolved, as Dolly the consummate show woman burst into life. Thirty faces looked up and creased into warm smiles. Nothing was more anticipated than the sight of Dolly and her gleaming urn on Trout's daily tea breaks.

'Thank Gawd you're back,' yelled a voice from the back of the floor. 'We didn't 'alf miss yer.'

These hard-working seamstresses were relying on her, not just to dispense mugs of hot, strong tea, but also to keep up morale. Goodness knows that's what the factory foreman, Archie Gladstone, had told her often enough. 'As long as we've got our Dolly Do-Good' – as he affectionately called her – 'on our side, we'll win this war.' His garrulous laugh was so loud it almost took the roof off Trout's, and

Dolly always laughed along too. How could she reveal to Archie and the girls the private war she was waging?

Parking the tea trolley by the high windows of the former workhouse, Dolly stuck the brake on and grinned at her boss as he strode from his office.

'Welcome back, Doll,' Archie winked, as he perched on the corner of a workbench. 'You ain't 'alf a sight for sore eyes.'

'Nice to be appreciated, Arch. I might go away more often if this is the welcoming committee. All right, girls, what comes after "S"?' Dolly asked her attentive audience.

'"T"!' roared back thirty voices.

'How does Moses make his?'

'Hebrews it!' groaned Archie, rolling his eyes in mock despair.

'Enough of the jokes. Hurry up and get pouring, Doll. Me tongue's 'anging out,' shot back a veteran worker by the name of Pat Doggan. 'And don't yer dare go away again.'

A gale of raucous laughter rang round the room as Dolly picked up her giant pot and started to pour. The banter was good-natured. Dolly's patter was always the same: corny, predictable, but above all reassuring. And goodness knows they could do with some stability at troubled times like these.

The war was eight months and seven days old now, and the Bore War, as they had jokingly called it, was now firmly over. In the East End, there had been none of the jingoistic flag-waving that had accompanied the first war. The loss of so many good men was still felt in every quarter. Each narrow street in Bethnal Green contained the ghost of a man, shuffling about, begging or selling matchsticks under the arches at Wheeler Street just to survive.

Dolly had lost her own beloved father, Harry, one suffocatingly hot day in late June 1922, shortly after she had turned eighteen. It hadn't been trench warfare that had killed Harry, but the deadly gas he had inhaled that had finished him off years later. Coming so soon as it had after her other loss, his death had had a profound impact on her. If she closed her eyes, she could still picture the white rags in her hand staining crimson with blood, her father having coughed and gasped his last. War had turned her big, jovial bear of a father into a corpse. Dolly had lost not one but two very precious things that fateful week.

So today, she felt nothing but a weary resignation. News had been breaking on the wireless as she had left that morning that Holland, Belgium and Luxembourg might be next to fall. Dolly didn't even know where half these places were, just that every country that was invaded brought the Nazis one step closer to Britain.

Mind you, what they would make of it if they ever landed here in Bethnal Green Christ alone knew. They might have been just three miles east of the wide, tree-lined streets and gracious Regency mansions of London W1, but E2 – Dolly's postcode – was a very different neighbourhood.

Her eyes instinctively drifted to the open window and Dolly gazed out fondly at the familiar landscape below. Row after row of smoking back-to-back terraces stretched as far as the eye could see, punctuated by grocery stores, public houses, synagogues and backroom factories, all pumping putrid smells into the drowsy heat. It humbled Dolly every day to look out over her manor and think of all those thousands of people living, working and battling to survive.

In the street directly beneath Trout's, two children were playing, taking potshots at imaginary Germans, and further along the road, Dolly spied two women squabbling loudly over some flapping laundry in the yard of a tenement. She chuckled to herself as their shrieking voices carried on the breeze. The language was enough to make her gran turn in her urn, but no matter – they'd be firm friends again by dinnertime.

It might have been airless, parochial and an impossible place for an outsider to understand, but Bethnal Green, E2, was home. It was Dolly's beloved East End and she would sooner die than see a swastika flag flying on the roof of the town hall.

Sighing, she turned her attention back to the job in hand. Out of respect, Dolly always served tea for Archie first, then the older, veteran workers, swiftly identifying which mug belonged to whom by the small but brightly coloured rags she tied round the handles.

'Here you go, ducks. How's your rheumatics?' she smiled brightly to Pat, handing her a tannin-stained enamel mug with a bolt of vivid scarlet material wound round the handle. Dolly took pride in matching the colour of the rag to the personality of the mug's owner.

'Mustn't grumble,' grinned Pat, taking a noisy gulp of her tea. 'Blow me, Doll. No one can hold a candle to your tea.'

It was widely regarded that Dolly's brews – hot, sweet and so strong you could almost stand a spoon up in the swirling brown liquid – were the best in all the East End, and when it came to the drinking of them, no one could out-slurp Pat Doggan. Her tea-drinking was legendary in the factory.

'I'm so glad you're back,' she went on. 'Your replacement was next to bleedin' useless. Tiny little thing she was, so skinny she couldn't have knocked the skin off a rice pudding, and as for 'er tea! Talk about weak. I 'alf wondered if it weren't nun's piss she was serving up.' Pat sniffed in disgust, placing her tea down on her workbench to tighten her turban and anchor the metal curlers underneath. In one swift move, she extracted a Craven 'A' cigarette at the same time and popped it behind her ear. 'Your tea's the only reason I come to work, Doll. That and to get away from my useless lump of a husband. He was knee-deep in the beers last night and betting all my housekeeping on the nags. Waste of bleedin' space.'

Dolly chuckled. Yes. Pat was definitely a scarlet-rag person.

'Mind your language, Pat – there's young girls present,' rang out a terse voice from the other side of the factory floor. Dolly glanced up and through the steam saw the slight figure of Vera Shadwell, the factory forelady, marching towards her trolley, accompanied by a small slip of a girl.

Pat rolled her eyes and leaned forward conspiratorially. 'Don't know what's eating 'er recently,' she scowled, her gigantic bosom straining beneath her wraparound pinafore. 'She's been biting chunks out of everyone all week like I don't know what. Even Archie's copped it.'

Pat's eyes narrowed and she looked about cautiously as if she were imparting state secrets, not factory gossip. 'We had a trial run of using the shelter yesterday and she refused to come down, said she suffered from claustrophobia, whatever that is.'

Pat wasn't known as Trout's foghorn for nothing. Her voice was easily the loudest on the floor, drowning out the rumble of thirty or so Singer sewing machines and the gale of laughter and song that accompanied it.

Pat swiftly moved on as Vera neared the tea trolley. 'Blimey, would you look at 'er phizog. I'm off for my ciggie,' she muttered. 'Ta for the tea, Doll.'

'That woman,' snapped Vera, exasperated, as Pat stomped down the stairs to the small yard out back. 'No respect, that's her problem.'

Dolly smiled at her old friend as she passed her a mug of tea with a royal-blue rag wrapped round the handle.

'Pay her no mind, Vera,' Dolly said, patting her hand. 'It's been hard for her, for all the women, in fact, adjusting to the new workload.'

'You think I don't know that, Dolly?' Vera replied stiffly, dashing away a greying hair that had escaped from her tightly knotted bun. 'But we have a duty to our country. In the last war, my mother, Anne – God rest her soul – worked at a concern up Sugar Loaf Walk. Milns, Cartwright & Co. took on women to replace the men sent to fight, but, by God, those proud women proved their worth. She put in sixteen-hour days, seven days a week, making army uniforms for the troops.' She finished with a deep sigh of martyrdom. 'Women today don't know they're born.'

Dear old Vera. Dolly knew the troubles that plagued her old friend so well, and unlike her, she couldn't seem to hide her problems easily. Vera Shadwell fell out of the cradle as a factory forelady, and respectability and decency were the bywords that governed her life. Little wonder the women called her 'Kippers and Curtains' behind her starched back. At thirty-two, Vera was four years younger than Dolly, but with her prematurely greying hair, buttoned-up black blouse and old-fashioned, ankle-skimming black skirt, you would never have guessed.

As a forelady and a tea lady, at opposite ends of the social scale, their friendship was unusual to say the least, but having both grown up in Tavern Street in Bethnal Green, their roots in a shared community knitted them together as tightly as kith and kin. When neither had married nor raised children by the age of thirty, that bond had only deepened, and now Vera leaned on Dolly, emotionally and practically. Dolly knew her old friend could never cope with knowing her explosive secret.

'You're right, of course, Vera, and in time they'll come to see that,' Dolly said soothingly.

Vera sighed. 'Bless you, Dolly. I honestly don't know what I'd do without you here as my ally. You going away like that so suddenly made me realize how much I'd miss you if you weren't here. Maybe I should be more tolerant, but the work . . . The government just can't get us doing enough. Why, only yesterday Mr Gladstone received an order for eighty more consignments of field bandages to be delivered by the end of this week. They seem to think we're as big as London Brothers, but they must have nigh on a hundred workers there.

'Do you know,' she went on, 'I even heard that Cole & Sons in Stepney now insists the day workers do piecework from home in the evenings, on top of their daytime shifts, so they can meet their uniform deadlines? So you see, I'm not the slave driver the women would have you believe.'

'True,' agreed Dolly. 'But they have just installed a welfare room and given the women a rise.'

Agitated, Vera fingered the top button of her blouse. 'That's as maybe, but I don't know how we're expected to deliver, though deliver we must.'

Until recently, Trout's had been producers of children's wear, supplying the poshest stores up West – Marks & Spencer, Bourne & Hollingsworth and, rumour had it, even Harrods – but now, as it had in the Great War, production had switched to essential war work, sewing surgical field bandages and army and navy uniforms for the troops. The Irish machine used for embroidery lay silent and dusty in a corner.

Dolly knew that replacing delicate embroidered garments with army battledress had been a heavy blow for the machinists of Trout's, all of whom were highly skilled needlewomen and for whom working in the rag trade was bred in the bone. It had also brought the sobering reality of war into sharp focus. How could the women escape the heartache of having a loved one in the forces when it could very well be his uniform they were sewing?

Vera's face darkened, and she lowered her voice to a whisper. 'Can they really think that we will need all those bandages, that so much blood will be spilt by our menfolk?'

Dolly knew the question didn't really require an answer. Vera had listened to the news of the Nazis' advance across Europe, just as she had.

'So tell me, how did you get on at your auntie's? Is she feeling any better? Where is it she lives again?' Vera asked.

Dolly hesitated. She hated lying to her old friend, but there were times when small white lies were the kindest thing of all.

'She moved down the line to Dagenham,' she said. 'Poor old girl had another fall, and what with her being Mum's oldest sister, I promised I'd look after her until Mum can get up there herself. Thanks for granting me the time off, Vera. I promise to make the hours up.'

'I don't doubt it – you've not let me down yet,' Vera replied. 'No disrespect to your auntie, but this is what happens when people leave the streets they were born in for these fancy new builds in the suburbs. I mean to say, what use is a big garden to her now? Better to stay close to your own.'

Suddenly, the young girl standing a step behind Vera coughed, and for the first time in the conversation, both women seemed to become aware of her.

'Where's my manners?' grinned Dolly, grateful for the interruption. 'Are you a new starter, sweetheart? How do you like your tea?'

'Oh, please, ma'am, don't go to any trouble,' blustered the girl, who Dolly put at around eighteen.

Gracious, but she was a timid little thing, not like some of the cocky young girls at Trout's. Her slate-grey eyes seemed lost in the white pallor of her face, and her long curtain of chestnut-brown hair was scraped back into a bun. Dolly immediately wanted to feed her a big hunk of bread and dripping. Poor girl wasn't further through than a coat hanger.

'Nonsense. Nice mug of hot tea's just what you need by the looks of you,' she beamed, picking up a new mug from her trolley. After surveying the girl for a moment, she thoughtfully selected a delicate piece of soft dove-grey material from under her trolley, wrapped it round the handle, filled it to the brim with piping-hot tea and popped in an extra sugar lump.

'There you go, my darlin',' she beamed, 'and don't call me "ma'am". You make me feel ancient! I know I'm thirty-six, but I'm not on my last knockings yet.' She extended her hand. 'Dolly Doolaney's the name. I'm just the tea lady here – bit thick to do much else, truth be told – but I do serve up a decent cuppa. Welcome to the Trout's family. Don't mind this lot,' she added, gesturing to the rest of the factory workers, who had cranked up the wireless and were singing a rousing rendition of 'Wish Me Luck As You Wave Me Goodbye' while they guzzled their tea.

'I swear they never sang this much before the war. Anyways, they're a bit rough round the edges, but salt of the earth, all of 'em,' she joked.

''Ere, Doll. Who you calling rough?' shrieked one. 'I'll 'ave you know I'm dead posh,' she joked, cocking her little finger and wagging it in their direction. 'By the way, you still all right to sit for my two tonight while I nip out?'

'Course, lovey. I'm looking forward to it.'

Dolly was still chuckling as she turned back to the new starter. 'So sorry, darlin'. Wotcha say your name was again?'

'Flossy Brown, ma'am. Sorry, I mean Dolly. Old habits die hard. When I lived at the home, we always had to address Matron and the domestic staff as "ma'am", so calling people by their Christian names takes some getting used to,' she smiled timidly.

'I recruited Flossy from a small Jewish tailor's just up

the road,' Vera chipped in. 'She's a skilled hand seamstress apparently, so shouldn't take her long to find her way round a machine. Before that, she lived at a children's home in Shoreditch. Her welfare officer visited myself and Mr Gladstone last week. She felt working in a larger concern such as Trout's would be of greater benefit to Flossy and the war effort than simply hand-stitching suits in a small family firm, and I'm glad of the extra help.

'She's sorted her out with lodgings not far from us in Tavern Street. I've got another new starter, Peggy Piper, arriving tomorrow and I've sat them both together on the apprentice bench. I know you'll look out for them both while they find their feet, won't you, Dolly? Dolly . . . are you quite well? You're as white as a ghost!'

Dolly heard Vera's words, but they seemed to be echoing around somewhere in the back of her head. She had the queerest sensation, as if she had been sucked into a giant wave and was being tumbled through pounding surf.

Dolly was thunderstruck as she gazed on the young girl's pretty face. She had thought there seemed something familiar about her when she first clapped eyes on her. Flossy Brown. How could it be? How? Today of all days . . . Her past seemed to be gaining on her as surely as the German juggernauts' advance across Europe. Fate had a hand in this; of that Dolly was sure.

Quickly recovering her composure, she put an arm round the shy orphan and squeezed her shoulder reassuringly.

'Don't you worry about a thing, Vera. I'll look after this lovely young girl.'

'Splendid,' replied Vera, smiling for the first time that day. 'I knew I could rely on you, Dolly.'

With that, Vera turned to her newest recruit. 'Flossy, I'm sure you and this other new girl will be firm friends in no time.'

Vera glanced down at the watch on her birdlike wrist and the look of brisk efficiency returned at once. She placed her mug back on Dolly's trolley with a resounding clatter and clapped her hands together. 'Tea break's over, girls,' she said curtly. 'Back to your stations. There's work to tend to.'

＊

From the moment Dolly Doolaney had swept onto the factory floor pushing her trolley, Flossy had been captivated. Dolly was not like any other woman she had ever met. There was something else too. Something Flossy couldn't quite put her finger on. As she had watched her pour tea and crack jokes with the factory workers, Flossy had felt the strangest of sensations wash over her, an overwhelming sense of familiarity.

Settled behind her sewing machine, Flossy had to pinch herself once more at her good fortune. She really had been most grateful when her welfare officer had secured her employment at the tailor's, but it was such a tiny firm. Just Flossy, a rather strict pattern-cutter and one other elderly woman, sat on tiny wooden stools, hand-stitching suits in the gloom and silence of the governor's front room. The time had crawled by so slowly that a minute had felt like an hour. But one morning at Trout's and already Flossy could see it couldn't be more different.

The high windows of Trout's garment factory afforded little light, and the floor was strewn with cotton and waste material. The room was packed to the gunnels. There must have been thirty or so women of all ages, Flossy noted, from the fourteen-year-old apprentices right up to formidable-looking veteran factory workers, like Pat, in their fifties.

Flossy had never seen so many sewing machines, all lined up like soldiers. Under each machine lay bundles of material, and the benches contained wells into which the women threw their finished bundles.

Penny song sheets were gaily slung from machine to machine like bunting. Not that the women seemed to need them, for most of them were singing along at the top of their voices to be heard over the hum of the machines, their hands a blur of seamless activity.

Those who weren't singing were chattering away ten to the dozen, their faces animated as they loudly gossiped over the humming of the machines and the other women's song. The noise of it all was something else and already Flossy felt her ears ringing. It was also stiflingly hot, and the unseasonably warm May sunshine beat down on the windows, which had been crisscrossed with anti-blast tape. The furnace-like heat wasn't helped by a giant Hoffman clothes press, which pumped out clouds of steam at the back of the room. Not that the other workers seemed to mind the temperature, though a few of the women had tied rags to the wheels of their machines, which gave off a limp breeze as they spun round. This did little to permeate the intense fug of heat and hormones, Flossy observed with a wry smile, but she admired their ingenuity all the same.

In among the organized chaos, Dolly weaved her way round the floor, sweeping up rag ends and bantering back and forth merrily with the women. A mouse scampered across the concrete floor in plain sight of all. No one batted an eyelid! It was like entering a club, Flossy mused, where everyone knew the unspoken codes except her.

It was also extraordinary how different two East End factories could be. Not that she should be that shocked, she supposed. Having grown up in a children's home in nearby Shoreditch, she was more than accustomed to the sharp contrasts of life lived in the East End.

Inside the ruthlessly clean and carbolic-scented four walls of the institution that had been her home since she was a baby, Flossy was used to obeying rules. After a morning of prayers, domestic chores and schooling, the girls would troop single file back to their sparse dormitories to rest. Flossy would lie on her bunk and stare out of the windows of her dorm, down at the maze of narrow, unlit streets, filled with darkened brick terrace houses, which clustered around the Victorian home like naughty children at their governess's knee.

All life was out there on the streets, and they teemed with fun and boundless possibility. Day after day, month after year, Flossy had gazed down longingly at the shrieking children beneath as they roamed the neighbourhood in huge packs, swinging on gas lamps or playing dead man's dark scenery. Not for them the misery of enforced rest or monitored playtime. In fact, Flossy doubted the gangs of local kids had ever had to walk single file anywhere. The streets and cobbled alleys were their playground, and they were free to run, hop, skip or jump wherever their fancy took them, their vivid imaginations replacing toys. So absorbed had Flossy once been watching them career up the street in a go-kart made from a fruit box and some pram wheels that she hadn't spotted Matron come in for her daily dorm inspection.

'Wicked, godless children,' she'd shrieked loudly behind Flossy, before slamming the window shut.

That misdemeanour had earned Flossy an extra three hours in the laundry with a flat iron, but it hadn't been enough to stop her spying. By watching from her window onto another world, Flossy had worked out that East End mums were fiercely protective of their children. It hadn't been unusual to see fistfights erupt in the streets between two mothers when one child had been taking liberties with another. Those children were loved, and nurtured, a valuable cog in a wider neighbourhood of rich family life.

Closing her eyes, Flossy suddenly felt something twist and lurch painfully inside her. The truth was inescapable. For also out there, on those same narrow, cobbled streets, was a mother, her mother, who had abandoned her.

'Penny for 'em,' rang out a voice, and Flossy's eyes snapped open.

There was Dolly, crouched down beside her. The tea lady's soft face gazed at her inquisitively. Close up, she was even more perfect and Flossy longed to reach out and stroke her velvety skin to see if it felt as smooth as it looked. She smelt faintly of violet water, and her eyes were quite the bluest Flossy had ever seen.

'Sorry, Dolly. I was just wondering if I'll be able to pick up this machining lark,' Flossy blustered, struggling to make her voice heard over the din as she wiped her brow.

'Packed in like sardines, aren't we? When one breathes out, the other has to breathe in,' Dolly joked. 'But don't worry. You'll get used to it soon enough. Watch the old-timers like Pat and Ivy – they'll show you what to do. Just keep your eyes open and work hard. You're not afraid of hard work, are you?'

Flossy shook her heard vigorously. 'Oh no, Dolly, ma'am. We worked hard every day at the orphanage.'

'I know you did, sweetheart . . .' Dolly said. She seemed about to say something else too, but at that moment, the door to Archie Gladstone's office flew open and the burly little foreman bowled out.

'Stop your jawing and pay attention, girls,' he ordered in such a booming voice Flossy flinched. He was flanked by his forelady, Vera, standing so stiffly she looked like an army major on manoeuvres.

'Don't mind the gov'nor,' whispered Dolly. 'He may seem a little brusque, but he's a diamond in the rough. He'd give you his last shilling if you asked for it.'

Staring at the gruff little man, with his craggy features and broken nose, Flossy was quite sure she would never have the nerve to ask him for a farthing, much less a shilling.

'I'll get to the point. I have news,' Archie announced. 'It's official. The Huns have invaded Holland, Belgium and Luxembourg, and now they're marching on France. The days of stitching dresses are well and truly over for us, and something tells me it's only going to get worse before it gets better.'

A feeling of despair swept over the floor, but Archie was quick to pick up on the mood.

'Now listen here, girls!' he thundered. 'I'm relying on you to give your best and support your factory forelady so that we get the work done,' he said, staring pointedly at

Pat. 'Vera asks you to jump, you say, "How high?" You women – each and every one of yer – have a part to play, and you have to serve our country in her hour of need. Let's not be under any illusions: we have a hard slog and many sacrifices ahead, but I know my girls – we're all up to the job! I don't want no defeatist talk from anyone.'

'Too bloody right,' piped up Pat. 'That 'itler ain't marching into my country. Not while I've got a hole in my arse!'

Pat's vulgar joke lightened the mood and the women fell about in howls of laughter. Only Vera's lips remained tightly pursed together in disapproval.

'Not sure I'd have phrased it quite like that myself, Pat,' said Archie, with a throaty chuckle. 'But the sentiment's the right one. We must fight for Blighty. We drove Mosley's blackshirts out of the East End before the war and we ain't going to stand for none of that fascist nonsense now neither.'

Up until now, Flossy had been listening with a mixture of bewilderment and awe, but suddenly she realized the factory foreman was staring straight at her.

'You, new girl. What's yer name?'

Flossy felt her tongue cleave to the roof of her mouth as all eyes in the room swivelled to stare at her.

Dolly's hand reached out and squeezed her shoulder. 'Tell him your name, love,' she coaxed.

'F-Flossy Brown, sir,' she stammered.

'Well, young Flossy Brown, you and our new prime minister, Winston Churchill, have something in common.'

'We do?' she gulped, aware that her cheeks had flushed a high crimson.

'Yeah. You're both starting new jobs today. His might be

at number 10 Downing Street, Whitehall, and yours at Trout's, Bethnal Green, but your new role in life is every bit as important as his.'

Try as she might, Flossy couldn't see how her new job as an East End seamstress could compete with the prime minister's. In fact, she felt about as significant as the tiny mouse she had seen scampering for cover earlier on.

Archie drummed a stubby little finger down on the workbench before pointing it at Flossy. 'He has to find a way to win this war, but it's girls like you, Flossy, on the Home Front, that are giving him the tools to do it. Every stitch you sew is helping to win this war.'

Flossy felt he might have been overplaying her role somewhat, but she smiled back all the same and nodded her head.

'I won't let you down, Mr Gladstone,' she whispered shyly.

'Good girl. I know you won't. You're a part of the Trout's family now, and like all families, we bicker, we get fed up of each other, but above all, we've always got each other's backs. Understood?'

Flossy nodded and felt a little ripple of warmth spread through her. For the first time in her life, she was truly in the thick of things.

'Now for some brighter news,' the foreman went on. 'As you know, Empire Day's coming up. On the day, a lot of local factories will be raising money for the navy, which is admirable, and Vera will also be passing a collection bucket round too. I'll bet a penny to a pound half of you lot in here have a loved one working either in the merchant navy or in HM Navy, but I have another way in which we can show our patriotism towards these brave lads.'

His pale blue eyes sparkled as he pulled a crumpled piece of paper from his back pocket. 'On here are twenty-seven names of the crew of HMS *Avenge*, a British naval mine-sweeper. The men of the minesweepers are among the bravest there are and have one of the most dangerous jobs at sea. I know this 'cause my younger cousin is one of 'em on board, and he has requested pen pals for all his shipmates. They're risking their lives for our liberty and all they want is word from the Home Front and a few friendly letters. Who'll oblige?'

There was an instant show of hands and a clamour of excitement on the factory floor, especially, Flossy noted, among the younger women. All traces of the dark mood of earlier was now gone, replaced with renewed fight, thanks to their foreman's rousing speech, not to mention the prospect of contact with the opposite sex!

'That's the ticket,' Archie nodded approvingly. 'Dolly, if you'd be so kind as to hand round the names of the sailors to those that want to write . . .'

'Course I will, Arch,' chirruped Dolly.

'Oh, and one last thing, girls, before we get back to work. Two new starters are arriving tomorrow: another seamstress to lighten the load and a new odd-job man and mechanic. I know you've all been grumbling like mad since Alf's been called up. Lucky Johnstone is a lovely eighteen-year-old lad I know from my boxing club. Be kind to him, girls, will yer? Don't eat him alive.'

'Where's he from, Mr G?' asked a sassy-looking young machinist with a halo of bright copper curls. 'And more importantly, will we fancy him?'

'Well, he's got a pulse, so I'm sure you will,' Archie shot

back. 'He's from right here in Bethnal Green, as it happens
. . . Russia Lane.'

'Ooh blimey, I know Russia Lane all right,' she replied.
'Police only dare go in there in pairs.'

'So he'll know how to handle himself,' Archie retorted.
'And he'll need to around you rabble. Anyway, enough of
this yapping. Let's *extractum digitum*, as the ancient Romans
would say.'

'You what?' gawped Pat.

'Pull your finger out. Our boys are relying on us for
uniforms.'

As the floor settled down to work, Flossy glanced at the
empty seat next to her on the apprentice bench. It would
be lovely to have someone else to learn the ropes with. She
hoped this girl, whoever she was, was the friendly sort,
perhaps even the sort she could confide in. With that, she
gazed down at her handbag, tucked safely just beside the
treadle under her machine.

The package had arrived at her lodgings two days ago,
in plenty of time for her birthday.

It was the same every year on 10 May, only this time it
had been forwarded on from the orphanage to her new
address in Bethnal Green.

Flossy had hardly dared to hope that the anonymous gifts
would keep on arriving even after she left the home. She
had assumed that once she started a new life outside the
four walls of the institute, they would stop, especially now
the orphanage had been evacuated. So when the postman
had delivered the brown waxed-paper package to her tiny
digs, a sweet rush of delirium had filled her veins. There
had been no time to open the parcel that morning, as she

had no wish to be late on her first day at Trout's, so instead she had carefully placed it in her bag before walking to work. But she already knew what the package would contain, for each year it was the same: the most beautiful-smelling treasures one could ever dream of – bars of Sunlight soap, talcum powder and a snowy-white full-length cotton under-skirt. Small but thoughtfully chosen gifts that told Flossy someone cared.

The first time she recalled opening one must have been around her eighth birthday. It had only been a wooden red-and-blue spinning top, but the cheerful little gift had lodged in her child's memory.

As Flossy had grown and matured so had the gifts. The spinning top had been followed a year later by a charming rag doll with corn-coloured plaits, just the right size to nestle into the crook of a nine-year-old girl's arm, but then on her tenth birthday had come the gift that had given her the sweetest joy of all, a slightly dog-eared copy of Anna Sewell's *Black Beauty*, which she had devoured each night after lights-out by the moonlight seeping in from the dormitory window. It was just words on a page, but the story had transported her from a narrow view of ramshackle tiled rooftops to wide, rolling pastures.

Age thirteen, the books had given way to sensible under-skirts and soap, birthday gifts to mark her transition into adolescence.

Matron had been at pains to stress the parcels were prob-ably from an altruistic, wealthy local business, anonymously gifting the poor and needy. Flossy could still hear her barbed voice in her head now when she had first asked whether the gifts could be from a family member: *Young lady, remove any fanciful notions from your head immediately. The children who enter this home do so through the death, vice, neglect or extreme poverty of their parents, or because they are left abandoned as foundlings.*

But each year, as it would this evening, tearing open the package gave Flossy the only real hope she had ever known, for in her heart, she was convinced the sender could only be one person.

'And here's your sailor, Flossy.' Dolly's voice snapped her out of her reverie. 'Sorry,' she added, with an apologetic grin, as she handed Flossy a piece of paper. 'His name's the last on the list.'

'That's all right. I don't mind a bit,' Flossy replied quickly, glancing down at the paper. 'Tommy Bird! Golly, what a smashing name. He sounds like a comic-book superhero,' she chuckled. 'I hope he doesn't mind being stuck with me.'

'I'd say he's a very lucky chap indeed to be paired with you,' Dolly asserted.

As the tea lady bustled off, Flossy found herself wondering what words of comfort she could offer to such a brave young man, risking his life to defend his country.

She only hoped her letters would provide him with as much succour as her mystery parcels offered her each year.

When the final bell sounded to mark the end of the shift, Flossy rose wearily to her feet. Her ears were throbbing from the whirring of the machines, and her eyes were as dry as parchment. The rest of the floor was a giddy whirl of gaiety, though. The younger women were busy tearing out their curlers and doing their eyelashes. There was much fluffing of hair and pinching of cheeks. Fresh stockings were slipped on, perfume dabbed on behind the ears and lipstick touched up as excited young workers talked eagerly about which dance they were going to or speculated about their pen-pal sailors.

Flossy watched, wincing as the lively redhead who had bantered with the foreman earlier deftly pierced her pal's ears with a factory needle, still threaded with cotton, before setting about her eyebrows with some tweezers.

The recipient caught Flossy staring and winked. 'You admiring my beauty spot, sweetheart?' she asked. 'Shall I let you into a secret? It's the black bit outta a winkle. Looks the real deal, though, don't it?'

She extended a slender hand over the workbench and Flossy found herself intimidated by her verve and vigour. Her arched eyebrows and sophisticated victory rolls gave the appearance of an older woman, but Flossy guessed she about seventeen.

'My e's Daisy Shadwell, and this here is my best mate, Sal owler,' she smiled, gesturing to the redhead. 'Vera's my big sister, but don't hold that against me,' she added, wincing as she cautiously dabbed her tender earlobes with a hanky. 'Me and Sal are off to a dance up at Shoreditch Town Hall. Why don't you join us? I'm sixteen, nearly seventeen, but Sal's twenty-two, so Vera lets me as long as Sal chaperones me.'

'That's right. It won't cost you nothing either,' said Sal, who despite having a less refined beauty was still striking, with her wide, slightly crooked smile and vivid red hair. 'I got a mate who works there who always leaves the side door open. I can even tidy those eyebrows up for you if you like,' she added, snapping her tweezers in Flossy's direction.

'Go on – we're going to paint the town red tonight,' purred the forelady's younger sister, extracting a tube of Tangee lipstick from her purse and slicking it on.

'Erm . . . thanks ever so, but I have plans,' Flossy lied. She didn't like to tell these worldly-wise girls that she had never been to a dance before. She had never even painted the town pink, much less red.

'Suit yourself,' shrugged Sal. 'But if you change your mind, you know where we are.'

'Thanks, girls,' she smiled appreciatively. 'It's nice to be asked.'

Flossy watched as the pair teetered giggling out of the factory, their work pinafores and flat shoes tucked away in brown paper packages under their arms.

As she hastily grabbed her bag, the parcel fell out, just as Dolly reached the side of her workbench.

'I was just coming to see how you found your first day,' she said breezily. 'See you met our Daisy and Sal. They're quite a pair. Don't be fooled by Sal, though. I know she comes across as a bit of a saucy piece, but she's devoted to her two young boys, and now they've been evacuated, she misses them something rotten.'

Suddenly, Dolly spotted the parcel on the concrete floor and bent down to pick it up. 'Is this yours?' she asked, handing the package to Flossy. 'What is it?'

'Oh, nothing,' Flossy said, blushing. 'It's . . . Well, it's just my birthday. It's a gift that was forwarded on from the orphanage.'

'Just your birthday!' exclaimed Dolly. 'Fancy not telling me, you daft apeth! How old are you?'

'Oh, I didn't like to make a fuss. I've just turned eighteen. We didn't really celebrate birthdays at the orphanage, you see . . .' Her voice trailed off uncomfortably.

'Well, we do here at Trout's. Happy birthday, sweetheart,' Dolly beamed, enveloping her in an enormous hug.

Feeling the warmth of Dolly's arms wrapped round her, Flossy savoured her embrace and the comforting smell of lavender soap on her cheeks. Being hugged by Dolly Doolaney was like slipping into a warm, scented bath, she thought with a smile. It was only a cuddle – two arms holding her tight – but with that embrace came security and a powerful sense of belonging. And so that precious thing a friendship was born.

'Good to see you smiling,' Dolly said as she pulled back. 'So, do you think you're going to like it here, Flossy?'

'Very much so,' Flossy replied earnestly, her grey eyes shining like a soft, milky dawn. 'It's going to be the start of a whole new life for me.'

Flossy meant every word. Maybe starting at Trout's would give her the confidence she needed to finally set about uncovering the truth.

Another question lingered . . . Did she have the nerve to ask her new friend Dolly to help her? Would the street-smart tea lady think her stupid for wanting to search for a mother who had never featured in her life? Or worse, delusional for thinking that she might be behind the anonymous gifts?

Flossy gazed up at Dolly's face and tried to assemble her muddled thoughts into something resembling a question.

'What is it, love?' asked Dolly, her smile melting into concern. 'You look like you've got something on your mind.'

Flossy heard Matron's sharp, scornful voice tearing through her brain and she faltered, feeling foolish.

'It's nothing, Dolly. See you in the morning.'

Two

Dolly whistled to herself as she heaped tea leaves into the urn and listened to the creak and rumble of the giant kettles heating up in the staff-canteen kitchens. She loved this time of morning, half past ten, when she merrily set up her tea trolley and had some peace and quiet before the thirsty rabble descended. Although recently her own tumbling thoughts hadn't provided any respite from the growing turmoil both inside and outside her home. Still, today was a new day and she was determined not to dwell on the trauma of the previous week.

Spring sunshine streamed in through the open windows, dappling the white-tiled walls and splashing the old copper with dancing lights. Dolly was an optimist by heart and it seemed such a sin to be fighting a war when nothing but blue skies stretched overhead.

She had left early that morning to build in time on her walk to Trout's to detour past Victoria Park, and the flowers had been bursting into bud. They were certainly having a ravishing spring, and Dolly had savoured every breath of sweet air in her lungs. She had half wanted to stretch out on the grass and listen to the birdsong and the soft snuffling of the piglets in their pens next to the allotments. Baby pigs and potatoes in a city park? Whatever next?! Intriguing sights were certainly popping up all over, thanks to this war.

The image of Flossy Brown's sweet, hopeful face immediately sprang to mind. Shaking herself a little, she took out a clean, dry cloth and lovingly polished all the mugs on the trolley until the heavy tannin rings faded away and they shone like new pins. If only she could wipe away every last scrap of sadness from that poor little mite so easily. Her mind cast back to the hug she had given Flossy yesterday at clocking-off time. She could still feel those bony little shoulders in her arms. Flossy had felt untreasured, nothing but a girl with a heart full of unused affection. Well, she was here now, and that was what counted. Dolly was determined to make the orphan realize she was cherished . . . before it was too late.

There was something else too, something nagging deep inside Dolly, making her feel distinctly uneasy. As she set the mug down smartly on the trolley, her heart started to palpate. Twisting the frayed cloth between her fingers, Dolly realized that her hands were trembling.

The young lady's sudden appearance on the factory floor was bringing the events of that terrible day flooding back into sharp focus. Dolly's stomach lurched at the memory. Exactly how much did Flossy remember of her childhood? Could she possibly remember . . . ?

No, no, no.

Pushing down the familiar waves of guilt and panic, Dolly forced herself to take some deep, calming breaths. It was all such a long, long time ago, buried in the dim and distant past, and that's precisely where it should remain.

By the eleven-o'clock tea break, Dolly had managed to compose herself, and out on the factory floor, she spotted the new machinist, Peggy, straight away. It wasn't hard. She stuck out like a sore thumb. Dolly chewed her bottom lip pensively. Good grief! The girl looked like she had high-stepped straight out of the pages of *Vogue*. She wouldn't last two minutes at Trout's looking like that. Best get to her before Vera did.

'Morning, Flossy. You've met our new starter, then, I see . . . Hello,' she smiled, turning to Peggy and stretching out her hand. 'My name's Dolly. I'm the tea lady here and all-round dogsbody. What's your name, sweetheart, and how do you take your tea?'

'Peggy Piper,' the girl replied with a tight little smile, ignoring Dolly's outstretched hand. 'Darjeeling with a slice of lemon.'

Dolly's eyebrows shot up. 'Darjeeling, ducks? Not sure I've got any of that foreign stuff in my trolley,' she smiled, undeterred. 'But I do brew up a mean British cuppa.'

Dolly hesitated. 'Listen, love, I don't mean to be a nose ointment, but just a friendly word – the bosses here, they have a fairly strict dress code. There's no uniform as such, just a pinny to stop you getting covered in fluff, but they don't really like the girls wearing their hair down, as it's a danger if it gets stuck in machinery. Or high heels. They skid something rotten on this concrete floor. I should know,' she chuckled.

Peggy was done up to the nines. Her shining hair had

been styled into soft waves, which fell about her delicate shoulders; she wore a pearl necklace at her throat and, the thing Dolly knew would most get up Vera's nose, patent-leather high-heel T-bar sandals.

'I can fetch you a hairnet from the canteen if you don't have a turban?' she offered.

At the mention of hairnets, Peggy recoiled. 'Well, thanks awfully, Dolly,' she replied coolly, 'but if I wanted fashion advice from a charlady, I would have asked for it.'

The acoustics of the former workhouse, with its high, vaulted ceilings, meant that Peggy's unfortunate remark echoed loudly around the factory floor. A sudden hush fell over the room as the inquisitive workers stopped what they were doing to stare.

'Girls who wear patent shoes only do it so boys can see their knickers,' Pat muttered angrily under her breath.

Sal Fowler shot Peggy a death stare that meant she wouldn't be getting invited to dances anytime soon.

'Suit yourself, sweetheart,' smiled Dolly evenly. It would take more than this young upstart to upset her on such a glorious spring morning. 'Only, don't say I didn't warn you.'

The voice from behind Dolly was as cool as steel.

'Miss Piper. A word in Mr Gladstone's office, if you will . . .'

Dolly turned to see Vera, arms folded in front of her like a shield, her mouth crimped into a tight line of disapproval.

'In a minute,' said Peggy. 'I've just got to pop to the lavatory. Where is it? Outside, I presume.'

The temperature in the room seemed to plunge a few degrees as Vera's expression froze over. Dolly almost felt sorry for the girl.

'The lavatory?' Vera said crisply, arching one eyebrow. 'Why, yes, they're outside, and please, would Madam like a red carpet rolled out in her honour as well?'

Ten minutes later, Peggy emerged from Archie's office wearing a pinafore, her hair neatly pinned under a hairnet and her neck bare of jewellery.

'Got you a brew, love,' said Dolly, handing Peggy a mug of tea, the handle of which was wrapped with a flame-coloured red rag.

A tiny mischievous smile touched the corners of her mouth. 'It ain't Darjeeling, but it's hotter than hell and darker than brown Windsor soup. That's how we drink it in the East End.'

*

When Dolly moved off, Flossy turned and nervously eyed the new girl. Everything about her looked refined – even her cheekbones looked as if they had been chiselled from marble – and thanks to her proud, upright bearing, she had managed to make her hairnet look like a high-fashion item.

Gracious but she was beautiful, marvelled Flossy. Peggy's startling violet eyes had a feline quality to them and were flecked with threads of gold. Even her ears were small and perfect, a sign of good breeding, Flossy thought with a pang.

Flossy nervously tugged her own ears, which protruded out like two Toby-jug handles, then glanced down at her well-worn shoes. She felt herself sink lower into her seat and instantly Matron's words tore through her: *Straighten up, girl!*

Flossy didn't know if her slight hunch was born from having almost no self-belief or whether it was rooted in a medical problem, but anytime she felt inferior – which was almost always – she began to hunch over. As soon as it had become apparent, Matron had ordered her pockets to be sewn up to prevent her slouching further, and she had been placed on the delicate dorm, with all the sickly, less robust children.

Not only that but she had also had her precious copy of *Black Beauty* confiscated, and a fresh Bible put in its place in her bedside drawer.

'The reading of such frivolous literature is not aiding your condition,' Matron had said with a disapproving grimace. 'The Bible is the only book you need rely on.'

Black Beauty had never found his way back to her, and oh, how she had pined for him.

A stoop and scuffed shoes! Flossy suddenly felt about as treasured as an old discarded button and hot tears pricked her eyelids. Angrily, she blinked them back. Forcing a smile on her face, she remembered that Trout's was supposed to be her bright new start in life. She and Peggy were doing the same job now, so surely that put them on a level pegging, regardless of their background.

'I'm Flossy Brown,' she said. 'And you must be Peggy. I only started yesterday myself, so hopefully we can save each other from making too many mistakes. Is it how you imagined it to be?' she ventured.

'And worse . . .' Peggy snapped. 'That forelady is an absolute harridan. Do you know she confiscated my necklace and has placed it in a safe in the foreman's office?'

'I'm sure you'll get it back at dinner break,' Flossy replied.

'When is that, anyhow?' Peggy asked, eyeing her sewing machine as if it were a live grenade.

'One o'clock sharp, or whenever Mrs Shadwell comes out and rings the bell,' Flossy replied. 'We get forty-five minutes for dinner. A lot of the women here rush out to do their shopping, but yesterday I went to the canteen. Food's not terrific, chips with everything, but it fills the hole until the three-o'clock tea break, and at least it means you don't have to use your coupons up. We get two tea breaks as well, plus four minutes for toilet breaks.'

'How regimented,' Peggy snorted in derision. 'Sounds like the army.'

'I rather like it,' Flossy admitted. 'Least you know where you are, and yesterday, the day flew by. Why, there was even singing . . .' Suddenly, she felt foolish. There she was again. Showing herself up. Was she really so marinated in routine that the highlight of her day was chips at dinner break and a sing-song?

'Well, it's all pretty decent, I'm sure,' she mumbled. 'The girls are good sorts. They were ever so helpful to me yesterday, showing me the ropes. I can show you too and help get you started, if you like? The old-timers like Pat do the trickier work, sewing the uniforms together on an assembly line. Us apprentices are just on pockets and bandages at the moment, but who knows – work hard enough and we could end up on piecework like Pat . . .' Her voice trailed off as Peggy surveyed her curiously through long, spidery lashes.

'Look here, I appreciate your help, but I really wouldn't bother trying to befriend me if I were you, as I shan't be here long,' she said in a cool voice. 'This has all been a dreadful mistake, but you can show me how to work this wretched machine if you like just so I can get through the day.'

'I'd be happy to,' said Flossy, leaping from her seat to give Peggy a rundown of the machine. By the time she'd finished, Peggy looked baffled.

'If you don't mind my asking, why are you here machining?' Flossy asked boldly, her curiosity overcoming her nerves. 'You could be working up West as a shop girl,' she smiled. 'You've certainly got the looks to be one.'

'I told you,' Peggy retorted. 'It's a mistake. I used to work as a nippy at Lyons Corner House in Marble Arch, but we've had to move back to Bethnal Green, where my mother hails from. She went down to the labour exchange and they came up with this . . . this factory. But as I said, I shall only be here a day or so at best.'

'I wouldn't bank on it, love,' piped up a veteran worker by the name of Ivy, taking her foot off the treadle and turning round with a wicked grin. 'You're stuck with us lot now, or rather, we're stuck with you.'

'Whatever can you mean?' Peggy replied defensively.

'What I says,' sniffed Ivy. 'You're in essential war work now. Government won't let you just up sticks and work wherever takes yer fancy. I'd make the best of it if I was you, and stop agitating Vera an' all, or you won't half catch it off her. Pearl necklace to work . . . I asks yer. Whatever next? Pat manning the press in a cocktail dress? Our Doll pouring the tea in white gloves?' She cackled as if she'd said the funniest thing ever and returned to her work.

'Ivy's right,' said Daisy, seated next to the older woman. 'I tried to join the Land Army – fancied the uniform and getting out of Bethnal Green – but when they heard I worked here, they refused to release me. There's no getting out now.'

'We'll see about that,' Peggy snapped. 'My chap's high up in the MOI. He'll be able to wangle me out, I'm sure.'

'What's that, then?' quizzed Daisy. 'Sounds posh.'

'Ministry of Information, of course,' Peggy retorted. 'He won't stand for this.'

'Well, he better have friends in high places, love,' piped up Pat, grunting slightly from the row in front as she shifted her vast bulk on the tiny wooden chair. ''Cos something tells me stitching uniforms is a damn sight more important than serving scones.'

Flossy looked up to see Vera marching towards them, the heavy set of keys she wore attached to her waist clanking like a jailer's.

'Is there a problem, ladies?' she said when she reached their bench, glaring at Peggy.

'No . . . no,' flushed Peggy.

'Then could Madam please deign to start work? Or would you like the man on the moon to come down and join in your little chat too?'

As soon as the forelady was out of earshot, Flossy saw Pat lean over towards Ivy.

''Ere, Ivy. Times must be hard when the labour exchange's sending us bleedin' nippies. You're either born into the rag or you ain't. Betcha we'll be able to see her stitches from 'ere to Aldgate.'

Ivy nodded. 'She'll never manage eight stitches to the inch. Half-hour in and she's already rubbed me up the wrong way. She wants to watch 'er mouth or else she'll end up with a smack in the gob, and I don't care how high up 'er fella is in the Ministry of Whatnot.'

The words were whispered, but loudly enough to be heard on the bench behind, which was, of course, the point. Flossy witnessed Peggy's humiliation and vowed there and then that no matter how haughty her new workmate might be, she would try her hardest to bring her into the fold. She got the distinct impression that Peggy's rudeness was a front for something. She didn't know what, but instinct told her the new girl was hiding something.

As she watched Peggy snap her thread for the third time, she realized she would have a job on her hands.

'Allow me,' Flossy said, deftly threading Peggy's needle for her. 'I know you don't want a friend,' she whispered, 'but something tells me you might need one.'

The rest of the morning passed by without incident, and come dinner break, Peggy, with Flossy's help, had at least managed to get some bundles of work past the eagle-eyed passer, whose job it was to inspect the finished articles, and into her well.

As the bell rang throughout the factory, the air was filled with the sound of thirty women scraping back their chairs. The relief was palpable. When Pat and Ivy rose creakily to their feet, rubbing their backs and grabbing their string shopping bags, they shot Peggy a look that told Flossy it would take a long while before she was going to be accepted.

Seeing their venomous stares, Peggy tapped Flossy on the shoulder. 'Look here,' she said nonchalantly. 'I think I will come to the canteen with you after all.'

'Be my guest,' Flossy grinned back. 'It's right this way.'

Once seated at the scrubbed wooden table, the two girls tucked into their dinner. For Flossy, Spam fritters with chips; for Peggy, a bowl of watery soup and a marg-scraped roll. A stream of factory workers bustled past with their trays, relieved to be on their precious dinner break, and smiled warmly at Flossy. She couldn't help but notice the curious nudges that Peggy's presence aroused.

Peggy seemed not to notice as she stirred her soup miserably.

'Cheer up,' grinned Flossy. 'It's really not so bad here, you know. There's even a pen-pal scheme where you can write to serving sailors if you like. I wrote to mine last night. Tommy's his name. I'm sure there'll be a sailor who'd love to hear from someone as glamorous as you.'

'A sailor?' exclaimed Peggy, looking up sharply from her soup. 'I think not. Besides, I hardly think Gerald would approve. He'll go spare as it is when he finds out I'm working in this grubby little place.'

'Is Gerald your chap, the one you mentioned earlier who works for the Ministry of Information?' said Flossy, between mouthfuls.

At the mention of her sweetheart's name, Peggy's demeanour softened. 'Yes, Gerald Fortesque. We've been stepping out for six months now after I served him luncheon at Lyons.'

'How exciting. He sounds terribly grand,' gushed Flossy. 'I've never courted, but here's hoping. So is it serious between you and Gerald?'

'Not if he sees me in this ghastly thing,' Peggy shuddered, gesturing to her hairnet. 'Yes, it is, I think. Gerald hasn't formally proposed as such, but we have discussed it. Gerald thinks it's best we wait until after the war is over before we think about it. He's terribly busy in the ministry, but I'm working on him. After all, any woman not engaged at our age simply isn't trying hard enough.'

'Oh right,' Flossy mumbled.

'Besides, we shouldn't have long to wait,' Peggy sniffed. 'The war will be over in the next six months. All this talk of invasion is so ludicrous. You know the orchestra is still playing at Lyons?'

Flossy sighed and an image of the orchestra on board the *Titanic*, playing on as the ship slowly sank into the icy depths, sprang to mind.

'Where does Gerald live? In the East End?' Flossy asked.

'Hardly,' Peggy snorted. 'He lives in Belsize Park with his mother. Well, actually his mother has relocated to their country house in Wiltshire, just for the duration of the war. That's why I haven't been able to visit him at home yet. Gerald thinks it's not appropriate I visit his London property until his mother is there to receive me formally.' She smiled for the first time since entering Trout's. 'Dear Gerald, he is a little old-fashioned.'

Flossy smiled back politely. It occurred to her that throughout their entire conversation not once had she heard Peggy say what she felt was best for her.

'That's why I know he would prefer to see me working back at Lyons,' Peggy went on. 'The uniform there is far more becoming for a young woman, and waitressing is wonderful practice in the art of domesticity.'

Peggy glanced around the works canteen at the babble of lively machinists, tucking into their hot dinners with gusto, and could scarcely conceal her distaste. The heat in the room was something else, and even though the window was jammed open, the cloying smell of distemper that oozed from the flaking plaster walls mingled with the stench of fried food.

'I know this might not be a Corner House, but you'll get used to it,' Flossy said, following her gaze. 'The women really are lovely, if you just give them a chance, because honestly, Peggy, I have a feeling this war is only just starting. Besides, I'm sure your Gerald will support you working here. After all, like Pat said, you are aiding the war effort now.'

Peggy said nothing, just stared dully into her bowl. 'I don't want to talk about the war anymore,' she replied, finally taking a tiny nibble of her roll. 'Urgh, this margarine tastes like cart grease,' she winced, throwing the roll back onto her plate.

Flossy's curiosity got the better of her. 'So why is it you and your mother have moved back to the East End? You never said.'

Peggy stiffened. 'I said I don't want to talk about it, Flossy.'

And with that, she stood abruptly and swept angrily from the canteen, colliding with Kathy, causing her to drop her plate of meat pie and chips all over the floor with a loud crash.

'Oi, mind yourself!' Kathy shrieked as chips and gravy splattered over the scuffed linoleum floor. 'Ain't you even gonna say sorry?'

Peggy didn't even turn round. Flossy suspected Kathy would be waiting a long time for an apology. Peggy couldn't eat a bowl of soup, much less a slice of humble pie.

*

Dolly opened the door to Archie's office and ushered the new boy onto the factory floor. She knew what was coming and the women didn't disappoint. Poor lad, she felt like she was turning him loose into a lion's den, not a garment factory. The women were rowdy at the best of times, but, honestly, with a full belly after dinnertime, they were positively incorrigible.

Not that she could blame them. The lad might have been small, barely skimming five foot six inches, but he was strong and powerfully built, with a boxer's physique and a slightly crooked nose. But it had been his twinkling eyes, not his biceps, Dolly had found herself drawn to when Vera had introduced them just moments before in the foreman's office. They were the colour of milk chocolate and as warm and melting as hot cocoa.

His earthy good looks wouldn't half stir things up, though, she had also thought sagely as he had shaken her hand firmly in his. She had seen it before, after all. The last chap who had worked here as an odd-job man, Alf, had been the cause of that many a catfight he had been relieved to be called up. Dolly prayed Lucky had a thicker skin than Alf.

The lusty chorus of wolf whistles and catcalls that rang out now were deafening. Dolly chuckled as she looked about the factory at the workers, hooting with laughter. They were an uproarious tribe of women, and no one, not even Hitler, could put a dent in their spirits this bright spring afternoon.

'Calm down, yer daft mares! Blimey, a bit of meat pie and you're anyone's. Ain't any of yer seen a fella before?' Archie bellowed over the din, holding his hands aloft.

Sal stood up and teasingly blew a kiss in their direction. 'Not one as handsome as this lovely chap, Mr G. What's your name, sweetheart? My machine could do with some oiling.'

'Shut yer trap and sit down, Sal Fowler,' the factory foreman ordered. 'Watch that one – she can be trouble at times,' Archie muttered to Lucky. 'Come to think if it, they all are.'

'Don'cha worry about me, lad,' boomed imperturbable Pat. 'I got bottles of sauce in my cupboard older than you, but you ain't half a sight for sore eyes.'

'Give it a rest,' said Archie. 'Anyone would have thought I'd employed Ernie bleedin' Flynn.'

Lucky coughed. 'Actually, sir, I think you mean Errol Flynn.'

'Errol, Beryl . . . whatever,' sighed Archie, as the floor fell about. 'As I was trying to say, this is Lucky Johnstone, the new odd-job man I was telling yer about yesterday. Too many hens and not enough cocks in this factory. It's nice to have another bloke about the place, truth be told, even if he does have more hair than me.'

With that, Archie gave the young lad a gentle nudge and Lucky removed his cap, to reveal a fine mop of dark brown curls, and stepped forward with a bashful smile.

'Glad to be at your disposal, ladies,' he said in a voice as rich as treacle. 'Anything you need a hand with, don't hesitate to ask.'

'Yeah, but where can we have the hand?' hollered Sal.

Giggling uncontrollably, Daisy pulled her back to her seat.

'Hands off,' piped up Kathy. 'You're married.'

'Yeah, but a slice off a cut loaf ain't missed,' Sal shot back. 'I'm only joking,' she added. 'My Reggie would murder me if he found me doing the double shuffle.'

If Lucky seemed intimidated by the women's crude banter, he didn't show it. An affable grin creased over his strong, handsome face, and his brown eyes twinkled in the spring sunshine.

'I'm flattered, ladies,' he grinned, holding his flannel cap and placing it over his heart.

''Ere,' screeched Pat. 'Whatever happened to your 'and?'

'Pat!' scolded Vera. 'Don't ask such personal questions.'

'Please, it's all right, Mrs Shadwell,' replied Lucky. 'I don't mind. I used to work as a cabinetmaker on Brick Lane.'

The women all nodded approvingly. The area had a proud history of carpentry, and those who didn't work the docks went into one of the many small timber yards that clustered around Bethnal Green Road.

'I had an accident in the sawmill and lost the tops of two of the fingers on this hand,' he said ruefully, holding his right hand aloft. 'Ended my career in carpentry. 'Fraid they won't let me join the army neither on account of not being able to hold a rifle.'

'Not surprised, lad,' heckled Ivy. 'You'd be about as much use as a chocolate fireguard on the front line.'

For a moment, Dolly thought she saw a flash of shame, but he recovered himself quickly.

'You're probably right,' he grinned good-naturedly. 'Still, what doesn't kill you makes you stronger, right? And it means I get to work here. Trout's has, er, quite the reputation.'

'The British Army's loss is our gain, I say,' beamed Archie, clamping his arm round Lucky's shoulder. 'Trout's reputation is soon going to extend to being the most prolific producer of army and navy uniforms in the East End. Ain't that right, girls? We'll be able to rival London Brothers at the rate we're going. So yer see, Lucky, you're still doing yer bit to beat the Boche.'

Lucky nodded respectfully at his new boss, and there it was again, Dolly noted – pain and disappointment, flitting just beneath the surface of those mesmerizing eyes. It must have been a terrible blow to a young man like him not to be able to join his pals from Russia Lane and wear the uniform of the British Army. She knew all too well the misery of being let down by your body.

With one arm still slung protectively round Lucky's shoulder, Archie gestured to the silent army of sewing machines lined up on the workbenches. 'They ain't rifles, but they are our weapons in this war against tyranny. What was it Churchill said to the nation yesterday? "Our aim is victory!" Well, let's start stitching our way to victory!

'I wanna hear them machines sing from dawn until dusk, girls. You hear me? Sing, sing, *sing* I say!' he said with an explosive laugh as he slapped Lucky on the back. 'Right, chop-chop, back to work.'

'Archie,' coughed Dolly, 'you said I could have five minutes of the women's time.'

'Sorry, Doll, so I did,' he apologized. 'Our Doll has a cracking idea, so lend her yer lugholes.'

Dolly stepped forward. 'Vera and I had an idea how we can help our new sailor pals. Letters are all well and good, but what do you reckon our boys really need?' she asked.

'One thing springs to mind,' Sal laughed, arching her eyebrows suggestively.

'Behave, you dirty bugger,' screeched Ivy.

'Back at yer with knobs on,' quipped Sal.

'Comfort items,' said Dolly firmly. 'You know – socks, fingerless gloves, polo-neck pullovers, sea-boot stockings, wristlets, balaclavas and so on. The waters around this country that they are so bravely sweeping for mines are perishing cold.'

Dolly cleared her throat before going on. 'So . . . Vera and I thought we could start a sewing circle through the Women's Voluntary Services, of which she is a member, and send bundles for our boys through them. We've asked about it and they reckon it can be done, perhaps through the Mayor's Comforts Group. There has to be a way, they reckon, as long as it's Vera running it. The WVS can achieve anything. It's not beyond the wit of man,' she chuckled. 'Or should I say woman?'

She gazed about the floor expectantly. 'Well, wotcha think? Should be a piece of cake for you girls. There's not one of you who couldn't pick out a bit of material from Green Street Market in the morning, stitch up a nice dress at dinner and be wearing it come nightfall. You're the most talented needlewomen in all of the East End. You have a feel for fabric that goes beyond instinct. It's in the blood, and it comes from being raised in the heartland of the rag trade.'

The silence stretched on, so Dolly filled it, anxious to win the women over. 'We can make it a working party and knit and sew on breaks, evenings and Sundays,' she said eagerly. 'There are pattern books being issued by the Personal Services League. Not that you lot'll need 'em, mind.'

'That's right,' interjected Vera, sensing the women's

hesitation. 'There are millions of women just like us starting sewing bees. There are already three hundred and twenty active members right here in Bethnal Green, from nurses to factory workers. Why, even Her Royal Highness is in on the act.'

'Behave!' chuckled Archie.

'Honestly, Mr Gladstone,' Vera insisted knowingly. 'My contact at the WVS assures me that Her Highness holds two weekly sewing bees in the blue drawing room at the palace.' Vera was a staunch royalist, and Dolly had a suspicion that was why she had agreed to start a sewing bee in the first place.

'If it's good enough for the Palace, then it's good enough for Trout's. Right, girls?' Dolly grinned.

Pat frowned. 'I hear you, Doll. It's just that, well, we've got our work cut out as it is just keeping on top of uniforms. Besides, ain't the WVS for toffs?'

'All the more reason *to* start a sewing bee,' Dolly insisted. 'Vera tells me the centre organizer up at the Green Street branch is from Hampstead, and the Comforts rep is from Chelsea. Do we really want our neighbourhood represented by women who ain't even from Bethnal Green? Come on! We can sew them toffs under the table.'

The floor fell silent and Dolly started to worry that perhaps she had misjudged the hard workers of Trout's. But then, at the back of the room, she saw a figure rise to her feet.

'I'd like to join,' mumbled Flossy.

Dolly winked at her. 'Good girl. Anyone else? Cold, wet, sore feet are the enemy as surely as the German troops, so let's get our boys some warm socks.'

'Go on, then,' grinned Pat, shaking her head so that her metal curlers clanked under her turban. 'I must be certifiable. Stick me down. Half the lads what grew up in my street are in the merchant or on a destroyer.'

'I'd like to help too, Dolly,' piped up Lucky. 'I know I ain't much good with a needle and thread, but I have got access to a Tin Lizzie, so I can deliver the bundles to the depot. I've got a load of mates down Petticoat Lane what owe me favours and can pass me scraps and swatches.

'I also do a lot of coaching with youth groups down at the Repton Boys' Boxing Club in my spare time,' he added. 'A lot of those boys are pretty resourceful, so I'll get them involved in finding us material.'

'Oh, would you mind, Lucky?' gushed Dolly. 'That'd be smashing, love. The WVS have already told us their wool and fabric are in very short supply, so we'll have to foot the cost of the materials ourselves.'

'Mind?' he grinned. 'Why, I'd be honoured to do my bit.' With that, Lucky raised both his fists in a mock fight stance. As he did so, his overalls strained tight over his broad chest and a thick lock of his dark hair tumbled over one eye. 'They call me the "Pocket Rocket" when I fight. Thirty matches and I ain't never been defeated yet. No guts, no glory – that's our motto in the ring,' Lucky grinned with a swagger. 'But I think it applies just as much outside the ring. Way I see it is, we have a duty to help our boys any way we can.'

'Now you're talking, Lucky me lad,' beamed Archie, ruffling Lucky's hair. 'That's what I call using yer loaf. I knew you'd be a useful asset to Trout's. So, Flossy, Pat and Lucky are in. Who else?'

The change in mood was like the flick of a switch. At the mention of Lucky's involvement, a sea of hands shot into the air.

'Yeah, I could maybe spare some time after work or on Sundays,' offered Kathy, shooting Lucky her most winsome smile.

'Yeah, me and all,' smiled Daisy, looking as fresh as morning dew, despite being out late the night before at the dance. 'Don't want to miss out on all the fun,' she winked, smiling coyly at Lucky.

'I'll definitely be joining up if you're involved, Lucky,' purred a sultry young machinist. 'My name's Lily. Lily Beaumont. I expect you'll have heard of me.'

Dolly allowed herself a little smile. Lily had been crowned 'Miss Bethnal Green' in a beauty contest at the Arabian Arms two summers ago and she had dined out on it ever since.

''Ere, Doll, perhaps we can hold jumble sales or wool drives?' piped up Ivy.

'Or how about a singing competition to raise money?' added Kathy.

'Now you're talking,' said Lily, who was known throughout the factory for her beautiful singing voice.

A clamour of excitement swept over the floor as the women all chipped in with ways in which they could source the much-needed materials for the sewing bee. Dolly shot Vera a wry grin. She knew from years of working alongside these resourceful women that their famed ingenuity would come into its own in a wartime sewing bee. Funny how it took a man with muscles of steel and a smile like silk to make them see that.

She glanced over to where the man of the moment was standing, to see whether Lucky realized what an effect he was having on the women. But as she looked into his brown eyes, she realized his focus had shifted.

Lucky's gaze had cut through his sea of admirers and was trained firmly on the back of the room. Dolly realized he was looking intently over at the flighty new girl, Peggy Piper. Every feature on his face had softened as if he had just been struck by an epiphany.

Peggy appeared not to have noticed and was digging around in her handbag.

'Just one more thing before we get back to work,' Vera's voice cut in. 'The sewing bee needs a name.'

'There's only one,' shrugged Pat. 'The Victory Knitters!'

'It's perfect!' grinned Dolly, clapping her hands together.

'Spot on,' chipped in Archie. 'Our very own army of girls, knitting for the troops. Right, now that's settled, hop to it. Them uniforms won't sew themselves, and let's have a song while we're at it.'

The women dispersed and started to drift back to their stations, while Dolly readied herself to collect her broom and begin her afternoon sweep round. But when she looked up, Lucky was standing straight in front of her, blocking her path. The new odd-job man was grinning from ear to ear like a love-struck fool.

'Well, Lucky lad,' Dolly said with a chuckle, 'I'll say this – you've certainly made a big first impression on the girls.'

'Good. I really think I'm going to like it here,' Lucky replied. 'Everyone said I was mad to come to Trout's and I should have gone to London Brothers, what with them being a bigger concern and all, but this place, well, it seems

smashing so far . . . I was just wondering, Miss Doolaney
. . . Who's that girl at the back of the room?'

They both turned as one and looked over to where Peggy
had clearly found what she was looking for and was now
filing her nails.

'She's the most beautiful woman I have ever clapped eyes
on,' he breathed. 'She looks like she's stepped right out of
the silver screen.'

Dolly sighed heavily. 'Oh, Lucky. First, call me Dolly,
won't you? Second, take a tip from a good friend, because
I truly hope that's how you'll come to regard me, but trust
me, sweetheart' – her blue eyes softened with concern and
she touched the lad lightly on the cheek, causing a soft red
flush to bloom across his skin – 'that way only leads to
trouble. She already has a fella. Unrequited love is a heavy
burden to carry.'

She smiled to let him know she had his best interests at
heart. 'Even more than not being able to serve your country.'

Lucky's proud jaw stiffened as he replaced his cap firmly
and shot a last lingering look at Peggy. 'We'll see, Dolly.
Fortune favours the brave.'

With the details of the sewing bee all wrapped up, the
women resumed their duties. Soon the room was filled with
the sounds of industry, the humming of machines meshing
with the women's beautiful lilting voices.

'Goodnight Sweetheart' had a resonance that touched all
the women's hearts. Dolly leaned into her broom, resting
her chin on the handle, and stared out of the window at the
floating army of anti-aircraft barrage balloons hovering
silently in the blue skies of the East End. But for once,

instead of being comforted by their presence, she felt a haunting wave of fear break over her. She would need a far stronger line of defence to save her from the heartache that inevitably lay ahead, just as Lucky would if he continued on his foolish quest.

A cacophony of emotions tumbled through her. Dolly loved Trout's, and she adored the women within it. They were like family to her, and the factory was her second home.

The East End was filled with garment factories, from Horne Brothers in Hackney to the north to Stripes in Stepney to the south, with Bethnal Green slap bang in the middle. But of all the factories in all the neighbourhoods, Trout's was Dolly's place.

Her lifeblood pulsed through every joist and joint of this creaky old building, and she could probably walk round the whole place with her eyes shut. She had loved coming to work every single day of the past twenty-one years. Her desire to stay another twenty-one and see through her work was powerful, but as her head began to swim and she gripped the broom handle tighter, Dolly knew. Her time in the factory was running out.

*

At the end of the shift, Flossy waited until the floor had nearly emptied before tapping Dolly on the shoulder.

'Do you have a moment, Dolly?'

The tea lady was busy clearing down the benches and looked up, bemused. 'What you still doing here, Flossy love? The night shift'll be clocking on soon. I'm only staying on to make up my hours after being off. You get yourself home.'

'I know, but I . . . I wanted to ask you a favour.'

'Ask away, ducks,' Dolly grinned, her blonde curls working loose from her turban as she resumed her vigorous polishing of the wooden bench top. 'Least I can do after you offered to join in the sewing circle.'

'I thought I might stop off at the town hall on my way home, see if I can't ask about finding my birth certificate, and I wondered if you might come with me.'

'Your birth certificate,' Dolly replied sharply, looking up from her polishing. 'Whatever for?'

'Well, how do I put this . . . ? I know nothing about my real mother or father and why – or how – I came to be in the orphanage. Growing up there, we were discouraged from asking too many questions.

'Matron told us that we should regard the staff and Christ as our real family, and the orphanage our home. The problem was, Dolly . . . it never felt like a home, at least not to me, anyhow.'

'Oh, love,' said Dolly, pushing back the stray curls from her face. 'I can see how upsetting this must be for you, but why start searching now?'

'Because yesterday I turned eighteen. I can go my own way now,' Flossy replied, 'and, well, the town hall seems as good a place as any to start.'

She was surprised and a tiny bit disappointed to see a frown spread over Dolly's face. 'Oh, you think it's a bad idea?' she blustered.

'No, no, it's not that, but is it really what you want, Flossy?' she replied cautiously, choosing her words with care. 'I mean, digging away at the past ain't always such a good idea. At the risk of sounding like your old matron, why don't you see me and the girls as your family now?'

'Oh, Dolly, I'm so grateful to you all,' she replied. 'But I need to do this.' Flossy hesitated, stumbling over her words. 'The . . . Well, the package I received yesterday, somehow I just know it's connected to my past. Maybe even to the identity of my real mother. Now that I've left the home, I have the freedom to start trying to find out how. I know you'll think I'm daft.'

Dolly's face softened, and reaching over, she squeezed her hand. 'I don't think it's daft in the slightest, Flossy. We must all journey with hope in our heart.'

'So you'll come?' she asked eagerly. 'You'll help me try to unlock my past?'

Dolly drew in a deep breath. 'Of course I will. But I should warn you the town hall will probably be closed by now.'

'Oh no,' Flossy said brightly. 'I saw a poster on the way to work saying that it's staying open late as they're doing an ARP demonstration and the Red Cross are down there doing first-aid courses.'

Dolly shook her head in amazement. 'Determined little thing, ain'cha? Very well, let me finish up here and then we'll be on our way.'

The town hall was thronged with residents watching eagerly as a serious-looking man in a tin helmet demonstrated how to operate a stirrup pump, and efficient ladies from the WVS bustled about handing out tea and garibaldi biscuits. Kids ran shrieking and sliding up the parquet corridors on their knees.

'So many kiddies come back from being evacuated,' Dolly remarked, as they walked through the maze of corridors. 'I wonder at the wisdom of it, mind you.'

Flossy was saved from answering when they stopped abruptly outside the registrar's office.

'Please, miss. I'm just here to enquire about finding my birth certificate,' Flossy said politely to a clerk.

'We're closing. Come back in the morning,' she replied brusquely.

Flossy felt the familiar feeling of disappointment pool in her belly.

'She can't,' said Dolly. 'She works in a factory. Essential war work, so I'm sure you won't mind obliging her under the circumstances.'

'Very well,' snapped the clerk, irritated. 'Mother and father's full names, occupations and dates of birth.'

'But that's just it,' faltered Flossy. 'I don't know them. I can provide you with my details. Flossy Brown. I was baptized and raised in the Shoreditch Home for Waifs and Strays.'

'If you can't provide me with their details, then I'm afraid I can't help you. You'll have to go to the home and ask them to see your files.'

'But they've been evacuated,' Flossy replied.

'So write to them. Look here, I really can't assist you further,' she retorted, taking her coat from a peg. 'Besides, there is a war on, in case you hadn't noticed.'

'And a little kindness goes a long way, in case you hadn't noticed,' Dolly shot back, placing a defensive arm round Flossy. 'Come on, let's get out of here.'

Out on the pavement, tears flooded Flossy's cheeks.

'I feel like such a fool,' she sobbed.

'Oh, love, you're not a fool – far from it,' Dolly soothed. 'What does that snooty old cow know, anyhow? But maybe it's a sign that perhaps you need to look forward, instead of back . . .'

Flossy felt a fresh wave of resolve prickle up her backbone. 'No,' she replied. 'I don't see it that way, Dolly. Really I don't. I can't even begin to think of moving forward until I have discovered who my mother was and why she gave me up. How can I dream of a future when I have no clue whatsoever as to my past? My life feels a bit like a jigsaw puzzle with lots of missing pieces. All I want is to find out who I really am.' She stared at the crowd of mothers and children spilling out onto the town-hall steps. 'Everyone belongs to someone, don't they? Who do I belong to?'

Tears pooled in Dolly's big blue eyes as she delicately cupped Flossy's chin in her hands. 'You fit in at Trout's. I know that much.'

'Well, my face didn't fit at the home,' she wept fiercely.

And suddenly, right there on the street, as the sunlight bleached from the sky, Flossy found herself blurting out the truth about her adolescence to a woman she barely knew but instinctively trusted.

'All my life I've felt like a spare part, Dolly. Only the thought that one day my mother would come and claim me gave me any hope. When potential foster parents came to the home, they never even bothered looking in on the delicate children's ward. After all, who'd want the bother of a sickly child?'

Dolly stared at her, thunderstruck, and Flossy wished

she could stop, but something about the tea lady was urging her to be truthful.

'I don't even know why I'm telling you all this . . .'

'Go on, love,' Dolly coaxed.

'The worst moment came when my best friend, Lucy, was picked by foster parents and left without me even getting a chance to say goodbye.'

As the pitiful story tumbled out, Flossy felt herself begin to slouch again.

'Lucy was chosen by a childless couple from Wales. I'm not surprised: she was ever so pretty and in the peak of good health. A rumour went round the orphanage that they had renamed her Dilys, because apparently it means "perfect and true" in Welsh—' She broke off, her face pale and contorted with guilt. 'God forgive me for saying this, but I was so jealous that she was getting a fresh new start and leaving me behind.

'It was soon after that that I started to wet my bed and sleepwalk, which didn't much help matters with Matron.'

Flossy felt her head droop further in shame at the memory, and she stared hard into the gutter. 'I suppose what it all boils down to was that I just wasn't good enough for anyone.'

'Don't you ever think that,' gasped Dolly. 'It's . . . it's simply not true.'

'But don't you get it?' Flossy protested. 'Every time I saw another girl leave the orphanage with new parents, it just made me feel even more worthless. No one wanted me. I even began to half wonder if I wasn't invisible. So you see, Dolly? You see why I have to believe that the sender of those parcels is my mother, and why I have to find her?'

'I do see, love,' Dolly replied. 'I can't ever pretend to truly understand what it must have felt like growing up in a place like that. And I promise I'm not siding with Matron, but have you considered why she has never made herself known?'

'It's simple,' Flossy shrugged. 'I'm illegitimate. She probably had me out of wedlock. I don't know much about life admittedly, but I do know enough to know that plenty of girls get themselves in trouble and are forced to give up their babies. The gifts, well, I'm certain they are my mother's way of securing my forgiveness when she decides it's safe to make herself known. And I shall forgive her . . . when I find her.'

Dolly gazed at her, deeply shocked and saddened by all she had heard, and without saying another word, gathered her in her arms.

*

Peggy trudged past the town hall and spotted Flossy being comforted by that rather brassy charlady. For a moment, she thought about stopping, but instead, she put her head down and scurried past, her heels clipping on the pavement. Besides, she thought, what did that girl know about heartache? She had enough on her plate dealing with her own troubles without taking hers on board.

Dusk was descending on Bethnal Green, but it was still a stiflingly warm evening, and it felt like an age before she finally spotted her turning.

The tired-looking street of shabby terraces in which her

mother had rented a house seemed to stretch on forever, and Peggy's spirits plunged with every step she took.

'Damn this wretched war and double damn the East End,' she muttered despairingly. At the same time, she tore off her hairnet, allowing her mane of gleaming chestnut curls to tumble defiantly down her back. She glared at the ugly thing in her hand and angrily tossed it into the gutter. And to think, just a couple of days ago she had been working in the genteel surrounds of Lyons Corner House. There had been no noisy machinery or raucous singing there, just the soft tinkling of silver spoons against bone china and an orchestra in black tie gently serenading the clientele.

Since leaving her grammar school, Peggy had worked there as a waitress, and oh, how she had adored her job. She knew the iconic black-and-white dress showed off her trim waist to perfection; it had been what first caught Gerald's eye, after all.

As a nippy, she had been required to wear the coveted uniform, but in Peggy's mind, she had never been simply a waitress. Truth be told, she had only taken the job to meet a man with decent prospects, and twenty-five-year-old Gerald Fortesque was definitely a man with prospects. She didn't care what Pat, Flossy or anyone, for that matter, had to say on the subject. This cursed Hitler chap was not derailing her domestic plans.

Gerald had said he would be collecting her tonight at seven thirty prompt to take her out to a dance at the Lyceum, and she would be ready and waiting. She glanced down at the wristwatch her father had given her for her eighteenth birthday and realized in alarm it was later than she thought.

She had better hurry if she wanted to wash the smell of the factory off and be looking her best.

As she quickened her step, Peggy became aware of the twitching of net curtains as curious faces peeked out, which only depressed her further. When she arrived at her new home, she reached through the letterbox and tugged the key tied to a piece of string through it.

Peggy's next-door neighbour, a large woman, was sitting on a chair outside her door, with a fag dangling from her bottom lip, both feet plunged into a bucket of cold water, while she shelled peas into her pinafore. Council workers had sprinkled some sort of pink disinfectant around the drains in the kerb, but it did little to disguise the smell emanating from the sewers.

Peggy had hoped to get through the door without having to enter into conversation with the woman. No such luck.

'Blimey, it was cracking the cobbles today, weren't it, love?' the woman muttered through the cloud of cigarette smoke. 'Could've filled a bucket with me sweat. Him indoors says there's going to be a storm tonight, but he can't tell shit from clay.' With that, she shrieked with laughter, causing the peas to bounce off her pinafore-covered lap like jumping jacks.

'Welcome to Bethnal Green,' she grinned, extending a large pink clammy hand. 'I'm Kate, mother of nine, for my sins. What's yer name, ducky?'

Peggy gaped at the woman and frantically searched her mind for something polite to say, but was saved from answering when her mother, May, flung open the door.

'Oh, there you are, darling,' she gushed, her pretty

features a mask of worry. 'I've been sitting here on tenter-hooks waiting for you to come home.'

'Good evening, Kate,' May smiled politely to their new neighbour. 'I'll make sure to return that cup of sugar tomorrow.'

Kate waved dismissively as she lit a fresh cigarette with the embers of her old one.

'Don'cha worry about it, darlin'. Every little helps, as the old woman said when she pissed in the sea. Me door's always open, so pop in anytime for a brew.'

'I'll do that, Kate,' May called, as she ushered Peggy through the gloom of the passageway and into the small kitchen.

'Gosh, isn't she friendly? Now sit down, love. I've got your tea all ready, but first you must tell me how you got on at Trout's.'

'Oh, Mother, why did you cook?' Peggy snapped, pushing away the bowl of Spam casserole her mother had prepared for her. 'I'm going out dancing with Gerald tonight. Remember I told you?'

May's face fell. 'I'm sorry, darling, but, well, you just missed him. He said to say he's ever so sorry but something's cropped up at work and he has to take some important visitors out to dinner. He was terribly apologetic . . .'

'What! Why ever didn't you keep him here until I got home?' Peggy shrieked. 'I was so looking forward to seeing him.'

'I know you were, and believe me, I did try,' May protested. 'But he seemed in a dreadful hurry to get away. Let's try and look on the bright side, though. At least it means we get to spend our first proper night in our new home together.'

Peggy was so disappointed she thought she might cry.

'I'm sure you'll see him soon, love,' soothed May. 'Now, please put me out of my misery and tell me how you got on at the factory.'

'Well, if you must know, the forelady was absolutely rotten to me, and the rest of the women weren't much better,' Peggy cried, letting her emotions get the better of her. 'Please don't make me go back there, Mother. I beg of you.'

'It's bound to be hard on your first day. Things will feel brighter tomorrow,' May said, smoothing back a stray hair from Peggy's face. 'Whistle a happy tune and all that . . .'

Peggy pushed her hand away, irritated. She knew it wasn't her fault Gerald had stood her up, but in his absence there was no one else to take it out on but her mother.

'And what exactly will you be doing while I slog my guts out in this wretched sweatshop?' she muttered accusingly. 'It's all very well for you. After all, you're not the one who's going to suffer the consequences of our fall from grace. I'll bet the real reason Gerald couldn't wait to get away is because he couldn't stand to sit in this fleapit.'

May's sweet face crumpled at her daughter's acid remark. Her eyes were ringed with heavy dark circles and she looked like she hadn't slept in weeks.

'Please, Peggy,' she wept, feverishly wringing the edge of her apron. 'There's no call for rudeness. I don't like this situation one bit more than you do, but now we're all in it, well, we've just got to make the best of it. Think of it as an adventure,' she smiled bravely, sweeping her arm around their new cosy terrace, filled with packing boxes.

'I'll have finished unpacking this lot by the time you get back tomorrow and have the place looking much more like a home. Maybe we could even go to Smart's Picture Palace, take in a flick? I know it's not quite dancing up West with Gerald, but it could be fun, just you and me?'

'But it's not our home, is it, Mother?' Peggy wept. 'Our home and where we belong is back in Islington with Father. I don't want to go to the pictures. I just want to go home.'

May was by her side in a heartbeat, dabbing at her only daughter's eyes with a hanky. 'I know you're hurting, darling, truly I do, and I miss him too, but your father . . . Well, your father is gone now and we have to make him proud of us. Show him what us Piper women are made of.'

It was a brave attempt at cheer, but a stony silence fell over the small kitchen as Peggy stared hard at the warped wooden floorboards.

'I just don't understand why I can't continue working at Lyons,' she replied. 'At least it would be easier for me to continue seeing Gerald on his lunch hour.'

'We've been through all this,' said May despairingly. 'No one knows when or how Hitler will strike – gas attacks, so they say – and I don't want you travelling into the centre of town day after day on your own. It's simply not safe in London anymore. The threat of invasion is all anyone talks of these days, and if Gerald truly cares for you, then he will understand that.'

'Utter rot,' said Peggy, her voice querulous. 'Everyone has their knickers in a twist over this war, and in a few months, it'll all be over, you'll see. Why are all the evacuees returning home? Hardly seems like a country on the brink of invasion, if you ask me. Meanwhile, king and country now seem to come before home and hearth!'

'It's not just the war to consider, though,' cautioned May. 'The simple fact of the matter is, we need the money now we don't have your father's income from the business. Machining is a more secure – not to mention better-paid – job prospect in these troubled times than waitressing.

'Besides,' she added gently, 'there's nothing wrong with serving tea, but it doesn't call for the same guts. You'll aid the war effort far more behind a sewing machine than as a nippy, darling.'

Peggy rose stiffly to her feet and glared hard at her mother. 'Very well, Mother,' she said icily. 'But I shall never forgive you if Gerald refuses to marry me and I end up on the shelf . . .' Her violet eyes glinted with malice as she readied herself to twist the knife further. 'Just as I don't forgive you for not fighting harder to save Father.'

She threw the last accusation like a handful of needles and swept from the house, slamming the front door so hard behind her that the tiny aged terrace rattled from roof to foundation.

May rose to her feet, blinking back tears of hurt. Despite her daughter's cruelty and capricious behaviour, her instinct as a mother to protect her child remained absolute.

'Wait, darling . . .' she cried, running to the front door and calling up the darkening street. 'Where are you going? You haven't had any tea . . . At least take your gas mask.'

But it was too late. Peggy was already too far gone.

Three

Eight days on from Peggy's inauspicious start at Trout's, Flossy was saddened to see there had been no improvement in her new workmate's attitude. At least she was now wearing a hairnet, but the flimsy pink chenille fishnet still offered little protection.

In contrast, Lucky had settled in well and had quickly been welcomed into the bosom of the Trout's family. He was the perfect fit for the factory, and his quick banter and sunny smile already made him a welcome sight along the benches.

The Victory Knitters were going great guns too, with herself, Vera, Dolly, Pat, Ivy, Daisy, Sal, Lily and Kathy meeting every dinner break in the canteen and some evenings at Dolly's house. But so far Peggy had refused to join in, preferring to mope over her boyfriend, Gerald, instead.

Flossy had written to the evacuated orphanage, requesting that now she was eighteen and had left, she be allowed to see what information her files contained. She was confident they would write back. They had to, because from where she was sitting, she had nowhere else to turn.

She glanced up at the giant clock on the factory wall. It was eight o'clock on the dot. The official start time to the working day was now, but Flossy, keen to impress, made sure to clock on at least fifteen minutes early. The workload was simply so enormous and there were so many sewing arts to learn that she felt she would master none if she didn't put in the hours.

Peggy, in contrast, liked to sail close to the wind. At four minutes past eight, she burst through the door in a cloud of Evening in Paris, her chestnut curls gleaming under the coral-pink fishnet, and hastily punched her card in, ignoring Vera, who looked pointedly at her wristwatch from her desk outside the foreman's office.

'Working part-time, Miss Piper?' enquired the forelady in a voice as tart as sour rhubarb. 'If you're so much as one minute late tomorrow, I shall be docking you a morning's wage. You can take that as an official warning.'

Peggy's porcelain cheeks flushed. 'But that's hardly fair, Mrs Shadwell,' she protested. 'I'm still finding my way around Bethnal Green. All these streets look exactly the same to me.'

'My warning stands.' Vera dismissed Peggy with a flick of her wrist.

'Another day in paradise,' Peggy muttered sarcastically, as she flung her bag down and sat next to Flossy on the workbench. 'Honestly, that woman's got a tongue like a nine-thonged whip.'

'You should have said you were getting lost,' said Flossy. 'I could have knocked for you on the way. You're right about these streets looking the same.'

Peggy turned abruptly. 'You amaze me, Flossy Brown.

I've been nothing but beastly to you since I started, and you've done everything in your power to be kind. Why?'

Flossy shrugged. 'Why not? Kindness costs nothing, does it? Besides, it would be smashing if we could be friends.'

Peggy shook her head in astonishment. 'Very well, Flossy. If you insist. But you might need danger money for being my friend round these parts.' She swept a manicured hand down the line of chattering machinists. 'These lot have it in for me all right.'

'They might warm to you if you joined the sewing bee,' Flossy ventured. 'I really think you would love it, and it would improve your sewing and knitting skills no end. When you marry Gerald, it will be a very useful skill to have.'

'That's true,' Peggy nodded. 'Very well. I can't make any promises, but I will think about it. Though if I do join up, I ought to warn you Gerald is my priority.'

'Of course,' Flossy replied. 'Have you seen him yet since you moved?'

'No, not yet, but he has been terribly busy at work,' Peggy said defensively. 'Now, I best get working, before that forelady gives me what for again.'

It was a start. For now.

'Good to see you with a smile on your face, Peggy,' came a nervous voice behind their bench, and both girls whirled round to see Lucky Johnstone. Well, at least it sounded like Lucky, but Dolly scarcely recognized the chap standing before them. He was head to toe in soot and grime; only the whites of his eyes and his teeth shone out.

'Gracious, Lucky,' Flossy chuckled. 'You look like a chimney sweep.'

Lucky frowned and wiped his cheeks with his sleeve. 'Have I got dirt on me?' The question was directed at Flossy, but he couldn't seem to wrench his gaze from Peggy.

'Just a bit, Lucky,' replied Flossy, handing him the compact from her handbag and a hanky.

He took one look in the tiny mirror and burst into laughter. 'Blimey. Whatever do I look like? Archie's had me clearing out the loft. I wanted to make a good impression on him, so I've been at it since six a.m. What a game, eh! He wants it empty for when—' He shot a nervous look at Peggy and promptly dropped Flossy's compact with a clatter. 'Sorry, *if* Jerry decides to start chucking bombs at us. A full loft is a fire hazard, you see,' he burbled as he picked up the compact from the floor and handed it back to Flossy.

'The whole world's gone mad,' tutted Peggy, coming perilously close to impaling her thumb with the needle as she angrily fed a strip of khaki fabric through her machine. 'I hardly think defacing flowerbeds and getting rid of a few dead pigeons from the loft will save this place in the event that the Germans do decide to attack, which they shan't, in any case.'

'I wouldn't be so sure of that, Peggy,' said Lucky darkly. 'The Dutch have surrendered, and they reckon France will be the next to fall. Jerry is crushing everything in his path.'

'France will never give in,' sniffed Peggy.

'Yes, but we didn't think Belgium would either,' warned Flossy, suddenly feeling very weak. 'The future does look uncertain.'

'Well, I, for one, would rather die fighting than live the

life of a slave,' Lucky announced, his broad chest puffing out. 'Which is why I joined the Local Defence Volunteers up at the town hall on my dinner break yesterday.'

At the mention of this, half the floor whirled round in shock.

'You didn't!' shrieked Pat.

'I only did,' Lucky smiled, pulling an armlet emblazoned with the initials 'LDV' out of his pocket and proudly displaying it to the floor. 'You're looking at Bethnal Green's newest member. It's our job to be the eyes and ears, a secondary defence force in the event of an invasion. A quarter of a million men signed up within twenty-four hours of the government's radio appeal a week ago, so I says to myself that I should get in on the act.'

'Have you got your broom shank yet?' heckled Sal. 'I saw a load of 'em parading down Cambridge Heath Road the other day with theirs.'

'The army can't spare the rifles,' replied Lucky defensively.

'Well, I think it's admirable, love,' smiled Dolly, as she bustled past en route to the kitchens. 'I feel much safer for knowing you're in it, Lucky. Only, I worry you might have a bit too much on your plate, what with this place, the LDV, your ARP work and your boxing.'

'Don'cha worry about me,' he grinned, beating his chest. 'English heart of oak in here. I'm built for hard work. Besides, Miss Doolaney, idle hands are the devil's playthings.'

'Dolly, please,' she said on a smile.

'Sorry. Forget my head if it weren't screwed on,' he grinned sheepishly. 'Dolly.'

Peggy glanced up from her machine with a scathing look on her face and Flossy found herself dreading what she was about to say.

'It's nothing but a sop,' she said blisteringly. 'You know they're calling it "Look, Duck and Vanish"? From what I heard, that quarter of a million volunteers consists mainly of the old, the deaf and a handful in the advanced stages of venereal disease,' she smirked. 'Oh, and those too crippled to fight.'

Flossy could see Peggy realized her faux pas instantly.

'I-I didn't mean you, Lucky,' she blustered.

'It's all right, Peggy,' he said, flinching as his damaged hand crept up inside his sleeve. 'I know people regard it as a bit of a joke – see *me* as a bit of a clumsy joke, in fact.' His usual twinkly smile had evaporated from his soot-smeared cheeks and in its place was a look of ragged pain.

'Do you think I like not being able to get out there and fight with my pals? I put a good face on it, but I hate it. I'd do anything to be on the front line. Anything. I try to ignore the jibes, laugh 'em off, but I've been called everything from a parasite to an army dodger. But I ain't no ducker, see.' Defiantly, Lucky pulled out his hand and held it aloft for all to see. Thirty machines slowed as feet came off treadles and the women turned to stare.

'Some folks don't know why I grumble like stink about this hand. "We'd do anything to get out of conscription," they say. The laugh of it is, there's a doctor down on Brick Lane what hands out forged medical exemption certificates and here I am, exempt for real, and yet it makes me feel like half a man. So if I want to parade through Bethnal Green with a broom shank, or a bleedin' broomstick for that matter, I flamin' well will, and I refuse to feel ashamed. It's my East End and I'll fight to the death to protect it.'

Angrily, he stuffed his armlet back into his pocket. 'Every story has a beginning, and this is mine . . .'

A stunned silence settled over the floor as Lucky marched from the room. This was a side to the usually good-natured odd-job man that Flossy had never seen. Something about his plight resonated deep within her. Lucky, like her – and indeed Great Britain herself – was fighting hard to find a new identity.

'Now see what you've done,' hissed Lily.

Once the door banged shut behind him, Vera rose sharply to her feet. 'That young man needs all our support right now,' she snapped. 'Now stop gassing and get back to work.'

Peggy at least had the good grace to look embarrassed.

'I didn't mean him,' she muttered defensively to Flossy. 'Do you think I should go after him?'

'Best you leave him,' said Dolly.

'I happen to think he's right to join the LDV,' said Pat in a low voice so the forelady couldn't hear. 'This area certainly needs all the help it can get right now in defending us from enemy aliens. Bleedin' Huns.'

She scowled and picked up her copy of the *Hackney Gazette* from under her workbench. 'Says here there are sixty thousand of the buggers at large in London. Probably undercover Nazis, the lot of 'em.'

'That's right – the only good German is a dead German,' sniffed Ivy, brandishing her copy of the *Daily Mail* like a weapon. *Intern the Lot*, screamed the headline.

'How can you fall for that propaganda claptrap?' blazed

Peggy, her violet eyes flashing furiously. 'It's just utter rot,' she went on, angrily pumping her treadle underfoot. 'The vast majority of Germans in this country are decent civilians just like us. Someone's son, brother or husband, and— Argh!' she screamed, yelping in pain. 'Blast!'

Flossy took her foot off the treadle and peered over at Peggy's machine. What she saw made her feel quite faint. In her anger, Peggy had accidentally managed to drive the needle clean through her nail and into the thumb on her left hand.

'Help me,' whimpered Peggy, her face draining of colour as she gazed, stricken, at the needle plunged deep into her flesh.

'Over here, Vera,' called Dolly calmly when she saw what Peggy had done. 'And bring the first-aid kit too, will yer?'

When Vera saw Peggy's predicament, she tutted. 'There's always one, isn't there? You better not have broken the needle.'

As the forelady slowly turned the handle to remove the needle from Peggy's thumb, Flossy closed her eyes, unable to watch. When she opened them again, Vera was briskly bandaging up Peggy's thumb.

'You're lucky,' she muttered. 'The needle came out whole.'

'Yeah,' piped up Ivy. 'Only gotta do it another two times, gal, and then you're officially a machinist.'

Poor Peggy looked like she might faint on the spot as she slowly reached down for her handbag.

'And where do you think you're going?' Vera demanded.

'Why, h-home, of course. I just presumed . . .' Her voice trailed off.

'Well, you presumed wrong. I'm not sending you home for such a piffling little injury. Dolly, fetch her a sweet cup of tea, would you? I'll put you on the steam press until you feel recovered.'

Peggy sighed heavily, but instead of sitting down again, she moved away from the bench.

'I'm sorry, but did you not understand me?' Vera said coldly.

'I'm just going to the lavatory,' Peggy retorted.

'But you didn't put your hand up to request a toilet break,' the forelady replied.

Peggy closed her eyes and raised her hand weakly.

'Very well, permission granted. Remember, though, four minutes, and I shall be counting, Miss Piper.'

Perhaps it was the drama of Lucky's outburst or the shock of impaling herself, but Peggy flung her bandaged hand in the air in frustration. 'Oh, for pity's sake, what a rigmarole,' she muttered.

'Fetch your coat and go home,' ordered the forelady, a vein on the side of her head twitching dangerously. 'I've had just about as much of your cheek as I can bear for one day. I'm docking you a day's wages, and I suggest that when you return tomorrow, you adjust your attitude or you'll be getting your marching orders with no reference.'

As Peggy fled from the floor in tears, Flossy's heart went out to her. She could tell that Peggy was really trying hard, but why, oh why did she have to get herself sent home? Just when she was so close to persuading her to join the Victory Knitters as well.

*

As Peggy clattered down the stairs, pulling her cardigan tightly around herself, she passed Lucky coming back up to the factory floor. His shirtsleeves were rolled up to reveal his forearms, and he was clutching a bundle of heavy fabric and a box of buttons, which he promptly dropped when he spotted Peggy.

'Your buttons,' she murmured, as she bent down to help him pick them up off the stairs. She handed him the button box, and as her hand brushed the naked flesh on his arm, she saw his cheeks flush in the gloom of the stairwell.

'I—' they both went to speak.

'Sorry . . .' said Lucky softly. 'You go first.'

'I just wanted to say I'm sorry if I offended you earlier,' Peggy said. 'It's admirable that you've joined the Local Defence Volunteers. It's just that I find all this talk of the war very unsettling.'

'Don't worry,' Lucky replied. 'I wasn't cross at you, just at my situation. This war's not easy for anyone,' he confessed. 'I've three older brothers all serving and I feel next to useless. I can't even hold a box of buttons without dropping 'em. What hope would I have handling bullets?'

Close up and alone for the first time, Peggy was suddenly aware of how broad his shoulders were from a lifetime of manual labour and boxing. His chest looked as solid as a tank and yet his deep brown eyes were gazing at her with such gentle tenderness. He smelt of Lifebuoy soap and tobacco. He had obviously washed his face, but his muscled brown forearms were still covered in soot and grime from his morning's toil.

The crooked nose, dark eyes and lips that curled up at the edges . . . It all added up to a face that would never grace the cover of a magazine, yet there was something strangely compelling about it. She forced herself to think about Gerald instead, and his smooth, freckled hands, neatly combed sandy hair and tailored suits.

'Listen, Peggy, I wondered if you might allow me to take you for a cup of tea on Sunday?' Lucky said, cutting through her thoughts. 'I wouldn't presume the date to be anything more than one of friendship. I know you have a fella already. It will just be a pot of tea, maybe a teacake if you're lucky,' he joked. 'I could show you round Bethnal Green; then maybe you wouldn't get lost anymore.' His voice trailed off and he grinned hopefully at her from under his mop of dark curls.

Peggy suddenly felt a powerful urge to escape the stiflingly hot stairwell. This encounter was simply too uncomfortable for words.

'I'm sorry for what I said earlier, but I . . . . I just can't,' she blurted. 'Gerald wouldn't approve.' She pushed past Lucky and ran as fast as her feet would carry her onto the hot cobbled street outside.

Peggy leaned back against the high brick wall of Trout's and took a moment to gather her thoughts. She had no desire to be shown round Bethnal Green by Lucky Johnstone, or anyone else for that matter. For wouldn't that be like admitting that she really would be staying here?

After the gloom of the stairway, Peggy's eyes took some adjusting to the spring sunshine. At the end of the street, a tall grey factory chimney stack belched out smoke, and acrid fumes drifted into a hazy blue sky. In its shadow, a small huddle of raggedy-looking boys pushed a pram bundled high with firewood. She found it astonishing the sheer amount of factories that sat cheek by jowl with the houses. There were garment factories, breweries, tanneries, candle works and glue factories all pumping out noxious smells.

Peggy shuddered before she set off for the dismal terrace her mother now insisted on calling home.

When she arrived, she found her mother in the tiny kitchen, a pinny wrapped round her slender waist, stirring a pot of potatoes, turnips and carrots on the stove.

'Hello, love,' she smiled brightly. 'You've come home for your dinner? That's nice. You know, rationing's really not all that bad, though four months on, you'd have thought I'd have got used to the coupons by now. At least potatoes aren't rationed, so I thought I'd try out this new Woolton pie they recommend on the wireless. Not really sure why it's got such a grand name. It's vegetable pie when all is said and done. Still, Kate from next door gave me an Oxo cube to liven it up. I'd forgotten how friendly East Enders can be.'

'I'm not here for pie,' sniffed Peggy, sitting down heavily at the table. 'I injured myself, and instead of showing me any sympathy, that awful forelady sent me home and docked me a day's wages.'

Her mother's face fell as she whirled round, clutching her wooden spoon. 'Oh, love, no . . .'

'I know,' Peggy said, holding up her bandaged thumb. 'Not a single care for whether I was seriously injured. Wretched woman. No wonder she's a spinster.'

'I'm not talking about your thumb,' May went on, with a curious edge to her voice. Taking off her pinny, she sat down slowly at the table and took her daughter's hands in hers.

'Peggy, I don't think you seem to grasp the seriousness of our situation. We desperately need the money now your father's gone. I'm relying on your wage. The landlord's coming round this week for the rent money and now . . .' Her voice cracked.

Peggy realized with a jolt that her mother looked so much older since they had arrived in Bethnal Green. Her beautiful pale blue eyes had lost their lustre, and without the love of a husband who adored her, she looked stripped to the bone.

'What I'm trying to say is that we're living Friday to Friday now, Peggy, just like everyone else round here. We cannot afford to have you out of work. You mustn't rub that forelady up the wrong way.'

'Oh, please don't send me back to that hateful place,' Peggy pleaded, squeezing her mother's fingers tightly. 'I beg of you. How bad can it really be? Father will be home soon. He's done nothing to betray his country, after all.'

Something about her mother's slim, pale fingers felt odd, and when Peggy glanced down, she realized her mother's sapphire-and-diamond engagement ring was gone.

'Mother, your ring!'

'I had to pawn it, love,' May said, looking away sharply. 'I didn't want to, but I had no choice. I have to put food on the table.'

With that, she pulled out a telegram from her handbag and handed it to Peggy. 'I . . . I wasn't going to show you this, darling. It arrived a few days ago, but I can see now there's nothing to be gained from shielding you from the truth. Your father won't be home in a few days, or even a few months.'

Peggy read, and as she did so, a cold fist tightened round her heart.

'But he's done nothing to betray his country,' she repeated tremulously, throwing the telegram back down on the table in anger. 'They can't do this.'

May shrugged, and her face fell into worried lines. 'They can and they are. But now do you see? Things are about as bad as they can possibly be. You will return to Trout's, love, for we have no choice. You're eighteen now, a woman, and it's high time you faced up to things. We both know your father's innocent, but things won't ever go back to the way they were. We're all stepping out into the unknown now.'

*

Dinnertime at Trout's and every available surface of the tabletops was covered in balls of wool, knitting needles and handbags. *We Must All Stick Together* blared out from the Marconi radio sitting on the canteen hatch.

The Victory Knitters had commandeered half the canteen for its sewing bee, and Pat Doggan was holding court like its queen.

'I'm telling you, Miss High and Mighty's got herself a German lover,' she said knowingly to the group, as her pudgy fingers made a grab for her knitting needles. 'Or my name's not Pat Doggan. Did you see her reaction this morning when we were talking about enemy aliens?'

Next to her, Kathy held her arms out for the skein as

Ivy made up fresh balls of wool from an old jumper she had unpicked.

'You really think she's having it away with the enemy?' Kathy said, wide-eyed. 'I thought she had some high-falutin' fella already?'

'It's a front,' Ivy nodded sagely, as she deftly looped wool round Kathy's arms. 'I mean, has anyone actually seen him yet? She's been here eight days now and he ain't visited her once.'

'Never mind purling – my head's whirling,' Kathy quipped, her mischievous face alight. 'She'll find herself behind barbed wire if she ain't careful.'

'Or locked up in the Tower,' Pat muttered darkly as she cast off.

'Well, I can't think why Lucky is so taken with her,' sniffed Lily, over the furious clacking of needles. 'Have you seen how clumsy he gets round her? What a rotten thing to have said to him. That snooty cow's due one.' The factory's glamour girl had made no secret of the fact that she had set her sights on Lucky herself, and quite clearly her nose was still out of shape over it.

Dolly sighed inwardly and tried to tune out the women's idle chatter. As a discipline, Dolly found knitting and sewing oddly calming. It stopped her from thinking about what the future held and brought her right back to the moment. The repetitive rhythm of working the same stitch over and over wove in her a sense of peace and created an inner calm she rarely felt these days. There was also a strange magic in taking an unpromising ball of wool and turning it into something warm to wear. She thought of all those young lads out there on HMS *Avenge* and realized there was something more fundamental at work than the alchemy of turning yarn into clothing.

She glanced up from the scarf she was knitting and caught Flossy's eye. She hadn't uttered a word as the rest of the sewing bee bad-mouthed Peggy. Not that Dolly was surprised. She doubted there was a bad bone in the whole of that young girl's body. If only things could have been different. If only . . . Suddenly, Dolly started to feel light-headed. The women's babble was deafening, their voices fusing to a single high-pitched hum in her head. She laid her knitting needles down on the tabletop with a clatter.

'Come on, girls, give it a rest and stop your grousing, eh?' Dolly snapped. 'We're here to sew, not crow.'

The group all looked up in surprise.

'You all right, Doll?' asked Sal. 'You're as white as a sheet.'

Dolly tried to still her desperately pounding heart. The palpitations were so loud she half wondered if anyone else could hear them.

'I'm fine,' she said, breathing out slowly. 'I just think we should lay off Peggy a bit. She's not from these streets and we should treat her with a little more kindness.'

'But she ain't one of our own,' protested Kathy.

'All the more reason to give the girl a fair go,' insisted Dolly. 'We're all in it together now, remember?'

She picked up her favourite ivory needles – she had sent her steel ones to be melted down for the war effort – and forced a bright smile onto her face. 'Now, come on, girls – less chat, more work. I promised Lucky our first batch of comfort items would be ready for him to deliver up to the WVS by tomorrow. There's a postal boat going out next week to our boys and we want this lot on it.'

Despite their loquacious tendencies, Dolly had to hand it to the girls. Their thrift had run to new heights, and their output over the past week had been prodigious. New balls of wool were in short supply, but that hadn't fazed the women. Pat had rummaged at a jumble sale at the Methodist Mission and come up with a load of worn-out old jerseys, which they had unpicked, steamed and knitted into twenty-seven balaclavas.

Lucky and his boys from the boxing club had come up trumps and sourced no end of swatches and samples from their mates down the markets, which when sewn together, made fetching patchwork quilts.

Dolly herself was rather proud of the length of material she had persuaded the local bus depot to give her. It had originally been the roller on the front of the bus to tell you its destination, but she had given it a good soaking in the tin bath in the yard out back to get the numbers off and bingo – five heavy cotton blankets. The boys on HMS *Avenge* would have no idea they had once been on the number 22 to Hackney.

'Doll's right,' said Pat, conveniently forgetting her part in Peggy's character assassination. 'Look at this,' she said, proudly holding up a soft wool scarf. 'Unpicked my Sylvie's old matinee jackets and made this with it.'

'That's smashing, Pat,' said Dolly, feeling her spirits return and her heart rate steady. Say what you like about East Enders, they didn't half know how to live on their wits.

'Never mind the knitting,' said Daisy, with an enigmatic

smile on her face. 'What I wanna know is what you've all written in your letters? I enclosed a photo with my letter and asked him to send one back. Hope he's a dish.'

Daisy flicked her best friend, Sal, a sly sideways grin. 'And failing that, I've found another way to meet a fella.'

Sal closed her eyes and shook her head. 'Don't drag me into this, Daisy,' she replied.

'Ooh, whatever have you done?' asked Kathy. 'Come on, spill the beans, you little strumpet.'

'I've been popping letters into the pockets of uniforms once I've sewed them on, and in the bandages,' Daisy replied. 'Nothing too saucy. *If you're single, drop a line. If you're married, never mind* . . . That kind of thing. I'm sure I'll hear back from a nice handsome chap soon, and if I don't, well, no harm done.'

'Unless Vera finds out,' warned Dolly. 'There'll be blood on the moon if she catches you, sister or no sister. You're not quite seventeen, remember.'

A sudden thought struck her. 'How many of you girls round this table have done the same?'

Nervous laughter rippled round the canteen.

'Aah, come on, Doll,' piped up Daisy. 'There's no decent fellas about at the moment.'

Her eyes sparkled as she patted her pinafore pocket. 'Got another one right here: *If this war's driving you round the bend, you're sure of a warm welcome in the East End.*'

The girls howled with laughter. Dolly could hardly blame them. The workload was punishing, and when all was said and done, they were young women in search of romance and excitement.

'Have you written to your sailor, Tommy, Flossy?' Dolly asked.

Flossy flushed as her delicate hands worked her needles. 'Yes, I have. It's ready to give to Mrs Shadwell to be sent out. I've also knitted him a scarf and a pair of socks, and made this to send with it.' She pulled out a beautifully stitched drawstring bag from underneath the pair of gloves she was knitting. 'I've been collecting the rag ends off the floor and I made this with them. I thought it might be useful for Tommy to store his keepsakes in.'

Her face fell. 'You don't think Mrs Shadwell will mind, do you?' she panicked.

'Not at all, love,' Dolly soothed, patting her hand. 'It's a terrific idea. Very thoughtful.'

'You wanna slip a photo in there too, ducks,' winked Sal. 'You're ever such a pretty young thing. He's bound to go weak at the knees.'

Flossy's eyes widened. 'Oh, I could never be so forward,' she squirmed. 'Whatever would he think of me?'

'He'd think you were an absolute peach, trust me. Don'cha wanna meet a man?'

'Well . . . I . . . Oh, that sort of thing was never really encouraged at the home,' Flossy replied. 'Besides, I'm still under the care of the home until I'm twenty-one: any suitors have to be vetted and approved by Matron first before I can start courting.'

'Well, I don't need anyone's permission, and I for one intend to meet a man and get married this year,' said Lily assertively. 'Half of Bethnal Green seems to be getting spliced at the moment.'

'That's right. No point delaying, is there? You could be dead if you wait until tomorrow,' said Pat bluntly.

With that, the bell indicating the end of dinner break rang shrilly throughout the canteen.

'Right, back to the coal face,' said Pat, gathering her knitting and scraping back her chair.

Flossy made to move off, but Dolly caught her by the arm.

'Why don't you come to ours for your tea later, love? Mum's only planning a bit of corned-beef hash, nothing fancy, but it can't be much fun going back to your digs on your own.'

'Really?' Flossy asked. 'That'd be smashing. As long as you don't mind if I bring my knitting too? I may be able to finish these gloves off before tomorrow.'

'Course not.' Dolly smiled. She felt relief wash over her as they walked back to the factory floor together. It really would be lovely to extend a neighbourly welcome to young Flossy. But she did have an ulterior motive.

*

When 6 p.m. rolled around and the day's work was over, Flossy was stunned to see the bright spring sunshine had vanished, to be replaced by a thick green pea-souper. She had been that absorbed in her machining she had scarcely noticed it. But now, standing on top of a long ladder, as she and Kathy fitted the heavy blackout blinds to the windows, she saw that a ghostly fog had crept in down the narrow cobbled streets outside Trout's. A thick wall of white was already shrouding the windowpanes and clinging to the gas lamps.

'We'll have a right game getting home tonight,' remarked Kathy, as she fitted the final blind and gingerly made her way back down the ladder.

Dolly was waiting for Flossy as she shrugged on her coat and pinned on her hat.

'There you are, love,' she smiled. 'Shall we get cracking? It looks dreadful out there.'

The two linked arms and picked their way down the staircase. Once outside, the fog hit the back of their throats like needles.

'Crikey! It's bad this evening,' said Flossy, pulling a cotton hanky from her coat pocket and holding it over her mouth.

'Awful, ain't it?' agreed Dolly, doing the same. 'Can't see your hand in front of you.'

Conversation was impossible as the two carefully made their way down the road in the direction of Tavern Street, tapping their feet against the kerbstones as they went.

They had scarcely been going two minutes when Flossy heard Dolly start to cough, great rasping, shuddering gulps for air. As Dolly's arm grew weak in hers, Flossy whirled round. Something about her friend's pallor drew Flossy out by the roots.

'Dolly!' she shrieked, clutching her arm in distress. 'Whatever's the matter?'

Her breathing was shallow and she could scarcely draw a breath before she was hit by another convulsive coughing fit. Desperately looking around, Flossy spotted a low brick structure built up against the side of a wall. Flossy led Dolly inside and insisted she sit down on one of the long benches lining the wall.

'I'm fine. Don't fuss so,' Dolly protested weakly, as she clutched at her chest.

'Just sit here a while until you get your breath back,' Flossy ordered.

As Flossy's eyes adjusted to the gloom, she realized this must be one of the new street surface shelters the council were building all over Bethnal Green. It was no more than forty feet long and was filled with rows of benches and little else. It stank to high heaven, and Flossy spotted a rat sniffing about under one of the benches.

Her eyes settled on some writing on the opposite wall. *To let (furnished)* had been daubed in white paint. Some wag's idea of a joke, but Flossy didn't find it very funny. A darker, more foreboding place you would be hard pressed to find.

Next to her, Dolly shuddered. 'Grim, ain't it? Heaven forbid you have to shelter in here if the worst happens. I don't reckon it could stand up to a ball, much less a bomb,' she said.

'Dolly, are you all right?' Flossy asked cautiously.

'Course I am,' she replied. 'It's the fog – it plays havoc with my lungs. I just needed a sit-down, but look, I'm right as rain now. Come on, let's get out of here: it's giving me the heebies.'

Dolly's coughing fit had passed, but as they moved out of the shelter, Flossy noticed her stumble and she reached out her arm to steady her.

As they walked cautiously in the direction of Tavern Street, Flossy was still worried.

'Are you sure you're all right, Dolly? You went an awfully queer colour back then, and I noticed you had a funny turn earlier on too.'

'Honestly, I'm fine,' she insisted. 'I'm just a bit below the mark, that's all.'

Flossy said no more, but when they finally reached the doorway to number 20 Tavern Street, Dolly went to knock, but then stopped.

'Listen, Flossy,' she hedged. 'Don't tell my mum what happened earlier. There's a good girl. She'll only worry about me. Our secret?'

'Our secret,' Flossy murmured, but as Dolly pushed open the doorway and she followed her down the narrow passage, she had a feeling she might just come to regret her assurances. Their journey through the fog had a poignancy that she couldn't quite put her finger on.

Dolly's mother was every bit as warm and welcoming as Flossy had imagined, and she felt right at home the minute she stepped into the cosy terrace.

A coal fire crackled in the grate, and Dolly and Flossy set to their knitting as soon as her mum had plonked two large mugs of tea in front of them.

'Got me hands on a lovely bit of beef fat down the market earlier,' grinned Dolly's mum. 'Rendered it down in the range, so I thought we could have bread 'n' dripping instead of corned-beef hash tonight, if that's all right with you girls? I even baked the bread myself,' she said proudly, crossing her arms over her large bosom. 'A nice crusty white – none of this wholemeal muck the government's insisting is better for us – and rice pudding for after. I like to spoil our Doll and her friends.'

'Sounds smashing, Mrs Doolaney,' Flossy said.

'Good. There was some spiv selling some lovely lamb chops out of a box, but I thought I better not,' she remarked, as she lowered herself down into an easy chair beside them.

'Too right, Mum,' said Dolly, looking up from her knitting. 'You get your ration and you be thankful. It's only giving them black marketeers a leg-up, and it ain't playing fair.'

As Dolly and her mum bantered back and forth about the growing black market, Flossy watched them.

Mrs Doolaney was a large woman wrapped in a floral apron who smelt faintly of Sunlight soap. A smear of flour dusted her rosy cheeks, and two blue eyes twinkled inquisitively at Flossy. As for her humble home, it was so old it was only the wallpaper holding it up, and a framed oil painting of a country meadow scarcely concealed a damp patch on the wall. But despite all that, the house gleamed like a new penny.

That supreme symbol of respectability, a plaster-cast bust of King George VI gazed down at them from the mantel, which was clustered with framed photos of a smiling Dolly and her sister, surrounded by a gaggle of other lively-looking women.

'That's Mum's sisters, my aunties Jean, Polly and Sylvie, and Mum's aunties, Joyce and Mary, and my cousins – too many to name,' said Dolly, as she noticed Flossy gazing at the photos. 'Most of 'em live down Tavern Street, or no more than a few turnings away. You want to hear the noise of 'em when they all get together.'

Flossy's head was still spinning as Mrs Doolaney made a playful swipe at her daughter. 'Enough of your sauce, my girl,' she screeched, laughing so loudly Flossy feared she might topple off her easy chair. 'Least you was never lonely growing up. It's good to have your kin near, I reckon. Don'cha agree, Flossy?'

Flossy nodded, and her mind grappled with what to say.

'I mean, I'm glad I had daughters, not sons, truth be told,' Mrs Doolaney went on. 'Least I know they'll never leave me. How's the old proverb go? "My son's a son till he gets a wife. My daughter's a daughter all her life."'

'Well, you certainly have a lovely family,' Flossy said, but she couldn't conceal the sadness from her voice.

'Vera lives two doors up,' Dolly said, hastily changing the subject. 'She's pretty house-proud, but even she's put to shame by Mum. You're out there on that step with your birch broom, pail and hearthstone before the milkman's done his rounds, ain't that right, Mum?' she smiled.

'What can I say? A woman's judged by her step, Flossy,' chuckled Mrs Doolaney, holding up her hands. 'My house may lack many things but not cleanliness. I just want my girls to come home to a nice place. After their father, Harry, died, well, they're all I've got, Flossy. It's my job to look after them, even after they're all grown up. I've never had any money, but I've always had plenty of love.'

'That's true,' Dolly said, gazing at her mum fondly. 'She's always been the same, and I can't see Jerry changing that now.'

'Right, this chat won't get tea on the table,' said Mrs Doolaney, heaving herself out of her chair and bustling to the range. 'You girls must be famished.'

'Your mother's lovely, and so is your home,' Flossy said, when Mrs Doolaney was out of earshot.

'I know,' Dolly replied. 'I'm blessed in so many ways.'

Flossy hesitated and stared down at the knitting in her lap. Outside, the muffled cries of a rag-and-bone man drifted up Tavern Street.

'Have you heard yet, from the orphanage?' Dolly ventured.

'Not yet, but I'm sure I shall soon,' she replied. 'But if I don't, I've already decided to ask my welfare officer about it on her next scheduled visit.'

'I can't stop thinking about what you told me that evening outside the town hall,' Dolly blurted. 'About your childhood in the orphanage.' She hesitated. 'Were . . . were they cruel to you?'

'No,' Flossy replied thoughtfully. 'Lacking in affection, but never wilfully cruel.' She shot Dolly a wry smile. 'Not unless you count two church services on a Sunday as cruel, or having *Black Beauty* confiscated and replaced with a new Bible. I never knew any other life, don't forget, but I always felt that there was a better way of living, somewhere, or rather someone I could belong to. That yearning to belong, it never leaves you.

'It's funny, you know,' she added as an afterthought. 'The older I get, the more I remember of my childhood.'

'Such as?' Dolly asked, looking up sharply from her knitting.

'Today, for example, I suddenly remembered how when I was seven, shortly after my friend Lucy was fostered, Matron called me to her office and told me how I was lucky enough to have been selected for a new government programme to send orphaned children to the Dominions. I was to be given a fresh start, full of blue skies, sunshine and opportunity in the New World. Well, at least that's how Matron put it.'

'Well, I'll be,' said Dolly. 'Whatever happened?'

'When they sent me off for my vaccinations, they discovered I had measles and I couldn't go, but around that same time, I distinctly remember a fair-haired lady coming to see me at the home. She spent the morning playing and reading with me. I suppose she must have been a governess, or someone from the child migration programme perhaps, as I didn't see her around much after that. The ship set sail soon after, minus one Flossy Brown.' She grinned ruefully at Dolly. 'Always the one left behind, eh?'

Dolly said nothing in response, just stared down at the knitting in her lap, and Flossy realized she had embarrassed her new friend by being so candid.

'But what of you, Dolly?' she said. 'Did you not want to become a machinist?'

'Me?' she snorted, the sunny smile returning. 'Nah, I'm too thick for that.'

'No you're not,' Flossy scoffed. 'You said the same thing on my first day and I didn't believe it then either.'

'I'm kidding, love . . . sort of,' Dolly replied. 'Actually, I prefer being a tea lady. I've done it for as long as I can remember and it suits me. I have got my own Singer, though.' With that, she pointed to a beautiful black-and-gold sewing machine on the far end of a dresser. 'I keep my hand in running stuff up, and Mum does the odd bit of homeworking. No woman worth her salt in the East End doesn't have a machine.'

Flossy's curiosity got the better of her.

'Are you not tempted to marry and start your own family? You'd make a cracking mum.'

Dolly laughed. 'What, and leave all this? Mum's made it far too comfortable for me to move out. Besides' – she shrugged – 'I've never found a fella good enough for me.'

Flossy laughed along too, but she knew there was more to the apocryphal story than a desire never to cut the apron strings; besides which, didn't half the women in Bethnal Green get married and move their husbands in with their mums, anyway? It just didn't add up that someone as lovely as Dolly should end up a spinster. She didn't like to pry, but Flossy got the distinct impression that Dolly was putting on a front as sparkling as her mum's doorstep.

*

Once tea was finished, Dolly and her mother walked Flossy to her lodgings round the corner, before setting back off for home. The fog had cleared, and a few dark clouds scudded across the sky like they were being chased. She could scarcely see a thing in the blackout, but Dolly could already picture the look on her mother's face.

As soon as they let themselves back inside their home, she turned to her.

'I'm not daft, love,' she said, licking her thumb and wiping a smudge of dirt from Dolly's cheek. 'I know you brought that young lass back because you are trying to avoid being on your own with me. You have to tell Vera and Archie.'

'Please, Mum, not now. I'm tired. I'm just going to finish this scarf; then I'll be up. We've got to have this bundle ready to take up the WVS in the morning.'

'Well, at least let me fix you a nice cup of beef tea . . . Or are you still hungry? I've got some calf's-foot jelly in the pantry.'

Dolly shook her head and felt her stomach heave. 'Honestly, Mum, I don't want anything.'

Her mother hovered anxiously by the table, and Dolly wished she would just leave her in peace.

'Oh my days. Look at your feet,' she exclaimed, staring down at Dolly's painfully swollen ankles. 'You know what that means.'

'Yeah, I've been on my feet all day,' Dolly snapped, feeling her patience desert her. 'Please, Mum, stop wrapping me in cotton wool. I don't want beef tea, calf's-foot jelly or all the tea in China. I just want to be left alone to do my knitting.'

'Stop driving yourself into an early grave,' she implored. 'You're taking on far too much. Now, up the wooden stairs to Bedfordshire and sleep.'

'I'll sleep when I'm dead,' Dolly blurted.

Her mother's face froze and Dolly instantly regretted her glib comment. Stifling a sob, her mother turned and ran up the stairs. Dolly sighed and ran a hand through her strawberry-blonde curls. She was finding it increasingly hard to keep a lid on her emotions, but she knew why that was. She loved life with intensity and a passion, sharpened by the knowledge that it was running through her fingers like sand.

She walked to the scullery and steeped her hands in a bowl of cold water, before splashing her neck and chest. With her composure regained, Dolly returned to the table and picked up the scarf. But it was no good. Tonight, her head felt full of broken glass, not good intentions. As she knitted, an image of all the poor sailors risking their lives in the freezing oceans chased through her mind. How many times had she already switched on the wireless this year to hear a sombre BBC newsreader announce, 'The admiralty regrets . . .'?

Letting the soft wool slip through her fingertips, it occurred to Dolly that her lovingly created handiwork, knitted to warm and protect, was also destined to suffer the same fate as her pen pal. Could the scarf she was knitting now end up as a bloodstained garment in a cold and watery grave?

Shuddering, she wondered what fate had in store for HMS *Avenge*, for all of them, in fact. Her tears flowed freely and Dolly suddenly had the strangest sensation that it was she, not them, who was drowning. She didn't bother to brush away her tears. Better to do her crying in the dark of the blackout.

'Dolly, Dolly, wake up,' urged her mother, shaking her gently.

'I must have fallen asleep at the table,' she mumbled groggily. 'What time is it?'

'It's morning. You've been asleep here all night. I've just come down and switched on the wireless. It's bad, love. Really bad.'

'What is?' Dolly asked, confused.

'The Nazis have invaded France. Our boys are withdrawing. It's time you left too.'

Dolly's head felt full of wool as she attempted to gather her wits.

'Oh, Mum,' she sighed. 'Stop being so dramatic.'

Hugging her housecoat tight about her, Dolly's mum looked suddenly old beyond her years. 'Dramatic, am I?' she cried. 'Our country is under attack, and when the Germans reach these shores, London is the first place they'll head. You promised me you'd return to Bexhill, out of harm's way, if that happened.'

'Oh, Mum,' Dolly snapped. 'I'm not made of eggshells. I don't want to shrivel up and die in that awful home.'

'Well, at the very least you need to stop work . . .'

'Never,' Dolly flashed back. 'I will never become a useless mouth . . . a burden. You hear me? Besides . . . how do we even know that physician was right? They don't know for certain I've got it, do they? What was it he said? "Diagnosis can only ever be arbitrary." I don't even know what that means, but I do know it means there's a chance they're wrong. Look at me – I look healthy enough, don't I?'

'You're kidding yerself,' Dolly's mum wept. 'Besides, you've forgotten what else he said: "You cannot see the infirmities it causes: its cripples do not limp."'

Dolly knew she ought not to say it, but the words spilt from her mouth unbidden. Years of pain and anguish came roaring out.

'How do I know you and the doctor didn't cook this up between you to keep me at home, eh?' she sobbed. 'You couldn't stand to be alone after Dad died, could yer? What was it you said to Flossy last night? "My son's a son till he gets a wife. My daughter's a daughter all her life."'

'I didn't mean it like that,' she protested hotly, but Dolly, in her anger, wasn't finished.

'I was even sterilized because you and the doctor told me it was for the best after what happened.'

94

Her mother gasped, and her hand flew to her mouth.

'Well, invasion or not, I'm stopping here,' Dolly insisted. 'Fate has given me a second chance with Flossy. I'm not running away again.'

Four

Standing alone in the canteen kitchen, lost in her own thoughts amid a cloud of billowing steam, Dolly didn't notice Lucky until he was right by her side.

'Morning, Doll,' he said chirpily.

'Oh my days!' she shrieked, clutching Lucky's arm. 'You gave me such a fright. I was away with the fairies.'

'I can tell,' he grinned, reaching past her to turn off the whistling kettles. 'You all right?' he quizzed. 'You look a little pale, and you're jumping about as if you got a touch of the St Vitus's dance. You're not worried about invasion, are you? It's all anyone seems to talk of since Dunkirk.'

'Course I'm not worried,' she scoffed. 'Take more than a few Nazis to topple Dolly Doolaney off her perch.'

And in truth, she really hadn't been thinking about the possibility of an invasion, though all these weeks on, she was still haunted by the terrible things she had read about Dunkirk. All those thousands of Allied troops trapped and bombarded on the beaches, the nightmare of their escape on the small flotilla of civilian boats . . . The bravery of every soldier battling on the beaches had been an example. If they could refuse to surrender, then so could she.

'Now, what can I do for you, my darlin'?' she asked. 'I'm just getting ready to bring the tea trolley round.'

With a flourish, Lucky produced a posy of violets from behind his back.

'How beautiful!' exclaimed Dolly. 'Wherever did you get your hands on them? I thought they weren't selling flowers down the market anymore.'

'Aah, it's not what you know but who,' he winked, tapping the side of his nose.

'Who's the lucky lady? Peggy?'

Lucky shrugged his broad shoulders and smiled sheepishly. 'You guessed.'

'It's as plain as the nose on your face that you've taken a real shine to the girl,' Dolly replied. 'What I don't get is why. I don't wish to be rude, but I really don't fancy your chances. She seems quite taken with her chap in the ministry, or if you listen to the girls' gossip, she's having it away with Göring himself.'

Lucky let out a long sigh and leaned back against the white-tiled wall. His handsome face lit up as he clutched the violets tightly over his heart. 'I know she's taken, but it's no good, Doll,' he said throatily. 'I can't look at her without wanting to kiss her. She has this effect on me. One look from her and I just lose myself.'

He wiped a hand through his dark locks and suddenly the dreamy expression of moments earlier was replaced with steely determination. 'I know I'm punching above my weight, but if being a boxer has taught me anything, it's never to give up until the final knockout blow. You understand what I'm saying, Doll? As long I have breath in my body, I won't give up.'

Dolly nodded and found solace in his words. 'Actually, Lucky, I think I do understand. It's not over until it's really over.'

'Exactly, so you'll lend me a tray and something to put these flowers in, then?' Lucky smiled, cocking his head to one side. 'I've got a little surprise for Peggy to try and win her over.'

'How can I say no to my favourite handyman?' she grinned back.

As she bustled about preparing her tea trolley, Dolly realized that if she was going to survive, she had better take a leaf out of Lucky Johnstone's book and start looking up to the stars instead of down to the gutter.

*

Out on the floor, Flossy looked up to see Archie leave his office, and from the look on his face, he meant business.

'Shut the machines down, girls,' he ordered, banging a cotton reel against a workbench to get their attention.

Flossy nudged Peggy and she immediately shut down her machine and looked up attentively. It had been just over a month since the forelady had packed her off home with a flea in her ear after she had injured herself. Flossy didn't know whether it was the shock of losing a day's wages or if she was, at last, coming to terms with her new life, but Peggy was finally knuckling down. She still kept herself to herself, but she hadn't been so much as a second late or dared to cheek the forelady.

The mood in the factory in the eighteen days since the last of the Allied troops had been evacuated from France had been decidedly subdued. Already, army and navy uniforms had started trickling into Trout's for repair, and it had been a stark reminder of the horrors of what had happened on those blood-drenched beaches. The fetid smell of damp khaki had filled the factory when the first bundle was unwrapped for repair. Even glacial Peggy had looked moved to tears when reports of the evacuation had drifted over from the crackly old wireless.

When the rumble of machines finally died down, Archie hoisted a large bundle and a sack onto the nearest workbench with a grunt.

'Bit early to be playing Santa Claus, ain't it, Mr G?' heckled Sal.

'I ain't here to talk about St Nicholas,' he replied. 'Do you know how many of our boys – not to mention French troops – were rescued alive from Dunkirk? Three hundred and thirty-eight thousand! Nothing short of a miracle, is it? They were rescued by brave civilians, and of course by the likes of our own boys on board HMS *Avenge* – civilian and soldier, fisherman and sailor, working side by side. Do you know what that proves?'

The pugnacious little foreman paced the factory floor, hands on his hips, as the women pondered his question. He stopped and turned to face them all. 'I predict a new kind of warfare, and it's gonna involve all of us on the Home Front. Do you know what the talk is out on the streets? The last war was the soldiers' war. This one is everybody's.'

Flossy glanced around at the stricken faces surrounding her.

'The reason I tell you all this is because I'm sad to report I have just heard the news that France has officially fallen. Paris is now under the control of the Nazis. Our little island stands alone.'

He pointed to the sack he had brought in. 'Uniforms fresh from France for repair, and there will be countless more flooding in. We all have to find our backbone!'

Flossy felt the blood in her veins turn to ice at the catastrophic news, the news that they had all feared but dared not believe could really happen.

From her position behind Ivy, she could see the older woman's shoulders start to shake.

'But that's the problem, Archie,' Ivy trembled. 'I'm too old for this lark. I don't mind admitting that I'm terrified of an invasion, and the government must think it too. Why else have they removed the street signs in the country? The church bells are silent too unless they invade. There's nothing between them and us now. We're just waiting, sitting ducks . . .' Her voice trailed off as tears consumed her.

Flossy couldn't bear to see the woman's suffering and leaped to her feet to put her arms round Ivy.

'Bless you, sweetheart,' she sobbed. 'But surely I can't be the only one who's petrified, am I? No nation has defeated Hitler yet.'

'Yeah, but they ain't come up against us Brits, have they?' reasoned Pat, standing up and slamming her fist down on her workbench so hard her machine rattled. 'Over my dead body is a Nazi marching up Brick Lane! I'll go down there and fight them bloody Germans on the beaches of Dover meself if I have to, with me bare hands and a rolling pin.

Give us women the weapons and we'll do the job! Who's with me, girls?'

A cacophony of noise and chaos erupted on the floor as each seamstress strained to make her opinion heard over the din. Suddenly, the clanging of a loud bell chimed over it all, and a sickening silence fell over the room. Flossy felt the unmistakable prickle of panic.

'The bells,' shrieked Ivy. 'They're here already!'

'Silence!' ordered a shrill voice.

Thirty sets of eyes swivelled to where a clearly vexed Vera was standing clutching an old school bell by the entrance to the foreman's office.

'I knew this would come in handy one day,' she said coolly. 'Now that I've got your attention, can we please stop all this hysteria? This is lamentable conduct, ladies. There's no question of Britain being invaded. We must remain steadfast and dedicated to our work. As Mr Gladstone said, our duties are of national importance. But' – her voice dropped to a gentler tone as she looked over to where Ivy was sitting – 'I do appreciate your fears. Dolly's bringing the tea trolley round, so we will break early for morning tea break. We have replies to your letters from HMS *Avenge* too, which I shall be handing round to those who wrote.' With that, she strode to the wireless and switched it on.

'The Home Service have launched a new programme, *Music While You Work*, to keep morale and productivity up among us workers, and a splendid idea it is too,' the forelady said briskly. 'Let's listen to this while we drink our tea.'

As the lively strains of Joe Loss and his big-band orchestra floated through the factory, Vera turned to move off, but then added as an afterthought, 'Nature has fashioned our sex for endurance, and endure we shall.'

The silky music and the prospect of tea and letters were as soothing as balm, and peace was once more restored to Trout's. But Flossy sensed that nothing would really be the same again now.

*

Peggy had listened in incredulous disbelief to the foreman's speech informing them of the fall of France. She had the queerest of sensations, as if she were watching a motion picture of her own life and she still had no idea how it came to be that she was in it. The world had quite simply gone mad.

As little as two months ago, she had the perfect life. Her biggest conundrum had been what shade of dress to wear to one of the regular dances Gerald took her to. But now perhaps it was time to start facing some uncomfortable truths. She hadn't seen hide nor hair of him since she moved to Bethnal Green six weeks ago, and the knowledge that he might have thrown her over was a bitter pill to swallow.

How much more could she lose?

Before, the war had been nothing but a minor irritation, and then had come that knock at the door that had changed everything and brought her here, to this place. Her world had turned on its axis. But Peggy was intelligent enough to know that fighting against it any longer was futile. Her mother was close to breaking point, and if they were to survive, she would have to keep a cool head and try to make a go of this job. The pitiful wage she brought home each Friday in a brown paper pay packet seemed to mean so much to her mother.

She turned to face Flossy, who winced while she rubbed her neck. 'Are you all right?' Peggy enquired.

'Oh, I'm fine, honestly,' she replied. 'Just a bit sore.'

'I know what you mean,' she sighed. 'Sitting at these machines hour after hour, my back's throbbing by the end of the day.'

Peggy had a grudging respect for the shy girl who had spent her life in some godforsaken home. It must have been ghastly, but she never heard a word of complaint from her lips. Perhaps if she were to take a leaf out of Flossy's book, she might be as popular as her, or Dolly for that matter.

Flossy was certainly a better machinist than she, and Peggy had a feeling it wouldn't be long before Vera moved her up to piecework with the more experienced workers.

'Still, mustn't grumble,' went on Flossy. 'If it doesn't ache, it doesn't work, and we are earning good money to be here.'

Peggy opened her mouth to say something scathing about how ten shillings a week was scarcely putting them in the same league as a Rockefeller, but decided against it. This didn't feel like the time or place for sarcasm.

'Come on, Dolly's here – let's get a cup of tea,' she said instead.

The pair rose to their feet and made to walk towards Dolly's trolley.

'Peggy?' rang out a nervous voice.

She turned round to find Lucky standing wearing a hopeful grin and a waiter's apron over his grease-stained overalls. In his hands, he clutched a tray with a single violet, a mug of tea and a marg-spread bun. Flossy tactfully made herself scarce.

'I thought seeing as how you won't come for tea, I'd bring tea to you. Sorry I ain't got no scones – a bun's the best I could do – but I hope you like the flower,' he grinned. 'I put the rest on your workstation. Violets, to match the colour of your eyes.'

She turned, and sure enough, a posy of violets stood in an old glass jam jar.

'Flowers in a jam jar?' she exclaimed, raising one eyebrow.

'I know, but I'm afraid I couldn't find a vase. Do you like it? I thought it was quite apt – you know, you're the flowers; I'm the old jam jar. Made me think how unusual things can go together . . .' His voice trailed off nervously. 'I know it ain't Lyons, but I thought it might help you feel more at home at Trout's.'

'Dizzy luxury,' she murmured, staring at the margarine, which was starting to congeal on the surface of the penny bun.

Peggy felt excruciatingly uncomfortable. The women's chatter had tailed off and suddenly she became aware that her and Lucky's exchange was the focal point of the whole room. Lily glared at her with ill-concealed hatred.

'Are you mocking my fall from grace?' Peggy snapped.

'What? No . . . no, of course not,' he blustered, confused.

'Please, Lucky, won't you just leave me alone?' she pleaded in a low voice. The four walls of the factory seemed to close in on her, and the heat was ferocious. Peggy turned and ran.

Outside, by the gates to Trout's, Peggy leaned against the

high brick wall and stared enviously at best friends Daisy and Sal, giggling over a shared cigarette.

Why had she not spent more time with her friends at Lyons this last eight months, instead of devoting every spare moment to Gerald?

Just then she heard a cough. She whirled round. Lucky stood on the cobbled street, clutching the jam jar of violets, his face a picture of contrition.

'I'm so sorry, Peggy. I didn't mean to embarrass you in there, and I swear I ain't mocking you,' he said, gazing deep into her eyes. 'I just wanted to do something nice for you, that's all. Cheer you up . . .'

Standing in front of her, clutching his pitiful jar of flowers, Lucky didn't look like a big, tough boxer. He looked like a lost little boy.

'It's me who should be apologizing to you,' Peggy said with a grimace. 'I'm sorry. I know you were trying to be nice. I'm just . . . Well, my life's a little complicated right now.'

'But we can be friends at least?' asked Lucky hopefully.

'Friends,' Peggy agreed with a smile, 'but please, no more dressing up as a waiter.'

'Hand on my heart,' Lucky promised, beating his hand against his chest and sloshing water from the jam jar all over the front of his overalls.

'You are the clumsiest man I know, Lucky Johnstone,' Peggy giggled, pulling a hanky from her pinny and dabbing it against his broad chest.

'Well, this looks frightfully cosy,' rang out a plummy voice.

Peggy turned in shock. 'Gerald . . . whatever are you doing here?'

'Hello, darling,' he smiled smoothly. 'Perhaps I should be asking you the same thing?'

Seeing Gerald, her Gerald, standing in his pinstriped suit on the street outside Trout's threw Peggy and for a moment she forgot her anger. Especially when from behind his back he produced the most enormous spray of exquisite red roses.

'For you, with my most humble apologies for neglecting my favourite girl,' he smiled.

Confused, she took the flowers. 'Gerald, it's been six weeks now with no word since you cancelled our date. I've been worried sick about you. I thought you had decided to . . . Well, I don't know what I thought.'

'Darling, Peggy, have you not been listening to the wireless? No, I'm sure they don't pay attention to such matters in a factory, but since the evacuation of Dunkirk, I've been practically chained to my desk. Now France has fallen, well, it's making life in the MOI impossible. I can't discuss it, of course – national security, you understand . . .'

'Yes, of course I understand,' Peggy replied, not really understanding at all. Surely he could have got word to her. And what of the two weeks *before* Dunkirk? Gerald had conveniently neglected to mention that. Where exactly had he been then? Peggy felt her head spin with unanswered questions as she clutched his extravagant peace offering.

Gerald turned to Lucky and the two men locked eyes. Gerald might have towered over Lucky, but Lucky's swarthy physique dwarfed his. For the first time, Peggy noticed how small Gerald's shoulders were.

'And you are?' Gerald asked coldly.

'Lucky Johnstone. I'm the odd-job man here at Trout's.' He wiped his right hand on his overalls and extended it to Gerald.

But instead of shaking it, Gerald simply stared in disgust at the missing tips of Lucky's fingers.

'Odd-job man, eh? Jack of all trades, master of none,' Gerald snorted. 'Mind you, I suppose there's not much a chap like you can do with that hand.'

Lucky's jaw clenched and for a terrible moment Peggy thought he might strike him.

'Anyway, darling, I've been at a meeting in Liverpool Street and I haven't long before I have to get back to White-hall, but I can spare you a few minutes for a cup of tea. Only, I really am going to have to insist you take that ghastly hairnet off: it does you no favours.'

'I won't have time, Gerald,' Peggy protested, patting her hair defensively. 'We only get ten minutes for tea break. I'll get in dreadful trouble if I'm late.'

Gerald rolled his eyes. 'A quick walk, then? Surely you can grant me that, seeing as I've come all this way to see you!'

Peggy nodded, wondering how he had managed to turn the tables and make her feel as if she were the one in the wrong.

'Very well,' she said weakly.

'That's my girl,' he replied, placing an arm around her shoulder and fixing Lucky with a cold stare.

'Thank heavens for these roses,' Gerald snorted as he guided her away from the factory gates. 'The stench round here is quite foul. I don't know how you bear it. You know why they built the factories in the East End, don't you?'

Peggy shook her head.

'It's downwind of the West End, of course.'

He laughed heartily at his own joke and Peggy didn't dare to look at Lucky's face, but as they disappeared down the street, Lucky stared after them, still clutching his small jam jar of violets.

*

Back in her tiny attic-room lodgings that evening, Flossy looked around and sighed wearily as she rubbed her throbbing neck. Dusty evening sunshine filtered into the room, split into columns by the anti-blast tape that crisscrossed the pane. Walking to the window, she jammed it open as far as it would go and stared out across the jumbled rooftops of the East End. There wasn't a breath of wind, but she thought she caught a whiff of rain. Sure enough, in the distance, dark clouds formed.

Flossy turned back to her tiny room. It didn't contain much, just a single iron bed covered in a candlewick bedspread, a chair and a small chest of drawers for her clothes. The walls were bare of any pictures or photographs, just flaking, damp plaster.

The toilet facilities – such as they were – were down four flights of stairs of the former silk weaver's house and at the bottom of the garden, and they were shared with the other occupants of the house. She didn't know how many other people all lived squashed together in the other rooms, but she guessed dozens. The dark passages were always filled with the smell of cooking cabbage and the sound of crying babies, and when she left for work in the morning, there was always at least one poor mother bumping a heavy coach pram down the stairs.

Flossy had found the overcrowding in this area shocking, but she knew it was caused by poverty, and the tumbledown houses crammed with the hungry poor.

But for all that, Flossy adored her room, her street and the village-like atmosphere of Bethnal Green. It may have lacked wealth, but as she knew from visiting Dolly's humble home, it was rich in family ties, loyalty and community. It was also the first time Flossy had ever had a space to call her own. She was earning ten shillings a week and learning a trade. Before she had left that day, Vera had pulled her to one side and told her she intended to move her up to sit with the more experienced women the very next day, with the promise of more complex tasks and piecework. Flossy sighed happily and walked to the single gas stove in the corner and set about fixing herself a cup of cocoa. As the tiny flame warmed the pan, contentment swelled in her chest. In her bag was a letter from Tommy, her sailor. Unlike the other women, she hadn't ripped it open there and then. She preferred to savour it on her own.

When the cocoa was bubbling, she poured the frothy chocolate drink into a mug, sat down on her bed and pulled the letter from her bag.

The first thing she noticed was the official stamp at the top of the paper, *HM Forces on Active Service*. Suddenly, her own work as a seamstress didn't seem quite so important.

Greetings, Flossy Brown,

My name is Tommy Bird. Thanks ever so much for the comforts, which we have just gratefully received on board. There is no sight these days more welcome than that of the mailboat. When she comes alongside, you have never seen so many willing and able sailors ready to give the Fleet Mail Wrens a hand in bringing the mailbags aboard.

Life is hard out here at sea, but I don't want to burden you with tales of our hardship. I can't tell you where I am or what I'm doing, as I can feel the censor's hand getting twitchy already, but we are doing our damnedest to beat Jerry. I don't want to talk about that, though. I want to hear all about the land I love the most of all. Blighty!

I'm a simple chap. Before war broke out, I worked down the docks, at the Tate & Lyle factory, and lived with my mum, dad and five older sisters – yes, five sisters. (My dad wept tears of joy when I came along!) Life was never dull, that's for sure. There was that much squabbling over boyfriends and lipstick, and my mum was forever threatening to bang some heads together. 'I can't hear meself think,' she used to say, but I loved the hubbub, and truth be told, I miss all them women fussing over me. Our house smelt like a tart's boudoir at times, but I even miss that. There was always laughter and fun in my family and constant noise. My dad whistling, the wireless, my sisters' latest dramas, church bells on a Sunday, the factory hooters sounding out the new shift . . .

Flossy was so gripped her cocoa had formed a skin as she read on.

Sometimes, when I'm up on deck on a nightwatch and a thick fog rolls in, it's so quiet it's deafening, and I'd do anything not to be able to hear myself think, 'cause that's when the fear sets in. So I cast my mind back to my little house in the East End and I think of my mum's Sunday roast, or all of us piled round the table with fish 'n' chips on a Friday night, or bread 'n' dripping on my lap round the fire, while Mum and my sisters sewed and sang along to the wireless.

Family life. That's what I miss the most. You can't beat it. I was married once too, but my wife, Sylvie, she passed. Anyway, I shan't dwell on that. I was lucky to be surrounded by my sisters then, I don't mind telling you. They carried me through some dark days.

Hark at me, rattling on about my family. Tell me about your mob, Flossy. I hope you're as blessed. I'd love to hear all about them.

Cheerio, ducks. The future looks promising now.

Yours faithfully,

Tommy

Outside, there was a low rumble of thunder and a fork of lightning lit up the skies over the East End. The storm had broken and the rains began. As she carefully folded Tommy's letter, the tears flowed freely down Flossy's cheeks, dripping onto the paper and blurring the ink.

Tommy had just painted a picture of family life that she could only dream of. His love of Sundays had only been matched by her hatred of them. Sundays had been the worst time of all. For that was when they would be forced to don awful tweed suits and felt hats, and be marched to church in a crocodile line. Sunday service in the morning, followed by Bible classes, and after she had turned eight, a second church service on Sunday evenings.

Besides her clothes, all Flossy had to show for nearly eighteen years in the home was her ration book and her Bible. Home! What an emotive word that was, Flossy thought as she dabbed her eyes with the edge of a tea towel and stared out at the rain cascading off the guttering. It made you think of somewhere warm and inviting, with a kettle that was permanently whistling and a hearthrug on which to stretch out your toes.

The home Flossy knew had quite different connotations. Her past was a blank sheet, the walls of her room devoid of any photos bursting with the kind of rumbustious but loving family life Tommy had just described.

But there was little point feeling sorry for herself. This poor chap had lost his wife and was on active service. Flossy picked up her pencil and pad, and immediately began to compose a reply. She didn't hold back. What was the point? She might never meet this Tommy chap in the flesh anyway. France had been invaded, good British men had lost their lives, and thousands more were getting ready to be sent to their deaths. Didn't she owe him a letter from the heart?

Writing was cathartic. By the time she had finished, Flossy felt calmer. She had told Tommy everything about her start in life, her upbringing in the institute, her desire to discover her roots and her sorrow at hearing he had lost his wife. She was just signing her name when a sudden knock at the door startled her. Whoever could be calling at such an hour? Flossy popped the letter in her bag and tentatively opened the door a crack.

'Peggy!' she exclaimed. 'Whatever are you doing here?'

Pulling her black astrakhan fur coat round her shoulders, Peggy was a frightful sight. Her mascara had run down her pale cheeks in rivulets, and her lips were bitten white against the pale of her face.

'May I come in?' she asked. 'It's raining stair rods out there.'

'Of course,' said Flossy, ushering her in. 'I'll fix you a cocoa and fetch you a towel.'

Peggy settled herself down on the chair and watched as Flossy set about making her drink.

'I hope you don't mind my barging my way in here, but after today, and what happened with Lucky, and Gerald turning up like that out of the blue, I feel so confused. I don't know what to think anymore,' she whispered. 'This morning, on our walk, he assured me he still loves me and wants to marry me when the war is over, but with France now occupied, that possibility seems more remote than ever.

'And now he says it's going to be even harder to get away from his desk and that I need to be patient and not get all hysterical. Oh, Flossy, I must be the most dreadful girlfriend ever.'

Flossy bit her tongue as she poured Peggy's drink into a tin mug and topped up her own.

'Anyway, what I'm trying to say is, I could use a friend. I thought perhaps you could persuade the others to let me join the sewing circle . . .'

'Why, of course, Peggy!' she smiled, pressing the mug of warm cocoa into her hands. 'Nothing would make me happier.'

'This wretched war, it's not going to go away, is it?' Peggy asked.

'No, and I fear this is just the beginning,' Flossy replied. 'We're going to need all the friends we can get if we're to endure what lies ahead.'

'But what about all the others?' Peggy replied worriedly. 'I haven't exactly endeared myself to them.'

'You leave Pat and the others to me. I'll talk to Dolly. She'll fix it. Deal?'

'Deal,' Peggy smiled back.

The two women bumped mugs and Flossy realized that all their happiness lay in each other. In the absence of family, friendship was everything.

Five

The next morning and the work was flooding in thick and fast. True to her word, Vera had moved Flossy up to piece-work, and no sooner had she assembled one part of a uniform than the next was hot on its heels.

'Gotta work fast to bring your money up,' muttered Daisy from beside her as she passed her a jacket, onto which Flossy had to sew the arms. The sassy young seamstress worked with effortless speed, displaying such a deceptively casual expertise that Flossy wondered if she would ever keep up. She had scarcely had a chance to look up from her machine, but at least it had made the time go quickly and she glanced up in surprise to see Dolly wheeling in her tea trolley.

'Goodness, is it tea break already?' she murmured, wearily rubbing her index finger across her throbbing temples.

Flossy didn't know how they all did it, especially the fourteen-year-olds, but everyone was pulling their weight, even Peggy. At the thought of Peggy, Flossy hoped Dolly would make good on her promise to broach the subject with the others of letting her join the Victory Knitters. She had just had time before shift started to tell Dolly about Peggy's visit the previous evening.

The sight of Dolly and her trolley was a welcome one.

'Come and wet your whistle, girls,' Dolly called.

Once Dolly had served Archie and Vera, the girls all jostled round for a well-earned brew.

Flossy was just sipping her tea when young Kathy drew her to one side.

'Flossy, I hope you don't mind me asking this, only I can't really talk to me mum about it,' she muttered.

'Of course, Kathy, if I can help?' she replied.

'Only, I've got a cracking headache and I think I've started my "p"s.'

'Sorry, I don't understand,' Flossy said apologetically.

'You know, me monthlies, the curse,' she went on. 'Only, I ain't too sure and I'm too embarrassed to ask any of the older women.'

'Sorry, Kathy, I see. Tell you what, let me talk to Dolly on your behalf. She'll know what to do.'

Flossy's heart went out to the fourteen-year-old. Poor Kathy. She might have the gift of the gab, but when it came to bodily functions, she was as clueless as she had been at her age.

Dolly was as kind and sensitive as Flossy knew she would be, even fishing a sanitary towel discreetly from her bag for Kathy. 'Use that, love, and don't worry about your headache. It'll pass in a day or two.'

Kathy bustled off to the loo gratefully, just as Pat loomed large.

'Here, Doll,' she laughed, 'what's up with your trolley?'

Just under the brightly coloured hand-stitched sign

reading, *Dolly's Trolley*, which the women had thoughtfully made her last year to celebrate twenty years of service, Dolly had attached a number of brown paper bags.

'Don't laugh, girls, but I'm going into thrift and salvage,' she replied. 'I heard a government appeal on the wireless for scrap metal and other remnants that can be reused for the war effort. It's all about the three "r"s.'

'Rum, rest and roll-ups?' Pat quipped.

'Get away,' Dolly said, laughing. 'Reuse, recycle and return. This bag is for bits of iron and old saucepans, this one dead batteries,' she explained. 'This one is for scraps of cotton, this one old clothes and so on. I want you all to bring your leftovers in and then Vera can take them down the WVS when they're full. Never let it be said that Trout's has fallen foul of the squanderbug.'

'Blimey, Doll,' laughed Sal. 'Never had you down as a rag-and-bone man.'

Dolly chuckled along too.

'Believe it or not, this will all go towards the national effort. Today's tatty old clothes are contributing towards tomorrow's Spitfire, Hurricane or tank.'

'Buggered if I can see how my Bill's old drawers will get a Spitfire up in the air,' grimaced Pat. 'But if you say so, Doll, well, of course we'll all do what we can to help.'

'That's the spirit, girls,' she grinned back.

'There is one more thing you can do to help me, actually,' she said, putting an arm round Peggy's shoulders and gently drawing her to the front of the group. 'Young Peggy here would like to join our sewing bee and I told her we would be delighted to have her.'

'I thought you was too good for the likes of us,' sniffed Pat.

'Behave, Doll,' screeched Lily. 'After the shocking way she treated poor Lucky yesterday? Well, I say no.'

A murmur of agreement rippled around the group.

'That's enough,' said Dolly sharply. 'Peggy may not have got off to the best of starts, but she wants to join in now, and that's what counts.'

The voices quieted, but the faces still glared back at her, as still as stone.

'We're fighting one war already; let's not start another,' warned Dolly.

Peggy cleared her throat nervously. 'Look here, I really am sorry that I behaved badly when I first arrived,' she said, with a shake in her voice. 'I know many of you must think I'm a . . . well, you know . . .'

'A snooty cow?' offered Lily helpfully.

'Yes, one of those,' she replied. 'But I would like to try and make amends. Please would you give me a fresh start and let me join the Victory Knitters?'

'Everyone deserves a second chance, so it's a yes from me,' said Sal.

'Very well. I don't mind,' said Pat. 'As long as yer give Lucky an apology for running out on 'im yesterday.'

Peggy nodded. 'I did already, Pat, but I think perhaps I owe him another.'

A strained silence fell over the group, broken only by a gush of hot wind and a strange whooshing noise. Pat's turban was blasted from her head with such force her metal curlers pinged off and clattered onto the concrete floor.

'What the jiggery-pokery . . . ?' the older woman jabbered.

Her hair stood up in great greasy grey tufts, yet she still managed to clutch her mug of tea in her hand, and looked down in shock to see a single roller bobbing about in it.

'What on earth just happened?' breathed Dolly, fishing the roller out of Pat's tea.

'Er, sorry, Pat,' piped up a sheepish Lucky from the far corner of the factory floor. 'I got my hands on an old war rifle for the LDV. I was using the steam from the works' boiler to clean it out and a pellet of grease shot out the barrel.'

Pat scowled. 'Bleedin' hell, Lucky, I ought to shove that rifle right up your—'

'Language, Pat,' interrupted Dolly.

'Yeah, well, all the same,' she huffed, as she tied her turban back on. 'You could have killed me. As it was, you nearly gave me a lobotomy, lad.'

'How would we have noticed, though, Pat?' cackled Sal.

There was a brief moment of stunned silence; then the whole floor fell about, helpless with raucous laughter. Even Peggy joined in, her rich, throaty laughter pealing above the others'.

'Ooh, you wicked sod,' screeched Pat, hoisting a beefy arm round Sal's neck and getting her in a headlock.

The laughter only stopped when Kathy re-emerged from the toilet . . . to a stunned silence.

'Oh, Kathy love,' said Dolly. 'I didn't mean the pad was for your headache.'

Poor Kathy. In her confusion, she had looped the ties to the sanitary towel round both ears and was wearing the pad across her forehead.

'Just when you think this place can't get any stranger,'

said Archie, poking his head out of his office at the commotion and doing a double take at Kathy. 'You're certifiable, the lot of yer.'

'You wouldn't have us any other way, would you, Mr G?' Daisy heckled back.

'Don't tempt me,' he sighed. 'Lucky lad, I know you take your defence duties seriously, but I'm not sure cleaning out a rifle complies with the fire regulations of this factory.'

'Sorry, Gov'nor,' apologized a bashful Lucky.

'Come on, girls, glug back that tea and back to your stations,' ordered Archie. 'Let's get some momentum going. How about a round of my favourite song "We're Going to Hang Out the Washing on the Siegfried Line"? Sing as you sew, girls, sing as you sew. Let's have a good day and give 'itler one in the eye!'

The women returned to their stations, as Dolly tactfully led Kathy back to the toilets. Flossy gazed about the room in astonishment; she truly had never encountered anywhere like Trout's in all her life.

*

It was nearly dinnertime and Peggy was engrossed in her work when suddenly her machine came to a great juddering halt.

'Botherations,' she muttered. She had managed to get her thread stuck round the race. Usually she would just ask Flossy to help her fix it, but now she had been moved off the new-starter bench, that was impossible. She had broken five needles last week and now this! Mrs Shadwell would skin her alive, or worse, dock her wages again.

Nervously, she eyed the forelady, who was inspecting some uniforms, four benches along. She would reach Peggy's bench in no time.

'Come on,' she urged, tugging helplessly at the snarled-up thread.

At that moment, Lucky walked past.

'What's wrong, Peggy?' he asked, kneeling down beside her.

'I've broken the machine again,' she said despairingly. 'If Mrs Shadwell sees, she's going to blow a gasket and put me back on the steam press, and that thing plays havoc with my hair.'

'Come here,' smiled Lucky affectionately. Whipping a screwdriver out, he deftly unscrewed the disc, removed the bobbin case, unwound the tangled thread, pulled it out and had the disc back on in a jiffy, before giving the machine a quick oil for good measure. 'There – good as new,' he grinned.

'Thanks, Lucky,' sighed Peggy, relieved. 'You've saved my bacon. That Vera could do battle with the best of men.'

'She's not such a bad old stick,' Lucky grinned back.

'Listen, Lucky, I really am sorry about yesterday. Your flowers truly were very thoughtful.'

'Sorry they weren't roses,' he grinned, replacing the screwdriver in his tool belt.

'That's all right. Don't tell Gerald, but I actually prefer violets.'

'Our secret,' Lucky grinned.

'I'm also sorry Gerald was a bit offhand with you,' she added. 'He doesn't mean it. He's under a lot of pressure at work at the moment.'

Lucky shrugged. 'Nothing I can't cope with, and apology accepted, but only if you'll allow me to take you out for a cup of tea. As friends! I promise to put on my best bib and tucker.'

'You never give up, do you?' Peggy said, shaking her head, but she couldn't help but laugh as Lucky stepped back and dislodged some bundles from the station behind.

'Oops, proper Herbert, me,' he grinned, frantically gathering them up. His eyes were still shining when he turned back. 'I may be clumsy, but I'm as fit as a flea and strong as an ox – you'll see, Peggy Piper. I'm going to keep on asking in the hope that one of these days you might just surprise yourself and say yes.'

In alarm, Peggy realized that the forelady was nearly upon them.

'Very well, Lucky,' she whispered. 'Just one cup, as friends, and no funny business, mind.'

'Scout's honour,' he promised.

'Now go,' she urged, shooing him away. 'Or you'll get me in trouble.'

'I promise you won't regret this, Peggy,' he babbled excitedly. 'How about tomorrow, straight after work?'

'Erm, I think so . . . Look here, you really must go,' she said.

'Tomorrow it is, then,' he winked.

'Is there a problem here?' rang out the forelady's shrill voice. Vera regarded them suspiciously.

'On the contrary, everything's coming up roses, ma'am,' Lucky replied. He winked at Peggy. 'Or should I say violets?'

The forelady looked confused and annoyed, as Peggy burst out laughing.

'Very well, move along, then, Lucky,' she ordered.

As Lucky bounded off like an overexcited puppy, he shot a last backwards glance. 'I won't sleep tonight, Peggy.'

Peggy rolled her eyes despairingly, but when she turned back to her Singer, she found she was smiling.

*

Flossy pondered her strange day as she walked home alone after work. She had only been at Trout's a short while and yet already she could feel herself changing. Excelling at machining and gaining the trust of the forelady was instilling in her a self-belief she had never known. Her childhood in the home had made her feel like a pencil drawing that was slowly being rubbed out, but thanks to Dolly and the girls, she no longer felt invisible.

Flossy had just wearily started to climb the linoleum stairs to her attic room when one of the mums who lived in the downstairs room poked her head out of the door.

'Letter for you, lovey,' she called out in the gloomy passage.

Thanking her, Flossy raced upstairs and lit the tiny oil lamp. Without taking her coat off, she tore open the letter and started to read. She recognized the spidery handwriting instantly. It belonged to Audrey Braithwaite, her welfare worker at the home.

Miss Brown,

We note your request to see the contents of your personal files. Now that you have turned eighteen, we

*are obliged to supply you with them. Your files contain
no information other than that you were a foundling
when you were admitted at the end of June 1922.
Based on an examination by a midwife, you were arbi-
trarily assigned a birthdate of 10 May. Flossy Brown is
the name you were given by this institute to legitimize
you, and you were baptized as such. Your birth name is
unknown, as are those of your mother and father.*

*We are morally and spiritually duty-bound to urge you
to draw upon the benevolence, education, cleanliness and
resilience that we hope we instilled in you to achieve
your full potential as a respectable and upstanding
citizen.*

*The forelady of Trout's garment factory has written to
us to inform us of your satisfactory progress within the
factory. I will take this opportunity to remind you of
the words of our founder: 'Girls who walk on a straight
road never lose their way.' I hope this serves as a
timely reminder to you of the virtues of decency and
chaste behaviour as we enter the most testing times in
our country's history . . .*

Flossy stopped reading and angrily crumpled the letter
into a ball in her fist. What rot! She hadn't wanted a regime
of resilience; she had wanted affection, love and cuddles,
but cutting through her anger was a stronger emotion.
Shame. She was a foundling. An abandoned child! What a
very strange word that was. It suggested she had been
'found', when it fact it meant only one thing. Her mother

had left her. Up until now, she had assumed her mother had officially signed her care over to the home, but in fact she had dumped her like a discarded wrapper and run. Her life had no more worth than a piece of rubbish.

An exquisite pain tore through her like razor blades and suddenly she was blinded by tears.

'I've had enough,' she yelled out, shaking with frustration, 'of being ignored . . .' Then the tears came. 'Oh . . . oh God,' she cried, shaking as great sobs erupted out of her tiny body.

A thump on the floorboards made her jump.

'Keep it down up there,' yelled a muffled male voice.

Flossy crashed back on the bed and covered her head with a pillow, to mute the sound of her anguish. She loathed herself that even in the depths of her despair, she still did not like to upset the neighbours.

In the sudden darkness, her pain continued unabated as she turned over the possibilities in her mind. Had her mother swaddled her in blankets and left her on the cold concrete steps, or had she had the decency to hand her over to a member of staff before fleeing?

How could anyone leave an innocent baby to such an uncertain destiny? As yet another door slammed shut on her, Flossy was more conscious than ever before of being alone in the world.

Putting the pillow to one side, she dried her eyes and picked up her sailor Tommy's letter from her bedside table. Now here was a man who understood the importance of family. His letter at least made sense.

*

The next day – the occasion of Peggy and Lucky's date – dawned and there wasn't a cloud in the sky. Before she had gone to bed, Peggy had prayed for a thick pea-souper to descend so that their date might be called off. But when she awoke and ripped down her blackout blinds, the morning sunshine had streamed defiantly in, as golden and sparkling as a glass of ginger beer. Never had the weather felt so at odds with the mood of the country, or the trepidation in Peggy's heart.

It wasn't that Peggy disliked Lucky; on the contrary, she had actually grown fond of seeing his sunny face about the factory. It was precisely these feelings of attraction she feared most of all. Her future lay with Gerald, but as she carefully eased her last pair of silk stockings over her slender ankles, she couldn't help but smile to herself. The man was so strong he looked like he could lift a horse, and yet when it came to matters of the heart, he was as soft as a lamb. Sighing, she smoothed her cotton summer dress over her camiknickers, tied on her pinafore and got ready to leave for the day's work.

It was still early, but downstairs, May was already in the small yard out back, pegging out the washing. When she spotted her only daughter, she carefully made her way through the sea of flapping laundry and kissed her warmly on the cheek. May smelt of lily of the valley and wore the faintest flush of lipstick the colour of raspberry jam.

'Morning, darling,' she said. 'It's going to be a fine day today, so I thought I'd get the washing out early. There's some sarnies wrapped up on the side for later, as I know how you hate the canteen food, and I've had the kettle steaming to freshen up your hat. I need to make a start, as . . . well, I have a job interview later in the City,' she admitted.

'But you haven't worked in years!' cried Peggy.

'I know, but now your father's gone, there's really no excuse for me to mope around the house doing nothing. Besides, I want to pull my weight. It's only part-time clerical work in an office – typing and filing – but I do hope I get the job. The extra money will certainly come in handy.'

May hesitated. 'In a funny sort of way, I'm quite looking forward to working. When you're gone, I do get rather lonely.'

'But what if Father comes home and finds you gone?' Peggy exclaimed.

May's face crumpled. 'Your father isn't coming back anytime soon. I'm just trying to be practical, darling.'

The factory at the end of the road hooted out a new shift and Peggy wearily turned and made to leave, resigned to her new life.

By six that evening, Peggy had snagged her last pair of silk stockings. Clothes rationing hadn't yet come in, but silk stockings were becoming increasingly hard to come by, which meant she would have to start staining her legs with gravy browning or buying paint-on hosiery like the other girls in the factory. The thought was a depressing one.

Outside, by the high wrought-iron gates to the factory, Lucky was waiting. He was wearing a smart shirt and jacket, and his boots had been buffed to a high shine. Peggy could see he had tried his hardest to tame his thick mop of dark curls by greasing them back with some brilliantine, but already an unruly lock had sprung out of place. When he spotted Peggy, a deep flush of red spread up his neck.

'You came. I worried you'd changed your mind,' he said, nervously twisting his cap between his fingers. 'You look the business, Peggy.'

Just then, a crowd of girls tottered past to start the night shift. When they spotted Peggy and Lucky, the air was filled with a chorus of wolf whistles.

'Oooh, hello, girls! What a lark. Looks like Lucky might get lucky after all!'

Lucky flushed an even deeper red as they screeched with laughter. 'Ignore 'em,' he grinned, rolling his eyes. 'Shall we step out?'

Once they were seated in a smart dining room on the Tottenham Court Road, well away from the East End, Peggy started to feel herself relax. She knew the place well from the early days of her courtship with Gerald. He used to bring her here all the time, and it felt like a place where even the war couldn't intrude.

The dark wood tables were laid out like stalls and all sealed off from each other by high wooden sides so that a couple could sit in perfect privacy without being seen from the street. The copper countertop was laid out with all manner of delicious cakes, and the gleaming chromium tea urn was so hot the windows of the dining room had steamed up.

'Blimey, this is a different gravy to what I'm used to,' remarked Lucky, shrugging off his jacket. 'Order whatever you like, Peggy. This is my treat.'

'Are you sure?' she asked.

'I'd use up a week's wages just to buy you tea. Don't

laugh, but I feel like the cat's whiskers to be sat opposite you.'

The arrival of tea eased the atmosphere, and as Peggy poured, Lucky chatted away happily about the East End and his work with the Repton Boys' Boxing Club.

'Isn't it a bit rum – you know, encouraging boys to fight?' Peggy ventured as she handed Lucky a cup of Darjeeling.

'I don't think so,' he replied thoughtfully. 'Boxing's in the blood for a lot of these lads from Bethnal Green: they're always gonna fight. Rather they have a fair fight in the ring than out on the streets. Some of the lads from my building are madder than scrapyard dogs. The club is respectable; it gives them self-belief, teaches them discipline and drive.'

Lucky gave a soft chuckle. 'I went with the mission last summer when they took a load of 'em down on a beano to Margate. It was the first time any of them had seen the sea. They all ran straight into the waves with their clothes on.'

'You're very fond of them, aren't you?' smiled Peggy.

His face lit up like a sunbeam. 'That I am, Peggy. I love 'em like little brothers,' he said. 'Since my own brothers joined the Kate, the folk down the club are like family to me.'

'Kate?' puzzled Peggy.

'Sorry – Kate Carney . . . army.'

'Cockney's a different language to me,' she sighed.

'You'll get the hang of it eventually,' he replied, slathering cream on his scone. 'It took me a while to learn my mother's tongue, but I got there in the end. Talking of France, I'd love to take my boys there. If they thought Margate was something else—'

'You speak French?' interrupted Peggy in disbelief.

'Not that well, but yeah, I do,' Lucky admitted. 'My mother's side are French, came over with the Huguenots in the seventeenth century and settled in Spitalfields as silk weavers and silversmiths. Apparently, this area was full of mulberry trees back then. I still love 'em today. They remind me of my mother. She's passed now, God rest her soul.'

'Tell me about her,' Peggy said.

'Well, she was an Agombar before she married my father and became a Johnstone. So beautiful she was – eyes and hair as dark as a gypsy's. She's been gone ten years now, but I still see reminders of her everywhere. There are French churches all over the East End – and mulberry trees if you know where to look. I miss her every single day. What's your mother like, Peggy?'

'Well, I suppose you could say she's devoted to me,' Peggy replied. 'I've been a bit rotten to her lately. Perhaps I should take more time to let her know how much I appreciate her.'

'You should,' agreed Lucky. 'You only get one mother, after all. What's Gerald's mother like? Do you get on with her?'

'Well, I'm sure I will,' Peggy replied, 'when I meet her. She's in the country for the duration of the war. Gerald wants to wait, and now he's so busy goodness knows when that will be.'

'If you were mine, I wouldn't be able to wait to show you off to my family. In fact, I'd want the whole world to know you were my girl.' As he spoke, Lucky's eyes bore into hers and Peggy felt herself flush and look down at the tablecloth.

A bell tinkled as the cafe door swung open and the silence was broken.

'Well, like I say,' Peggy said, looking up, 'he's busy.'

'Not that busy,' Lucky remarked. 'He's just walked in.'

Peggy swung round sharply in her seat. 'What on earth . . . ?' she breathed.

Sliding into a nearby booth was Gerald. Peggy watched, frozen in shock as his arm snaked round his female companion's shoulder. With a lecherous smile, he leaned over and whispered something in the young blonde's ear. With a great shriek of laughter she picked up the menu and playfully bashed him on the arm, before snuggling back into his embrace. Peggy didn't know what she found more shocking, the brazen way they were conducting themselves or the fact that the young lady was wearing a Lyons Corner House uniform! She was on her feet in a flash.

'This is you chained to your desk, is it?' Peggy yelled.

Gerald's face blanched of colour and he leaped up from the table. 'Peggy darling, it's really not what it looks like. You're confusing friendship with something more. Astrid here is a friend, that's all.'

'Don't you "Peggy darling" me. I'm not confused. In fact, things have never been clearer. This is the real reason why I haven't seen you. How could you, Gerald?'

She gestured to the confused-looking blonde. 'Do you really like her, or do you just have a thing for nippies?'

Gerald recovered himself quickly, and his lips twisted into a cruel sneer. 'Peggy, this really is frightfully tiresome. I can assure you there is nothing serious between me and this girl, but in any case, you can't honestly think that I would marry you now?'

She felt the blood drain from her face. 'W-what do you mean? But you said . . .'

Gerald sighed. 'Mother could just about have accepted

a waitress into the family, but a factory girl? Especially one whose father is . . .' He raised one eyebrow tauntingly. 'I'll spare your blushes, but you know what I'm referring to.

'In many ways, I'm relieved you saw me here today – saves us both a rather awkward conversation down the line, wouldn't you say?'

Peggy felt as if she had been struck round the face, as his companion stared at the ladder in her stockings and stifled a snigger.

Up until now, Lucky had remained silent. Rolling up his shirtsleeves, he stepped forward. 'You betta apologize to the lady immediately,' he demanded.

Gerald took one look at him and burst out laughing. 'Aah yes, the odd-job man. Please . . . I'm not taking orders from your sort. Put your guttersnipe back on his leash, Peggy.'

'In that case, you leave me no choice.' With that, Lucky drew back his fist and with one blow sent Gerald crashing onto the floor.

Lucky stood over him, his shirtsleeves strained across his biceps, as a dreadful hush descended over the dining room. 'Now apologize,' Lucky ordered.

Gerald's hand leaped to his nose to stem the trickle of blood.

'Lucky . . . what on earth are you playing at?' Peggy gasped, reaching for a napkin and crouching down beside Gerald. 'You could have killed him!'

'W-what?' stuttered Lucky. 'I-I was trying to defend you.'

Adrenaline pumping through her, she glared angrily up at Lucky. 'I don't need you to fight my battles for me, Lucky. This is all just . . . just so humiliating.'

Gerald wiped away the blood from his nose and smiled

up from the floor, his hard gaze mocking. 'Hard luck, old chap. Punching above your weight, I'd say.'

'Suit yourself, Peggy,' Lucky snapped, ignoring Gerald's jibe. Reaching for his jacket, he threw down enough money to cover the bill and stormed from the dining room. 'You clearly don't need help from *my sort*.'

*

The following day, Flossy tried in vain all morning to get some idea of how Peggy's evening with Lucky had gone, but Peggy had been totally absorbed in her work. When morning tea break finally arrived, she couldn't wait to hear the details.

'Come on, then,' smiled Flossy. 'I'm dying to hear how your date went.'

Peggy shrugged and played with the red rag tied round the handle of her mug. 'It wasn't a date,' she said abruptly. 'I need to go to the lavatory. Excuse me.' With that, she turned and hurried from the factory floor.

'What's eating her?' Flossy asked.

Dolly shrugged as she polished her tea urn. 'Search me.'

Flossy stared after Peggy as the door swung shut behind her; then she remembered the letter she had brought in to show Dolly.

'This arrived from the orphanage the night before last. I've been meaning to show you. It's hardly encouraging, is it?'

Dolly scanned the crumpled letter and shook her head before handing it back to Flossy. 'Oh, love,' she sighed. 'I don't know what you expected. But perhaps it's for the best.

Perhaps it's time to stop your search. I can't bear to see you hurt even more.'

Flossy jutted her chin out defiantly. 'I thought you understood, Dolly. I'm not giving up! I'm going to go down the records office, then the police station, then the library. Somewhere there has to be a clue as to who I am.'

Her neck gave a twinge of pain. Angrily, she rubbed at it as she blinked back tears.

'Oh, Flossy, please calm yourself,' soothed Dolly. 'I didn't mean to upset you, love. I just think that your mother, if she's still alive, well, perhaps she might not want to be found. Have you considered that?'

'Yes . . . No. Oh, I don't know,' she said despairingly. 'I just have a feeling, Dolly, a feeling I can't describe that my mother is alive, and that she's near.'

Dolly stared hard at Flossy, her blue eyes softened in concern. 'I think, love, that you should get yourself down the doc's and get that neck of yours looked at before you start hotfooting it all round the East End in search of your mother. It's really bothering you, I can see that.'

'It's the new workload,' Flossy admitted. 'Since Mrs Shadwell's moved me up to piecework, well, there's more uniforms than ever. War work is punishing. I don't know how the younger girls like Kathy do it.'

Flossy paused and thoughtfully rubbed at the soft grey rag tied to her mug handle. 'Talking of Kathy. Poor girl, she didn't know where to put herself when she got the wrong end of the stick over that sanitary towel, did she?'

Dolly shook her head at the memory. 'I know. She didn't half get some ribbing over that. She comes across so cocky

I sometimes forget she's only thirteen—' Dolly stopped and clamped a hand over her mouth.

'Kathy's only thirteen?' Flossy exclaimed. 'I thought you had to be a minimum of fourteen to work here?'

'Oh blimey, that just slipped out,' Dolly mumbled. 'I promised Kathy and her mum I wouldn't say nothing. Kathy's mother badly needs the extra money now that her old man's away serving. A private's wage don't stretch very far when you've six mouths to feed. Kathy's mum has to stitch Union Jack flags at night when all the kiddies are asleep. They're barely keeping their heads above water as it is, and without Kathy's wage . . . Please don't tell Vera.'

'I shan't breathe a word,' Flossy promised, but deep down she began to wonder what other secrets her friend was hiding.

Dolly looked relieved as Lucky walked past the tea trolley. 'Lucky!' she exclaimed. 'Wait up, love – you haven't had a cuppa yet.'

'No time, Doll,' he mumbled. 'I gotta run the wireless batteries down the oil shop to be recharged. Pat'll string me up if the wireless runs low.'

'You can always make time for a nice cup of tea,' Dolly said. 'A man can't go to work without a nice hot cup of Rosie inside him. Why do you reckon Napoleon lost the Battle of Waterloo? He ain't had his morning cuppa!'

Flossy groaned and giggled, but Lucky simply nodded, his face a mask of misery.

'Oh, Lucky, whatever's wrong, lad?' Dolly asked. 'I've never seen you look so down.'

'I've been a total fool,' he admitted, and the whole sorry story came tumbling out.

'I should never have been so stupid as to believe someone like Peggy could like someone like me. Honestly, Doll, you should have seen the way she looked at me after I landed one on that Gerald. I know I shouldn't have, but I couldn't just stand by and listen to him insult her like that, and now she hates me.'

His voice grew thick with emotion. 'It's because I'm a half-crown hero,' he whispered, running his hand despairingly through his dark hair. Abruptly, he turned and strode off.

'How could she treat him like that?' puzzled Flossy, staring after Lucky. 'What a shocking thing to do when all he was trying to do was stand up for her. I had a bad feeling about that Gerald all along.'

'Hold your horses, love,' counselled Dolly. 'We haven't heard Peggy's side of things yet.'

'I know what it's like to be rejected, Dolly,' Flossy mumbled angrily. 'Lucky's such a lovely chap and he really doesn't deserve this.'

By dinnertime, Flossy found her anger hadn't abated. In fact, if anything, she was even more cross with Peggy. She had stuck up for her right from the very beginning and insisted that everyone give her a chance.

'Flossy!' Peggy called out as soon as she walked into the canteen, patting the seat next to her. 'I saved you a seat. I thought I might try my hand at one of those drawstring bags you made.'

'Never mind all that,' Flossy muttered as she sat down. 'I know what you did to Lucky last night.'

Peggy's beautiful face fell, and at the mention of Lucky's

name, Lily's head snapped up from the other side of the table.

'It's not what you think,' Peggy replied, shifting uncomfortably.

'However could you take Gerald's side over Lucky's after what that snake did to you? Lucky was only trying to defend your honour and now he's heartbroken.'

At the sound of the girls' voices raised in anger, the rest of the Victory Knitters stopped their sewing and knitting, and conversations tailed off.

'Girls, give it a rest, eh,' Dolly warned in a low voice.

'Sounds like Peggy deserves what she's got coming, if you ask me,' chipped in Lily.

'You don't get it, do you?' Flossy cried, ignoring Dolly and Lily, and throwing her knitting needles down on the table in frustration. 'You've had such a privileged upbringing. You haven't wanted for anything, so you think it's perfectly all right to disregard Lucky's feelings and trample all over him.'

Peggy's violet eyes flashed angrily as she rose suddenly, scraping back her chair. 'How dare you? You don't know the first thing about my life. If I didn't know better, I'd say you were jealous.'

Flossy was aware the whole canteen was now watching, eagerly awaiting her response. She knew how the other women regarded her. Mousy little Flossy who never answered back, the forelady's favourite because she never dared to step out of line.

'Jealous of you? Never,' she snapped. 'I may not have a mother, but at least I have morals.'

Peggy had opened her mouth to protest when Dolly rose to her feet.

'That's enough!' she fumed, her cheeks drained of colour. 'How can you be arguing at a time like this? The full might of the enemy is just across the Channel! We should be pulling together.'

Dolly's hands started to tremble violently and she dropped her cup of tea, sending hot liquid skidding all over the floor. She ran from the room, stifling a sob.

Flossy and the rest of the group stared at each other, flabbergasted. A black cloud of uncertainty surged through her. What was happening to them?

Peggy waited a moment, then slowly gathered her sewing together. 'I know you won't believe me, Flossy, but the last thing I wanted was to hurt Lucky's feelings, or yours for that matter. I'm sorry.'

Flossy looked down, shamefaced. 'No, it's me who is sorry, Peggy. Dolly's right. We shouldn't be falling out at a time like this. I know how hurt you must have been to find out about Gerald.'

She stretched out her hand and laced her fingers through Peggy's. 'Please don't go. Stay and sew with us.'

'Thanks, Flossy,' Peggy murmured. 'But if it's all the same with you, I won't. I feel like some fresh air.'

No sooner had she set foot out of the factory door than she bumped into Lucky, coming back from the oil shop. He looked so handsome and strong, his thick, wavy dark hair gleaming in the sunshine. How she longed to return to the blissful state of intimacy they had enjoyed the previous evening, before everything had gone so badly wrong.

His face fell when he spotted her.

'Lucky,' she whispered, as he made to walk past her. 'Please wait.'

He stopped and stared at the pavement, his eyes downcast and dull.

'I'm so sorry for talking to you like that when all you were doing was trying to protect me. Please forgive me,' she pleaded. 'You're twice the man Gerald is.'

Lucky slowly raised his gaze and Peggy found she was holding her breath, waiting for his response.

'It's all right, Peggy,' he said quietly. 'I could tell you were ashamed to be seen with me, and you clearly don't need me to fight your battles.'

'No . . .' she protested. 'I was hurt and angry and confused. No one's ever stood up for me like that before.'

He shook his head. 'Don't worry – I shan't be bothering you again. The world's made up of different sorts of people, see, Peggy, your sort and my sort.'

Six

For the rest of that tense, hot and dusty summer of 1940, Peggy, along with the rest of the world, had watched bewildered at the devastating developments of the war. Countless British ships were attacked in the Channel, and a battle for Britain broke out in the skies above as the Luftwaffe fought for air superiority so that the German Army could invade. Bethnal Green had even had several screaming bombs dropped not one week ago, tragically leaving nine dead. How Peggy hoped that was an end to it.

In response, the women sang louder than ever before. Pat had even pinned a note to the door of the factory – *Go home, Huns. You will never take Trout's* – but the gallows humour did little to disguise the fear that cloaked the factory floor.

And to think Peggy had thought the war would all be over in a matter of months. How hollow her protestations sounded now. She had been wrong; in fact, she had been wrong about so many things. With that, she looked up from her machine just as Lucky was passing by her workbench. They locked eyes and she smiled, but he quickly looked the other way. She had tried her hardest to win his forgiveness, but she had wounded him far more deeply with her words than he had Gerald with his fists, and now that he had started courting Lily Beaumont, she had given up trying. The factory glamour puss had had Lucky in her sights from the moment she had clapped eyes on him, and Peggy had known that a steely, ambitious girl like Lily wouldn't rest until she had made him hers.

Besides which, Lucky kept himself so busy with work and the Local Defence Volunteers, which had changed its name to the slightly snappier-sounding Home Guard, he scarcely stayed still for a moment.

As for that rat Gerald? Peggy was still stunned at how blind she had been to his betrayal. How many other Lyons Corner House waitresses had he wooed in that dining room? He clearly had a penchant for the uniform, and as soon as she had left, her appeal had diminished. To think she had genuinely believed he loved her and wanted her for his wife, when all she had been was just a bit of fun.

Peggy supposed she ought to be grateful that she could finally see Gerald for the man he really was, but her heart ached with loss and regret. Worse still, there was only one person to blame . . . herself! Lucky was a diamond in the rough, and she had thrown away something priceless.

Flossy, meanwhile, seemed to spend every spare minute she wasn't in the factory pounding the cobbles, searching through every available record to see if she could find clues to her past. She knew Dolly worried about her desperately, but for all her fragility, Peggy knew her friend was a determined little thing. A ring of steel ran through those mysterious grey eyes.

Even Peggy's own mother was scarcely around now that she was working so hard in her new office job, and for the first time in her life, Peggy had had to pull her weight around the home, cooking her own meals and helping to keep the house spick and span when she wasn't in the factory.

Peggy watched as Lily rose from her workstation and tweaked Lucky's ear suggestively as she sashayed past. Lily shot Peggy a triumphant grin before flouncing to the toilet, pulling Lucky by his tool belt behind her.

Curiosity drew Peggy to the grimy window and she gazed out at the small yard that housed the old soot-stained brick toilet block. A few moments later, Lily and Lucky ran giggling into the yard, her pulling him by the hand until they reached the furthest secluded corner. Hands entangled, they leaned together against the wall, melting at the shoulders. Peggy watched enviously as Lily nestled into the crook of Lucky's strong arm and gazed up at him.

Lucky had such a powerful physical presence – close her eyes and Peggy could still feel him opposite her in that steamed-up dining room that fateful evening. As for Lily, she was so pretty and curvy, all saucer eyes, husky voice and shiny black hair. Little wonder she had scooped Miss Bethnal Green 1938. What man could resist her? Obviously not Lucky, as a second later, he removed his cap, bent down and brushed his lips against hers. Lily responded by eagerly throwing her arms round his broad shoulders and kissing him back passionately.

It was like a leaden blow in the solar plexus, and for a dreadful moment, Peggy thought she might be sick. Tears blurring her eyes, she stumbled away from the ledge and back to her workstation.

Thank goodness for the sewing circle and her friendship with Flossy, both of which were thriving. Thanks to Dolly's tireless fundraising, the Victory Knitters had managed to purchase a reasonable quantity of wool and they had just completed a second bundle of comforts for the sailors on board HMS *Avenge*. When it came to her involvement, Peggy sensed she hadn't been totally accepted, or forgiven, and would always be something of an outsider to the tough tribe of feisty factory workers. How could she blame them? She had been so offhand and snooty when she first arrived at Trout's, mistaking resilience for wretchedness, time and time again. For layered beneath the squalor of the housing bubbled a vibrancy of life that helped Bethnal Green to survive. The question was, did Peggy have what it took to survive? Throwing herself into the work of the sewing bee might or might not bring about her redemption, but at the very least it provided a respite from her heartache.

Two hours later, at Friday dinnertime, Dolly and Vera called a meeting of all the members of the Victory Knitters in the staff canteen.

'Ladies, I'm deeply gratified to announce our sewing circle as one of the most successful in the East End,' announced the forelady with a rare smile. 'No one can hold a candle to it. I'm so proud of you all, and really feel I can hold my head up high in the WVS. Some of the other work parties only managed half of the comfort items we've produced. Why, Cole & Sons factory sewing bee only made a paltry twelve items,' she added smugly.

'Not that it's a competition,' Dolly chipped in. 'Every little bit helps.'

'Yes, quite,' the forelady added hastily, and Peggy stifled a giggle as Flossy nudged her under the table.

'However, our reserves of wool are dwindling,' Dolly warned. 'We urgently need more and there is no money left in our funds. So, any ideas?'

'Oh, here we go,' piped up Ivy, as she rummaged through her knitting bag. 'Don't tell me – we can start unravelling our socks, unpicking our old man's long johns. I've already donated me spare pans for Spitfires; the rate this war's going on, I won't have a pot to p—'

'No one's asking you to do any such thing, Ivy,' Vera interrupted sharply. 'Hear Dolly out, won't you?'

'Yeah, hear Doll out,' teased Sal. 'Last I heard, your old man was sewn into his long johns anyway.'

'Why, you cheeky beggar!' screeched Ivy, playfully punching Sal on the arm.

'I just wondered if anyone had any ideas how we can get our hands on more wool and fabric,' said Dolly. 'There's rumours that clothing's next to be rationed and then we really will be stuck.'

The voices quieted at the dread of yet more rationing. For the first time ever, Peggy had seen her mother flustered when she returned from the shops the previous evening. She had queued for the best part of an hour after work, only to have the shopkeeper slam down the shutters in her face when she reached the front, as his meagre stock had run out. They'd had to content themselves with a bread roll and a mug of Oxo for tea. Now, Peggy found the grumbling in her tummy had the unusual effect of sharpening her brain.

'How about entering a singing competition?' she suggested.

'I remember seeing one advertised for every Friday evening at a public house up by Columbia Road. They had a small cash prize, a pair of glass peacocks and a tea set for the winner. We could raffle the tea set off too if we won.'

'Ooh, not half!' said Kathy. 'And there was me thinking you was all meat and no potatoes.'

'I think what Kathy is trying to say is that is a really excellent idea, love,' said Dolly, beaming at Peggy. 'Don't push your luck, though, Kathy,' she added. 'You're far too young for the pub.'

Peggy felt a little glow of happiness to be singled out by Dolly.

'Who's going to sing, though?' Flossy asked. 'We can't all get up on stage.'

All eyes in the canteen swivelled to Lily.

'I could do that new Vera Lynn number, blow them other turns out the water. Lucky reckons I look a bit like her,' Lily said modestly. 'I am used to being up on stage after all. I was crowned—'

'Miss Bethnal Green 1938. Yeah, yeah, we know – you have mentioned it once or twice,' interrupted Sal, winking at the rest of the group.

'Actually, sweetheart, I know you have a smashing voice, but I was thinking perhaps it would be nice to let Peggy do it,' suggested Dolly, trying to head off the row before it broke out. 'Seeing as how it was her idea. Also, Peggy, I've listened to you singing on the sly. You've got a cracking little voice, darlin'.'

'I . . . Oh, I don't know about that,' Peggy replied, flustered, as she saw Lily's green eyes narrow to slits. 'I'm happy to let Lily take the stage.'

'Nonsense,' insisted Vera. 'I'm sure Lily will be happy to take a back seat for once.'

'Well, if you insist,' Peggy said. 'But when? I shall need some time to prepare.'

'No time like the present,' said Dolly, grinning. 'Let's go after work tonight.'

'Tonight?' Peggy blustered. 'Oh, I don't know . . . I think my mother needs me home this evening to help with chores.'

'Sorry, Peggy, but didn't you tell me your mother had a work social this evening?' said Flossy with a little grin.

'You swine,' she mouthed.

A clamour of enthusiastic voices filled the air.

'Oh, come on,' urged Pat. 'Gawd knows we could all do with some light relief. We've been working our fingers to the bone and a night out is just what the Victory Knitters need. Besides, I heard half the mob from London Brothers are going tonight. We can't let that lot bag it from under our noses.'

'Very well, then,' Peggy sighed, knowing she was beat. She had to admit it would feel good to earn the women's praise, and who knew, it might even help take her mind off Lucky.

*

At seven o'clock that evening, Flossy found herself in Peggy's terrace, after agreeing to go to the competition with her.

Once the girls had eagerly devoured the cold luncheon meats and pickles May had thoughtfully left out for tea, they sat back in their seats and warmed their toes by the embers of the fire she had lit before she left for the evening.

'Your mother is a really wonderful woman,' sighed Flossy, as she stared into the golden glow of the fire. 'She never seems to stop thinking of ways to make your life more comfortable. I hope you appreciate her.'

A flash of shame crossed Peggy's face. 'That's what Lucky said.'

A strained silence fell over the room and Peggy forced a smile on her face. 'Why don't you let me doll you up a bit, Flossy? You're about the same size as me. An eight, yes? I could lend you a dress.' She hesitated. 'I don't wish to sound mean, Flossy, but if you spent a little more time on yourself rather than searching for your mother, perhaps you might find more contentment.'

Flossy shook her head vehemently and winced as she felt her neck stiffen. 'No, thanks,' she mumbled. 'I'm quite happy the way I am.'

'Suit yourself,' Peggy replied. 'I know it's hardly the Albert Hall, but no way am I getting up on stage wearing my work pinny. Make yourself at home. I won't be long.'

Peggy turned and clattered up the creaky wooden steps of the terrace. Once she heard her bedroom door slam shut, Flossy pulled the letter from her pinafore pocket and felt her heart give a little flip.

Tommy's reply to her second letter had arrived at the factory that very morning.

Taking it out, she carefully laid it on the table and began to read.

My dear Flossy,

What a total fool I am – fancy me rambling on about my family without stopping to think. Trust me to put both my size-ten feet right in it. Please forgive me. You sound as if you've had a sorry start in life, but you've dusted yourself down and got on with things. I admire that in a woman. Your words about life in the factory make me smile. They remind me of my days down at Tate & Lyle, and I think you and I could be good friends.

It's hard for me to express in words how important letters are on board this ship. A letter from a wife, sweetheart, parent, child or even a stranger is all it takes to give us that connection to the home we are fighting for. The contents of the mailbag, well, that can make or break the mood at camp or on board. Jerry ain't making things any easier and we sleep in our life-jackets now. What little time off we have, we try and sleep, but who can do that these days? Instead, we play Uckers. We play for cigarettes, Martins. Horrible things, they are. The Red Cross send 'em. I don't even smoke, but you can't gamble for money on board.

The next three lines had been blacked out by the censor, so Flossy was unable to read whatever it was Tommy had shared, but the end of his letter certainly had her smiling.

I hope I'm not being forward, but, well, we've both endured our fair share of heartache and we're still here to tell the tale. Thanks ever so for the comforts, which arrived this week. I can't even begin to describe the pleasure on the men's faces when they collected their bundles. It really makes all the difference during the long, cold hours on duty. My feet are lovely and snug

*in these new socks. They say the way to a man's heart
is through his stomach, but on board this ship, I reckon
it's by giving him warm toes! If there weren't hundreds
of miles of ocean separating us, I should have married
you on the spot. Thanks, Flossy. You're a diamond. You
haven't just warmed me up. You've brightened my life
up.*

Yours,

Tommy x

A childlike feeling of excitement tingled up Flossy's spine.
Tommy had signed his letter off, *Yours*. Maybe, just maybe,
she could belong to someone after all.

She was still grinning like the cat who had got the rationed
cream when Peggy re-emerged from her room. The transformation was quite spellbinding.

'Oh, Peggy,' breathed Flossy. 'You really are a picture.'

And she really was. Peggy was pure molten glamour.
Flossy had become so accustomed to seeing her in her drab
factory attire and headscarf that she had forgotten quite
how beautiful her friend was.

Her hair had been brushed out and her glossy chestnut
curls gleamed in the firelight. A sweep of hair had been
pulled back by a single diamanté hairslide. Her tall, willowy
figure was encased in a column of shimmering coral silk,
and on her feet she wore the same patent-leather high-heel
T-bar sandals that had got right up Vera's nose on her first
day.

Peggy spotted Flossy looking at them and grinned wick-
edly. 'Well, we're not in the factory now, are we?'

Flossy shook her head. She didn't know where her friend got the nerve. You could take the girl out of the West End . . . 'Come on,' she chuckled, 'or else we'll be late. Best take my arm or you'll break your neck on the cobbles.'

'It's the only smart way to totter,' Peggy winked, taking Flossy's arm.

Flossy had a hunch that she might just have dolled herself up in the hope that a certain brown-eyed boxer might be watching from the audience.

Outside, it was dusk and the sun was sinking, burnishing the soot-caked buildings in a fiery glow. The street was filled with the scent of cooking and coal fires. The girls paused on the doorstep and became aware of Peggy's neighbour, Kate, perched on her window ledge in a wrap-over apron, smoking a fag.

'Evening, girls. Don'cha look lovely?' she said. 'Mind how you go – especially you, Peg. One blast o' wind in that dress and yer drawers'll fly off.'

'Who says I'm wearing any?' Peggy shot back, before teetering off, leaving Kate and Flossy to stare after her open-mouthed.

*

Dolly paused outside the pub door and attempted to smother a yawn with her hand. She hadn't gone home after work like most of the factory workers; instead, she had helped Lucky load up the borrowed Tin Lizzie to deliver their second consignment of comfort items to the depot, stopping at the WVS to drop off some tins of Klim powdered milk and her salvage.

Dolly needed a night in a smoky pub like a hole in the head. She longed for a hot mug of Ovaltine and to curl up in her nice warm bed. But that was hardly putting a good face on it, was it? All the girls were expecting her and she didn't like to let them down. Besides, another part of her knew her mother would only beg her to stop in with her and rest had she gone home. Her mother had always been protective of her, but recently . . .

Dolly gazed up past the impressive tiled facade of the old Victorian public house, its windows already heavily blacked out, and saw the sun sinking in the west, drenching row after row of smoking chimney pots in a honey-coloured glow. Skeins of smoke drifting over from the factories were lit up a dazzling pink in the fading light.

These streets were usually such a grey and bleak landscape, coated as they were with centuries of industrial grime and coal dust. Dolly took a moment to stop and drink in the spectacle of colour.

Her eyes were drawn to a poster nailed to the community noticeboard facing the pub door, as if to warn tongues who had imbibed too much ale, *Careless talk costs lives.*

Dolly breathed in deeply. For a moment, she caught an infinitesimal trace of an odour she didn't recognize in the evening breeze. She had the queerest of sensations, not so much a premonition, more an instinct that something was brewing in the skies above. Anticipation hung heavy in the air as the sun went down over the East End for another day.

Shaking herself, Dolly pushed open the door to the pub. A wall of smoke and noise hit her, and gasping slightly, she wove her way through the tables. The pub was heaving with groups of women, from office and shop workers to rag-trade factory groups, most of whom Dolly knew, all cock-a-hoop that it was a Friday and, more importantly, payday.

She had never seen so many exuberant women per square metre than were crammed joyfully into this pub. She spotted the Victory Knitters first; it wasn't hard. They were easily the noisiest people in there, all huddled round a table nearest the makeshift stage, guzzling watered-down ale in a fug of cigarette smoke. Their garrulous laughter filled the saloon bar. How she loved her gossiping sisterhood, desperate to find fun despite of, or maybe even because of, this war.

Sal spotted her first and her face lit up. 'Oh, here she is. Wotcha, Doll. Shift up, everyone,' she ordered. 'I got you your usual, a gin and lime.'

'Thanks, Sal, but I don't feel like drinking tonight – you have it and I'll grab a lemonade in a bit. I'm dead on my feet.'

'Blimey. You sure you're feeling all right, Doll?' said Sal, jokingly touching her forehead. 'Not like you to be on the wagon. Come to think of it, you do look a bit peaky. You've got a proper flush on yer cheeks.'

'I'm fine,' she reassured. 'I just want to keep a clear head so I can make sure I remember the look on the faces of London Brothers when we scoop the prize from under their noses.' She said it loud enough for her pal, a seamstress at the nearby factory, to hear.

The wiry woman with quick blue eyes looked up and a wicked grin creased her face. There was nothing her old mate Babs, a machinist of twenty-odd years' experience, loved more than a bit of verbal fisticuffs.

'Behave, Dolly Doolaney,' she cackled, drawing heavily

on her cigarette. 'You Trout's girls are going home with nuffink tonight except sore heads. London Brothers can sing you lot under the table.'

'Well, Babs, I suppose every dog has its day,' chipped in Pat with an arch smile. 'So maybe tonight you might get lucky. Talking of which, how's your Neville? Still spending money like a man with no arms?'

'No better or worse than your Bill,' Lil shot back, blowing a long stream of blue smoke in Pat's direction. 'Still got a set of teeth on him like a Whitechapel graveyard at midnight, has he?'

Pat's laugh was booming as she slammed an enormous hand on the table. 'Do you know what we say about you London Brothers mob? *The girls from London Brothers pretend they're saints to their mothers, charming lasses, full of airs and graces, but you wanna see their lovers. I've seen better-looking nags at the Kempton Races!*'

Rising to the challenge, Babs mashed out her cigarette in a glass ashtray, rose and slurped back her beer, before wiping away the frothy moustache with the back of her hand. '*There was a factory called Trout's. The workers had a reputation for being devout. So how come there are sailors queuing up outside? Is it something to do with the saucy letters they hide?*' Babs raised her eyebrows teasingly and a chorus of lusty wolf whistles rang out round the saloon bar.

Dolly felt a smile return to her dimpled cheeks, but poor Daisy and all the other girls who had been secretly leaving notes in the uniforms flushed a deep red. You really couldn't keep anything secret for long in the East End.

'Filth and nonsense,' Pat blustered.

'Ladies, I enjoy a bit of factory rivalry as much as the

next, but let's keep this a clean fight, shall we?' laughed Dolly. 'Honestly, what a caper!'

Her words were drowned out when somewhere in the corner of the room, a piano started up.

'Crash, bang, wallop!' boomed the publican, who looked to Dolly as if he had been enjoying too much of his own beer. He bashed his tankard down on the bar with a thump that made poor Flossy jump in her seat. 'Come on, then, girls. Less jawing, more singing!'

London Brothers were up first and Dolly recognized a sweet local girl she knew by the name of Ethel take to the stage. Her frizzy hair was scraped back, and she had an unfortunate boss eye that meant you weren't quite sure where she was looking, but what she lacked in looks, she made up for in enthusiasm, and soon she was belting out a proud but slightly warbling rendition of 'It's a Long Way to Tipperary'.

As she reached the crescendo of the song, Dolly spotted two men at the bar nudging each other.

'*It's a long way to Tipperary!*' screeched Ethel.

'Too bloody long. Wish you'd hurry up and get there!' one man shouted.

A great peal of laughter rang out round the pub as Ethel gamely sang on.

The crowd gave up listening after a while, and by the time poor Ethel trudged off the stage, half the pub had resumed their conversations or nipped to the lav.

Next up was a very nervous-looking Peggy. Dolly squeezed her hand in support as she walked past.

Soon her stunning voice filled the pub and the room fell silent, as if under a spell. She sang the number-one Frank

Sinatra hit everyone was talking about, 'I'll Never Smile Again'. Dolly knew she was talented, but by golly, she didn't know she was this good. Her crystal-clear voice was utterly mesmerizing, her shimmering looks beguiling. The lyrics of loss and love were haunting and seemed to resonate with everyone. Even the heckler at the bar had fallen silent and seemed to have something in his eye, judging by the way he kept wiping it.

'There aren't enough tears in my eyes,' murmured Ivy, misty-eyed.

Flossy gazed open-mouthed. Only Lily sat sulkily, glaring into her port and lemon.

As Peggy reached the crescendo of her song, she closed her eyes and tilted her head back, her chestnut hair sliding over one milky shoulder.

Just then, a movement by the door caught Dolly's eye and she watched as Lucky slipped in and removed his cap. He stood motionless by the heavy red velvet curtains, as he watched Peggy sing through the clouds of smoke, and Dolly knew in a heartbeat . . . The man was still infatuated. He could not wrench his gaze from Peggy's smoulderingly beautiful face.

Lily spotted him too and rose sharply. 'I've got a headache. I'm going,' she muttered under her breath to Dolly. A moment later, she and Lucky left.

Peggy finished her song, and for a split second, you could have heard a pin drop, before a round of thunderous applause filled the room.

'That's one in the eye for you,' crowed Pat triumphantly to Babs.

That night, Dolly fancied that Peggy had won more than

just prize money and a pair of glass peacocks. She had finally won the approval of all the women. Her time on the sidelines was now over.

Seven

The next day was a Saturday, and by late-afternoon tea break, still all anyone could talk about was Peggy's triumph the previous evening.

'You should have seen their faces when the compère handed you the prize money. That Babs had the right hump!' crowed Pat, slinging an arm round Peggy's shoulders.

'Yeah. Why didn't you tell us you had such a good voice, love?' said Ivy. 'You're so good I reckon you could sing up at one of Tate & Lyle's factory socials.'

'I should say,' agreed Daisy. 'Or even the Hackney Empire.'

'I don't think I'm that good,' said Peggy. 'Besides, I didn't exactly try very hard with you when I started.'

'Never mind all that,' blustered Dolly, filling up her mug. 'You're one of the girls now.'

'That's right – you're one of us, you little dark horse,' said Pat.

'Isn't she just?' interrupted Lily coldly, folding her arms. 'A dark horse, that is.'

An uneasy silence fell over the room.

'Am I the only one who is still intrigued by why you suddenly washed up in the East End?' she spat. 'A nice fine lady like you from such a lah-di-dah background.'

'Lily,' warned Vera. 'Watch your mouth.'

'No, I won't,' she blazed suddenly, her green eyes flashing dangerously. 'She didn't want a bar of us when she first started, looked down her nose at all of us, not to mention how she walked all over poor Lucky. I, for one, think she's nothing but a little hussy. A hussy with a German lover . . .'

'You don't know what you're talking about, Lily,' Peggy muttered.

'Wanna bet?' Lily crowed. 'This lot might be taken in by your little Miss Perfect act, but I saw your reaction when Pat started talking about German spies.' With that, she reached out and pushed a goading finger hard in the middle of Peggy's pinafore. 'But I got your number, see? I know you're bedding a Boche.'

Everyone stood stock-still, waiting for Peggy's response, but she never got the chance to reply. A deep, wailing drone rose up and filled the factory floor.

Archie walked out of his office, rubbing the crown of his bald head with one hand and holding a half-eaten garibaldi in the other.

'All right, folks. Probably a false alarm, but after last week's bombings, let's not take the chance, eh? Let's get down the shelter quick smart. Just when I thought I might actually be able to leave on time and catch the end of the West Ham game.'

A heavy groan of resignation rang out.

'I know, I know. Bloody 'itler. Come on, girls, Moaning Minnie's telling yer to shift your backsides.'

'What's Moaning Minnie?' Flossy blurted, regretting her words before they were even out of her mouth.

'Wotcha think it is?' Archie exclaimed despairingly. 'An invitation to do the conga? It's the bleedin' siren, of course!'

A cold finger of fear drew up Flossy's spine. She had dreaded this moment above all else. It was time to go underground.

*

Shakily, Peggy gathered up her belongings and followed the slipstream of workers clattering down the stairwell, but when she reached the door to the factory, she realized she had left behind her wristwatch. She always took it off before she started work in case she scratched it, and left it by the side of her machine. It was the last thing her father gave her before . . .

By the time she had retrieved it and turned back, Peggy realized with a start that she was the last machinist left on the floor. Lucky was standing by the door, his hand on the light switch.

'Come on, Peggy, don't dilly-dally,' he urged, placing a hand on the small of her back. 'Archie's just shutting down the machines; then we have to get out of here.'

Peggy paused, aware of his touch burning into her skin. A voice whispered in her head, *Do it. Tell him everything* . . . Months of heartache and loneliness crystallized together into a bolt of pure emotion. The realization was startling. She was in love with Lucky.

'L-Lucky,' she stammered, over the relentless wail of the siren. 'I haven't been straight with you. Last night, when I was singing . . . it was you I was singing those words to. I saw you by the door, watching.'

His face fell as he quickly turned away. 'I don't wanna hear it, Peggy.'

But Peggy knew. It was too late to turn back now.

'I beg of you, Lucky, don't avoid me any longer. I know you're with Lily now, and I don't wish to do anything to hurt either of you, but I owe you an explanation for my behaviour.'

The words spilt from her lips. 'I'll tell you everything, the real reason why I'm here. Please meet me later.'

'I thought I was born on the wrong doorstep for you?' he mumbled.

'Oh, Lucky, I've been a total fool and I'm not ashamed to admit it,' she cried.

'This isn't the time . . .' he said, nervously scanning the cloudless skies outside the high windows.

'Please,' she begged. 'This evening. Say you'll meet me.'

'Very well, Peggy,' he sighed, shaking his head. 'But right now, I want to get you safely underground.'

'Where will you be going, Lucky?' she asked.

'I'm heading down to the ARP headquarters on Lyte Street. Archie is staying here on fire-watching duty. But I can't leave until I see you to safety. Now hurry, there's not a moment to lose.'

Below ground, Peggy felt terrified, relieved and excited all at once. She had never been in a public shelter as big as this one. It was housed in the basement of a neighbouring factory – now requisitioned by the authorities as a public shelter – and every worker within a square-mile radius seemed to be crammed in here, seated on the narrow wooden slatted benches that lined the damp brick walls. The basement was dark, hurricane lamps threw out dim lighting, and Peggy could only just make out an Elsan chemical closet partially screened off by a canvas door in the furthest corner. Frantically, she scanned the benches for a face she recognized.

'Over here, Peggy,' called out Flossy. 'I've saved you a place next to me.'

The Trout's girls were all sitting huddled together; many had grabbed their knitting bags on the way out and were already starting to work on their knitting.

'Is this it?' Peggy asked, as she took her place next to Flossy.

'What were you expecting? The Ritz?' sneered Lily, who, despite the interruption, clearly hadn't forgotten her earlier outburst.

'Don't worry, love,' smiled Dolly, sitting opposite. 'I shouldn't think we'll be down here long.'

'Wanna bet?' said Pat darkly. 'We've had it coming a long while.'

'That's enough, Pat,' snapped Vera. 'No one knows how long we'll be down here, so we need to stay collected.'

Her breezy words spoke of a determination to stay calm, but through the gloom, Peggy could see she was wringing the hem of her skirt feverishly with her fingertips.

'I hope Mr Gladstone remembered to switch off the machines,' she muttered, agitated.

Without saying a word, Peggy noticed Dolly slip a comforting arm round Vera's shoulders.

Suddenly, her thoughts strayed to her mother and her whereabouts.

'I do hope my mother is safe,' she said to Flossy. 'The City firm she works for usually closes early on a Saturday, so she may be on her way home from work already.'

She felt Flossy's slight hand reach through the darkness and her tiny fingers thread through hers.

'I'm sure your mother will be quite safe in the City. I hear there's plenty of shelters there.'

Flossy's words were reassuring, but the quake in her voice didn't go unnoticed by Peggy.

'Flossy,' she whispered, so the rest couldn't hear, 'are you all right? Your knees . . . They're rattling like a door knocker.'

Flossy stifled a sob. 'I don't like confined spaces. I never have done, ever since the home put me in a tiny isolation room when I suffered from measles. But please, don't tell anyone. I shall just have to be brave.'

Peggy said nothing, just squeezed her friend's hand reassuringly in the darkness.

'Might as well have a natter about the sewing circle while we're down here, eh?' said Dolly, her bright voice cutting through Peggy's thoughts. 'Though we may have to change our name to the Underground Sewing Circle.'

'Give over,' cackled Ivy. 'That makes us sound like we're a black-market sewing bee.'

'Do you mind? I ain't no bloody spiv,' shot back Sal, standing up and doing her best impression of a ducking-and-diving dealer.

A chorus of raucous laughter rang out through the dingy basement, and Peggy felt Flossy's stiff little shoulder start to relax.

'You sound like the unruly top deck of a works-outing charabanc,' snapped the forelady. 'We're in a public-authority shelter – show some decorum.'

But the relief of laughter was infectious and soon not a single occupant of the shelter could contain their helpless giggles at Sal's little skit. For a while, their laughter was so loud it drowned out the background noise, but gradually the droning grew louder. The forelady was the first to hear it.

'Hush,' she ordered, gripping Dolly's hand. 'What's that noise?'

The laughter stopped abruptly and the basement fell eerily silent. Peggy listened in the strangled silence. At first, all she could hear was the sound of dripping water, but then from the very bowels of the earth rose an unholy roaring and the benches began to shake and vibrate beneath their skirts.

'What's happening?' whimpered Flossy, gripping Peggy's hand so tightly she could feel her nails digging into the flesh on her palms. Peggy scrambled for words, but the noise was so deafening she felt her skull might just split in two. The faces of her fellow workers seemed frozen, a ghostly white tableau of fear against the dirty brick wall.

The noise rose and fell in sickening waves that drew Peggy out by the roots, a sickening pulsing that seemed to punch at the solar plexus with each throb.

Wave after wave of enemy aircraft droned relentlessly overhead, blackening the cloudless blue skies.

'What is it?' sobbed Flossy hysterically. 'I can't stand it. What is it?'

'It's them, ain't it,' said Pat gravely. 'They've come.'

With exquisite timing, the Luftwaffe chose that moment to drop their deadly cargo. An enormous boom rocked the underground shelter, followed a second later by another.

In all her days, Peggy had never heard anything like it.

Explosion followed explosion, a twisted orchestra of noise playing out in the basement. A high-pitched whistling, followed by an ominous silence, then an almighty juddering whoosh that made Peggy feel as if her eyeballs might just be sucked clean out of their sockets. The pressure from the explosions was immense, causing a vacuum in the basement that left her ears ringing. It was a queer sensation, like someone tuning a wireless in and out. One moment, she was deafened; the next, her hearing came flooding back, more acute than ever and she could make out the heavy crack of shrapnel dancing off the cobbles overhead.

With each blast, the heavy metal door to the shelter seemed to ripple from the force of the compression and every woman sat rigid with fear, staring in horror at the door as if imagining what fresh hell lay the other side.

Sal broke the screaming silence first.

'They're bombing the docks, aren't they? Stands to reason. They want to cut off our supplies of food and fuel. Force us to surrender.'

Just then, a bomb crashed so loudly the hurricane lamps jumped off the floor.

'You sure it's just the docks?' Kathy gasped, her eyes out on stalks. 'Sounds like Jerry's having a ball right over our heads.'

No one said a word or moved a muscle, as if by doing so, they might just alert the planes to their presence. Only the forelady moved, compulsively making the sign of the cross, over and over, as she fervently murmured the Lord's Prayer under her breath. Vera's face was so grey with terror it was almost the same colour as her hair.

The tomb of darkness was filled with the sickening crump of buildings collapsing overhead, and all the while Vera muttered her prayers, her desperate voice filling the blackness between them.

She paused. 'Who'll join me in prayer? There is no safety unless one abides in His presence.' No one uttered a word, but the forelady was not to be deterred. '*Our Father, which art in heaven, hallowed be Thy name. Thy kingdom come; Thy will be done, in earth as it is in heaven . . .*'

Flossy was the first to crack.

'I can't stand it any longer. We're finished,' she whimpered, her fearful voice echoing around the basement. 'Please make it stop, Dolly. That terrible throbbing, it sounds as if they're saying, "For you . . . for you . . . for you . . ."'

A distant voice rang out from the far side of the room. 'Will someone shut 'er up? It only takes one to lose their nerve and we're all done for.'

'Listen, darlin', you've gotta take hold of yerself,' said Pat bluntly. 'If there's a bomb with your name on it, there ain't nuffin' you can do about it. Besides which, if we go, at least we all go together.'

'Not everyone is as stoic as you, Pat,' scolded Dolly crossly. 'She's hysterical and in shock.' The timbre of Dolly's voice commanded attention and Pat muttered a hasty apology.

'Wrap her in this,' Dolly ordered, quickly handing Peggy the scarf she had nearly finished knitting.

With trembling hands, Peggy did as she was told, gently winding the scarf round Flossy's rigid neck.

'We are going to be just fine, Flossy,' Peggy whispered, taking her pale little face in both hands. Flossy stared back at her in the gloom, her cheeks icy cold and her pupils dilated with fear.

'I promise you, Flossy, you're not alone,' she urged, rubbing her cheeks gently. 'Nod yes if you can hear me.'

Flossy gave a tiny little nod.

'That's my girl,' Peggy smiled. 'If it makes you feel better, I'm perfectly terrified. My legs are shaking.'

'What do you know about suffering?' goaded Lily, her voice dripping poison from the bench opposite. 'I bet you've never felt a moment's fear in all your life.'

'Oh, give it a rest, would yer, Lily?' Dolly snapped, at the same time placing a firm but gentle hand over Vera's to prevent her fevered recitation. 'We're all in this together.'

A bolt of rage seared through Peggy's heart. Enough. Perhaps the bombs had dislodged something deep within her, or maybe the fear of impending death was driving her to confess, but the need to be truthful was exploding in every nerve ending.

'It's all right, Dolly,' she said. 'Actually, Lily, you don't have the monopoly on suffering here in Bethnal Green. I don't know much about your life, but you know even less about mine.'

Lily glared back at her from the other side of the shelter, eyes as cold as flint.

'I don't have a German lover, Lily,' Peggy went on. 'But I do have a German father.'

Peggy almost laughed as she gazed upon the stunned faces of Trout's machinists. She might as well have tossed a live grenade into the shelter.

Pat's eyes snapped open, and Vera's muttered recital of the Lord's Prayer abruptly tailed off.

'You what?' Ivy gaped.

Lily's voice lashed at her. 'It's as bad as, if you ask me. Where is he?' She jerked a thumb angrily up at the ceiling. 'Up there with the rest of those bastards bombing the hell out of us?'

'I shouldn't think so,' Peggy replied. 'Right about now, I'd say he's probably midway across the Atlantic, either above or below the water.'

'Is he, well, in the German Navy?' ventured Flossy. Peggy's confession seemed to have brought her friend to her senses and she was blinking at Peggy now in confusion.

'No, Flossy, he's not,' Peggy replied. 'He would sooner die of shame than wear the uniform of the Third Reich. My father is a peaceful and respectable businessman. He has lived in London for decades, running his own successful manufacturing business. My mother worked for the firm too. They fell in love and married.'

Above ground, the sound of hundreds of tons of high-explosive bombs roared through the skies, but inside, at that precise moment, you could have heard a pin drop in the gloomy basement.

'Over time, he came to regard himself as British,' she went on. 'He gave so much to this country, contributing regularly to the Children's Fresh Air Mission and other charitable institutions in the East End, where my mother comes from. He wanted to give something back to the land he had grown to love.'

'So what happened?' asked Ivy, dismayed.

'The war happened, Ivy,' she said with a brittle little laugh. 'Very early one morning in May, not long before I started at Trout's, there was a knock at the door of our old home in North London. Mother answered it to find two British military policemen standing there. The country was gripped by spy fever at the time. I even read of one Lincolnshire vicar arrested for transmitting wireless messages from his vicarage.'

Peggy snorted. 'What hope did my father have, a German running his own manufacturing business? They explained he was to be taken straight to Holloway Prison, where he would be held until he was called before a special tribunal. The last we saw of my father, he was being bundled into the back of a Black Maria.'

'How awful for you and your mother,' Flossy said, unable to hide her shock. 'No wonder you were so uptight when you started at Trout's!'

'It has been pretty wretched,' Peggy nodded. 'Our lives were thrown into chaos. His business was forced to close, I had to leave my job, and we had to sell our home and find lodgings in Bethnal Green. The fear was that he would be sympathetic to the Nazis in the event of an invasion. What a joke! My father loathes Adolf Hitler and all that he stands for.'

'Is that why you were so convinced the war would all be over in a matter of months?' asked Sal.

'It's what I hoped, Sal. I just kept praying it would all

end so my father would be released,' Peggy agreed. 'But I was being naive. About a week after I started at Trout's – I remember it well, actually: it was the day you sent me home, Mrs Shadwell, after I ran the needle through my finger – we received a telegram. My father managed to get word to us that, along with thousands of other internees, he was to be shipped to Canada. The pain of driving that needle into my thumb paled in comparison to the agony of realizing that I may never see my father again.'

'But why ever not?' asked Vera. 'Surely he will be allowed to return once the war is over?'

'In July, the *Arandora Star* left Liverpool bound for Canada carrying German and Italian internees. It was torpedoed and sunk . . .' Peggy's hand trembled as she picked at a stray thread on the frayed hem of her skirt. 'Eight hundred people drowned, or so they said on the wireless.'

'What are you saying, Peggy?' asked Kathy.

'We don't yet know whether my father was on that boat, Kathy,' she replied. 'If he is still alive, it doesn't look good. They seem determined to ship internees as far away as possible, to camps in Australia and Canada.'

Her beautiful face crumpled in anguish. 'There was an outcry about it in Parliament recently, and now they are starting to release internees, but we haven't received a single word from my father. I fear it may be too late for him.'

The emotion caught up with her and, finally, Peggy surrendered to her pain. Hot tears splashed down her cheeks, dripping onto her pinafore lap.

Flossy wrapped her arms round Peggy, while Dolly dug out a hanky from her bag.

'He's no more a Nazi than you, Pat,' Peggy wept, gratefully taking the hanky from Dolly and attempting to mop up her tears. 'He was making plans to join the Home Guard the day before the military police turned up. He's just a civilian who happens to come from Germany, and now I don't know if I'll ever see my dad again.'

'But that's shocking,' Ivy exclaimed. 'How can they do that to innocent men?'

'We're on the brink of invasion: they can do what they like,' Peggy snorted. 'Besides, you know how people feel at the moment. The only good German is a dead German. You said it yourself, Ivy.'

'Did I?' she mumbled.

'Blimey,' said Kathy. 'Makes you sorta see things in a different way, don't it?'

'I should say,' agreed Daisy. 'And I thought it was only our boys suffering.'

'It's war!' Sal's voice chimed in the gloom. 'It's always the innocent who suffer.'

'Well, I for one think Peggy is very brave to have shared that with us,' said Dolly. 'I think this is a lesson to us all not to be so quick to judge.' She glanced pointedly over to where Lily was sitting, studying the floor of the shelter intently.

Lily raised her gaze. 'I owe you an apology, Peggy. I should never have said them terrible things about you.'

Peggy blew her nose and managed a weak smile back at Lily. 'Thank you, Lily. Apology accepted. But I have to remind myself that my predicament is no different to any other woman in here who has a loved one serving. Everyone's fate is uncertain.' She shrugged. 'I have no other choice but to keep going and hope that one day my father returns home to London . . . where he belongs.'

'Well said, Peggy,' Vera remarked, nodding approvingly. 'I shall pray for your father.' With that, the forelady glanced over to where her headstrong younger sister was sitting. 'Adversity can bring out extraordinary qualities in us all.'

'Let's hope you're right, Mrs Shadwell,' Peggy smiled sadly. 'One thing's for certain: seeing another side of life, well, it's opened my eyes.'

The girls fell silent in contemplation. It was Kathy who broke it.

'Listen!' she exclaimed. 'It's the all-clear.'

Wearily, the girls rose and started to make their way back up the concrete steps, blinking into the light, fearful at the scenes that awaited them.

As Peggy pulled on her coat, it suddenly occurred to her that her tears of earlier had not just been for her father, but for the other man in her life she had lost. Lucky.

*

Dolly stepped onto the street from the underground shelter and instantly retched into the gutter. The air was thick with acidic yellow smoke, which roiled into the horizon, and the acrid smell of sulphur. Instinctively, she reached for her hanky and clamped it over her mouth to prevent the toxic fumes seeping into her lungs. She hadn't been able to think straight in that godforsaken shelter; the bombs, Vera's muttered prayers and then Peggy's confession all jumbled into a blur, dulling her senses. But right now, every instinct in her body burst into life and cold, hard fear clamped her heart. The scenes were unlike anything she had ever witnessed before.

Screams of disbelief punctured the air and mingled with the clanging of bells from the streams of fire engines racing past them in the direction of the docks. She had gone down into that basement on a gloriously sunny afternoon and emerged into pandemonium. Now it felt impossible to tell day from night. Dolly's eyes stretched upwards and followed the searchlights crossing and swooping through the skies, cutting great silver swathes through the darkness.

The movement disorientated her, and for a moment, Dolly felt faint, stumbling from the pavement into the gutter.

A heavy hand wrenched her back onto the safety of the pavement, just before a fire engine loomed up out of the smog and roared past her in an angry flash of red.

'Dolly!' gasped Vera. 'Watch yourself.'

Dolly went to respond and found she couldn't. Her breath was so ragged she started to wheeze and then cough, struggling for every last breath in her lungs.

'Quick,' urged Vera, taking her hand and dragging her after the rest of the workers, the sound of crunching glass splintering underfoot. 'Let's get inside. It's not safe out here.'

Inside, the factory floor was just the same, except everything was coated in a thick layer of grey brick dust. Every window was shattered beneath the brown sticky tape, and a couple of heavy green enamelled pendant lights had crashed down, smashing onto the sewing machines beneath.

Slowly, Dolly started to feel her breathing steady and she looked about the place in disbelief.

An awful thought occurred to her. 'Where's Archie?'

Vera's face drained of colour. 'He was fire-watching . . . on the roof.'

Vera turned and pelted towards the door to the rickety iron staircase that led up onto the flat roof of Trout's, and Dolly stumbled after her, clutching her chest. Frantic with fear, the forelady took the stairs two at a time, her heavy black skirts sending up clouds of dust into Dolly's face.

Once outside, they spotted Archie instantly. He was standing at the far end of the roof, with his back to them, silhouetted by an ominous red glow. He didn't move a muscle, and for a terrible moment, Dolly feared he might be dead, until he picked up the spade next to him and dug it defiantly down into a bucket of sand.

Dolly placed a gentle arm on his shoulder. 'You had us worried sick, you daft beggar,' she smiled. 'Got yerself a ringside seat up here, didn't you?'

Archie's shirt was drenched with sweat, and a thick crust of soot was welded to his cheeks. The grime was pitted with tiny slivers of glass from the blown-out windows on the factory floor. He stared without blinking in the direction of the docks. A fierce crimson glow bathed the skies blood red.

'I ain't never seen anything like it in all my days, Dolly,' he breathed, gesturing to the horizon. 'The planes filled the skies, wave after wave of 'em; they just kept coming. Thank God I had Lucky clear out the loft and bring buckets of sand up here.'

'How many did we catch?' asked Dolly fearfully.

'Must have been ten incendiaries landed on the roof, maybe more. I managed to put most of 'em out with that before they took hold,' he replied, gesturing to the bucket of sand and a small stirrup pump. He jutted his chin out defiantly. 'No one sets fire to my factory!'

'Mr Gladstone!' exclaimed Vera. 'Your arm.' A thick red gash on his forearm oozed blood.

Archie looked at it as if it was the first time he'd seen it. 'Just caught a bit of shrapnel. It'll be fine.'

'Hellfire,' murmured Sal, who, along with the rest of the girls, had joined them on the roof and was gazing with horrified fascination at the strangely enthralling spectacle. 'You could read a paper by the light of those fires.'

Dolly followed the beacon of flames and, in mounting horror, realized they stretched in a perfect arc round the East End, encircling them, in places almost white with the heat from the conflagration. Fear stopped her breath. The immediate London landscape as she knew it was changed beyond recognition. Broken glass, debris, flattened houses and, the sight that curiously disturbed her the most, giant rats streaming from a bombed warehouse nearby, leaping over the jumble of fire hoses that snaked up the cratered streets.

Peering over the railing, she recognized the corner shop at the end of the street where she and the girls got their sweets on a Friday dinnertime. It was now a smoking hole. A great pall of greasy black smoke mushroomed over the whole diabolical scene.

It was just too nightmarish to comprehend. Somewhere out there was her mum, probably scared witless. Please God let her have gone straight to the brick shelter on Tavern Street when the sirens sounded, just like Dolly had shown her. She had prayed that if the worst happened, she would be able to make it back from Trout's to Tavern Street in order to look after her, but there had simply been no time.

Now the worst had happened! As for Lucky, last seen heading to the ARP headquarters, he would be out there in the thick of this chaos.

Dolly could smell and taste death in the air and pulled out her soot-stained hanky to smother the scream that was threatening to burst from her mouth.

'London's burning,' rasped Archie, finally wrapping his handkerchief round the cut on his arm to stem the bleeding. 'We're standing in hell's kitchen.'

Hot tears stung Dolly's eyelids as she gazed out over the second great fire of London and the decimation of the place she loved the most.

How could the East End survive this? How would she ever survive it? Perhaps her mother had been right: maybe she should have left London for her own good. She banished the thought before it took hold. No. Bethnal Green was her home, and running away from it would be nothing short of cowardly.

An equally strong burst of hatred clawed at her chest. What kind of vile perpetrator could inflict such suffering on innocent civilians? But just as quickly she suppressed that too. Fear and loathing would not serve her East End. She was a working-class woman. She had survived the suffering inflicted on her childhood, and so too would she survive this.

Slowly, she drew back her handkerchief.

'Will they be back, Archie?' she asked.

He nodded sadly. 'They will, as sure as day follows night, Doll. Especially now they have the fires to light their way.'

'God help us,' sobbed Ivy, the outline of the fires reflected in her pale rheumy eyes. 'God help us all.'

Eight

Two hours later, at 8.30 p.m., the siren had sounded again, and this time the raid went right through the night and lasted until dawn on Sunday morning. Squadrons of Heinkel and Dornier bombers came in waves to drop high-explosive bombs on an already devastated East End. Fires still smouldering from the previous raid were quickly reignited. It was an unprecedented, catastrophic inferno of noise and flames . . . and Flossy had found herself trapped right in the middle of it.

Dolly had refused to let her go home alone after the afternoon raid and so she, along with Dolly's mother, Vera, Daisy, Sal and the rest of Tavern Street holed up in a brick street surface shelter built at one end of the road. They had tried to persuade Peggy to join them, but she had insisted on returning to her home to shelter with her mother. Sensing Dolly's relief at being safely reunited with her own mother, Flossy understood why she had let Peggy go without too much of a fight.

As Flossy stumbled into the dark and narrow shelter, she had the strangest sensation of stepping into her own coffin. Her mind cast back to Dolly's fateful words when they had paused to rest in one shortly after her arrival: *Heaven forbid you have to shelter in here if the worst happens. I don't reckon it could stand up to a ball, much less a bomb.*

How poignant Dolly's words felt now as the bombs crashed down around them. Unlike the underground shelter they had used earlier near Trout's, this one was small, and absurdly, or so it seemed to Flossy, *above ground*! Try as she might, she just couldn't see how this would protect them should they take a direct hit. She supposed the authorities must know what they were doing when they built them.

Flossy found she could do nothing but squeeze her eyes tightly shut and cling to Dolly in the darkness. When the waves of panic at being enclosed in such a crowded space threatened to engulf her, she used every fibre of her being to cast her mind to another place, to wonder at what Tommy, her dear, sweet sailor pen pal, looked like. She mentally drew a map of his face and vowed that, should she survive this night, she would write him the most perfect of replies to his letter. Could it really be just twenty-four hours since she had sat in Peggy's parlour before the singing competition and dreamily savoured his letter? Already it felt like a lifetime ago. Time lost all meaning. In so few hours, Flossy had tasted base fear and bewilderment. Now she listened as it turned to anger.

'How can they think this is a suitable place to shelter?' raged a deep male voice. 'We got our pride. This place ain't fit for a dog, much less human habitation.'

'Smells like a dog's been using it an' all,' piped up another. 'Watch what you're treading in.'

Another voice, dripping with vitriol, speared the darkness. 'It's all right for them, the establishment, holed up in their steel-lined dugouts or their country retreats. I'm a labourer by trade; rumour has it these shelters are dodgy. Penny-pinching authorities have substituted sand for concrete. If we cop it, the roof's gonna come down in one solid piece.'

'That's as may be, but it's obvious why we're in here, ain't it?' rang out a sharp female voice that Flossy thought might have been Sal's. 'If a bomb lands on us, it's easier to dig the dead out of one place than go through the houses individually.'

Flossy felt Dolly bristle in the darkness.

'Oh, come now,' she chided. 'Enough of this defeatist talk: it's not helping anyone. Let's try a sing-song, shall we? How about "There'll Always Be an England"?'

Her words were drowned out by a high-pitched whistling. Flossy buried herself so close into Dolly's side she felt her ribs, sharp and brittle beneath her skin. The bomb did not have their name on it . . . but the colossal boom seemed to lift the brick walls from their very foundations.

'Bloody hell, there nearly wasn't an England here then,' quavered a voice.

Speechless with fear, Flossy waited before opening her eyes a fraction. Through a crack in the door, she saw the flash and spark of flames, then a sudden movement in the darkness.

'I'm not sitting in this death trap waiting for half a ton of masonry to come crashing down on my head!' Vera shrieked. 'Come on, Daisy, we're going home. We'll take our chances under the stairs.'

Her sister's defiant voice shot back, 'No chance, Vera. Them houses are centuries old. It's only the paint holding 'em together. I'm staying put, thank you very much.'

'Vera, please sit down,' pleaded Dolly, reaching out through the darkness and gripping her old friend's waist in both her hands. 'We're safer together. United we stand; divided we fall.'

Vera batted her hands away. 'I . . . I'm sorry, Dolly,' she wailed. 'I . . . I just can't stay in here a moment longer.'

'I beg of you, as one friend to another, don't go out there,' implored Dolly. 'Don't . . .'

A sickening silence filled the shelter, followed by the blast of air as Vera opened the door.

'Look after Daisy for me, Dolly,' she cried, before the door slammed shut behind her and she vanished into the smoke.

No one said a word, and Flossy felt Dolly's body sag in defeat next to her. Had Vera sealed her fate, or would she in fact be the only resident of Tavern Street left alive come daybreak? In silence, Flossy reached over and threaded her slim fingers through Dolly's in the darkness. United they remained.

Exhaustion overwhelming her, Flossy wasn't aware she had drifted into a fitful sleep until the wailing of the all-clear pierced the smoky twilight air.

Wiping the grit from her eyes, she looked about her and half wondered if she hadn't died. Every occupant of the shelter was coated from head to toe with a thick grey dust that gave them a ghostly pallor, and they were slumped, defeated and exhausted, against the freezing, damp wall. But it was Dolly's appearance that gave her the biggest jolt. Her skin was so pale it was almost translucent, save for a high shine of purply red on her cheekbones that looked like a streak of blood. Her lips had that strange tinge of blue about them that Flossy had seen before, and her breathing was shallow.

'Dolly,' she whispered, clutching her icy hands. 'Dolly, wake up.'

Dolly started and, wiping her blonde curls back, made a heroic effort to smile. 'Well, we survived,' she murmured shakily, hauling herself to her feet and holding on to the wall as her body spasmed into a volley of uncontrollable coughing.

'I think I must have breathed in half the brick dust in London,' she wheezed. 'But no matter. We're here to see another day. I might be a bit battered and bruised, but once I've had a nice hot cup of tea and a wash, I'll be ready to face the day.'

'I think we should all go home, and you need to rest,' ordered Dolly's mum. The note of warning in her voice did not go unnoticed by Flossy.

'I'm going to have a cup of tea, and then, Mum, I'm going to go down the WVS and help out at whatever rest centre they point me in the direction of,' she said with steel in her voice.

'That's the spirit, Doll,' remarked one of her neighbours as he threw open the door to the shelter. 'The East End stands defiant.'

*

It was Sunday morning, but instead of getting ready to go to church, the inhabitants of Bethnal Green were staggering, shell-shocked and dazed, from their hiding places. Out from cold brick shelters, cramped cupboards, draughty church crypts, damp Andersons, railway arches. Crawling from underneath tables and scrabbling out of muddy trenches in the park. Folk stumbled into the dawn of an uncertain day.

The morning sun tried and failed to break through the dense blanket of smoke, and Dolly knew that unless she tried harder to put on a brave face, she too was in danger of vanishing.

Wearily, she linked arms with Flossy, and in silence they picked their way up Tavern Street, followed closely behind by Daisy and Sal.

Outside number 24, Vera was waiting.

'Thank God you're all right,' Dolly exclaimed on seeing the forelady.

'A couple of houses at the far end have copped it,' Vera said. 'The water's been cut off, but I've found a standpipe in the next street that's working. I've brewed up. Come in for a quick cup; then we had better get going to the WVS. We'll be needed.'

'Of course,' Dolly said. 'Flossy, you coming?'

'No, I'm going to go and check that Peggy and her mother are safe. Then we'll come and join you to help.'

'Good idea, love,' Dolly replied.

Once inside the terrace, Vera waited until Daisy and Sal had gone out back to wash off the debris, before turning to Dolly.

'I'm so scared,' she whispered.

'We all are, love,' Dolly replied. 'And I have a horrible feeling this is just the beginning. I do wish you'd shelter with us all . . .'

'No, not about that,' Vera replied. 'Last night . . . It never ended. Explosion after explosion. Eight hours solid they were bombing us, so they're saying, though it felt like an eternity. The bombs . . . It's like they were blowing God clean out of my head. I called on Him to stop the planes in their tracks and still they kept coming. For the first time in my life—' Her voice broke off and in alarm Dolly realized her old friend was struggling not to cry. 'I found myself questioning my faith. I have always been His obedient servant, but how can any God allow this? Without Him, who am I? How can I help keep Daisy on the straight and narrow, help all the girls to fulfil their war duties for that matter?'

'You can and you will,' Dolly insisted. 'Perhaps this is His way of showing us that we have to fight to rid the world of evil and tyranny. This is our part to play, our destiny.'

Vera closed her eyes, and when she opened them, she nodded. 'You're right, Dolly. I had never thought of it that way before. Thank you.'

'Come on,' Dolly said. 'What was it you said to Peggy yesterday afternoon in the shelter? "Adversity can bring out extraordinary qualities in us all." You're stronger than you might think, Vera.'

The sights that greeted Dolly and Vera as they picked their way through the debris en route to the WVS were beyond all belief.

Exhausted firemen, faces blackened by the fires they had spent all night battling, were slumped on the kerb in a daze, housewives bringing them out hot jugs of cocoa. So many homes were reduced to nothing but a smoking pile of rubble, as if a massive steel fist had reached through the clouds of grit and indiscriminately punched holes in them.

The women walked in silence down the cratered streets overlaid with thick coils of hosepipes and the swill of sooty water. Dolly found the silence eerie, the only noise the crunching of glass underfoot and muffled sobs. So many streets were closed off Dolly scarcely recognized the neighbourhood she had grown up in. It had been reduced to rubble, charred timber and debris.

As they turned into the main street, the crowds intensified. Streams of women and children pushing perambulators and handcarts walked past them, exhausted and dazed.

Dolly recognized a woman she used to go to school with, clutching a terrified girl to her chest.

'Vi!' she called. 'Where you going?'

'Where do yer think, Doll?' she croaked, her eyes wild with fear. 'As far away from here as I can. I've lost everything. Me home's gone. Everything I own is in this pram and I ain't stopping to see them bomb that when they come back. I'm heading to Epping Forest. I'll walk the whole bleedin' way there if I have to.'

Without saying another word, she turned and carried on trudging eastwards to the open countryside, along with columns of other bewildered refugees. Dolly could hardly blame them, but she knew the only way she would leave the East End would be in a box.

Dolly and Vera carried on walking in silence, ignoring the desperate cries of 'Have you seen?' until they turned a corner, and glancing up, Dolly saw a sight that turned her heart to stone. She stopped in her tracks. The side of a house had been blown clean off, revealing a home perfectly torn in two, the contents on show for the whole world to see. In horrified fascination, she took in the pretty, faded wallpaper, the neat dresser and a child's wooden toy duck, incongruous with the landslide of rubble covering the other side of the house. ARP, policemen and civilians worked side by side, frantically digging their way through the cumbersome concrete slabs, but without heavy lifting equipment, they were making slow progress.

'Oh no!' Dolly cried. For there, like a macabre signpost, a child's hand emerged rigid from the masonry. 'Don't look, Vera,' she urged, tugging her sleeve and pulling them on their way. She had salvaged the forelady's faith once already this morning; she didn't think her belief in God would stand up to seeing such a grisly sight.

Instinctively, her mind drifted to her young Flossy, such an innocent. Please God, protect her and keep her safe from harm.

By the time they neared the WVS centre on Green Street, Dolly had recovered herself and drew strength from the spirit of her neighbours. For despite the carnage, there were sights that caused pride to swell in her chest. Housewives out sweeping up the glass, arranging the debris into piles for the borough workmen to collect, attempting to create order out of chaos. Boy Scouts were gently helping the elderly to the nearest rest centre, while mobile canteens served hot tea and sandwiches to the bombed-out.

The WVS swiftly despatched Dolly and Vera to a nearby school that had been converted into a rest centre, and Dolly was tasked with serving tea to shaken survivors and the freshly homeless. Behind the tea urn, she quickly felt her vigour and gayness return. The people here had lost their homes, and she was determined to put on her brightest front, as usual.

'Oh, hello, Dor,' she called out to a woman she recognized from the neighbourhood. 'See you got your Sunday best on.' The older woman was caked head to toe in soot, and her clothes were ripped and filthy.

It was gallows humour, but Dolly instinctively knew it was precisely what this woman needed.

Her blue eyes sparkled defiantly as Dolly handed her a hot cup of tea. 'I tell yer, Doll, that 'itler's done me a right favour,' she replied. 'How many times have I grumbled to you about that hole I lived in? Well, it's flat as a pancake now and I'm bleedin' glad. I was sick of the wallpaper.'

Dolly chuckled and patted her arm. 'That's the spirit, Dor.'

But as the day wore on, the grim humour gave way to exhaustion and bewilderment. Added to which, Flossy and Peggy still hadn't turned up. A sense of jagged unease nagged Dolly. Just where were they?

Every other minute, it seemed, the door swung open and another East Ender, homeless and shaken, surged in, in need of tea, food and fresh clothing, not to mention the practicalities of life, like where to get new a ration book and identity card. She, Vera and every other member of the WVS were working their socks off to deal with the casualties, but at times it felt like a losing battle and the queue of homeless families stretched out through the door. Fortunately, Dolly found she had a knack of knowing when someone wanted jocularity or just a sympathetic ear.

Vera was in charge of handing out second-hand clothing from behind a trestle table set up in one corner, and when Dolly took her over a cup of tea, she shook her head in despair.

'We're running out of blankets and socks, Dolly,' she exclaimed. 'And rumour has it nearby rest centres are filled to the brim. They're turning people away. There's so much anger. The Tube is shut, so no one can shelter down there, and I'm not the only one who refuses to go in those street shelters. They're death traps, I tell you.'

Her shrill voice started to rise. 'It will be nightfall before we know it, and where are people to go? Folk are up in arms. One woman just told me there's hundreds of women and children crammed into a school in Canning Town waiting for transport out . . . They're sitting ducks. We all are . . .'

Dolly gripped Vera firmly by the arm. 'Now you listen to me – it's important that we stay positive,' she said. 'We might share their anger, but we can't show it. We have to keep a cool head, however desperate things might look.'

'Dolly's right, Vera,' cut in a deep male voice.

'Archie, thank God,' smiled Dolly, whirling round to look into the face of the foreman.

'We can and we will take it,' he went on. 'We have to keep going. We've got no other choice. I've managed to get my hands on some blankets, and Lucky's on his way here to help out. I warn you, though, he's had a hell of a night. He'll be in need of one of your strong brews, Doll.'

'Course, Arch,' Dolly winked, feeling her spirits rise.

As she walked back to her urn, the door opened and Flossy, Peggy and Peggy's mother, May, wearily trudged in.

'Oh, there you are, girls,' Dolly called, relieved. 'I was starting to worry.'

All three looked shaken to their core.

'Have you seen the sights out there?' said Flossy.

'We have. It's carnage all right,' Dolly replied.

'There but for the grace of God,' said May. 'But we're here to help. Now, what can we do, Dolly? I'm a trained first-aider, and I've brought what medical supplies I could get my hands on.'

Within no time, May was helping to tend to the injured, assisted by Flossy and Peggy. As the afternoon wore on, Dolly kept sneaking little glances over at the girls and felt moved to see them both working so calmly and diligently together – just eighteen, the pair of them, but not a flicker of fear or complaint. They were a credit to Trout's.

Peggy in particular seemed to be keeping her wits about her splendidly and didn't flinch as her mother helped to dress an elderly woman's badly burned feet. The woman's howls of pain were ear-splitting, but Peggy gently held her hand and gave her sips of water. When her mother finished bandaging her feet, Peggy slid an arm round the shaken woman's shoulder. 'There, all better. See, I told you your dancing days weren't over yet.' She winked at the woman, before rushing to the door to help a mother struggling with three wailing children.

It was funny what war did to women. Dolly had a hunch that since her confession in the basement yesterday afternoon, they were finally starting to get a glimpse of the real Peggy Piper.

*

By late afternoon, Peggy was starting to flag. Her eyes felt filled with grit, and she had seen so much suffering and anguish she wondered at how much the human spirit could endure.

Her mother touched her lightly on the shoulder. 'I've just heard word that the authorities are sending a coach here to transport women, children and injured out of London,' she said wearily. 'There's every likelihood the bombers will return tonight. The hospitals are apparently already at capacity, and, well . . . I promised your father I'd keep you safe. I think you should go too.'

Peggy jutted out her chin. 'I will do no such thing! I promised Father I would look after you, so I'm staying right here by your side. The East End is my home now. I'm not abandoning it, or you.'

May smiled and touched her daughter's cheek softly. 'Your father would be very proud.'

Just then a movement by the door caught Peggy's eye. A lump rose in her throat. Lucky walked in, plainly exhausted and with a face as black as coal. The last time she had seen him had been when he had ushered her down to the shelter, just before the bombers had arrived. So much had happened since then, yet her feelings for him remained the same.

'Lucky,' she murmured. 'Where have you been? I've been so worried.'

'I've been working for the Civil Defence, delivering messages on my bike to the emergency services where they can't get larger vehicles through. Though, there were a few occasions when I thought I wouldn't get through, mind.

'I got blown off my bike twice, my wheels caught fire,

and a burning girder missed me by a cat's whisker, but I'm the lucky one . . .' His voice, oddly flat, trailed off.

'What is it, Lucky?' she urged. 'Tell me.'

'It's Lily,' he said shakily. 'She's . . . she's dead.'

Peggy's hand leaped to her mouth. 'Oh, Lucky. W-what happened?'

'It was last night. She was in a large public shelter under Columbia Market with hundreds of others; they thought they was safe underground. Well, you would, wouldn't you? There was even a wedding party going on.'

'I don't understand,' Peggy frowned, realizing a small crowd had gathered to listen.

'Yes, lad, go on,' urged Archie gently.

'It must be a million-to-one chance, but a fifty-kilogram bomb entered the ventilation shaft. It only measured three feet by one and whistled straight down underground into the basement and exploded. People nearest didn't have a hope.'

He stumbled on, his voice cracking. 'Lily . . . Lily, her mother and sister were asleep next to the shaft, apparently. I was despatched to help. By the time I'd got there . . . Oh God, no . . .' Lucky broke down and covered his face, his huge shoulders shaking under the weight of his sobs, and Peggy, along with everyone else, listened stricken. 'She was being carried out on a stretcher to a waiting ambulance. I knew she was dead the moment I set eyes on her. Her face . . . oh, her beautiful face . . .' Lucky squeezed his eyes shut and moaned. 'It was slashed to ribbons, bits of brick embedded in her cheeks. I knew she would have hated to be seen like that, so I covered her with a sheet. My Lily deserved dignity in death. God knows no one deserves to die like that.'

'I'm sure it would have been a quick end, lad,' said Archie softly. 'Did you go with her in the ambulance?'

Lucky sighed and shook his head. 'I wanted to, believe me, Arch, but there was no time. I knew it was too late for Lily and her family, but there was time left for the living, so I set to work. It was utter chaos . . . Smoke and screams. Those cries will haunt me to my dying day.' Lucky ran a filthy, trembling hand through his hair, and suddenly Peggy felt very afraid. 'Perambulators and corrugated iron all twisted together. It was a bloody mess. I started to dig through the rubble, trying to see if anyone had survived. I felt a tiny body in the darkness and I pulled it out.' His voice broke off and a solitary tear coursed down his soot-blackened cheek. His eyes stared past the crowd, to some unknown place of horror in his head.

'It was a baby . . . So help me God, it was nothing but a little baby. The body fell apart in my arms. I don't even know where the poor mite's mother was. I spent hours there trying to dig people out, but in the end, they sealed the site off.'

Fresh tears flooded his face and his fists bunched in frustration. 'You have to believe me, I tried . . . I really tried! I was still there this morning when the authorities arrived. I looked up at this fella inspecting the site. Pale as a ghost he was. It was the King. His Majesty himself, in full field marshal's uniform. I don't know who looked more shocked to be there, me or 'im.'

No one uttered a word as they listened in horrified fascination.

'I still remember listening to his speech last Christmas. "Give me light that I may tread safely into the unknown," he said. I remember thinking, What the heck does that mean? Well, I think I know now . . .'

'You're exhausted! Come and have a cup of tea, lad, and rest a while,' Archie said, attempting to guide him to a chair, but Lucky shrugged him off.

'No! I don't want to drink tea, Arch,' he replied angrily. 'I wanna know what kind of war this is where innocent civilians are bombed in their homes, where they should be safe. I can't get rid of the image of Lily's face, and that poor little baby . . .' Lucky scrubbed despairingly at his face. 'Just a baby, for goodness' sake. It was too dark to tell if it was a boy or a girl, but it had the softest hair, the body – or what was left of it – so tiny. Later on, we found the mother, bleeding from a head wound and screaming blue murder for her baby. She was that hysterical when she found out that a doctor had to sedate her. I bet she wishes she died along with her baby.

'Can someone please tell me what Nazi did they ever hurt?' Lucky stared around the group, but no one could summon the right words to respond.

'I'm sorry,' he choked, crumpling into his grief. 'I need some air.' He wheeled round and rushed from the school hall.

Peggy went to follow, but felt a hand pull her back.

'Leave him,' counselled Dolly. 'He'll need some space. He's seen sights no man should ever have to witness.'

'But he needs comfort,' Peggy wept angrily. Her tears weren't just for Lucky, but for Lily, Lily's family, the baby's mother and all those other poor souls who perished. How was that poor mother to continue living without her baby? And Lily! Vivacious, vital Lily. How could she be dead? How?

Peggy hadn't always seen eye to eye with the young seamstress, but she felt the grief of her passing, in every corner of her being. Lily was a beautiful young lady with so much to offer the world. And now she was gone.

'I don't think anything you could say can ease his suffering, do you, love?' Dolly whispered, suddenly looking as afraid as Peggy felt.

'Dolly's right,' said May. 'That poor man will be haunted by that memory, and by his loss.'

'If decent folk aren't safe in huge public shelters like that, then where exactly are they safe?' Vera muttered angrily. 'Why aren't the Tubes open to shelterers? Where are the deep shelters? The East End has been hung out to dry. Lily and her family never did anyone no harm.'

'I just can't believe Lily is dead,' murmured Flossy.

'The first and, please God, the last of Trout's casualties,' said Archie.

An ominous silence swept over the group.

'Peggy and Flossy,' said Dolly at last. 'Would you both go and fetch the bundle of blankets we made for our boys from the Tin Lizzie parked outside Trout's? Me and Lucky loaded them up to deliver Friday night, but obviously we never got the chance. Vera tells me we're nearly out, and hopefully they're still there. I don't mean to sound callous, but our concern now rests with the living.'

'Of course, but aren't they for HMS *Avenge*?' queried Flossy.

Dolly swept a despairing hand around the packed school

hall, filled with the bombed-out homeless getting ready to bed down for the night on the hard floor.

'I reckon our boys won't mind if we bring them down here instead,' reasoned Dolly. 'I think these poor souls' need is greater. At times like this, the East End lives collectively, not individually. We look out for our own, Flossy, and we owe it to Lily to keep going.'

'Of course,' said Flossy. 'Come on, Peggy, let's go.'

'Wait. Take this torch,' Dolly said. As she passed it over, her small fingers gripped hard on to Flossy's hand and for a moment she wondered if she would let go. 'Stay safe, love,' Dolly said in a curious voice.

Outside on the streets, Peggy felt Flossy's arm slip through hers as they walked in the direction of the factory.

'I just can't believe Lily's dead,' Peggy whispered, still thunderstruck at the news. 'We were sat opposite her just yesterday afternoon. Please God Archie's right and she felt no pain.'

'I know. Poor, poor Lucky,' said Flossy. 'I always admired Lily. You know, somehow she felt invincible to me.' Flossy turned suddenly to Peggy, her lips bitten white against the pale of her face. 'What will happen now?'

'I don't know,' Peggy replied, honestly. 'I suppose it's like Dolly said – we keep going. For Lily.'

'I'm really worried about Dolly too,' Flossy continued. 'Have you noticed how pale and exhausted she is? She's got a rattling cough, and her ankles have swollen up like barrage balloons too.'

'Dolly?' said Peggy, surprised. 'I'd say she's the last person we should worry about. Strong as an ox, she is.

Besides, who isn't exhausted after the night we had last night? My lungs are filled with brick dust. I can feel it in every crevice of my body.'

'I can't put my finger on what it is, but something's not right,' Flossy insisted. 'She was out of sorts at the singing competition too.'

Flossy's voice blurred away as Peggy spotted something that made her stop dead in her tracks.

'Look, Flossy,' she exclaimed. 'It's a mulberry tree, growing at the far end of that school playground.'

'Oh yes, what of it?' Flossy asked, confused.

A bomb blast had stripped the tree clean of its leaves, and its splintered branches rose stark against the grey skies, as if winter had arrived early. Peggy felt a painful twist of sorrow slice through her.

'Lucky loves mulberry trees. They remind him of his mother,' she murmured.

They fell into a contemplative silence as they walked, but soon the chaos and turbulence of the bombed streets consumed them. The crowds of people intensified, and as they turned onto a main thoroughfare in Spitalfields, panic slammed Peggy's heart. A huge crowd surged up the road, sucking them in and carrying them along with the throng.

'Flossy, I don't want to lose you. Take my hand,' Peggy ordered over the clamour. Flossy gripped her hand and laced their fingers tightly together.

Down the cobbled streets, faces were twisted with anger, and tempers were reaching flashpoint as people struggled to free themselves from the tightly packed and fast-moving crowd.

'What's going on?' Flossy asked the man nearest them.

'We've all just come from Liverpool Street Station,' he replied. 'We was trying to get down the Underground to shelter, but there was policemen barring the entrance. It's flamin' madness. I'm going to head up West. Apparently Dickins & Jones have got a huge shelter.'

'You're joking, ain'cha?' commented a woman next to them. 'I was up there earlier. There's hundreds queuing round the block to get down there. They can't let any more in.'

'Have you heard the rumour about the big bomb?' yelled a hysterical voice over the crowd. 'It can take out the whole of London. We gotta get underground.'

'Wotcha think we're trying to do, mate?' a man next to him snapped.

'Oh, shut up, will yer?' shouted another.

The terrible realization dawned on Peggy that they were trapped. Her epiphany was as dark as it was sudden. Moans and wild cries filled the darkening skies. The anger of the crowd was raw, visceral even. The race for human survival was stripped to its most primal form.

'Flossy, let's wait,' she panted. Using every last ounce of her strength, she pulled them back and they managed to flatten themselves into a slender brick doorway until the crowd had passed.

'Oh, Peggy, whatever are we to do?' trembled Flossy, staring bewildered at the retreating crowd, a seething mass of impotent rage.

'Let me think,' said Peggy, her heart banging inside her chest. But there was no time, for the skies were suddenly filled with the wail of the siren. A bilious dread rose sharply in her throat.

'Oh no,' Flossy cried, panicked. 'They're back already.'

'Stay calm and move quick,' Peggy urged. 'I think we passed a street shelter a few turnings ago. Turn the torch on to help us.'

Flossy did as she was told, and clasping each other's hands, the pair started to run, glass cracking sharply underfoot, the torchlight bouncing off the cobbles.

'Turn that torch off and take cover,' boomed an ARP warden striding down the street towards them. 'Take cover *now*.'

Hustling them to the nearest street shelter, he wrenched the door open and ushered them into the darkness. The steel door slammed shut behind them.

Flattening herself against the shelter wall, it took a few moments for Peggy's eyes to adjust to the gloom, and when she did, she was dismayed. Scared faces peered out of the dusty darkness, clutching candles and lanterns, waiting breathlessly for the second night's instalment. A strange, damp, bitter smell pervaded the air. Not a solitary toilet or light in sight. You could taste the fear in the shelter.

Peggy was desperate to *run*, to escape this sticky, dark hole. Only the relentlessly wailing siren overhead forced her to stay put, reminding her that whatever was about to erupt outside was infinitely worse than being trapped in here.

'Is this like the one you sheltered in last night?' she gasped.

Flossy nodded wordlessly and squeezed her hand.

'We managed to get into the crypt of St John Church. We may have been sheltering with the dead, but it was a darn sight better than this,' Peggy whispered.

There was no time for a response, for the crack of the ack-ack guns filled the air, drowning out all rational thought.

'That's it, boys – give 'em some back,' urged a lone voice.

Flossy whimpered and huddled into Peggy's side like a child might its mother. The anti-aircraft guns were swiftly followed by the steady throb of enemy aircraft droning overhead. The whine and crash of bombs sounded like an out-of-control brass band. How much louder the enemy sounded when you weren't underground.

Peggy listened.

The whine was soft to begin with; then it grew louder. And louder still. The shelter collectively held its breath. Instead of dying away, the screaming whistle reached a fever pitch in Peggy's head, and in that instant, she knew. This bomb had their name on it. In that moment, she was aware of nothing, not herself, not the blood-curdling screams of the other people in the shelter, just the all-pervading instinct to protect Flossy, the girl with no mother, the girl with no home to call her own . . .

The world seemed to go into slow motion as the sky fell in on them.

'Get down,' Peggy cried above the roar. With a crash, she pulled Flossy to the floor and flung herself over her body like a blanket.

'You're safe, Flossy,' she said, with an unnatural calmness. It was the last thing she remembered saying. A second later, the ceiling came down in one solid sheet.

*

Was she dead or alive?

'What happened?' mumbled Flossy, but found for some reason the words were muffled. She spat and mouthfuls of debris and saliva spooled from her mouth.

She was alive, but the roaring of blood in her ears was so loud Flossy wondered for a moment if she was deaf; then suddenly everything came flooding into focus with dizzying force. The blast, and oh God . . .

'Peggy!' she cried in the darkness. 'Where are you?'

Her shaking hand crept out over the mound of bodies . . . but all she could feel was damp fabric and cold skin. The soft moans of the mortally injured pierced the evening air. Remembering the torch, which by some miracle was still clamped rigid in her fist, she flicked it on and cast it around the tomb of trapped bodies. Forcing down great waves of nausea, she swung the beam around, but every face she settled on, waxy and blood-soaked, did not belong to Peggy.

Shattered masonry was piled high, an odd tangled limb protruding here and there from the debris. The sights were unimaginable. Grisly fragments of bodies lay strewn everywhere. A middle-aged woman, plainly in shock, her intestines ruptured and spilling from her, chattered hysterically as she gripped her handbag for dear life.

It would be so easy to close her eyes against such horrors. Flossy felt so weak, so weak and cold. Then an image of Peggy's mother flashed through her mind. No, she owed it to May to fight for her daughter's life.

With a colossal effort, and ignoring the stabbing pain in her ribs, Flossy pulled herself up onto one arm. As she did so, the torch swung and settled on a mound of rubble nearby.

Something gleamed in the torchlight. Tentatively, Flossy brushed it to reveal a familiar watch face. The watch was attached to a pale and slender arm.

'Oh, Peggy,' she sobbed. Relief coursed through her as she flung aside the rubble and bricks covering her body. Peggy was lying on one side. Her breathing was dangerously shallow, but she was alive. Though her upper body was free, her lower body was a different story. A huge slab of concrete and debris had her legs pinned fast to the floor of the shelter. Flossy pushed against it, but the vast weight of it was immovable.

'Peggy? Peggy, can you hear me?' she sobbed, brushing her chestnut hair from her face. Peggy's eyelids flickered at the sound of Flossy's voice, and her dry lips opened slightly.

'Wake up, Peggy. I'm going to get you out. You hear me? I'm going to get you out.'

She took Peggy's pale, dusty fingertips in hers and pressed them individually, pad by pad, hoping to elicit some response.

Just then, an enormous crash nearby caused the rubble to bounce, sending up clouds of brick dust. In mounting disbelief, Flossy's eyes were drawn to the gaping exposed hole in the ceiling of the shelter. It was as if someone had lifted the lid of hell.

Overhead, a stream of dark planes circled like predators, sticks of bombs falling from their undercarriage one by one and exploding onto the rooftops below. Spectacular flashes lit up the gloom, and the searchlights prowled the darkness. In any other situation, the dramatic skies would be thrilling. Except this was war.

It was hopeless. More bombs screamed into the furnace,

and the earth spewed blood and bones. Flossy's eyes flickered to the end of the street. One side of the road was a solid wall of flame. The deafening roar of water filled the air as a fireman battled to bring an inferno under control.

Flossy gasped and jumped as a pigeon with its wings on fire swooped low, fluttering past her face before landing with a thud against a pile of bricks.

'I don't want to die!' screamed a woman trapped near Peggy.

The screams roused Peggy and her eyes opened a fraction.

'Flossy . . . go . . .' she croaked, over the low groans of the dying.

Settling down on her haunches, Flossy took out her hanky from her pocket and, gently wiping the dust from Peggy's eyelids, shook her head. 'I should never live with myself if I left you here.'

And so there they remained, silhouetted against the raging fires as death rained from the skies, two friends from across the divide but united in their desire to stay alive.

Flossy talked and talked until the breath in her lungs nearly ran dry, anything to keep Peggy conscious.

'Come on, Peggy, stay with me,' she urged. 'Together we can thread this needle. We will work a way out of here, but you must keep your eyes open.'

'What an absolute fop you must think me,' Peggy smiled weakly.

'You saved my life, Peggy,' Flossy replied incredulously. 'And when we get out of here, I'm going to tell everyone.'

It could have been ten minutes, it could have been hours,

but finally Flossy saw figures in tin helmets and a white vehicle with a cross on the front bumping up the pitted road.

'Thank God,' she cried, springing to her feet and waving her arms wildly. 'We need help over here.'

An ARP man pushed his helmet back and squatted down beside them. 'Hello, love,' he said to Peggy. 'We got ourselves in a bit of a pickle here, ain't we?'

'I don't think she's lost any blood,' Flossy babbled. 'We just need to move this slab off her legs.'

The man frowned as he ran his torch over the masonry that was pinning Peggy fast. 'That's a job for heavy lifting.'

He pulled some smelling salts from his bag. 'This will help keep her round until they get here.'

Flossy felt her body tense with frustration. What use were smelling salts?

The voice cutting through the darkness was familiar and for a moment Flossy felt completely disorientated.

'Flossy? Peggy, can you hear me?'

In a heartbeat, Flossy was on her feet and waving her torch about. 'Lucky! Lucky, we're over here!'

The plucky messenger hove into sight, scrambling through the wreckage of the crater and leaping over the buckled steel door.

It could have been the smelling salts, but Flossy rather fancied it was the sound of Lucky's deep voice that brought Peggy round.

'Hello, angel,' he said, half smiling, half sobbing as he dropped to his knees and gently pulled her body in towards his. 'I went back to the rest centre after the siren sounded and Dolly told me you'd headed this way. I've searched half the shelters in Bethnal Green. Now, we're going to have you outta here in a jiffy.'

Peggy looked up at him groggily, managed a weak smile of recognition and promptly fell unconscious.

'You're going to be right as rain, you hear me,' Lucky urged, his voice cracking. 'You hear me . . .'

'But how?' cried the ARP man. 'We ain't got no lifting equipment.'

'I already lost one of the girls from my factory; I ain't losing another,' Lucky said through gritted teeth. '"No guts, no glory" is the Repton's motto. It's never failed me yet.'

Lucky delved into his satchel, and pulling out a jemmy and an axe, he set to work. An ambulance woman arrived on the scene and started to administer morphia to Peggy, while Lucky worked. Flossy stumbled back and closed her eyes, scarcely able to look. But when she opened them again, Peggy was free. Using sheer brute strength, Lucky had removed the concrete slab in no time at all.

As Peggy was carefully transferred onto a stretcher, she reached her hand towards Lucky to hold. Her skin was so pale it was translucent, and her eyes lurched dangerously in her head.

'What is it, Peggy?' Lucky cried. 'Remember, before all this madness broke out, you wanted to tell me something.'

'I . . . I never deserved you,' Peggy said, her voice barely above a whisper.

Then she was gone, as the ambulance door slammed shut, the vehicle going as fast as it dared up the cratered street. Her fate was now in the hands of the medics.

Lucky watched the ambulance until it was out of sight, before his face crumpled and he broke down in Flossy's arms, helpless with sobs. Tears washed runnels in the dirt on his face.

'I know it's just the morphia talking,' he whispered. 'She probably don't mean it, but please don't let her die. I love her so much, you see. Please God, I feel so guilty for saying it, after Lily, but I couldn't stand to lose her.'

The all-clear droned out over a landscape of desolation and Flossy drew back.

'Come on, let's go and find the others.'

There was nothing more that either of them could do now but pray.

Nine

The ramifications of the first week of the London bombings stretched further than Bethnal Green. Night after remorseless night the East End copped it. But to Dolly's shining pride, everyone apart from Peggy was back at their workstation on the Monday morning after that first dramatic weekend, and one week on, they may have been a little battle-wounded, but the brave and tenacious machinists were still going strong.

By night, Dolly and the rest of the girls took their sewing and headed down to the crypt at St John Church, and in the morning after a quick wash – or if they were lucky, a free shower in the Lifebuoy van if it was parked outside – they would hotfoot it to Trout's to check it was still standing before clocking on.

The immense relief and joy Dolly felt each morning when she turned the corner to see the factory silhouetted against the ash clouds, a Union Jack flag fluttering out of the window and a *Still open for business* sign tacked to the door, was hard to put into words. Though Dolly had a hunch that the fact the factory was still standing had more to do with Archie's insistence on staying there overnight to deal with incendiary bombs than with mere good fortune alone.

It was a Saturday afternoon, precisely one week on from Black Saturday, as it was now dubbed, when the man himself called all the machinists to order.

'Shut them machines down, ladies, and listen,' Archie called. 'I have some news. Peggy's mother, May, just called in on her way back from visiting her at Bethnal Green Hospital. I'm delighted to say the docs are pleased with her progress. It could be a while before she's discharged – by all accounts her legs ain't a pretty sight, but she's alive, and that's what counts. I told Mrs Piper that Peggy's job remains open until she is well enough to return. Meantime, I think we all know who we have to thank. Stand up, Lucky and Flossy.'

Dolly watched as Flossy blushed. 'I didn't do anything,' she mumbled. 'It was all Lucky.'

But the women gave her a proper Trout's chorus of approval, whooping and banging their cotton reels with their empty enamel mugs.

'Peggy owes you her life, and May still has a daughter because of you both, and don'cha forget it,' Dolly said over the clamour. 'You were very brave not to abandon her in her hour of need.'

'Dolly's right,' insisted Archie. 'All my girls are brave. I'm so proud of you all. Watching you clock on this morning, not a minute late, I don't mind admitting I had a lump in my throat.'

The foreman cast his eye over the floor with a tender smile of propriety. 'I counted you all in personally, and I don't want to lose another one of you.'

With that, everyone's eyes instinctively drifted over to Lily's workstation, where Archie had symbolically draped her sewing machine with a Union Jack flag.

'We will never forget Lily Beaumont,' he said, gulping deep in his throat. 'But in her memory, we will fight harder than ever before.'

He glanced at the clock on the wall. 'In ten minutes, it will be four forty-three p.m., precisely one week from the start of the bombs. I'd like us to have a minute's silence in honour of Lily; then Doll's going to bring round a whip, so we can all put a bit of money in to send Lily's older brother, who's away serving. He's God knows where in the army fighting for his country, and back home, he's lost his mother and his sisters. His whole family wiped out . . .' An awful silence turned the room over as each and every one of them digested Archie's sad words.

Pat shook her head and folded her arms over her vast chest. 'Some Home Front he's going to return to. Poor bugger.'

'And he's PBI too,' Dolly found herself remarking. 'Poor bloody infantry,' she added, when she spotted Flossy looking confused.

'We can't pretend to know when the end will come, but I suspect 'itler's gonna try his hardest to bring us to our knees,' Archie went on.

'Let 'im try,' jeered Sal.

'And he will, Sal, make no mistake,' warned Archie. 'My mate down at the control tells me there were over five hundred incendiary bombs extinguished in Bethnal Green that first night alone. I felt like half of 'em landed on our roof.

'For that reason, I'm going to keep Lucky posted up there during working hours. He's gonna keep a sharp eye out for enemy planes, and he's rigged up a buzzer system so we can keep working after the siren goes off. One buzz for "Keep working"; then if they get too close for comfort, two buzzes and we head down the shelter.

'I'm also gonna close the factory up early, at five p.m., so you can all get yerselves sorted for the long nights ahead. I'll pay you an extra four shillings a week danger money; anyone not happy with that can leave now. I hear the Rego down Curtain Road are hiring.' He planted his hands on his hips and gazed round the room expectantly, but no one moved a muscle.

'That's my girls,' he grinned. 'On a brighter note, the bombing of our fine city has caused the Yanks to sit up and take notice, and Vera tells me that the Red Cross are sending through an urgent consignment of free wool to the WVS, so the Victory Knitters won't have to scrimp and save anymore.'

'That's right,' added Vera. 'Our little sewing bee is more important than ever before, though we will have to turn our attentions away from HMS *Avenge*. Having said that, I would urge you to continue writing your letters. We may not be able to provide comfort items for them, but we can provide words of comfort.

'We can use our time in the shelters during the raids to great effect. The WVS urgently need blankets for hospitals and first-aid posts, armlets for emergency helpers and layettes for bombed-out families with babies.'

A heavy sense of fatigue settled like a blanket over the floor.

Sensing a drop in morale, Dolly grabbed her knitting needles and held them aloft. 'Come on, girls,' she urged. 'They ain't guns, but it's our way of fighting back. Let's get knitting for victory.'

Pat rose from her bench and folded Dolly into her arms. 'God love you, Dolly Doolaney. Where would we be without you? Don't worry – we won't let you down. It'll take more than a few bombs to stop the Victory Knitters.'

Pressed into Pat's voluminous chest, Dolly smiled as a chorus of cheers and general approval rang round the floor.

'Bleedin' hell, Doll,' teased Pat, pinching her side. 'I know decent grub's in short supply, but you're wasting away, gal. Don't lose any more weight, will yer?'

Dolly was saved from answering by Archie clearing his throat.

'All right, girls, it's time. Silence, please.'

Every single member of Trout's stood stiffly behind their sewing machine and reverently bowed their head, in tribute to the short life of Lily Beaumont. Dolly couldn't help but sneak a look at poor Lucky, who had removed his cap and was staring hard at the floor, a black armband encircling his shirtsleeve. He might have lost his sweetheart, but how she hoped he had finally gained the sense of worth he craved. Night after night he had proved himself, dodging bombs and digging out bodies.

The cataclysmic turn of events would surely make or break them all, but for Dolly at least, the real danger lurked within.

*

At the end of Saturday's shift, Flossy was just wondering whether she had time to stop at the shop on the way home to replenish her meagre food provisions before the sirens went off when Sal tapped her on the shoulder.

'Upstairs in the canteen,' she muttered under her breath, casting a furtive glance about the factory. 'And don't tell Vera.'

Intrigued, she followed Sal into the works canteen and was surprised to find every member of the Victory Knitters – bar the forelady – seated round a large table.

'All right, girls, it's like this,' said Sal, when at last the hubbub had settled. 'Who here is angry about the lack of shelter in the East End?'

An angry murmur rippled round the group.

'Look at this,' spat Sal in disgust, as she flung a copy of a newspaper across the table.

Flossy could just about make out the headline: *The Cockney Is Bloody But Unbowed.* Sal picked it up and started to read: '"East London paused for a moment to lick its wounds after what had been planned by Hitler as a night of terror. I saw only quiet calm that amazed me. Even homeless chatting smilingly."'

'Codswallop, ain't it?'

'A load of old guff,' agreed Daisy.

'But it's all, you know, what do they call it . . . ? Propaganda, ain't it?' said Kathy. 'The East End can't be seen to be cracking.'

'And I agree with you, Kathy,' said Sal. 'But don't we have a basic right to safety? All them months the politicians knew this war was coming. Why weren't they building deep shelters, instead of shaking hands with the enemy?'

Sal jutted her chin out defiantly, and her red hair shimmered in the fading light of the deserted canteen. Lighting a cigarette, she inhaled deeply before blowing a long stream of blue smoke into the air. 'Now the day of reckoning has arrived and what we got? A few feeble brick shelters that I wouldn't keep an animal in. Either that or we have to take over church crypts, goods depots or railway arches. Why should we have to? It's all right for them lot – they've packed their kids off to America and they're dining out in the basements of posh restaurants, or sitting in their steel-lined dugouts, safe as houses. Except our houses aren't safe, are they? They're so bleedin' old it's only the wallpaper holding 'em up, and who here has space in their yard for an Anderson?'

'I ain't got room to swing a mouse, much less a cat in my yard,' snorted Ivy.

'Exactly,' said Sal. 'You heard what Her Royal Highness said yesterday after Buckingham Palace was bombed? Reckons she can look the East End in the eye now. Don't get me wrong, I'm all for Her Highness, and she does some sterling work, but it's a little bit different, ain't it? She's sheltering in a palace; meanwhile I'm in a pisshole.'

Sal mashed her cigarette out and started to pace the canteen. Flossy watched, riveted. The twenty-two-year-old seamstress radiated anger, from the roots of her fiery red hair to the tips of her calloused fingers.

'Fifty-eight people, including our Lily and baby twins, killed in Columbia Market, and now I've heard of another "incident", as they so charmingly like to call 'em. Four days ago, hundreds of bombed-out women and children were awaiting evacuation from a school not five miles from here in Canning Town. Three days they was waiting for the coaches that never arrived. On the fourth day, a parachute bomb split the building in two and fell in the basement. Lucky's mate over there on rescue reckoned as many as six hundred poor souls were buried alive – said they had warned the authorities time and again to get them out. After a few days, they had to give up digging.'

Her words were unflinching, but Flossy could see she was struggling not to cry as she lit yet another cigarette with a shaking hand.

'All those poor mothers and their innocent children buried alive.'

No one breathed a word as terrifying images tumbled through their minds.

'We can't go down Bethnal Green Tube, can we?' Sal went on. 'But thousands of lives would be saved if folk could shelter down the Tubes. Honest, decent, hard-working folk are getting killed night after night. It just ain't right. It's us in the eye of the storm, after all.'

'I heard two thousand swarmed down Holborn Underground a few nights back and slept on the platform,' piped up Ivy. 'No one tried to keep 'em out.'

'Yeah, but they're working stations, so the doors are always open. They'd have a job on their hands keeping huge crowds out, but Bethnal Green ain't a finished station yet, so the doors are bolted.'

'What I don't get is why?' asked Kathy, baffled.

'Simple, ain't it?' sniffed Sal. 'Whitehall, in their infinite bloody wisdom, seem to think that if we go down the Underground, we'll never come back up again – "shelter mentality", they call it. They think the war effort would grind to a halt. Bleedin' high-falutin' politicians.'

Scornful laughter pealed around the canteen.

'I ask you, don't that go some way to showing you they have no clue what our day-to-day lives are really like?' said Pat, her top lip curling in contempt.

'We still gotta earn a crust; we still gotta clock on each morning. If they had to scratch for a shilling like what we do, then they'd understand that going underground and never coming back up ain't even an option.'

'I hear what you're saying, Sal,' said Dolly, who had remained silent up until now. 'But the question is, what do we do about it?'

Sal stopped pacing, and her turban-topped figure cast an imposing shadow on the canteen wall. Flossy had the queerest sensation she was facing a general addressing his army.

'We stop the hand-wringing and take action,' Sal blazed, her dark eyes full of fire. 'There's a group from our neighbours in Stepney, led by an ARP fella and a newspaper reporter, going up to the Savoy Hotel, up West, to protest about the lack of shelter and the Tubes being shut to shelterers. They're going to stage a sit-in to make a point.'

'Why the Savoy, Sal?' Flossy couldn't help herself from blurting.

'Good question, Flossy,' Sal replied. 'Because all the American newspaper correspondents are staying there. It's the only way to get word out.'

'When?' asked Dolly.

Sal glanced at the clock. 'One hour.'

'Hell's teeth,' screeched Ivy. 'Jerry will be here then if the last week's anything to go by. We'll get caught out!'

'Look,' said Sal, her features softening. 'I don't want to put anyone in harm's way, and I wouldn't think less of you for not coming. But the way I see it is this: we're sitting in the backyard of the richest square mile of Britain, but does any of that wealth or privilege filter our way?'

'Does it hell, Sal,' muttered Pat, pulling a cigarette from underneath her turban and drumming it on the tabletop. 'But I don't see how staging a sit-in up at some fancy hotel's going to change a bleedin' thing.'

Sal calmly took the cigarette from Pat's feverish hand, lit it and passed it back to her. 'I'll tell yer how. Remember the Match Girls from the Bryant & May factory in Bow?'

Heads nodded in recognition.

'I'm sorry, Sal, but I don't,' Flossy ventured.

'That's all right, sweetheart. The Match Girls were famous in 1888. They were working-class factory girls from the East End, just like us, except they had to work in shocking conditions. The white phosphorus they handled gave them painful and disfiguring injuries. Not only that but it was a sweatshop: they slaved for a pittance.'

She shook her head in disgust. 'We might have a grumble about Vera from time to time, but the Bryant & May foreman would strike 'em for not working hard enough.'

Flossy's grey eyes widened in dismay as Sal went on. 'It only took a few brave girls to go on strike and soon fourteen hundred of 'em had joined in the spirit of solidarity.

'Who cares about the rights of working-class women? was what the authorities thought back then. Fifty years on and I don't reckon that belief has changed much.' Sal's eyes gleamed mutinously as dusk settled over Bethnal Green.

'Those girls were my inspiration. Would they have sat around waiting for whatever providence decides to dish out to them, or would they have fought for their right to safety?'

An unnerving hush descended on the canteen.

'They had the guts to make their voices heard,' Sal cried into the silence, her hands bunching into fists. 'Now it's *our* turn to fight. Come on, girls, where's our mettle? Who's in?'

A handful of arms shot up. The other women looked to each other nervously.

Ivy rose creakily to her feet. 'I'm too old – my knees ain't up to a sit-in – but I wish you the best of luck, Sal. Do us proud, eh, dearie,' she sighed.

'Thanks, Ivy,' winked Sal, patting her on the shoulder as she passed.

'Sorry, Sal, but I can't,' said a pale-faced Dolly. 'I can't leave Mum in a raid. Besides, Vera's a friend. I know she wouldn't approve, and I don't want to upset her. She's been good to me over the years.'

'I understand, Doll,' Sal replied. 'So who's joining me?'

'I will,' Flossy heard herself say.

Dolly's head whipped round in surprise. 'Flossy, are you sure?' she asked.

'Quite sure, Dolly,' she nodded. 'I should be too scared to utter a word, I'm sure, but I'd like to be there to support the girls.'

Flossy thought back to her cowardice that first afternoon underground, when she had felt hysterical with fear. She knew Dolly would tell her not to be so foolish, that she had proved her bravery by sticking by Peggy's side. But a part of her felt she still had something to prove, if only to herself.

'Count me in too,' rang out a voice from the doorway.

'Lucky!' Sal exclaimed as he stepped out of the shadows. 'How long you been there?'

'Long enough to know what you're up to. I'll probably get in hot water for being late for my ARP shift, but some-one's gotta keep an eye on you girls,' he replied.

With that, the group rose to their feet and started to gather their coats and bags, ready to make their voices heard outside of the East End.

Dolly was waiting outside the canteen and stopped Flossy as she passed by.

'I don't like this one little bit, Flossy,' she said. 'Remember you are still under the care of the home – if either Vera or Matron find out, they will have your guts for garters. To say nothing of how dangerous it is.'

'Please, Dolly,' said Flossy. 'All my life I've never dared step out of line. Who am I? The girl who grew up on the delicate ward, the girl who never quite made it to the New World, the girl who doesn't even know her past . . . Well, it's time to take a gamble on my future. When I finally meet my mother, I want her to be proud of me.'

'And what if I forbid you?' Dolly flashed back.

Flossy felt an emotion so potent she couldn't put a name to it sear through her. 'I mean to go,' she replied, her jaw clenching in determination.

Dolly closed her eyes, and Flossy fled down the darkened stairwell to catch up with Sal and the others.

Outside on the cobbled street, Sal and her band of protestors huddled in a doorway with a dimmed torch.

'Little brightener, anyone?' Sal asked, pulling a hip flask from inside her blouse with a trembling hand.

'I could use some Dutch courage, Sal,' said Daisy, taking it and having a swig.

'We're meeting the rest of the group over in Stepney; then the plan is to make our way to the Savoy en masse,' said Sal. 'Keep your wits about yer, and, Lucky, you keep an eye out for young Flossy chops here.' She tweaked Flossy's chin and grinned, just as the sirens started to wail.

'Uh-oh, right on time,' Sal muttered. 'Let's go. There's not a moment to waste, but remember this: we might just be ordinary seamstresses, but our cause is extraordinary.'

Flossy felt a sense of unreality settle over her, as if her body was walking of its own accord, as they set off, moving quickly down the darkened streets. Overhead, a blanket of stars brushed the skies silver, which would have been a beautiful thing were it not for the huge bomber's moon casting them in an ominous spotlight.

*

From a tiny chink in the factory's blackout blinds, Dolly watched them with a sinking heart, until they were nothing but a smudge in the distance. She understood what Sal was doing, but dragging a young innocent like Flossy into it . . . well, it was downright irresponsible. Despair and helplessness eddied inside her. She wanted to scream and drag Flossy back into the factory; she would do anything to protect that young mite from harm. But right now, sadly she had more pressing matters to tend to. An urgent appointment that could not be delayed any longer, bombs or no bombs. Dolly pulled her hat down firmly over her face and set off into the moonlit night.

*

Flossy didn't know what had stunned her the most. The noise of the sirens, the endless rubble, dodging flying debris as they ran through the streets . . . or the horrified faces of everyone in the Savoy's underground banqueting hall, who stared flabbergasted at the East End gatecrashers. More and more protestors had joined them as they had marched up West, and now there must have been nearly eighty of them filling up the large, plush room.

Flossy stayed huddled at the back, glued to Sal's side, her eyes out on stalks. The group of women diners nearest them looked them up and down as if they had just crawled out from under a stone. Flossy couldn't help but marvel at their clothes, such exquisite beaded gowns and mink coats – she had never seen the like. They had obviously interrupted the shelterers' supper, as forks loaded with Dover sole froze mid-air. A soft light glowed from the chandeliers suspended from the ornate ceiling. Nervously, Flossy pulled her old scratchy wool coat around her. This was a world not for the likes of her.

Sal nudged her. Her face was a mask of disbelief, shot through with scorn. ''Ere, Floss. I can't believe me eyes. There's a woman over there with a Labrador. See – even dogs have better shelter than us.'

Suddenly, a protestor in a black coat leaped onto a chair

and held his hands aloft. 'This is a peaceful protest, but we want to see the Tubes opened,' he began, and soon the room was filled with their fierce chants.

'Open the Tubes! Open the Tubes!' Their cries filled the banqueting hall, and Flossy soon found herself carried away and added her voice to the battle cry. Journalists picked up their notepads and frantically began to scribble, and Flossy blinked as the pop of flashbulbs blinded her. The atmosphere inside the hall was electric.

'This is simply preposterous,' spluttered a woman over the hubbub, clutching a crystal wine goblet in a heavily jewelled hand. 'The effrontery.'

'I agree,' said Sal, deliberately choosing to misconstrue her words. 'Hundreds of women and children getting killed night after night in the East End because they won't allow the use of the Underground as shelter. We're ratepayers: we have a right to safety.

'You can write that down an' all,' she said, nudging a journalist.

The woman's mouth opened and shut like a stranded goldfish.

'Your sole's getting cold,' Sal smiled impishly.

Before long, the police arrived and the main protestor tried to explain his position.

'What would you do if your wife was in the situation of that woman over there?' he asked the inspector, pointing to a woman from Stepney who had four young children all clinging to her knees.

Wearily, the inspector shook his head, knowing there was no easy answer to that question.

To Flossy's surprise, the waiters then began calmly

serving cups of tea in bone china on silver trays, and the protestors insisted on paying tuppence a cup.

Sal, Lucky, Flossy, Daisy and the rest of the Trout's protestors paid their tuppence, then settled down on a spare patch of carpet, their backs against the ornate wall, cradling their cups in disbelief.

'Hark at us,' giggled Daisy, crooking her little finger as she sipped at her tea. 'I ain't never taken tea at the Savoy before.'

'You all right, Lucky?' Sal asked. 'You look like you've seen a ghost.'

Without saying a word, Lucky rose to his feet and the girls watched in astonishment as he walked a few yards to a table where a smart young couple were sitting, tucking into their cheese course.

'Gerald Fortesque, as I live and breathe.' Lucky was smiling as he spoke, but his voice was as cold as ice. 'Fancy seeing you! Bet you never thought you'd see *my sort* up here, although I have to say, I'm a little surprised you're not dining at a Lyons Corner House!'

The man's face was a picture of confusion as he scrambled to place Lucky; then the penny dropped and he shifted uncomfortably in his seat.

'Gerald, who is this chap?' barked his dining companion. 'Aren't you going to introduce us?'

'I'll save you the effort, Gerald. My name is Lucky Johnstone. I'd love to tell you how we met, but I can't – national security, you understand.' He winked at Gerald. 'Let's just say Gerald and I have a mutual friend, Peggy.'

The woman looked irritated and confused, as Gerald squirmed lower into his seat. 'Well, I don't care who you are,' she said shrilly, as she played with a vast emerald-and-diamond ring on her finger. 'You have ruined mine and Gerald's five-year anniversary supper with your hullabaloo. As if life's not trying enough as it without you folk breaking in here and causing all this fuss and bother.'

'Oh, I do apologize for the interruption, ma'am,' Lucky said subserviently. 'And please, do let me offer my congratulations on reaching five years of *happy* marriage.' Lucky drew out the word 'happy', his voice dripping sarcasm, before turning his gaze on a horror-stricken Gerald. 'Only, the problem is, while you've both been tucking into your anniversary dinner, not three miles from here hundreds of innocent men, women and children are dying because of inadequate shelter. Mothers killed protecting their children, babies swept from perambulators and blown to pieces . . .' Lucky's voice trailed off as he fought back angry tears.

'Peggy is in hospital after the roof of the measly brick shelter she was in caved in on her after it took a direct hit. She's lucky to be alive . . .'

Gerald and his wife stared up at Lucky, gobsmacked.

'Anyway, you think on that. Enjoy your cheese,' he said, before striding angrily back to where the girls were sitting.

'Who was that you was talking to?' asked Daisy.

'Who, him?' Lucky replied, glancing over to where Gerald and his wife were embroiled in a heated argument. 'He's nobody.'

Presently, the all-clear sounded and the group ended their occupation of the plush hotel. Their point had been made. The battle between the people and the government would now be known.

Outside, Flossy found herself strangely euphoric at having entered a brave new world of adventure. She and the other protesters linked arms and ran giggling down the deserted streets.

'Did you see their faces?' whooped Sal, still glowing from her bravura performance.

'Not 'alf,' giggled Daisy. 'Not sure we'll be welcome back, mind.'

'Not sure I care,' Sal laughed.

'Sal, you got a chip in your tooth,' Lucky pointed out as they walked.

'Blimey, so I have,' she said, running a pink tongue over the jagged edge of her front-left tooth. 'I knew I'd caught a bit of debris when we was running to the hotel, but in all the commotion, I never clocked it. Oh well, all the better to cock a snook at the authorities. I have a feeling they won't be able to ignore us East Enders for much longer.'

Maybe it was the relief of hearing the all-clear, the wide, deserted moonlit streets or the delightful delirium coursing through her veins from the protest, but in a fit of madness, Sal whirled round and round in the middle of the road, her hands stretched high over her head, her dress skirts billowing in the breeze.

'You hear that? You silly sods in yer nice, congenial private shelters!' she yelled at the top of her voice. 'You can't put us cockneys down. We won't crawl into them pathetic shelters and think ourselves grateful. We're from the East End, see. Proper. You don't mess with us.'

Her gravelly voice echoed up the road; the vast white stuccoed townhouses with their taped-up windows stared back, silent and reproachful.

'Sal,' Lucky hissed, tugging at her arm. 'You'll get us arrested.'

'Oh, who cares?' she said. 'I could be dead tomorrow.'

By the time they made it back to Bethnal Green, Flossy found herself alone with Lucky. They paused outside the town hall and she leaned back wearily against a pile of sandbags. Her eyes flickered to a sign on the town-hall noticeboard. In bland terms, it listed the numbers of dead and injured from each 'incident'. She despaired. Weren't the departed souls of Bethnal Green so much more than a bleak statistic?

'What a night,' she said, wincing as she rubbed her sore neck. Life was being lived so intensely; danger, excitement and the constant nearness of death left her exhausted to the bone.

'That man you were talking to at the Savoy,' she began warily. 'I couldn't help but overhear snatches of your conversation. That was Gerald, wasn't it?'

Lucky nodded. 'Turns out he was married all along, so he was cheating on his wife *and* Peggy with that other waitress. Some men just don't know when to be happy with their lot.'

'The swine,' Flossy gasped.

'He's certainly that all right,' Lucky agreed. 'He's so crooked he couldn't lie straight in bed, but do me a favour, Flossy – don't say nothing to Peggy, will yer? I worry it will only set her recovery back. Besides, she's had enough bombshells to cope with of late.'

'I agree,' Flossy replied. 'On the subject of Peggy, I think I may go and see if I can sneak a quick visit to her at the hospital. I know it's outside visiting hours, but I shouldn't think it will hurt to see if we can try. Come with me, Lucky,' she urged. 'I know you haven't been up to see her yet, but she'd love to see you.'

Lucky hesitated. 'I . . . I don't know, Floss. It's complicated.'

'Please,' she begged. 'It's just a quick visit. Seeing you will be the best medicine ever.'

The duty nurse at Bethnal Green Hospital looked too exhausted to much mind that it was outside visiting hours. The poor woman looked like she hadn't slept in over a week, which in fairness she probably hadn't.

'Ten minutes and not a second more,' she whispered to Flossy and Lucky, pointing to a bed at the far end of a darkened ward, now operating out of the basement. 'Otherwise, you'll get me in no end of trouble with Matron.'

'Bless you,' Flossy mouthed, clasping her hands together in a gesture of thanks.

Lucky could bob and weave his way round a boxing ring and duck bombs in a raid, but in a hospital ward, he looked as nervous as a kitten.

Quickly, he removed his cap and plastered back a curly lock of his dark hair.

'Wish I'd had a chance to go to the barber's and get me ears lowered,' he muttered anxiously.

'Peggy won't care,' Flossy whispered, taking his hand and dragging him along the silent ward.

The ward was overflowing with bomb victims. Flossy couldn't bear to see all the faces of those poor injured folk, so looked straight ahead until she reached Peggy's bedside.

Peggy was asleep, her beautiful face chalk white against the pillow, her long lashes sweeping delicately onto the corners of her eyes. Her right leg was encased in plaster and hoisted above the bed in traction.

'She's asleep. We should go,' Lucky said, turning to move off, until Flossy clasped his hand tightly.

At the sound of his voice, Peggy's eyes flickered open, and for a second, she looked confused. Then she spotted Lucky and an avalanche of emotions crashed over her face.

'Lucky,' she whispered. 'You came.'

Their eyes locked and the intensity of the look that passed between them took Flossy by surprise.

'How you feeling, Peggy?' he smiled, his features softening. 'I'm sorry I didn't bring nothing.'

'Oh, don't worry about that. Look here, I don't remember anything about that night. The last thing I remember is going into the shelter with Flossy; then it's a blank.' She turned her head a fraction and managed a weak smile at Flossy. 'Except Flossy's filled me in, told me how heroic you were that night to save me.'

Lucky blushed and fiddled with his cap. 'It's Flossy you should be thanking, Peggy. She refused to leave your side.'

'So says the humble hero,' Flossy teased with a smile.

'I'm so very grateful to you both,' Peggy replied. 'The way I treated you when I first started . . . I'm quite sure I didn't deserve to be saved.'

An awkward silence hung over the hospital bed, before Peggy filled it.

'Lucky, I'm so sorry about Lily. So very sorry for your loss,' she said quietly.

A dark shadow flickered over Lucky's face. 'The only

comfort is that they don't think she will have felt much pain. She was killed instantly.' He hesitated. 'And I'm sorry too, about your father. Dolly explained everything to me, him missing and all.'

'I haven't given up on him, you know,' Peggy replied.

'I'm going to leave you two alone to talk,' Flossy said. As she turned and tiptoed as quietly as she could from the ward, Flossy doubted either of them would even realize she had gone. She knew it would take time for Lucky to recover from Lily's death, as it would for Peggy to admit that her father might never return. She just hoped that, when the time was right, they could repair their fractured relationship and find solace in each other's arms. Something good just had to come from so much destruction.

As she walked, she pondered on something else too. The chances of finding her mother in all this chaos were growing ever slimmer now. But after the events of the past few hours, she felt a stronger, more capable woman. And she knew just who to try and explain her feelings to. It had been a little over a week since she had received Tommy's letter, and didn't she ever have news to tell him.

'What on earth are you doing here?' a startled voice rang out from the darkened ward. 'I thought you were at the protest up at the Savoy!'

Flossy whirled round and found herself standing face to face with Dolly. 'I was, but it's over and I decided to stop in and visit Peggy,' she murmured, feeling confused. 'W-what are you doing here?'

Dolly shifted uncomfortably. She opened her mouth and then faltered, pressing her lips together.

Dread rushed through Flossy. 'What is it, Dolly?' she

urged, gripping her wrist, which felt painfully bony. 'You can tell me anything. Anything.'

Dolly gazed back at her, her beautiful blue eyes feverishly bright in the gloom of the passage. Flossy felt an unexplained jolt of fear. Dolly always looked so in control, always quick with a ready retort. Now, she just looked, well, crushed.

'Mind your backs, girls,' called a hospital porter, clattering up the passage with a trolley. And just like that, the moment was gone.

'Visiting a friend of mine with some nasty burns,' said Dolly. 'Now come on, let's get out of here and down the crypt. The raiders will be here again soon, I shouldn't wonder.'

Dolly was clearly flustered, so Flossy decided it was wise not to push it further and they left the hospital together in brooding silence. Events were moving at a bewildering pace, and Flossy scarcely knew what to expect next, but as they scurried up Cambridge Heath Road towards the crypt at St John, she knew with a certainty. Her friend *was* hiding something. Secrets between friends could be corrosive. How she hoped, in time, Dolly would come to trust her enough to reveal hers.

Out on the street, the sirens started up again for the second time that evening. Dolly gripped Flossy's hand in hers and they started to run.

Suddenly, from out of the darkness, Flossy made out a fast-moving crowd of figures heading towards them. As they loomed closer, she started. Men and women, faces twisted in anger, clutching sticks, brooms and shovels.

'Irene, whatever's going on?' gasped Dolly to a lady she recognized in the thick of the group.

'All right, Doll. Rumour has it a Luftwaffe pilot's been shot down and he was last seen bailing out over the Hackney Road.' She gripped her shovel so tightly her knuckles turned white. 'We're going to see if we can find him, teach him a lesson he'll never forget.'

Flossy was taken aback at the vitriol in her voice.

'I owe him one for my boy at Dunkirk. You coming?'

Flossy felt Dolly's arm grip hers. 'No . . . no, Irene, we're going to shelter.'

'Suit yourself,' she replied.

Then the lynch mob disappeared, retreating into the darkness to exact their bitter revenge, adrenaline and anarchy still pulsing in the spot where they had stood.

'That's one battle we ain't fighting,' muttered Dolly, as they continued on their way.

When they reached the church, a small and excited crowd had gathered outside with dimmed torches.

Flossy spotted Sal in the thick of the crowd.

'Dolly! Flossy!' she called, when she saw them. Her cheeks were flushed as red as her hair.

'Someone's managed to get into the Tube. It's happening. People are going down. Quick, come with me.'

Instinctively, they both hesitated.

'Come on,' Sal urged breathlessly. 'What are you waiting for? All over London, people are taking over the Underground. This is what we're fighting for, ain't it?'

Flossy found herself staring longingly at the door to the church.

'The crypt's already heaving. Daisy, Pat and loads of the other girls have already gone down. Dolly, your mum's with them. Please follow me,' Sal begged. 'There's not a moment to lose.'

Dolly shot Flossy a nervous look, and gripping her hand firmly, they both followed Sal without saying a word.

The entrance to Bethnal Green Underground was directly opposite St John Church. As they descended the small, slippery stairwell, Dolly paused for a second. She glanced over her left shoulder, back at the church, and crossed herself before they descended into the bowels of the earth.

Safe haven or hell? Only time would tell. Further and further into the inky depths they plunged. Using every ounce of concentration so as not to fall, Flossy pounded down the out-of-use escalators, her breath ragged in her chest, the blood whooshing in her ears.

The steps never seemed to end, and because of the sheer numbers streaming down, she couldn't get a sense of how much further there was still to go. Up ahead, she could just make out Sal's red curls bobbing above the crowd and the occasional flash of torchlight, and from behind she could hear the wheezing lilt of Dolly's struggling breath.

'Dolly, are you all right?' she called.

'I'm fine. Just keep moving,' Dolly urged. 'Don't stop whatever you do – we'll get crushed.'

Abruptly, the escalator steps stopped and the crowds forked right and streamed through a heavy steel flood door onto the westbound platform.

'Floss! Doll! Sal! Over here!' hollered Pat.

Flossy glanced to her right and, to her astonishment, saw that most of the Victory Knitters had already commandeered a space in the pits of the unfinished tracks, and laid down bedding and blankets. Pat's mighty bulk and sheer presence alone seemed to have secured a generous piece of space. She was perched regally on a faded green-and-pink patched eiderdown, like some sort of Queen of the Underground, cheeks flushed, chins wobbling excitedly.

''Bout time, girls,' she exclaimed. 'I nearly had to take me skirt off to save yer a space!'

Every available patch of cold concrete floor was occupied by a jumbled mass of men, women and children. It was hard, in fact, to see where the platforms ended and the pits began.

'Oh my giddy aunt,' Flossy breathed, attempting to slow her wildly pounding heart.

Sheer amazement prickled up her spine, and her breath hung like smoke in the freezing subterranean air. Flossy knew that for the rest of her days, she would never forget this moment.

In a dark, desperate and chaotic fashion, the East Enders had taken over the Underground station – well, if you could call it that. As Flossy gazed about, she realized it resembled a building site more than a Tube station.

Dim electric bulbs, suspended from the ceilings by a cable, cast a low, flickering light over the platform. Railway sleepers and piles of rubble lay discarded in the pits, and cables snaked up the wall. There were no tracks laid yet, which mercifully meant people could at least occupy the pits where the trains were meant to run.

Hundreds were bedding down for the night in the dark, gloomy and fetid atmosphere. Shelterers were clearly trying to respect each other's decency, as women were changing behind held-up blankets, but pressed together cheek by jowl, privacy was a hopeless wish.

Others were unpacking flasks of tea and sandwiches, or tucking into fish-and-chip suppers. A baby slept soundly in the pits, tucked up in a suitcase, next to a couple squabbling like they were in the privacy of their front parlour. Family groups calmly knitted or played card games. At the far end of the platform, a man played an accordion and a merry rabble had gathered round and were singing along. The acoustics of the curved platform roof meant his tune was carried the length and breadth of the station, over the babble of a hundred conversations. A strange cloying smell of fried fish mingled with the scent of wet concrete and sewers.

'Mind yerself, love,' called a man, pushing past Flossy to join his wife and kids in the pits.

'You remember to shut the windows and put the cat out?' she joked.

Laughter rippled round at her gallows humour. Like it mattered. Chances were her home wouldn't be standing in the morning, anyhow.

Life was continuing. Underground. And Flossy realized that this was neither heaven nor hell but somewhere in between.

'It's astonishing,' Flossy murmured, when at last she had picked her way through the tightly packed bodies and wriggled into the small space between Pat and Dolly.

'It stinks,' sniffed Daisy, pulling a bottle of smelling salts from her pocket. 'And I swear to God I just saw a rat the size of a small dog scuttle past a minute ago. Urgh!' she screamed, slapping at her thigh. 'And something just bit me. It's a bleedin' bug hole.'

'Not only that but have you seen the facilities?' gaped Kathy. 'It's a bucket behind a curtain.'

'Least you got a curtain,' Pat quipped. 'Though I do wish some of them blokes would piss a bit quieter.'

'I can't argue with you, girls – it don't smell too pretty, and it certainly ain't no Savoy,' said Sal, chuckling. 'But being down here will save lives. No doubt about it.'

'Sal's right,' Dolly said. 'Listen.'

The group fell silent and strained to hear above the babble of cockney voices and the accordion player.

'What we listening for? I can't hear no bombs,' said Pat.

'Exactly. We must be, what – nearly seventy feet down here?' Dolly smiled, as she unpacked her knitting. 'We won't be able to hear a thing.'

'Thank Gawd for that,' sighed Ivy. 'I don't reckon me nerves could take much more.'

'Are you quite sure we won't get into trouble?' Flossy asked worriedly.

'What choice have we got, Floss?' said Sal. 'It's happening night after night, after night. Not having a safe place to stay is soul-destroying.'

'Sal's right,' Dolly said, putting down her knitting and sliding an arm round Flossy. 'No one is *trying* to break the law; it's do or die, self-preservation. Now, how about we distract ourselves with some work for the sewing circle? Vera and I promised the WVS we'd have some layettes ready by next week.'

Grateful for the distraction, the girls started to pull out balls of wool and knitting needles from their bags, and soon the accordion player's melody was joined by the rhythmic clacking of needles and relieved laughter.

'If you don't mind, there's a letter I have to write first,' Flossy whispered to Dolly. 'I've been meaning to do it all week.'

'You go right ahead, love,' Dolly winked. 'I bet that sailor's dying to hear from you.'

Flossy pulled a small notebook and pencil from her bag and, without pausing, started the letter she had been meaning to write since the siren's call changed all their lives just over a week ago.

Dearest Tommy,

I was planning to respond to your lovely letter straight away, but, well, the very worst has happened. I don't even know where to begin. I'm sure you will have heard, but the bombs we all feared have begun to drop, and we have gone from the Home Front to a battle-front.

I'm so sorry I can't write with better news, but we all feel we understand a little of what you brave men have been enduring now, and in a way, that helps us. We can look you in the face and say, 'We understand.'

The day after I read your letter, the bombings began and life is more of a challenge than it's ever been. But having you to write to, well, it's given my life some purpose.

I do so hope your family have escaped harm. I know they live near the docks and I have been praying for their safety. Would you believe I am writing this nearly seventy feet underground on the unfinished tracks of Bethnal Green Underground Station? My bed for the night! We, like every other law-abiding citizen of London, have taken over the Tubes as shelters. Earlier this evening, we also staged a sit-in at the Savoy in protest at their closure. Me! A girl who never even dared to leave the top off the toothpaste and never once failed dorm inspection. I can scarcely even believe it as I write the words. It all feels like a dream, as if somehow it's happening to someone else, if that makes sense, Tommy.

I should never have thought I had the gumption to be a rule-breaker, but I suppose you never know what you're really capable of doing until you're up against it.

In my heart, though, I know it's the right thing to do. Please don't think ill of me, but after a very near-miss in a street shelter the day after the bombs began . . . well, I'm convinced that this is right. Being down here will save lives. I can't pretend it's comfortable, but at the very least we can no longer hear the bombs.

When I read your letter, life was normal. Now, well, you can't help but feel anything could happen. Why, only yesterday I had a shower in a Lifebuoy soap van parked on the street! The weekly wash in the tin tub seems like a distant luxury!

In a funny way, I don't mind sleeping and washing surrounded by perfect strangers. You feel you're not

*facing it alone, and there's great camaraderie down
here.*

*Many years ago, I missed out on a passage to the brave
new world. Back then, I was distraught; now, well, it
may sound funny, but I'm pleased I did. I think
Britain is the brave new world. I don't know why I'm
confiding in you like this, Tommy. Perhaps because you
were man enough to confide in me about your loss.*

*We'll keep sending comforts as much as we can, but
there are many bombed-out now in urgent need of blankets and clothing.*

Flossy paused and looked around furtively at the girls,
many of whom were engrossed in their knitting or, like her,
were writing letters to their pen pals or loved ones. Suddenly,
she felt a fit of impulsiveness bubble through her veins, the
same raw emotion that had gripped her earlier that evening,
when she had agreed to join the Savoy protest.

*I have no idea whether I'll ever meet you in the flesh,
dear Tommy. Who knows now what the future holds for
either of us? But just in case I don't . . . Next time you
wind that scarf round your neck, imagine it's me giving
you a warming hug.*

Yours with devotion,

Flossy x

With that, she tucked the letter back inside her bag, rested
her head against Dolly's shoulder and surrendered to the
waves of exhaustion.

'That's it, darlin' – you rest,' whispered Dolly in the half-light, as she gently covered her shoulders with a blanket. 'Sleep tight. Don't let the Tube bugs bite.'

That night, deep underground, in the bosom of her fellow factory workers and friends, Flossy slept soundly for the first time in seven days.

Ten

25 SEPTEMBER 1940

Setting her broom down smartly, Dolly felt her heart begin to race.

'I'm just nipping to the toilet, Vera,' she said hastily.

The forelady hardly had time to nod her approval before Dolly was clattering down the factory steps to the privacy of the brick outhouse. In the yard, she gasped great gulps of fresh air into her lungs and tried to quell the palpitations beating wildly in her chest.

Once in the toilet, she laid a trembling hand over her sternum and breathed out slowly. Dolly stared hard at her reflection in the cracked mirror over the basin. A shaft of pale autumn sunshine broke in through a gaping crack in the brick wall, and myriad threads of dust swirled in the air. In the darkness of the shelters, everyone looked the same, but now in the unexpected prism of light, she saw herself as if for the first time. Pale, exhausted and growing steadily thinner as the flesh melted from her bones.

Eleven days and dark nights on from the dramatic night of the Savoy sit-in and the taking-over of the Tube, and Dolly found it impossible to remember ordinary life as she had once known it. Eighteen consecutive nights so far, death had droned overhead and no part of Bethnal Green had escaped, from the library to the power station and too many houses to count. Three nights ago, they had even had their first parachute mine, which had elegantly drifted down before blasting the Allen & Hanburys factory sky-high. When word of it had reached them the next day, everyone had but one chilling thought. Would Trout's be next?

Many had left streets now pockmarked by rubble and ruins – 'trekkers', they were calling them – fleeing to the countryside. Dolly could hardly blame them, but the folk left behind were knitted from a strong moral fibre and were adapting and surviving, beating Hitler at his own game. The steady acclimatization to life under fire had already begun. The mass panic and riots in the street that some had predicted? Dolly had seen none of that, just a plucky resolve to sit it out and get the job done.

After their takeover of Bethnal Green Tube, the authorities had quickly sealed up the entrance once more, condemning them back to the church crypt, but all over London, the shelterers' cat-and-mouse game with the authorities was dominating the news. Try as they might, the police and the transport authorities couldn't keep Londoners from taking over the Tubes. Huge crowds were scrambling underground, and by nightfall, there wasn't a spot to be found from Hampstead to Leicester Square. Dolly had felt a burning pride when she had read news of it, only matched by her anger that Bethnal Green Tube hadn't yet been sanctioned for use. But she knew it was only a matter of time before they would be forced to open up their Underground station. The people had spoken. The government would be forced to listen and take action. She was sure of it.

In a funny sort of way, the urgent fight for sanctuary, combined with the bombs, was doing her a favour. Life had been thrown into such turmoil she had found it far easier to hide her condition from the rest of the girls. Although if that doctor was to believed, that would be increasingly hard to do now.

Dolly cast her mind back to that night in Bethnal Green Hospital, when she had bumped into Flossy, and shivered, despite the warmth of the late-September morning. It had all felt like a dream when she had left her appointment, turned the corner and stumbled into the young seamstress. How perilously close she had come to revealing her secret. Thank goodness they had been interrupted by that hospital porter, not that it mattered much: in the fullness of time, Flossy would know.

Dolly would no more be able to hide the painful truth than the government would be able to keep Londoners from getting underground. The outcome of both was inevitable. The fight for life and its preservation was the rawest, most fundamental of all human struggles.

Soon enough, everyone would know what she had been hiding and her secret. The letter had been written, sealed up and placed within the small package, hidden under her mattress for when the time was right. Then Flossy would have some of the answers to the questions that consumed her. Only the dreadful burning guilt that had haunted Dolly since that fateful day prevented her from revealing its contents now.

How Dolly prayed she had the fortitude to survive the

truth, though judging by her transformation since the bombs began – from a shy young lady who had lived in the shadow of her clinical upbringing to a woman on the brink of finding out what she was really capable of – Dolly had no doubt she wouldn't just survive but thrive. How she wished she would be around to see it.

At least Peggy and Lucky finally seemed to have seen sense. In between day shifts at the factory and nights spent delivering messages to the emergency services, the devoted odd-job man had spent as much time as he could by her bedside, reading her snippets of news from the paper or just sitting gazing at her as she slept.

Peggy and Flossy had both changed so much since their arrival at Trout's just over four months ago, and something told Dolly that they would do just fine. But the Lord had other plans for her. She knew that now. The physician hadn't minced his words. He had forbidden her from sleeping in cold, damp or draughty places, explaining how it would exacerbate her symptoms, but even as he had been saying the words, she could sense he saw the bald futility of his statement.

'I can't persuade you to leave the East End, Miss Dool-aney, for the good of your health?' he had asked.

'Leave London? Not likely,' she had exclaimed, before adding with a feeble attempt at humour, 'I've got the East End written right through me like a stick of rock.'

The doctor had not returned her ready smile; instead, he had ordered her to stop working with immediate effect.

'You know what they call people who can't contribute to the war effort as well as I do, Doctor,' Dolly had retorted. 'I will never be called a useless mouth, and my mother relies on my wage. Besides, what difference would leaving London really make to my condition?'

He had peered at her sternly from over the top of his half-moon spectacles. 'Miss Doolaney, may I be frank? You have a disease, not a condition, and we need to treat this with the gravity it deserves. At the very least, I urge you not to shelter at the Underground; the conditions are wretched from what I hear.

'If I had a spare bed on the ward, I would admit you immediately for a minimum of three months' bed rest and observation, but alas . . .' He had thrown his hands up in a gesture of despair. 'You are strong in mind if not in body, but I will insist you attend the London Chest Hospital regularly for tests.'

'I'll come in for the tests, but I won't leave my friends and family. Where they go, I go,' she had replied firmly, a fierce pride burning in her eyes. 'Every day I'm alive is a gift. I won't squander it by going into exile. Besides,' she had added, with a forced smile, 'what can't be cured must be endured, ain't that right, Doctor?'

'Intentions are a poor medicine, my dear,' he had replied, more gently.

'So is a daily dose of aspirin and the small tidal wave of beef tea my mother insists I drink,' Dolly had snapped. 'It's doing little to hold back the advance of my condition. Sorry, Doctor, disease.'

At her defiant words, the physician had shrugged, knowing when he was beaten, and in silence they had both stared down at the X-rays that sat between them like an unexploded bomb.

It was the build-up of fluid in her lung tissue, he had

explained – that dark mass on the scan – that was making it so hard for her to breathe. He had rattled off more terms – oedema, malar flush . . . But Dolly had stopped listening. She didn't require the medical terminology: her body was telling her everything she needed to know.

The weight loss she could mask by bulking up with extra layers and vests; the purplish flush on her cheeks could be blotted out with a thick layer of panstick, the bluish tinge to her lips disguised with a touch of her treasured Coty rouge lipstick. Thank God for warpaint! The terrible explosive coughing fits she had attributed to the powdered brick dust coating everything. The blood that seeped into her hanky afterwards could alas not be concealed with clever make-up and clothing. Until now, she had hidden her disease in the darkness of shadows. But a new day was chasing the shadows away. She was running out of places to hide.

Dolly turned on the taps and gasped slightly as the cold water spattered over her thin wrists like icy needles. When at last her pulse had slowed, she carefully pulled down the roller towel and dried her hands, before dabbing a little violet water behind each ear. With that, she smoothed down her pinafore and returned to her duties.

*

Up on the factory floor, it seemed to Flossy that since the bombings had begun, the women were singing louder than ever before, or maybe it was because *Music While You Work* was now pumped out through a tannoy system, which Archie had had Lucky install to drown out the thump of bombs, to the general approval of all the women. Before the bombs, they had sung simply to keep up momentum; now, it felt as if they were singing for their very lives.

'Ooh, lovely, my favourite,' Daisy gushed, as Glenn Miller's 'Moonlight Serenade' flooded through the garment factory. 'Turn it up, won't you?'

'This song melts me insides,' Kathy sighed.

'Cor, not much,' agreed Sal.

Soon, all the women on the line were swaying as one, as the silky melody drifted over the workbenches. To the exhausted workers, who weren't clocking up more than a few hours of sleep each night, the music was as calming and soporific as being swaddled in a pure wool blanket.

Hands steadily fed strips of khaki material through Singers, but minds and hearts were elsewhere, hundreds of miles away, dreaming of loved ones wrenched from them by the war.

The romance of the music stirred Flossy deep inside. She knew she risked a telling-off, especially as Vera had eyes in the back of her head, but seeing as the forelady was in Archie's office, she took a punt and removed her foot from the treadle. In a fit of spontaneity, she pulled Tommy's letter out of her pocket and couldn't resist reading it again. It had been waiting for her when she arrived home from work the previous evening. She had read it that many times in the shelter last night that the paper was already curling at the edges.

Judging by his words, Tommy hadn't received her previous letter and their missives had crossed one another over the dark oceans. The fact that he hadn't waited to hear from her before sending another filled her with joy. She mattered to him.

Dearest Flossy,

I know I haven't received your response to my last letter, so please don't think me too forward, but, well, I think the time for social niceties has passed. When I heard about the London bombings, my heart was filled with dread and I knew I had to write straight away.

The most terrible news has reached us about what you are all enduring. Please God you are reading this alive and well. I am praying for the same reassurances from my own family.

When I saw the pictures of the East End, my East End, burning, it filled me with rage but stiffened my resolve. I know this war we are fighting is just. The cause is the right one. And to think that you, a sweet factory girl on the Home Front, are now in as much danger as we are on a minesweeper makes me even more determined to get the job done. Germany may have started it, but we will damn well finish it. Until then, please, Flossy, write as soon as you can and put my mind at rest. The thought of you and your plight is as distracting to this lonely sailor as a siren's call.

Your Tommy x

P.S. If I may be so bold, I would love a photograph of you if you could see your way to sending one, so that I may have a reminder of what I am fighting so hard to protect.

As Flossy came to the end of the letter, Glenn Miller's tune faded out, jolting her from her reverie. Hastily, she stuffed the letter back in her pocket and resumed her machining just as the forelady emerged from Archie's office.

'Where's Dolly?' Vera tutted, checking her watch. 'She can't still be in the toilet surely? That's long past four minutes.'

'Dunno,' sniffed Sal. 'But I wish she'd get a wriggle on. I dunn'alf fancy a cuppa. I feel like I've run up a whole platoon's worth of army overcoats!'

'Leave it to me,' Pat muttered under her breath, before nudging Ivy.

Flossy knew the impertinent sparkle in Pat's blue eyes spelled trouble.

Ivy leaned over and whispered to Sal. The whisper was repeated round the room, up and down the banks of work-benches, like falling dominoes.

Finally, it reached Flossy's ears.

'Hold the wheel,' hissed Daisy.

'I-I don't understand,' Flossy stuttered.

'Hold the wheel,' Daisy mouthed, as she frantically motioned to her sewing-machine wheel, which she gripped tightly in her hand. 'And put your foot down on the treadle.'

'But surely that will . . .' Flossy's words were drowned out by the rumble of thirty sewing machines groaning to a sudden halt. '. . . fuse the power.'

The foreman's door swung open.

'Power's gone. Might as well break now for tea.'

Pat shot the room a sly grin and pulled a cigarette out from under her turban, just as Dolly pushed her trolley in in a cloud of violet water.

'Oh, here she is, thank Gawd. 'Bout time, Doll. I was

starting to think you'd gone AWOL,' said Sal. 'My tongue's hanging out.'

Flossy stared hard at Dolly from over the top of her Singer. The tea lady had freshly applied her make-up, but there was something different about her, like a silver spoon that had lost some of its lustre. Her banter was just the same, though.

'All right, girls, don't have a hairy canary – I'm coming,' she said, blowing Sal a kiss. 'Now I know how Polly must have felt, someone always nagging her to put the kettle on.'

'I'm only pulling yer leg, Doll,' Sal replied, blowing her an even bigger kiss back. 'We wouldn't swap you for all the tea in China, would we, girls?'

'Not bloomin' likely!' sang back a lively chorus of voices.

Flossy chuckled along with the rest of the girls as she rose to her feet and started to weave her way over to the tea trolley for a well-earned ten-minute break. Halfway across the floor, she became aware of Archie calling her name.

'Flossy and Sal, a quick word in my office if you will,' he called. The usually avuncular foreman was in a brisk mood as he stood waiting for them, tapping the door frame to his office impatiently.

It was funny how the wailing of the air-raid siren no longer filled her with dread, but the sound of her boss's voice summoning her into his office could bring her out in a cold sweat.

'Is this because the power got fused?' said Flossy worriedly to Sal, as they walked to his office.

'Nah,' she replied. 'Mr G wouldn't get his knickers in a twist over that.'

Inside the office, the foreman took care to pull the blind down over the glass door before gently closing it behind him. He pulled a copy of the *Sunday Express* out from his drawer and slid it over the desk towards them.

'You girls know anything about this?'

Flossy felt her heart plunge to the soles of her feet, and even Sal seemed to shrink a little.

For there on the front page, in undeniable black and white, was a photograph of Sal and Flossy in the shelter of the Savoy with the other protestors. The photographer had got an uncanny close-up of them both, which gave the unfortunate impression that Sal was leading the protest. Flossy didn't need to read the text to know what it would say.

'One of me ARP pals gave it me last night, assumed I'd already seen it last week. What have you to say for yourselves?' the foreman asked.

'Oh, Mr Gladstone, I'm ever s-so sorry,' Flossy stammered. 'We didn't mean to bring Trout's into disrepute. Will you be informing Matron?'

Archie said nothing, just kept on staring at the blasted photograph. Flossy inwardly cursed. Why had she not looked away when the photographer pointed his camera at them?

Sal straightened up in her seat and defiantly flicked her tongue through the chip in her tooth.

'I'm sorry too. Sorry that you had to learn about it this way, Mr G,' she said. 'I think the world of you – all the girls do, if you must know. But I'm not sorry I went along. It was me who talked Flossy into going, so you mustn't lay any blame at her door. We weren't some foaming-at-the-mouth mob – we was courteous – but I don't regret standing up for what I believe in. I'd do it all over again tomorrow if I had to, but if you have to give me my marching orders, then so be it.'

Archie steepled his fingers together and stared long and hard at the girls. Mentally, Flossy was preparing herself for a return to her old job at the tiny tailor's when finally he spoke.

'Sack yer? Give over, you daft mare.' His blue eyes twinkled mischievously, and the corners of his smile creased into dimples. 'I'm proud of you both.'

'You are?' asked Flossy, gazing back at her boss with big, bright eyes.

'Yeah, I am,' he nodded, sitting back in his chair with a deep sigh and crossing his arms over his rotund belly. 'You've got the guts to stand up for what you believe in. Takes me back to the battle of Cable Street, when we drove that fascist Mosley and his no-good blackshirts outta the East End.'

Archie was still pontificating over his past when Flossy leaped to her feet. She didn't know what came over her – perhaps it was the relief of not being turned out of her job – but the next thing she knew, she had leaned over the desk and pressed a grateful kiss onto the foreman's warm cheek.

'Thank you, oh thank you for not sacking us, Mr Gladstone,' she gushed.

'Sit down, you dozy Dora,' he ordered, but he was chuckling as he did so, his round little cheeks flushed as pink as plums. 'I would never sack you for standing up for something you believe in. I like to think I've always had the guts to be counted, and I expect my girls to behave the same. Takes more than a bleedin' Nazi to scare me.'

'I say, Mr Gladstone,' Vera's voice rang out from the

doorway, and she wore an expression that could curdle a milky drink. 'Did you not hear me calling? Why on earth have you pulled down your blind?'

The factory foreman leaped to his feet like a man who had just sat down on a pin, while hastily shoving the news-paper under his desk. 'Sorry, Vera,' he blustered. 'I didn't hear you. I'm all ears.'

Flossy allowed herself a wry smile. Nazis might not scare her boss, but prickly East End foreladies certainly kept him on his toes all right.

'If you're not too busy in here, there's an announcement on the wireless you all might be interested to hear,' she remarked coolly.

Archie strode from his office, but as Flossy and Sal made to leave, the forelady stepped in front of them, barring their way.

'By the way, girls, don't think I don't know where you were the night of Saturday the 14th,' she added, her green eyes narrowing. 'Fools rush in where angels fear to tread. I just hope you conducted yourselves in a way that brought no shame on Trout's.'

Outside on the factory floor, every single worker, including Lucky, was gathered round the wireless, listening intently.

'Quick, girls,' said Daisy breathlessly, when she saw them. 'Get your lugholes over here and listen to this.'

The wireless was tuned to the BBC Home Service, on which the newsreader was making a sombre announcement. His plummy voice sounded incongruous in the factory floor of Trout's, as it echoed loudly through the new tannoy system: 'Here is a special bulletin. The use of Tubes has now been officially recognized, according to a declaration to the press released today by the government. The Home Secretary has declared that although the Underground is primarily for transport, all Tube stations will now be fitted out for the occupation, and all facilities and refreshments will be provided to make them habitable for shelterers.'

The roar of approval was so loud a pigeon resting on the window ledge flapped off in alarm, and suddenly, Flossy also found herself hoisted into the air as Sal swept her off her feet and spun her round until her skirts flew up.

'My knickers!' she giggled helplessly.

'Sod yer knickers,' Sal whooped. 'We're celebrating a victory. Victory for the working classes. We did it!'

Flossy's head was still spinning when Sal planted her back down and ruffled her hair, but she shared in her friend's deep joy at the news.

'So does that mean they'll be opening up Bethnal Green Tube now?' asked Kathy.

'Too bloody right it does, Kath,' said Pat. 'Not that we need a formal invite, anyway, thank you very much.'

''Bout time,' nodded Archie approvingly.

'Well, the government better pull their finger out and get to the job in hand and fast,' said Dolly. 'Jerry will be back tonight.'

'I honestly don't know why you want to shelter down the Tubes,' sniffed the forelady, who, up until now, had remained silent. 'It'll be a breeding ground for germs and put even more pressure on the cleansing stations of Bethnal Green. How does the old rhyme go? *I had a little bird. Its name was Enza. I opened the window. And in-flu-Enza.* You mark my words, those tunnels will be riddled with disease in the time it takes to say "scabies",' Vera snapped, clicking her bony fingers together.

Daisy shook her head in exasperation. 'Hark at Mrs Mona Lott. You don't 'alf know how to rain on our parade.'

But not even the forelady's dark mutterings could cast a dampener over the machinists of Trout's, who, for the first time since the bombings began, had been thrown a lifeline.

'Well, at least we'll all sleep a bit easier in our shelters tonight, eh, girls. I reckon that calls for a nice cuppa to celebrate, don'cha you think?' Dolly said with a relieved smile.

Abruptly, the wireless went dead, and each and every woman froze and looked to one another. A sickening silence cloaked the room, for they all knew what it meant when the wireless cut out.

'Wait for it . . .' Dolly murmured.

A heartbeat later, the familiar wail of the siren pierced the air.

'Knew it. Jerry didn't want to miss the party,' Dolly quipped sarcastically. 'Should have known really – it's been a bit Blitzy today.'

'I'm going to head up to the roof, Gov'nor,' Lucky said to Archie. 'See how close they are.'

The sirens regularly went off in the day, but experience had taught Flossy and the girls that the daytime alerts were mostly nuisance raids. It was the night-time bombers they need fear most.

'Come on, girls. Let's sit this one out in the stairwell, away from the windows, shall we?' ordered Archie, flicking a look at his wristwatch. 'Wish they'd hurry up. We got work to do.'

But as they walked towards the factory door, the machines started to rattle and the ceiling lights danced, as the noise of the planes quickly engulfed them.

'Blimey!' shouted Sal, over the noise. 'Sounds like they're right overhead.'

Thirty seconds later, Lucky was back, his face blanched of colour.

'It's Jerry all right. There's a whole squadron of Dorniers and Heinkels nearly on us. Let's get down the shelter sharpish.'

The noise rose to a deafening roar that seemed to swallow the factory whole and Flossy felt the floor vibrate under her feet.

'No time,' yelled Archie. 'Quick, everyone, get under your workstation.'

The floor was a mass of confusion and noise as every machinist flung herself under the nearest workbench in a tangle of limbs.

Time seemed to freeze as Flossy frantically wove her way along the line of workbenches looking for a spare spot to shelter. The droning of the planes was deafening her, disorientating her.

'Get down, Flossy!' screamed a distant voice.

The explosion was so loud it tore through the building. Flossy crashed to the concrete floor and felt the breath rush from her body. A second later, a pair of arms hooked under her armpits and hauled her under the nearest work-station.

Dolly threw her arm over Flossy just as a second almighty boom ricocheted around the factory. It sounded to Flossy as if a hundred roof tiles were raining down to earth, and a great cloud of choking grey smoke mushroomed through the factory.

The floor lay silent and still as the workers attempted to gather their wits. Slowly and steadily, Dolly clambered out from underneath her workbench. Coughing and brushing shards of glass from the blown-out windows off her pinafore, Flossy followed. Soon, all the workers were crawling out from their hiding places, their faces coated in a thick layer of dust.

The women gaped at the scene.

Trout's hadn't taken a direct hit, but from the looks of it, a factory two doors down had. Flossy peered out of the shattered windows and saw that a canning works was now nothing but a smoking hole. The reverberations from the blast had caused a chimney pot on the roof of Trout's to topple, smashing clean through the ceiling and onto Flossy's workstation. She stared in dismay at the crumpled remains of her Singer sewing machine, now covered in masonry, and her wooden stool, smashed to smithereens.

'Blimey, Floss. Ten minutes earlier and it would have been curtains for you,' remarked Ivy. 'Goodnight, Vienna, an' all . . . You must have a fairy godmother looking out for you.'

'No. Just Dolly,' she replied, looking over to where a shaken Dolly was standing.

Pat hauled herself out from under her workbench. 'I always said these were bloody good tables,' she muttered grimly. 'I thought me last hour had come. Cor, don't we all look a sight?'

It might have been hysteria, or simply the relief of being alive, but Flossy started to laugh, and soon, all the women were laughing along too, shakily lighting cigarettes or retying their turbans.

In no time at all, Archie and Lucky had cleared Flossy's workstation and the rest of the girls had rallied round to sweep up the worst of the mess from the factory floor. Flossy's machine was beyond repair, but on Archie's say-so, Lucky moved Lily's sewing machine onto Flossy's work-station. Flossy didn't know how she felt about using Lily's old Singer, but this wasn't the time for sentiment: uniform deadlines still had to be met.

Lucky managed to shore up the damage in the roof and haul a giant piece of tarpaulin over it to protect them from the elements.

'All right, girls, I think we've done everything we can here,' Archie announced, dusting down his hands. 'I suggest you take an early dinner break. Everyone clean yourselves up, and it's back here at two p.m. prompt and business as usual.'

'What a morning,' said Dolly, pausing with her broom to wipe back a tendril of hair that had escaped from her turban. 'I think I may use the longer dinner break to go up to the hospital and visit Peggy. I want to tell her about the Tubes.'

'Good idea. I'll come too,' said Flossy.

'Mind if I tag along?' piped up Lucky, who had been listening in. 'I found a bit of parachute silk and I've had Ivy run it up into a nice housecoat for Peggy. Thought it might make her feel a bit better while she's stuck in hospital.'

'Be our guest,' replied Flossy, impressed at his thought-fulness. 'I'm sure she'll be thrilled.'

*

Peggy felt a red-hot burst of anger implode within.

'What do you mean, there's nothing more you can do? Surely there must be something?' she demanded.

The doctor looked at her sympathetically. 'I wish there were, Miss Piper. Your kneecap was severely shattered in the blast and it is simply too early to tell how permanent and long-lasting the damage is. You will need to wear a plaster cast for the next six to seven weeks and then we can begin physiotherapy. I should warn you, though, it is possible that your right leg will never fully recover and you may need to use a stick. Time will tell . . .'

A weary smile flickered over his face. 'On the positive side, your left leg should make a complete recovery once the swelling and bruising subside. It would appear the right leg bore the brunt of the impact.'

'And my hand, Doctor?' she asked limply.

'Your damaged hand will heal, but you will need to work at it.'

'At least let me stay a little longer?' she pleaded.

He shook his head gravely. 'I wish I could, Miss Piper, but there is a war on and this bed is needed for incoming casualties. The nurse will be round in a moment to change your dressing and supply you with crutches and the necessary discharge papers.'

He paused and consulted his folder. 'You're a machinist at a garment factory in Bethnal Green, sewing army and navy uniforms. Is that correct?'

Peggy nodded miserably.

'Good,' he said approvingly. 'I see no reason why you

can't return to your duties with immediate effect. I will write to your foreman and suggest you be placed on hand-sewing. You won't be able to operate a treadle, of course, but needlework is the perfect thing to build up the strength in your right hand.'

'Thank you, Doctor,' Peggy replied.

The doctor went to move off, but almost as an after-thought, he stopped.

'Now you are out of apparent danger, you need to return to and embrace civilian life, and – dare I say it? – be grateful you still have a life. You are one of the lucky ones.'

With that, he bustled off to consult with his next patient.

Peggy stared forlornly at the crisp white bed sheet and watched helplessly as hot tears slid down her cheeks and dripped onto the starched linen. She knew it was selfish to admit, but she didn't feel like one of the lucky ones. Seventeen days she had been lying here in this hospital bed, hoping and praying that the damage to her right leg was repairable, but the doctor hadn't minced his words. The force of the impact had been too severe and she might well be permanently lame, only able to walk with a stick.

She knew the doctor was right, of course – she was lucky to be alive – but it was a blow all the same. Her right leg felt next to useless, her hand weakened and wasted from burns, and the deep laceration on one cheek would leave a scar. For a former nippy who prided herself on her immaculate appearance and slim little figure, someone who could zip from table to table, it was a cruel blow. She would look old before her time, hobbling around on crutches. Lucky's lovely face flashed her into mind. He would never want her now, surely? The thought caused a deluge of fresh tears to flood her cheeks.

'Peggy, you won't believe the day we've had,' gushed an excited voice, jolting her from her misery. 'The government's only done a U-turn and opened up the Tubes, and the factory's copped it, a great big hole in the roof. No one was hurt, but— Oh, you're crying, Peggy. Whatever's the matter?' The voice trailed off.

Peggy looked up and through the mist of tears saw Lucky, Flossy and Dolly standing by her bedside, their faces masks of concern.

'Peggy, what's happened?' cried Lucky, clutching a parcel in his hand.

'It's my wretched leg,' she sobbed despairingly. 'The doctor has just told me I might be permanently lame, which means I'll never get my old job back now, to say nothing of how frightful and ugly I look. Look at this scar on my face – just look at it.'

'Oh, Peggy,' said Flossy, patting her arm soothingly. 'I'm sure the doctor's got it wrong. You just need time, that's all.'

'Flossy's right,' said Dolly. 'That scar will fade in time, and you can work on your legs.'

Lucky seemed to be thinking very hard, before abruptly putting the parcel down on her bedside and pulling back the covers.

'Come on, let's get you out of bed,' he ordered.

Peggy's eyes snapped open. 'Are you quite mad? Did you not just hear what I said about my leg, Lucky? I . . . I can't.'

'Can't, or won't?' he challenged. 'Look here, you've had a knock to your confidence, I get that, but that's all it is,

Peggy, a knock, a temporary setback. You have to face your fears before they take hold.'

'B–but . . . how?' she stammered, gesturing to her leg. 'Look at me!'

'So?' he shrugged. 'I've managed to cope all these years with my hand. It's never held me back, and look at me now – I'm helping to save lives night after night.'

'He's right,' said Flossy. 'I've found a strength I never thought I had. You'll do the same.'

'I'm right here by your side,' Lucky said in a voice husky with emotion. 'And, well, I've been waiting a long time to say this. I know I oughtn't to, but hang it all. I love you, Peggy Piper. I have done from the moment I set eyes on you, and now, well, I love you even more. I don't give a fig what you look like. You have never looked more beautiful to me than you do now.'

'D–do you really mean that?' she asked.

'Never more sure of anything in my whole life, and when your father returns, I'd like to ask for your hand in marriage,' he said.

Peggy's hand flew to her mouth, and just like that, the pain and fear of the past four months melted away.

'I would like that very much indeed,' she admitted, with a tremulous smile.

'I'm not getting down on bended knee just yet,' Lucky grinned. 'I'll do that just as soon I have respectfully asked for your father's blessing. But in the meantime, I'll settle for a kiss.'

Peggy glanced over to where Dolly and Flossy stood watching, smiling through their tears.

'Go on, then, gal,' beamed Dolly, half crying, half laughing as she pulled out her hanky. 'What you waiting for?'

Without saying a word, Peggy held out her hand, and as tenderly as if he was picking up a newborn infant, Lucky scooped her into his arms and gently eased her to her feet.

Peggy felt herself stagger a little, but Lucky wrapped both arms firmly round her waist, anchoring her to the ground, until she felt a little safer.

'There now, told you you could do it,' he said softly.

He drew her body closer. Their eyes met. The time for words was over. Peggy tilted up her chin, closed her eyes and felt the softest of kisses brush over her lips. This kiss had been a long time coming and she savoured every delicious moment. When at last his lips left hers, she laid her head on his solid chest. She was grateful for Lucky's love, but also for his refusal to accept her father was dead. Thank goodness he had stuck with her. She had been too blind to see him for the man he really was, but now she had been granted a second chance.

She felt Lucky's breath, warm and tingling, in her hair. 'I'll take you dancing once this war is over,' he whispered. 'We'll be the envy of one and all, you'll see.'

And there they remained, wrapped in each other's love and acceptance in the basement of a bomb-shattered hospital, oblivious to everyone but each other.

*

Flossy knew they ought to leave, but there was something so spine-tinglingly romantic about the sight of Peggy enveloped in Lucky's strong arms that she and Dolly couldn't resist sneaking a last peek at the couple before they left the ward. To watch love blossom from the ashes of despair was a rare and precious sight.

'Gladdens your heart, don't it? Most East End men hide their love,' Dolly remarked. 'They don't want to be seen as sissies, got to act the tough nut.'

'Oh, don't be so cynical,' teased Flossy. 'There's someone special for everyone. "There's always someone nearby who loves you." That's what you told me. There'll be a special someone out there for you too.'

Dolly shook her head. 'Nah, not for me, love. It's too late. I'm too long in the tooth for all that caper.'

'You're only thirty-six. You're hardly past it yet,' she said with a quizzical smile.

'Just drop it, would you?' Dolly replied briskly. 'Now, let's talk about your chap. Have you heard from Tommy?'

'He's not my chap,' Flossy protested.

'But you'd like him to be?' Dolly said, with a wink.

'Well . . . no . . . yes . . . I don't know! I got a letter from him yesterday, actually. It was ever so sweet. He asked me to send a photograph, but I daren't really. I'm hardly the glamorous sort, am I?'

'Well, we can fix that, can't we!' said Dolly mysteriously. She glanced up at the clock on the hospital ward. 'Ninety minutes until we need to clock back on. That should just about give us time by my reckoning.'

'What do you mean?' Flossy asked, puzzled.

'You'll see,' laughed Dolly, grabbing Flossy's arm and leading her out of the hospital.

A short walk later and Flossy found herself standing outside Eugene's Perms on Cambridge Heath Road.

Dolly untied Flossy's turban so that her long brown hair fell around her shoulders. Instinctively, Flossy looked down at the pavement, but Dolly gently lifted her chin up so that their eyes met.

'Look at me, love,' she said. 'I reckon a nice wave in your hair and a touch of lippy; then we'll pop down Bethnal Green Road and get a photo taken. It's where all the girls go to have their picture taken for their sweethearts in the forces.'

Flossy frowned. 'I should never dare,' she mumbled. 'Doesn't it seem a bit forward? He might get the wrong idea.'

'Look around you, Flossy,' Dolly urged. 'What do you see? Rubble and bombsites. Who knows what tomorrow will bring? Haven't you already had enough near misses to realize that? He'll be happy as a sandboy. You're a smashing-looking girl, after all.'

'This sounds daft,' Flossy said haltingly, 'but I just wish I had my mother here.'

'Oh, sweetheart,' Dolly said with a catch in her voice. 'Your mother, wherever she is, would be very proud of you. She would want you to live your life to its fullest.'

Tenderly, she brushed back the long curtain of hair from Flossy's face. 'Your youth will pass. Life flashes by so quickly, trust me. Don't delay – do your living today.'

A sad smile quivered on Dolly's lips. 'You're an unpolished diamond, sweet girl. Don't be afraid to shine.'

'But I'm so . . . well, so ordinary, I suppose,' Flossy muttered.

'The ordinary is often extraordinary on closer inspection,' Dolly replied, gazing deep into her grey eyes.

Flossy stared wide-eyed up at her friend and, without saying a word, pulled open the door to the salon. Dolly was right. If she wanted to stop behaving like a downtrodden orphan, it was time to stop looking like one.

Ninety minutes later, Flossy and Dolly clocked back in at Trout's and a chorus of wolf whistles flooded the factory floor.

''Ere, Doll. You didn't tell me you knew Rita Hayworth,' Daisy joked.

'Leave it out, Daisy,' Flossy blushed. 'I've just had a wave put in my hair, that's all.' She had to admit, though, as she caught a glance of herself in Archie's glass office door, she had had quite the transformation. Her hair, instead of hanging limply down her back, now fell in soft waves about her face, and the soft coral rouge that dusted her cheeks brought out the silver in her pale grey eyes.

'Oh, sweetheart, you look an absolute picture,' Sal said from behind her machine, 'and if I'm not much mistaken, you're wearing a bit of lippy too.'

'She is too,' said Dolly proudly. 'Beauty is a duty. Us girls gotta wear our lipstick to show 'em our flag's still flying. Put your best face forward and all that . . .'

'Too right,' agreed Daisy. 'If you don't mind me saying, Flossy, when you started here, you looked like a proper drudge, and now, well, you're a new woman.'

'You doing it all for a special chap?' Kathy shouted over the rumble of the machines as they started up. 'Are we gonna have our first pen-pal marriage?'

Flossy said nothing, just smiled enigmatically as she sat down behind Lily's Singer. Hitler wasn't going to stop her machine from humming, not if Archie had anything to do with it. She traced her slender fingers over the cool black curves of the sewing machine and thought of glamorous Lily, singing at the top of her voice behind this very machine. The feisty seamstress had never let anything or anyone stop her enjoyment of life. Perhaps the very best tribute she could pay Lily was to live her life with the same zeal.

As Flossy started work, she also found herself musing on Kathy's question. It was true. A part of her had wanted to look more glamorous in her photo for Tommy – but the makeover experience with Dolly had been an uplifting one too. It might be just a bit of Pan-Cake and a perm, but it had brought with it a queer sense of liberation from her past.

At the end of yet another momentous day, Flossy was beat and chilled to the marrow. The gaping hole in the roof, although covered with tarpaulin, meant the factory was perishingly cold, and by the time the end-of-shift bell sounded, Flossy could scarcely feel her fingers or toes. Despite this, she was itching to get going. The photographer on Bethnal Green Road had said that her portrait would be ready to collect after her shift finished and she was dying to see it and get it sent off to Tommy.

'Before you all hurry off to the shelters, might I take a quick moment of your time?' piped up Vera, seemingly oblivious to the cold, or Flossy's love life.

'Make it quick, will yer? I need to get home and warm my cockles before we head down underground,' piped up Pat. 'It's cold enough to freeze the balls off a brass monkey.'

Vera wrinkled her nose in distaste, before continuing. 'I had a meeting with the WVS on my dinner break and the centre organizer informs me that the St Pancras branch managed to complete six hundred and three articles in the month since the bombings began, which is very creditable. They really have come up trumps.'

'As have the Victory Knitters,' added Dolly hastily.

'Quite,' said the forelady. 'But there is a desperate shortage of clothing in the borough. The rest centres are at breaking point, with people bombed out of their homes, and the WVS urgently need blankets, pillows and socks. To this end, and thanks to the kindness of the Red Cross, they have supplied us with fresh wool and material. Now the Tube is set to open, I hope you'll all use your evenings there to get knitting and stitching. The WVS also plan on going down there to distribute free wool to all shelterers, and any finished articles can be handed straight to a shelter marshal.

'I've also said that we can use our time down there to repair soldiers' cartridge belts to raise money for the comforts fund. Eighteen hundred bandoliers need repairing at a charge of a penny each,' added Dolly. 'And please don't forget to keep writing to your pen pals on HMS *Avenge*. I know some of you are closer to your sailors than others,' she said, winking at Flossy, 'but they're all relying on our letters for morale.'

'Count me in,' said Ivy. 'I'll do anything to keep my mind off the bombs. Plus I've become quite fond of my pen pal.'

'Me an' all,' added Sal.

'Very good,' replied the forelady, as she tore open the brown paper package from the Red Cross and got ready to begin distributing the wool. As she did so, a note fluttered out.

'You're not the only one who likes to send secret notes,' Flossy heard Kathy mutter to Daisy.

Intrigued, the forelady picked it up and began to read out loud. *'This wool has been sent from Hot Springs Red Cross Sewing Circle. It will have had a long journey: one hundred and fifty miles by plane, then another thirty miles by Dog Mail Run, and then carried on snowshoes across deep snow before its perilous journey across the Atlantic. We hope you can make good use of it.*

'When we heard on the wireless the terrible news of what the Nazis are doing to your beautiful cities, we wept. Then we gathered round the one television set in the village and saw with our own eyes the devastation wreaked on your city. What a barbaric beast Hitler is. We pledge to do all we can to help you British women, and our thoughts are with you from afar. From mothers, wives, and women to a far nobler, braver breed of women than us. We are in awe of you British women. Don't give up the fight. Knit for victory!'

When the forelady had finished reading, Dolly shook her head in amazement. 'Well, I'll be,' she murmured in astonishment. 'That proves it.'

'Proves what, Doll?' puzzled Kathy.

'That we're not alone,' she replied. 'Our little sewing circle is part of something far bigger, a women's production line that stretches from factory to office, village to town, and across the oceans.'

The girls were just about to take their leave with the strangers' kind words still ringing in their ears when the factory door opened and in peeked the frightened face of a girl. Flossy put her at no more than twelve. She was dragging a Tate & Lyle sack behind her, and her eyes darted nervously around the factory.

'Can I help you?' snapped the forelady. 'You're far too young to work here.'

'Pardon me, miss, but I ain't here about a job,' said the girl. She turned to Dolly. 'If you don't mind, I heard you ran a sewing circle. I seen yer in the rest centres and down the crypt. Can you help me? Only, I got a lot of mending for my six brothers and sisters. I see you're handy with a needle.'

The forelady bristled. 'Why can't your mother do it?' she asked.

The girl's face crumpled. 'Please, miss . . . She's dead. She got caught out in the open in a raid last week, and my dad was killed in Dunkirk, so it's all down to me now. I ain't gone a day without seeing my mum . . . I . . . I don't know what to do.'

A silence fell over the floor.

Slowly, Dolly bent down to the girl's level. 'Of course we'll help you, sweetheart. You've done exactly the right thing. Tell you what, I'll take you up the canteen now, make you a nice cup of tea; then you can tell me all about it.'

Archie poked his head out of his office door and tucked a ten-bob note in the girl's dress pocket.

'I couldn't help overhearing,' he said, his usually gruff voice soft with concern. 'Give us your address and we'll make sure you're looked out for, all right, love?'

The girl nodded gratefully as Dolly led her away.

Flossy stared down at her workstation and tears pricked

her eyes. Every day in the East End, fresh orphans were being made.

With no more words to say, wearily the women started to oil their machines in readiness to leave for another long night.

Dolly paused at the door, her arm still wrapped round the young girl's shoulder. Her sweet voice chimed around the floor. 'Goodnight, girls. God bless and see you in the morning, PG.'

'PG?' puzzled Flossy, out loud.

'Please God,' Dolly replied.

The next morning, God had answered their prayers. Every worker clocked on at 8 a.m. sharp. Including Peggy.

Thanks to the hole in the roof, it was so cold that overnight ice had formed on the inside of the cracked windowpane and Flossy's breath hung like smoke in the freezing air. But when she spotted Lucky tenderly carrying Peggy up the factory stairs, she felt a warmth ripple through her. Gently, he set her down and handed her her crutch, before attempting to escort her to her workstation.

'Please, Lucky,' she said, pushing his hand away. 'I need to do this by myself.'

Slowly, and with a bit of a wobble, Peggy made her way across the factory floor, leaning heavily on her crutches and smiling bravely. As she passed by Pat's workstation, the veteran seamstress rose to her feet and began to clap.

'Good on yer, gal,' she said, with a smile in her eyes. 'It takes guts to come back to work so soon.'

And then an amazing thing happened. Each machinist Peggy passed slowly rose to her feet and began to clap. By the time she had reached the new-starter bench at the back of the factory floor, the room was filled with thunderous applause and every woman was standing to attention behind her machine.

It was a short walk, but it had taken a lot out of Peggy and she sank onto her stool with a relieved sigh. Flossy smiled through her tears as she furiously clapped her friend. Talk about a turnaround! Peggy's journey from shallow and spoilt young nippy to brave and humble war-worker was complete.

'Thank you all so much,' Peggy said with a grateful smile, once the applause had died down. 'I can't tell you how good it feels to be out of that hospital bed.'

Even the forelady was grinning broadly. 'Welcome back, Miss Piper,' she said. 'It's good to have you back. The doctor tells me it's hand-sewing only for you from now on, but there's plenty of pockets that need doing. I've left a bundle on your station, and there's a parcel on there for you too.'

'Thank you, Miss Shadwell,' Peggy replied.

Flossy popped over. 'I best not stop long, but it's so good to have you back,' she grinned, squeezing her friend's arm. 'Lucky spilt the beans about it being your birthday. It's not much, I'm afraid,' Flossy said, handing over a small parcel. She had saved her rations to get Peggy her favourite short-bread biscuits.

'Thanks ever so, Flossy,' Peggy gushed, doing a double take as she glanced up at her friend.

'Gracious, look at you,' she said admiringly. 'You look ever so sophisticated.'

Flossy blushed and patted her hair. 'Oh, it's nothing. Dolly talked me into getting a wave after we left you at the hospital yesterday. I even had a photo taken, which I posted to Tommy last night. I hope he likes it.' She hesitated, and the flush spread to her chest. 'Sending a photo of yourself to someone you've never even met does seem a bit . . . well, loose.'

'What does it matter, in this day and age?' Peggy exclaimed. 'Besides, he'll love it. You look beautiful.' With that she tore open the recycled newspaper wrapping on Flossy's gift. 'Thank you, Flossy. You're a treasure. I'll share these with everyone on tea break.'

'Aren't you going to open your other one too? Is it from Lucky?'

'I shouldn't think so,' Peggy replied, ripping open the package. 'He already gave me a new pair of stockings this morning . . .' Her voice trailed off as the contents of the package spilt out onto her workstation. A pot of zinc cream, some much-coveted Max Factor panstick, a bar of Sunlight soap and a snowy-white full-length cotton underskirt.

'Oh my days,' Peggy exclaimed, delighted at the thoughtful gifts. 'This is so wonderful. It would take me hours to get round the market on my leg to get all this. Zinc is known to help scarring, and look at this make-up! I'll start to look like the old me with this. I wonder who on earth sent it.' She riffled through the discarded brown paper, but there was no note.

Flossy felt a sudden jolt of dismay tear through her. The parcel was nigh on identical to the ones she received each year on her birthday! Her treasured bar of Sunlight soap was still sitting in the enamel soap dish on her dresser. She regularly shaved off little slithers of it and mixed it with water to make it last.

Her mind spun with the possibilities, and then came the fierce stab of disappointment. They couldn't possibly be from her mother, for why on earth would she be sending gifts to Peggy? It made no sense. Just who was the mystery benefactor? And why had she and Peggy been chosen? Frantically, Flossy tried to reason it out in her mind, but she could reach no logical conclusion. All these years, the parcels that had arrived without fail on her birthday had been a tangible link to her past, a connection to a mother she was convinced loved her but couldn't have her in her life.

'How strange,' Peggy murmured. 'To send such a generous gift but no note to identify yourself.'

'Very peculiar,' Flossy agreed. In silent confusion, she returned to her workstation, the hope she had carried in her heart all these years extinguished.

Eleven

It had been six months since the bombs began to drop, and Lucky finally had his first night off. In that time, Peggy had fallen more deeply in love with him than she had ever believed possible. Against a ceaseless backdrop of nightly raids, she had seen him transform from a man held back by his own self-doubt to a gallant hero on the Home Front. When he clocked on for work each morning, shattered Lucky never mentioned what scenes he had witnessed in the mayhem of the long nights, preferring instead to stay smiling for the sake of all the workers' morale.

No part of Bethnal Green had been untouched by war now, and their ordeal went on. Countless homes, churches, schools, factories, shops and even whole streets had been destroyed. Sal, Pat and Ivy were just some of the workers whose homes were now nothing but smoking rubble.

One night last December, so many hundreds of incendiary bombs had dropped on the borough that the Bethnal Green Road had been a solid wall of fire, with even the wood blocks that surfaced the street itself catching fire. It had burned fiercely until daylight.

In an absurd way, Peggy mused, the fact that it happened night after night somehow made it easier to bear. Unlike the poor folk of Coventry, whose devastating attacks had come at random, London knew to expect it every night, come what may.

It had been the longest, hardest winter of all their lives, but spring was stirring. Peggy had smelt it on the breeze that morning on her slow and laboured walk to work, even over the stench of burned buildings, and she had seen it in a beautiful little crop of saffron crocus pushing their way through the charred earth of a bombsite. She saw it too in the faces of proud housewives out on the streets each morning, sweeping away the glass and debris, determined never to give in, or die trying. It proved that beauty, strength and optimism could be found in even the darkest of places. The East End might be burning to the ground, but its heartbeat was stronger than ever before.

Since her injury, Peggy had found her appreciation of life all the brighter. A hot bowl of soup, a final stitch in a pair of socks she had been knitting or even a good belly laugh . . . The little pleasures were all the more vivid for having nearly lost her life, or maybe it was simply because she was a woman in love.

As Peggy waited for Lucky's arrival, she fixed her face in the mirror over the mantel and couldn't help but smile to herself; even the jagged scar that zigzagged down her right cheek no longer bothered her as it once had. After all, it didn't seem to bother Lucky, so why should it her?

Her leg was now out of plaster, and the physiotherapy sessions Lucky insisted on accompanying her to were helping slightly, but there was still a long way to go and Peggy was never without a stick to help her walk.

It was funny the way things worked out. She might not have met a man who could keep her in fine style, but in these shattered war years, worries over his class had been swept aside. After all, Lucky had more class in his little finger than dishonest Gerald possessed in his whole rotten body, but she didn't care to dwell on him.

She was blessed to be alive and in love. Lucky had saved her life, and his care of her since her injury left her breathless. Their dates had taken on an almost dreamlike quality. Wrapped in each other's arms in the corner of a steamy cafe, huddled in the darkness of the picture house, snatched kisses in the factory yard on tea break . . . precious moments rescued from the spiralling madness of the war. Always living for the moment, for who knew what tomorrow might bring?

A soft knock at the parlour door startled her from her reverie.

'Visitor for you,' smiled her mother.

Thanks to May's increasing work and Lucky working flat out, the pair had not yet met. Lucky was wearing a freshly pressed shirt in honour of the occasion, and he had even attempted to plaster back his mop of unruly dark brown curls, but the slight tremor in his hand betrayed his nerves. Peggy loved him all the more for it.

'For you, Mrs Piper. Delighted to finally make your acquaintance,' Lucky said nervously, holding out an exquisite flower whittled from wood. 'I made it when I worked as a cabinetmaker on Brick Lane. It used to be my hobby,' he grinned sheepishly. 'I couldn't get any fresh blooms, I'm afraid.'

May took the hand-carved gift and her face flooded with emotion. 'Oh, Lucky,' she said, a catch in her voice. 'I think it's the nicest thing anyone's ever given me. Peggy's father has talents in that direction too.'

And then the pair were off, chatting away ten to the dozen about where she had been raised in Bethnal Green and Lucky's upbringing. Turned out May had even met Lucky's late mother at a community-group beano to Margate one summer.

'You feel like one of the family already, Lucky,' she beamed. 'I just know Peggy's father will be thrilled to bits that you've found each other . . .' May's voice tailed off.

'Is there any news on that front?' Lucky gently enquired.

'Only that we know now for certain that he wasn't on the doomed vessel that sank, thank goodness. Despite that, we still have no news of his whereabouts, but I pray every day, and in my heart, I feel he is still alive.' She touched her chest lightly and sighed deeply.

'Anyway,' she said, a touch more brightly, 'I dare say you young lovebirds would like a little privacy. I shall fix you some tea.'

When the door clicked behind her, the couple moved towards each other, arms outstretched. Swallowed into his strong physical embrace, once again Peggy marvelled at the effect Lucky had on her. She still remembered the first time she had felt it, all those months ago on the stairwell at Trout's, when the slightest touch of his hand had sent ribbons of electricity shooting through her.

Lucky sat down and perched nervously on her mother's chaise longue and Peggy giggled.

'You make it look like a piece of furniture in a doll's house.'

'Come here,' he grinned, holding out his hand, and Peggy snuggled in beside him. Usually, being with Lucky made her feel so safe, but talk of her missing father had unnerved her.

'Oh, Lucky,' she cried, 'what if this war never ends? What if my father doesn't come home, and we never marry? What if you get killed on duty tomorrow night? I'll be left with nothing.'

Lucky's grip tightened. 'I can assure you, Peggy Piper, I ain't going nowhere. You hear me?' He tilted her face up and gently kissed her on the tip of her nose. 'You're going to wake up next to this face for the rest of your days, and your father will be there to walk you down the aisle.'

Silhouetted against the flickering fire in the hearth, Lucky looked so solid that Peggy instinctively believed him. She was in the arms of the man she loved and nowhere on earth felt safer.

Tenderly, she reached out and touched his war-wearied face. 'What keeps you going?' she asked.

'You,' he answered without hesitation. 'I loved you from the very first moment I set eyes on you. That you now love me too is extraordinary to me, so you see, to have hope in your heart pays off.'

Peggy smiled as she traced her fingers down his proud jaw.

Suddenly, the music playing softly from the wireless in the background died. The young couple didn't say a word, for they both knew what it meant. A moment later, the sirens began.

'Jerry's come early tonight,' Lucky groaned, rising to his feet, as May walked in with a tray of tea.

'Please don't go out tonight, Lucky,' Peggy begged. 'It's your night off.'

But even as she was saying the words, she knew nothing on earth would stop him joining his team in the ARP.

'I'll see you and your mother down the Tube first,' he promised, as May handed him his coat and tin helmet.

Silent tears started to slide down Peggy's cheeks. She was helpless to stop them.

'Peggy, what is it?' Lucky asked, confused.

'I just couldn't bear it if anything happened to you,' she wept.

'Nothing will, I promise you,' he reassured her, buckling his helmet.

'You can't possibly say that,' she said, her face wet with tears. 'My father was there one minute, and the next he was gone. The same could happen to you.'

Lucky moved quickly across the room, the broad sweep of his shoulders swallowing her in his embrace. 'Listen, angel,' he murmured in her ear. 'All I can offer you is my love. That love and the will to return to you is what will keep me safe tonight. All right?'

She gazed up at him, large eyes glittering with tears, and nodded. Never had she felt so deeply in love, or so afraid.

Outside on the streets, for speed's sake, Lucky scooped Peggy into his arms, while May carried a ready-packed attaché case containing all their important documents and a bundle of bedding for the night, and they strode in the direction of the Tube with hundreds of others. It was such a familiar routine by now that they could almost do it with their eyes shut, but something she saw made Peggy urge Lucky to stop. Sequestered down a tiny cobbled yard, hidden from the street, was a mulberry tree, its ancient, gnarled trunk lifting green branches up to the skies.

'Look. It's growing new shoots.'

A wide grin creased Lucky's cheeks as he paused to gaze up at the branches of his favourite tree. 'Well, I'll be . . . Come on, let's get you and your mum to safety.'

*

Dolly looked around the packed ward of the London Chest Hospital in Bethnal Green and shuddered. She had a deep fear of this old red-brick building ever since coming to visit her father here. He had drawn his last breath right here in this very hospital, and the fact that her physician ordered her to come here for her regular tests felt like a bad omen to her.

She tapped her fingers impatiently against the iron frame of her hospital bed as she waited to be seen by a doctor. She could ill afford to be cooling her heels here, not when she and the rest of the girls had so much work on for the sewing circle that she should be getting on with down the Tube. They had only just received word that their pen-pal sailors on board HMS *Avenge* would be getting leave in three months' time, and at her instigation, the girls had started sewing a quilt with all their names and those of their sailors woven into it, to present to them as a keepsake. She had hoped to get it finished that evening.

'Do you know when I can expect to be discharged?' Dolly asked a passing nurse politely.

The nurse's reply was drowned out by the sudden wail of the siren.

*

Flossy had grown to love the Underground even more than her own tiny digs. It was hardly surprising really. It might not be everyone's idea of a dream home from home, but to her, her little patch of space in the pits represented safety and companionship. She had come from a solitary room with a single gas ring to a place of total community spirit.

As she waited for Peggy, Dolly and the rest of the girls to join her in their usual spot, she gazed about the place with a sense of belonging she had not once felt in all her years in the children's home. It was astonishing. You could barely recognize the place from that first desperate night they had sheltered down here on bare concrete, when the bombs had started to drop six months ago. Gone were the rubble and discarded railway sleepers, and in their place light, warmth and organization had sprung up. Since the government had sanctioned its use as a shelter, the home secretary had stayed true to his word and transformed the rest centres and Underground shelters.

Bethnal Green Tube had been scrubbed and fumigated, the walls whitewashed and an extractor fan fitted to deal with the damp. The latrines were now partitioned off from each other, and thanks to regular maintenance, you didn't need to put a bag over your head any longer or have smelling salts to hand when braving them.

A shelter committee had been formed, and an ARP lady built like a tank ruled over the children who slept down there with a rod of iron. The tiny tea station had been replaced with a warm and bustling canteen staffed by a smiley lady called Alice, who made the best bacon sarnies Flossy had ever tasted.

The Salvation Army band toured regularly, playing uplifting hymns, and the WVS were on hand to sell cheap cups of tea, bundles of wool and knitting needles, and had even arranged a children's crèche to give mothers a much-needed break. Groups to rival the Victory Knitters were being formed nightly. From bingo to book groups, there was no excuse to be bored underground.

There was even a doctor's quarters and first-aid post that reeked of Jeyes Fluid, and regular hygiene inspections meant the outbreaks of disease Vera had gloomily predicted had yet to occur. Flossy had spotted the odd rat, but you couldn't have everything.

Rumour had it they were even planning triple bunks, a library and a shelter theatre. Flossy couldn't wait for that. Yes, she adored Tube life. Frankly, she was in awe of the local community, who had seamlessly taken the camaraderie on the streets up above and sunk it deep down into the subterranean town below. It might have been a town devoid of natural light, but the Underground was an important safety valve. Flossy knew the neighbourhood could not have gone on much longer as it was without it.

In the early evenings, gangs of kids roamed for miles up the tunnels playing kiss-chase, she and the Victory Knitters would get down to some serious knitting, and impromptu sing-songs would burst into life. Now they felt truly safe, the sewing circle's output was prodigious and they were churning out socks and gloves at a rate of knots!

At around 11 p.m., the lights would dim and the station would settle down for the night. At dawn the following morning, the mass of sleeping bodies would wake, and Flossy and the rest of the girls would quietly go about their business, emerging blinking into the light to get a quick wash and breakfast before clocking on for work. So much for refusing to come out! Chance would be a fine thing, Flossy thought to herself – Vera would give them what for if they were a minute late, bombs or no bombs.

The transformation had breathed fresh heart into all the girls, and she felt proud as punch of the small part she had played in it. Almost as proud as she was of her blossoming relationship with Tommy!

While she waited for her friends to join her underground, she couldn't resist sneaking a quick peek at his latest letter, which had arrived at the factory that morning. Most of the women had ripped theirs open there and then, dissecting them accompanied by great hoots of laughter and lewd innuendo, but Flossy still preferred to read hers in private.

Opening it ever so carefully, she found she couldn't wipe the daft grin from her face. Could there be a greater pleasure than the promise of an unread letter? The oceans between them rolled away as she read.

My dearest Flossy,

We're all so proud of you women back home. For the first time since I lost my wife, I find myself thinking of another woman. You, Flossy Brown. You are prettier than I could ever have imagined. Don't get me wrong,

I loved the socks and gloves, but the sight of your beautiful face, well, that warms my heart more than anything. Your photo is the best gift by far, and I shall cherish it.

One good turn deserves another and so I enclose my own photograph. Sorry it's taken so long, but I had to wait until we were granted twenty-four hours' shore leave, and, well, to be honest, I hesitated, being that much older than you.

I make the age gap ten years, but age suddenly seems unimportant. If my life so far has taught me anything, it's that we should grab our happiness where we can find it.

I know I'm not the most handsome of fellas, Flossy – in fact, my sisters call me 'Face Ache' – but if my photograph doesn't make you want to run for the hills, perhaps you might be there to greet me when I return . . . ?

Yes, Flossy, that's right. We've been granted shore leave for this coming June. Please say you'll be there, waiting on the quayside, because I have something very important to ask you.

I know this sounds corny, but the only thing that brings me any measure of joy is the knowledge that the world is round. So wherever I am, dearest Flossy, I know I will always be sailing back to you.

Yours in hope,

Tommy xx

Flossy felt her heart quicken as the photograph slipped out from between the folds of the envelope and she turned it over.

'Tommy Bird! Oh my . . .'

He had lied in his letter, for he was handsome. Quite dashing, in fact. Gazing back at her was a strong, proud man who radiated goodness. His wide smile was brimming over with sincerity, and his eyes, though baggy with exhaustion, sparkled with warmth. Flossy couldn't help herself and traced her finger over the dimples creased into his smiling cheeks.

'Face Ache indeed,' she murmured. Far from it! Tommy was definitely what Daisy would term 'a catch'. She didn't want to run for the hills; in fact, she wanted to run straight into his arms!

Nothing on earth would keep her from being there to greet him and find out what he wished to ask her. Carefully, she tucked the letter and photograph into her cardigan pocket, and a small pang of sadness surfaced. If only she was closer to unravelling the truth over her mother, then life would be about as good as it could be under the circumstances. No more had come of the mystery parcel, and Peggy was as clueless as she was.

'Aye-aye, no prizes for guessing whose letter you're hiding away there,' screeched a voice. Flossy jumped and looked up to find Sal, Daisy, Kathy, Pat and all the others tottering down the platform towards her, their faces emblazoned with mischievous grins, flasks of hot tea and bundles of bedding and sewing in their arms. They were followed closely behind by Peggy and May.

'Your sweetheart's coming home on leave,' said Daisy

with a wink, as she plonked her bundle of bedding down next to Flossy. 'Betcha can't wait to meet him.'

Flossy felt herself blush pink, but she couldn't find the energy to deny it as Daisy playfully whistled the tune to 'There's a Boy Coming Home on Leave'.

'Spill the beans,' grinned Peggy, as she allowed her mother to help her down onto the floor of the pits.

'Stop teasing her, all of you,' said Pat. 'I think it's lovely. I can't wait to meet all the boys off HMS *Avenge*. If I was twenty years younger, I'd be greeting mine with a great big sloppy kiss an' all.'

The group's raucous laughter echoed up the tunnel, but when it died down, Flossy realized something. 'Where's Dolly?' she puzzled.

'She said she was going to catch up with a mate and shelter further up the line at Liverpool Street Station tonight,' remarked Pat, as she took out the part of the quilt she had been piecing and her sandwiches.

'Don't know why she's bothering,' sniffed Sal. 'I've slept on every platform on the Central Line, and trust me, Bethnal Green's the best.'

'That's a bit strange, isn't it?' murmured Flossy. 'Especially as she seemed so keen to try and get this quilt finished.'

'Give her some space, eh, love?' said May tactfully. 'She does do an awful lot for you girls at the factory and the Victory Knitters. She's running herself ragged at the moment.'

'That's true,' said Sal. 'She's got a rattling cough. I heard her in the lav coughing her guts up the other day.'

'Who hasn't got a nasty case of shelter throat?' said Kathy.

'It's not the shelter throat that gets me,' said Daisy. 'It's the bleedin' snorers. Some fella on the wireless reckoned he's done a survey and one in seven people sleeping underground snore.'

'Yeah, well, he obviously ain't been down Bethnal Green. This Tube's full of the seventh person,' Sal bantered back, to a gale of laugher.

'Come on, enough of this moaning. Let's have a good old sing-song while we finish this quilt,' suggested Pat. 'Let's not wait for them to entertain us. Let's entertain them.'

With that, she struck up a rousing version of 'Pack Up Your Troubles in Your Old Kit Bag'; before long their neighbours joined in, and in no time at all the song could be heard reverberating up and down the underground tunnels. Flossy smiled and joined in the chorus as she sewed.

Even after all these months, it was still an astonishing sight to behold, and made the hairs on the back of her neck stand on end. A jumbled mass of humanity, pressed up against each other, all with different jobs and roles to play above ground, but each night, deep underground, singing one song. She couldn't wait to tell Tommy all about it when she finally met him in the flesh.

Three hours later, the quilt was nearly finished and half the station dwellers were asleep, with the rest settling down for the night as the station lights dimmed.

Flossy took the opportunity to pen a hasty reply to Tommy's letter.

Dear Tommy,

I am intrigued and cannot wait to hear what it is you wish to ask me. Of course I shall be there to greet you. Your age does not matter. Not to me, at any rate. I am counting the days. I too shall cherish your photograph.

Impulsively, and because despite her new-found confidence Flossy found she was still too shy to tell Tommy that she thought she loved him, she signed the back of her sweetheart's letter with the acronym 'ITALY', for 'I trust and love you.'

She popped it in the envelope and quickly sealed it before she could change her mind.

Warm and dozy, Flossy was drifting on the periphery of sleep, slipping into a delicious dream about the moment she greeted Tommy, when a lone voice pierced the shelter, startling her back into full consciousness.

'The Chest Hospital's copped it.'

*

Dolly had never felt so terrified or vulnerable in her life. Please God, was it not bad enough to be so ill without the German Army trying to hasten the process? She had been waiting to be seen by the doctor when the bomb had hit.

Immediately the wards had been plunged into darkness. Closing her eyes, she could still hear the patients' terrified screams ringing in her ears. Images came to her like snapshots. A nurse pushing her through the wards in a wheelchair, breathlessly steering her past piles of smoking timber and fallen masonry. Every door they had tried to exit had been ringed with fire. All had been confusion and fear.

The situation had been so desperate, but not once had the nurse entrusted to get Dolly out safely wavered, even when escape had seemed impossible. At one stage, they had no choice but to discard the wheelchair, and with Dolly leaning heavily on the nurse, they had followed a stream of frantic patients and taken the dark steps to the basement so that they might seek shelter there. Dolly had finally lost her cool when they staggered down into the room and straight into six inches of filthy, freezing water.

'It's flooding,' she had howled in despair, as the swill of dirty water soaked into her shoes. 'Oh, please God, Nurse, what are we to do? If we stay here, we'll drown. If we go up there, we'll burn.' Hysteria clamped her heart. 'I can't die in here!'

The nurse gripped her firmly by the shoulders. Her kindly brown eyes had not once left Dolly's, and her voice was firm but reassuring.

'Now you listen here, Miss Doolaney. No one is dying on my watch. You hear me?'

Dolly allowed herself to be led back up the steps into a ward fast filling with smoke. Finally, from out of the ash clouds, a fireman had emerged and guided Dolly and her nurse to safety.

That wonderful nurse had not stopped holding her hand and murmuring reassuring words of comfort, even as they stepped out into the hospital grounds and saw the firemen's hoses trained on the burning hospital roof.

A solid wall of fire bellowed and roared into the night sky, while enemy planes droned overhead. Unable to bear it a moment longer, Dolly had buried her head into the nurse's shoulder with a strangled sob, as the roof finally gave way and crashed into the wards below with a gut-wrenching boom.

A few hours on, and by what Dolly could only conclude had been some kind of miracle, the entire hospital had been evacuated to Parmiter's School, a hundred yards away. Except it was the strangest kind of hospital Dolly had ever been in. Every window in the school hall had been blown out, over a hundred patients lay in makeshift beds, and teams of doctors and nurses worked diligently by the light of dimmed hurricane lamps.

The large-scale evacuation had been a masterclass in dogged determination and British grit, and by 3.30 a.m., Dolly was stunned to see a normal routine returning, with the WVS on the scene dispensing hot tea and the ARP working hard to salvage what they could from the hospital and bring it to the school.

The nurse who had led her to safety even stopped by to take her temperature.

'I honestly don't know how I will ever be able to thank you, Nurse,' Dolly whispered, so as not to disturb her fellow patients. 'You're my guardian angel. I feel so foolish for losing my head like that in the basement. If it hadn't been for you, well, I don't think I'd have made it out of there alive.'

'Nonsense, Miss Doolaney,' scoffed the nurse, with a self-deprecating smile. 'Of course you would have.' She glanced about before leaning closer to Dolly. 'Don't tell Matron, but truth be told, I'm glad I had you by my side.

I don't mind admitting I was shaking like a leaf when the roof caved in.'

Dolly wasn't sure about that, but she was certain of one thing: every nurse, doctor, fireman, ambulance driver, WVS lady and ARP chap working so diligently on this dark night was a true hero. Gazing about the makeshift hospital in awe, it dawned on Dolly that, despite the threat of tyranny and constant destruction, the bombings had also brought out the very best in people. The East End had found its soul. *This* was the time to be alive!

She turned back to the nurse with a grateful smile. 'Well, I shall be writing to your matron and the town hall when I get out of here to tell them of your courage . . . When will that be, anyhow?'

'Oh, not for a bit, I shouldn't think,' the nurse replied.

'But please, Nurse, I need to leave now. I'm absolutely fine,' Dolly insisted, struggling to sit up. 'I was only here to have some routine tests when I got caught up in the blast.'

'You need to wait and be seen by a doctor before I can discharge you,' she insisted. 'And as you can see, they are all busy. Please, Miss Doolaney, I urge you to try and rest. You've had quite an ordeal.'

Dolly slumped back against her pillow as the nurse left to tend to her next patient. She knew the nurse was right, but her mother would be worried sick about her, and she had to be home in time to clock on for work. She had told the girls she was visiting a friend at another shelter. As she gazed about the dimmed room, she shook her head. In her heart, she knew this was madness. How long could she go on concealing this before events forced her hand?

'Dolly . . . Dolly, is that you?' came a shaky voice through the gloom. 'Why, I mean . . . what are you doing here?'

Lucky's soot-smeared face gazed down at her, concerned, from under the rim of his ARP helmet. 'I don't understand. Are you helping out with the WVS? Are you injured?'

Too exhausted to spin a lie, Dolly smiled weakly. The game was up.

'No, love. I'm a patient. I'm . . . well, I'm dying.'

Dawn was breaking when at last Lucky escorted Dolly back through the shattered streets to her home, his strong arm looped protectively round her shoulders the whole way. By the time they reached her doorstep, he had extracted the whole truth from her, and she, in turn, had the promise that she would be the one to tell the girls.

A pale spring sun struggled to break through the smoky air as the pair faced each other.

'I won't betray your secret, Dolly,' he whispered, his face flickering with concern as she staggered slightly. 'But I think you need to tell Archie, sooner rather than later.'

Steadying herself by holding on to the blackened brick surround of her door, Dolly straightened herself. 'I have my pride, Lucky. It's about all I have left. I don't want anyone's pity. Besides, there's nothing anyone can do to help me,' she shrugged, without rancour.

'It's not a case of pity. We all care about you, Dolly,' he pleaded. 'I don't understand why you're keeping it from them. They'll want to look after you, that's all, see you're safe.'

Dolly's blue eyes teemed with emotions so nuanced Lucky could not divine their meaning.

'It's my job to look after them, Lucky,' she replied simply.

And then, because she could see a man's brain could never truly hope to fathom a woman's, she touched him lightly on his broad shoulder and smiled softly. 'I appreciate your concern, Lucky, truly I do. Peggy's a lucky lady to have you, and don't worry – I shall tell them. When the bombs stop. Until then, you say nothing.'

Without saying another word, she turned and walked through the door, shutting it heavily behind her. Once inside her bedroom, Dolly slid her hand under the mattress and felt comforted to feel the slim package still there in its hiding place. The time was drawing near.

Less than five minutes' walk away, Flossy was also arriving home after her night underground in the Tube for a quick wash before she clocked on, but when she turned the corner to her street, she found a crowd of people gathered there.

Her heart picked up speed and she began to run. When she neared them, she saw precisely what they were looking at.

A strangled wail escaped from her lips. The house where she rented the top-floor bedroom was sliced clean in two, with the four houses to one side nothing but a smoking hole in the ground. The air was thick with the burning stench of exploded lyddite. All around her, her neighbours stood sobbing and dazed.

Every morning that Flossy emerged from the Tube she had half expected to be greeted by this sight – it was, after all, always someone's turn to cop it – but now that it had actually happened to her, Flossy felt bereft. She had so little in the world and all that she owned was in that tiny attic bedroom.

To anyone else, it was a fleapit, a hot, stuffy bedroom in a house that smelt of damp and cooking cabbage. But to Flossy, it had been her sanctuary, the first place she had ever really had to call her own.

Her bed and mattress, now dripping wet and coated in thousands of slivers of glass, were balanced precariously out of the top floor of the ruined house. Every item she owned had been wrenched violently from its pride of place and was now lying shattered on the pavement.

Flossy spotted her spare work pinny, which she had carefully washed and hung out to dry the previous evening so it would be ready for work this morning, now wrapped round the top of a gas lamp, and a doily she had spent weeks crocheting in the home was a sooty, pulverized mess in the gutter next to a set of someone's false teeth.

A flash of yellow caught her eye in the landslide of dull grey debris. Cautiously, Flossy picked her way over the rubble, taking care not to lose her footing, and tugged at a piece of yellow fabric trapped beneath a pile of charred bricks.

'Oh no!' she choked despairingly, as it came loose in her hands. For clutched in her pale fingers was the cheerful little rag doll she had received at the orphanage on her ninth birthday. Her corn-coloured plaits were scorched black on one side, one of her button eyes was missing, and the stuffing spilt out of a tear in her sodden gingham dress. A dull ache spread across Flossy's chest. It was pathetic really. It was only a child's toy, not a life, but in that moment, Flossy felt like she was losing her grip on everything: her past, her present and her even more precarious future.

'She's ruined,' Flossy murmured out loud to no one.

'Miss, whatever are you doing up there?' cried a voice from the street.

Flossy whirled round to see the green-uniform-clad figure of a WVS worker.

'It's not safe there. Come down immediately,' she ordered. 'They're about to start sealing this site off.'

Wordlessly, Flossy scrambled back down the wreckage, still clutching the doll. Once she was safely back on the road, she started to shake, either out of shock or cold, stuffed the remains of the doll in her bag and trudged to work feeling like she scarcely had the strength to pick her feet up off the floor.

Flossy held her tears in until she got to Trout's. It was early and no one would be there yet, so she planned to go and wash in the toilets and try and find a cup of tea somewhere, but when she opened the door to the fifth floor, she was surprised to find Dolly already there.

The tea lady whirled round, and even in her shock, Flossy was taken aback at how exhausted she looked. She had shadows under her eyes like bruises, and her bloodless lips were thin with exhaustion.

'Don't,' Dolly smiled weakly. 'I know I look a sight. I sheltered with my mate up at Liverpool Street last night, but it's not a patch on Bethnal Green and I didn't get a wink of sleep. I gave up trying at dawn and came here instead. What you doing in so early, sweetheart?'

Flossy tried to speak, but no words came, only the tears she had been holding in. By the time the whole story came out, Dolly had led her upstairs to the canteen, put the kettle on and was drying her eyes with a clean hanky while the water boiled.

'Forgive me,' Flossy said, sniffing as she twisted the hanky between her tiny fingers. 'I feel so selfish complaining when goodness knows how many people will have died last night. Did you hear the Chest Hospital was bombed? How awful to be in hospital with a raid going on!'

'Was it? No, I didn't hear,' Dolly murmured, rising abruptly to turn off the whistling kettle. 'But you've lost your home, love, and that's important. A home is . . .' She paused and gazed at Flossy through the steam. 'Well, it's the shape you've grown, ain't it? But you mustn't worry. I'll ask Archie to telephone the home and inform your welfare worker, and I'll take you down the town hall at dinnertime and we'll get you sorted. We'll apply to the Mayor's Relief Fund for a cash advance so you can get clothes and look into new housing. I'd say stay with us, but looks like we'll be down the Tube every night for the foreseeable.'

'Honestly, Dolly, I hate to be a burden,' Flossy replied. 'I rather like the Tube, anyhow, but I would be glad of your help sorting myself out. Those forms are bewildering.'

Dolly finished making the tea and placed it gently in front of Flossy. 'There you go, my darlin'. Tea's a great healer.'

'What would I do without you, Dolly?' Flossy sighed, smothering a yawn and curling her fingers round the warm mug.

'You'd find a way,' Dolly said, gently removing a stray hair from her face.

'Maybe,' Flossy replied dubiously, 'but thank you all the same for patching me up.' Suddenly, she remembered her rag doll, and reaching under the table, she pulled the battered old doll from her bag. 'I rather think she may be beyond patching up, though,' she remarked sadly. 'I've had her since I was nine.'

Dolly's jaw clenched, her expression unreadable as she picked up the fragile remains of the toy. 'We'll see about that.'

Twelve

10 MAY 1941

Eight weeks after the bombing of the London Chest Hospital and it was still the talk of Bethnal Green. The hospital's Gothic chapel, the north wing and the nurses' home had been completely destroyed. Over a hundred patients transferred with the loss of only one life, so they were saying. Flossy had also heard about Lucky's heroic role in the evacuation, and that it was he who had recovered the crucifix from the rubble in the chapel. Lucky had remained modest about his involvement; in fact, he had stayed tight-lipped about the whole incident, changing the subject whenever it was brought up.

Flossy had decided to take a leaf out of his book this morning and make no mention of the fact that it was her nineteenth birthday. Today, 10 May, also marked another milestone. It was exactly a year since she had started at Trout's, and so much had happened in those twelve months, not least the fact that her new home was now a patch of floor in an underground Tube station!

The brown paper parcel had been delivered to Trout's, and Flossy was once again stunned that the mystery sender of the birthday gifts knew so much about her life and was obviously keeping close tabs on her. It seemed highly unlikely now that whoever it was was her real mother, for why else would they take the trouble to send Peggy a gift? But the knowledge didn't slice so deep any longer.

She found herself pondering on it as she fed strips of khaki material through her Singer. She might not have found her mother, but in some ways, she no longer cared. Flossy had found family in Dolly, Peggy and all the girls in the Victory Knitters; their love and close protection of her this past year had been her salvation. Not to mention the romance she had found with her pen-pal sailor. The very thought of Tommy – her Tommy – caused a little shiver of delight to tingle and swirl through her tummy.

In just three weeks' time his ship would be docking and she, along with all the girls in the sewing bee, would be there to greet him. The local paper had got wind of the sewing circle's friendship with the sailors on board HMS *Avenge* and were sending along a photographer that very afternoon to picture them for a propaganda piece.

Flossy was so lost in her daydreams and the comforting background swell of chatter that she scarcely even noticed when the machines shut down for mid-morning tea break. The floor was so quiet, though, that she soon found herself looking up to see where everyone had gone. A second later, the factory door burst open and Dolly wheeled in a cake, blazing with nineteen candles, on her tea trolley.

'Surprise!' she grinned. 'I baked you a cake. Sorry it ain't got no icing, or much sugar in it, and it's mainly made of grated carrot.'

It was the smallest cake Flossy had ever seen, but it had

been carefully decorated with chopped-up nuts, glacé cherries and candied peel.

'Wherever did you get your hands on those?' asked Flossy, impressed. 'It looks divine.'

'Oh, it was nothing,' said Dolly, waving her hand dismissively. 'I've been saving my rations, and I had the cherries and peel pre-war. I've been saving them for a special occasion. I'm sorry it's not a bit more fancy.'

'It's perfect,' Flossy insisted, deeply touched at Dolly's thoughtfulness.

Soon, the floor was filled with the loudest, lustiest 'Happy Birthday' Flossy had ever heard as the girls belted out a full-throttle rendition. Flossy put her head in her hands in mock embarrassment.

'Did you really think Dolly would forget your birthday?' Peggy whispered from next to her with a grin.

'No birthday's complete without the bumps,' whooped Pat, casting a mischievous wink Flossy's way.

'Oh no . . .' she quavered, rising to her feet and backing up against the factory wall. But it was too late to escape, and soon Pat, Sal and the rest had wrestled an arm and a leg each and Flossy found herself being thrown up high into the room.

When at last she was allowed back down to earth, she was as red as a berry and her sides ached from laughing.

'Here you go, love. You look like you could use a brew,' chortled Dolly, handing her her mug. 'Happy birthday, darlin'.'

Gratefully, Flossy sipped the piping-hot mug of tea.

'My rag – you've changed the colour,' she remarked, suddenly noticing that the pale grey piece of material Dolly used to mark out her mug from the rest had been changed to a gay and bright cerise one.

Dolly smiled fondly at Flossy and cocked her head. 'You're not the same shy young girl that walked through these factory doors a year ago. You've blossomed into a lovely young lady. You're more a cherry red now than a dove grey, I'd say.'

On impulse, Flossy reached out and threw her arms round Dolly, knitting her tiny body tightly to hers. She wanted to say that Dolly was not the same as when she had started either, that she was a ghost of herself. The tea lady wore the same sunny smile, but her cheekbones jutted out from her pale face, and there was an aching sadness in those blue eyes. Only the scent of her remained the same, the calming aroma of violet water that gently perfumed the air around her and had come to personify Dolly almost as much as her pillarbox-red lips.

As winter had thawed to spring and the mercury had risen on the thermometer so too had Flossy's disquiet over Dolly. Somewhere along the way, they had swapped places. Flossy was now the strong one. By claiming her right to sanctuary and daring to fall in love, she had proved to herself that she had the strength not to be defined by her childhood in the orphanage. She was no longer just a foundling but a woman in control of her destiny.

Dolly was now the pale, vulnerable-looking one, and try as she might, Flossy just could not put her finger on why. She wanted to attribute it to the past eight months and the horror and heartache they had all endured, yet something told her Dolly's deterioration was something more.

Instead, she kept her counsel and returned her smile.

'Thanks, Dolly. For everything you've done for me. I was scared witless when I started here and you took me under your wing and looked after me, and you've been doing it ever since.'

Dolly stared back at her, her blue eyes shining as fiercely as beacons from her slender face. 'I think the world of you, love, that's why. I've grown to love you like . . . well, like a . . .' she hesitated, 'like a member of my own family . . .

'Oh, I nearly forgot,' Dolly added. 'I got you a little something else, love.'

With that, she reached behind her tea urn and pulled out a small package.

'You didn't have to do that, Dolly. The cake was more than enough . . .' Her words trailed off as she pulled apart the packaging. For clutched in her hands was her old rag doll, beautifully bought back to life with bright new button eyes, blonde plaits and even a new pink dress covered in a smattering of tiny blue flowers.

'Oh, Dolly, she's better than before,' Flossy marvelled. 'She's absolutely perfect, in fact. Thank you!'

'It's nothing,' Dolly said with a shrug. 'I just think some things are worth holding on to.'

Suddenly, both women became aware of Archie calling everyone to attention.

'All right, girls, it's time to scrub up. The photographer and journalist from the *East London Advertiser* are here,' he announced.

'What, already?' squawked Daisy. 'I thought they weren't coming until this afternoon.'

'Yeah, well, they're early, so look lively.'

The news caused an excited commotion on the floor as

every woman dived for her handbag and started fishing out tubes of lipstick and combs.

'It's only the *East London Advertiser*, not *Woman's Own* magazine,' said Archie, shaking his head in bewilderment.

'Women,' sighed Lucky, pausing on his way to the loading bay with an armful of bundles. 'London's on fire and they've still gotta have their face on.'

In no time at all, the photographer had arranged all the workers round a Singer sewing machine, with Peggy standing in the middle, supported on either side. Protective Lucky had tried to ensure she remain seated, but she had proudly insisted on putting her stick on the floor.

Flossy couldn't help but smile when she found herself elbowed to the side by Daisy. Not that she cared. She was more than content to let the factory glamour girl take centre stage.

Dolly nestled in next to her, looping her arm through hers. 'Hark at us,' she whispered to Flossy, as the photographer raised his camera and the flashbulb started to pop. 'Reckon our little factory will be famous?'

'If Daisy has her way,' Flossy replied under her breath.

She felt Dolly stifle a giggle, before her body was wracked with coughs.

'Are you all right, Dolly?' Flossy murmured.

'Fine,' she spluttered, waving her other arm dismissively as she whipped a hanky from her pocket.

'Look here, girls, my editor tells me you've knitted and sewed a record number of blankets, socks, woollies and mittens, more than any other sewing circle in London apparently,' said the journalist, glancing down at his notebook. 'There's three hundred and twenty-one women in Bethnal

Green in sewing circles. What's the secret to your success, girls?'

'Why, our devastating looks and charm, of course,' replied Daisy with a flirtatious smile.

'The WVS was gifted three thousand three hundred and sixty pounds of free wool from America, which was allocated to boroughs most in need . . .' interrupted Vera, but the journalist wasn't listening, his gaze was fixed firmly on Daisy, who was gazing up coyly from beneath her long eyelashes.

'We've knitted everything from comforts for the troops to baby clothes,' Daisy purred. 'We like to do our bit.'

'I bet you do, miss, and I'm sure receiving anything from you is a great comfort,' the journalist flirted back.

'We ain't stopped knitting, all through the bombs, over a million of us in the WVS, from charladies to duchesses,' piped up Pat. 'We're the army Hitler forgot, or so the WVS tells us.'

'And let's not forget our Doll,' chipped in Sal. 'There might be hundreds of sewing bees, but there's only one Dolly Doolaney. It's her what's been driving us. I don't think she's slept in the last eight months. Working class and staunch to the bone she is. Our Doll's one of the best!'

A murmur of agreement rang out, and smiling, Flossy turned to look at Dolly. The smile froze on her face.

'Dolly . . . Dolly!' she gabbled. In horror, she felt Dolly's arm grow loose in hers and her face faded to the colour of mist. The tea lady slithered to the factory floor in a heap.

*

Dolly heard her name being called, but the voices were muffled, as if she were a hundred leagues under the sea.

Gradually, she came to, but when she struggled to sit up, her body felt as heavy as lead and she slumped back.

Concerned faces hovered over her.

'Stand back, everyone,' ordered Vera. 'Give her some space to breathe, for pity's sake.'

'I'm all right, Vera,' Dolly protested weakly.

Lucky and Archie gently lifted her to her feet and helped her into the office. Once she was settled in a chair, Dolly felt a burning shame sweep over her. She could hear the hubbub from outside, and the photographer had resumed taking photos of the girls, but she was acutely aware she had ruined the moment.

'I'm so sorry,' she blustered, closing her eyes. 'I don't know what came over me.'

'Well, I do,' said the forelady sternly. 'You haven't stopped this past eight months. Look at the state of your ankles. They're so swollen. You're to go home, put your feet up and rest.'

Dolly sat up and immediately felt her heart start to race. 'No,' she said, wheezing heavily. 'I haven't had a sick day in years. Besides, who'll do the teas this afternoon and clean up? I'll be right in a minute.' She drew a clenched fist into her chest, as if to quell a spasm of pain before exhaling slowly.

'Besides,' she joked feebly, when the palpitations had subsided, 'apart from that week off to care for my auntie in Margate last May, I'm never not here. Those girls don't know one end of an urn from the other.'

Vera scrutinized her with a puzzled frown. 'I thought you said your auntie lived in Dagenham?'

Dolly could have kicked herself. 'Sorry, Vera, I meant Dagenham. I'm getting myself confused.'

Vera said nothing, just looked at her strangely.

'Whatever, Doll, it don't matter,' rang out Archie's gravelly voice. 'But the bottom line is this: Vera's right. You're to go home and rest, and that's an order. We can cope with making our own tea for one day.'

Dolly sighed and slowly rose to her feet. 'Very well.'

'Lucky, see Doll gets home all right, would yer?' ordered Archie.

'Okey-dokey, Gov'nor,' agreed Lucky, taking Dolly's arm in his.

Outside on the cobbled streets, Dolly could scarcely bring herself to look up at Lucky's face as she leaned in heavily to his arm. By the time they reached Tavern Street, Dolly was so out of breath she could barely speak.

Lucky's question took her by surprise. 'Where were you really last May? You obviously weren't looking after a sick auntie in Dagenham.'

Dolly found she didn't have the strength left in her body to deny it; besides, she was sick of the lies.

'Mum found me unconscious on the scullery floor one morning, so I was admitted to hospital for a week to monitor my disease,' she stated in a flat voice. 'How could I admit that to Vera and the girls?'

Without saying another word, Lucky stopped and whipped Dolly's handkerchief from her coat pocket.

'No, Lucky . . .' she protested weakly, but it was too late. He held the bloodstained hanky aloft, the dark red stain of blood vivid against the white of the cotton.

'This can't go on, Dolly,' he cried in anguish. 'I've kept your secret now for nearly two months, but so help me God, I won't stand by and watch you keel over and die on the factory floor. I could never live with myself.'

Dolly felt tears prick angrily at her eyes, but she was helpless to stop them and soon they were spilling down her cheeks and dripping onto the soot-stained cobbles beneath her feet.

'Please, Lucky, just hold me, would you?' she sobbed. 'I'm scared.'

In silence, Lucky folded her into his broad arms. She rested her head against his warm chest and listened to the steady drum of his strong heart beating in her ear. She felt her own heart splinter into thousands of tiny pieces.

And just like that, Dolly knew. It was over. The end was not far. Her body held ancient and unique wisdom, intuition and powers beyond medical logic. Now was the time to make her peace.

Upstairs and alone in her bedroom, she took the small package out from its hiding place under the mattress and placed it in the drawer of her bedside table. Then she lay down and folded her hands over her chest in prayer.

11 MAY 1941

The night of the photo shoot with the *East London Advertiser*, the bombers had returned with one of the most earth-shattering raids of all. Flossy had gazed up fearfully at the huge full moon hanging in the sky as she had descended the steps to the Tube, and the lyrics to 'They Can't Black Out the Moon' played ominously through her mind. When she and the girls had emerged the next morning, it was to scenes of unparalleled devastation. The Luftwaffe had taken advantage of the full moon and a low tide to start almost 2,500 fires and nearly 1,500 people had been killed.

In the factory, it was all anyone could talk about.

'Look at this,' Sal said, holding up a copy of the paper on their tea break.

Everyone gathered round and read, stunned. The front page showed a picture of St Paul's silhouetted against the flames. Flossy drank in the majesty of the splendid cathedral rising up through the smoke, seemingly indestructible. By some act of God, the much-loved London landmark hadn't been destroyed, but according to the reports, many other institutions, from the House of Commons to Westminster Abbey, had been damaged. The Rego garment factory in Bethnal Green had copped it too, and Archie was there now, helping the foreman salvage what machines he could from the wreckage.

'At least they didn't get St Paul's,' remarked Ivy. 'I couldn't have stood it.'

'Why?' asked Kathy.

'I don't know,' she replied. 'It's like the heartbeat of London, ain't it? Like our soul.'

'Like Dolly is to Trout's, you mean?' said the girl, with a wisdom that belied her tender years, Flossy thought privately.

'Yes, just like that, Kathy love,' Ivy replied, and with that the women all lapsed into a reflective silence.

It had felt strange not having Dolly with them down the Tube last night after her fainting fit, stranger still that she wasn't here today manning her giant tea urn as usual. One of the canteen workers had stepped in, but not having Dolly's comforting smile to look at behind the trolley was like taking a sip of tea only to find it was missing the sugar.

'She'll be back very soon, I'm sure,' remarked Vera. 'Her mother popped in yesterday afternoon to say the doctor had called round. She's not looking too bright and he's ordered five days of complete bed rest.'

'She'll be right as rain soon, I'm sure,' remarked Pat. 'Tough as old boots our Doll.'

A ripple of agreement rang out around the floor, and Flossy noted that only Lucky was not joining in, his usual chipper demeanour strangely guarded as he looked up at the giant patch of tarpaulin that covered the hole in the roof.

'I'm going up on the roof. There's a hole in that cover, I'm sure,' he muttered darkly, setting down his mug and stalking from the floor.

'Who's rattled his chain?' asked Daisy.

'He's tired,' said Peggy. 'He had quite a night last night, as I'm sure you can imagine.'

Flossy nodded her head sympathetically, but inside she wasn't so sure that was it. First Dolly, now Lucky. What was happening to them? A feeling of deep unease crawled the length of her spine.

Thirteen

16 MAY 1941

Five days later, Peggy stepped sleepily blinking into the morning light and felt a rush of relief when she spotted Lucky casually leaning against the railings by the park next to the Tube, his cap perched at a jaunty angle.

In his hands, he clutched a paper bag and a rolled-up newspaper, and on his face, he wore a broad smile.

'Morning, beautiful,' he called, holding up the bag. 'I've brought you breakfast. Fresh rolls made with ham straight off the bone.'

'Oh, thanks. I'm famished! The Tube was so packed last night the cafe ran out of food,' she grinned, thinking how much she was going to love being greeted by Lucky every morning for the rest of her life.

'I can't wait to bring you breakfast in bed when we're married,' he grinned. 'Not outside a Tube station. Come on, let's get going.'

'You're full of the joys this morning,' Peggy said, sinking her teeth gratefully into her crusty ham roll.

'Well, that's because we had another quiet night last night,' he revealed. 'That's the fifth night now with no bombs. I spent most of the night in my cot down the ARP post. Still didn't get no sleep, mind. I think I've forgotten how to lay me head in peace anymore.'

'Really? You don't think . . . ?'

'Too soon to say, and I wouldn't want to jinx things,' he replied, 'but let's try and be cautiously optimistic, shall we? Perhaps that was his final great raid.'

Since that last catastrophic night when the City of London had taken a battering, the night skies had been curiously quiet of planes. In fact, save for one night in November when the weather had been foul, this had been their first break from the nightly bombardment for eight months. The relief of having a fifth raid-free night certainly showed on Lucky's face.

'God willing, that's it,' Peggy replied. 'We've certainly had our share.'

At Trout's, the workers, buoyed by yet another quiet night, fed off each other's optimism. Peggy knew no one dared suggest that might be it, but a weary and cautious hope prevailed as everyone got ready to do a day's work behind their machines. After a week's bed rest, Dolly was due back to work today. Maybe, just maybe, some normality could return at long last.

Lucky nipped to the toilets to change out of his ARP outfit and into his overalls, and when he returned, he held the newspaper aloft. 'I nearly forgot, girls – you're in the paper!'

Peggy giggled as Lucky's words caused a near stampede, with everyone clustering round him to look at the newspaper.

'Ooh, would you look at that?' babbled Daisy excitedly, spreading the *East London Advertiser* out across a workbench.

'We're only on the front page, and oh look – is Doll back in yet? Someone fetch her. They've made it all about her.'

Peggy glanced over Daisy's shoulder and sure enough, there, under the headline – 'The Daring of Miss Dolly Do-Good' – was a photograph of a very young Dolly.

'Look at Dolly,' said Peggy admiringly. 'Isn't she the spit of Ginger Rogers in this picture? How old is she here?'

'She must be, what – eighteen, nineteen? Same as you two, Flossy and Peggy,' said Pat. 'It was taken about three years after she started at Trout's. That must be near on nineteen years ago.'

'That's right. She was quite the head-turner back then,' said Archie, who along with the rest of Trout's had come to take a look. 'I hope she won't mind but I gave the journalist that photo. He wanted one of Doll on her own, but she had to leave suddenly after that funny turn, so I gave him one of her on Trout's first ever beano down to Southend. I took it on my old Box Brownie.'

Archie smiled wistfully at the memory. 'We stopped halfway down to the coast for a loo break and I took this photo of Dolly in a field while we were waiting for the girls.'

Dolly wore a gingham dress cinched in at the waist, with white gloves, white hat and white sandals, which showed off her slender ankles. The works' charabanc was parked on the edge of a cornfield, and Dolly was leaning back casually against an old wooden gate as if she didn't have a care in the world, her smiling eyes bright and warm as the drowsy late-summer sun.

Peggy looked fondly at all the factory old-timers and suddenly realized the photo had opened a window onto a golden past. Funny how a single photograph could do that.

'Cor, life was so straightforward back then – no ducking bombs and sleeping down the Tube,' murmured Ivy. 'We had no idea.'

'Not much,' agreed Archie, with a wan smile as he picked up the paper and started to read. '"The *East London Advertiser* calls for Dolly Doolaney, or, as she is affectionately known by her work colleagues at Trout's garment factory in Bethnal Green, Dolly Do-Good, to be awarded a medal for setting up and running the finest sewing bee in the East End of London."'

'Too right,' interrupted Pat.

'"A boatload of our sailors and bombed-out locals have been supplied with warm clothing, not to mention the endless mugs of hot tea she made for bomb survivors. If the war could be won on tea and smiles alone, then Dolly Doolaney could claim a victory."'

Chuckling, Archie put the paper down and looked about. 'Well, what about that? So come on there, where is the lady herself? She'll get a real kick out of this.'

'She hasn't clocked on yet,' said the forelady, frowning.

Peggy suddenly noticed Flossy, standing on the edge of the group, staring at the photo of Dolly with a curious look on her face. She seemed oblivious to everyone, until suddenly she looked up with the queerest expression.

'Please, Mrs Shadwell, permission to go and check that Dolly is all right,' she blurted.

'Really, Flossy, must you be so melodramatic?' chastised the forelady. 'I'm sure she is perfectly well. She's probably just running late, though I'll admit it is out of character.'

But Flossy wasn't listening; she was hastily gathering her bag and coat, and heading to the door of the factory with a stricken look on her face.

'Flossy Brown,' the forelady called after her, 'where on earth might you be going? I take a very dim view of this.'

*

Flossy scarcely registered Vera calling after her, or the stunned expressions plastered on the faces of her fellow workers. There was no time to stop. She had to get to Dolly's house.

As she ran in the direction of Tavern Street, her legs pumping over the cobbles, she felt as if her brain was spinning out of control. The realization had struck her like a thunderbolt as she had gazed on the image of the young Dolly dressed in her Sunday best, almost as if an invisible hand had come and gently lifted a piece of gauze from the shrouded memories of her past.

The image of Dolly in her best white hat and gloves had jogged something from her subconscious, and now she realized, it was so glaringly obvious. Why had she not registered it before?

Dolly was the fair-haired, smartly dressed young woman who had visited her in the children's home when she was a child. The kind young lady who had taken time to read books and play with her was no governess or official from the child migration programme. It was Dolly! She had known her before she started at Trout's. Their past lives were entwined together in ways only Dolly knew.

A thousand questions buzzed through her mind like a hive of clashing bees. In her haste, Flossy collided with a telegram boy on a bike and fell crashing to her knees on the cobbles. 'Watch yourself!' he called, but Flossy didn't even pause to dust herself down. She picked herself up and started to run again, the blood from a gash in her knee soaking into her work pinafore.

Breathless, Flossy skidded to a halt outside Dolly's front door and through her ragged breath realized that despite the bright spring sunshine, the blackout blinds were still drawn. Horror drummed in her chest as she frantically scanned up and down the street . . . Most of the houses in the road had their blinds half lowered. She had lived in the East End long enough to know that was a sign of respect. An awful, wrenching fear rolled over her as she pounded on the door.

One look at Dolly's mother as she opened the door confirmed her worst fears. Mrs Doolaney's round face was raw and etched with grief. It was like looking at a stranger. The last time Flossy had seen her plump, flour-dusted cheeks, they were creased into a permanent smile. This woman here had the light of madness shining in her eyes.

'Dolly . . .' Flossy ventured, her words breaking off.

The older lady simply nodded, and held the door open.

'Oh, my dear, I was just about to send word to Vera . . . She's with the angels.'

Inside in the gloom, Flossy cradled her cup of tea and stared in disbelief at the cooling brown liquid. Seated round the kitchen table of the tiny terrace, dressed head to toe in black, were the faces of women she had seen in photos. Dolly's aunties, Jean, Polly and Sylvie, along with what felt like half the neighbourhood, had all come to pay their respects. Older women were quietly moving around the kitchen, cleaning and providing a never-ending stream of tea for the visitors. Dolly's mother sat stock-still in the middle of it all, quietly dignified, but in a state of profound shock.

'I don't know why I feel like this,' she said at last. 'It's not as if I didn't know it was coming. The "dread disease", they call it.' She snorted and angrily brushed away a tear. 'Well, I've been dreading it since she first got it, aged seven. Thirty years I've been waiting for this moment, so can someone please tell me why I feel so surprised?'

Her sister Polly patted her on the hand. 'It's the shock.'

With that, Dolly's mother started to cry, great heaving sobs that seemed to consume her body, and Flossy watched in horror.

'It just ain't fair. It ain't bleedin' fair,' she wept bitterly. 'It was the bombs. They were the final straw. Her heart was just too weak to stand up to much more. I came down this morning to find her asleep in the easy chair. Well, I thought she was asleep . . .'

She stared at Flossy, her eyes wild with grief. 'Do you wanna hear the funniest thing?'

Flossy nodded, dumbstruck.

'It looks like the bombs have stopped. She lasted through the worst of it, and now they've stopped and she's dead. Where's the justice in that? Mind you, where's the justice in any of it? My poor darling girl never had a bad bone in the whole of her body. Why did God choose her?' She gazed round the table, a broken woman. 'Why?'

'Come on, Mum,' soothed a lady Flossy took to be Dolly's older sister. 'I think you need to get upstairs and rest.'

Dolly's mother was led up the stairs and Flossy gulped slowly.

'Please, ma'am,' she said at last to Dolly's auntie Polly. 'What . . . what did Dolly die from?'

'Didn'cha know?' she gasped. 'She had rheumatic heart disease. She caught rheumatic heart fever as a girl and it never left her.'

'No, ma'am, I'm afraid I didn't know,' Flossy replied.

'Time and again the poor mite was struck down with an episode of it. By the time she was ten, she'd been hospital-ized with it that many times. They hoped her body would be strong enough to recover, but each bout just damaged her heart that bit further, left her with severe cardiac damage. It cast such a dark shadow.'

The woman's gaze drifted to the blacked-out window. 'My sister wanted to let Dolly live, but it blighted her whole childhood. The girl couldn't so much as throw a ball in the street without my sister dragging her inside. Not that I can blame her for being so protective. It's a horrible disease. Licks the joints and bites the heart, so they say. The fear of it haunted the whole family. Poor girl was even sterilized so she couldn't . . .' Her voice trailed off. 'I've said too much already.'

'I'm so sorry,' Flossy heard herself say. 'But please, ma'am, may I know this? How long have you known time was running out?'

Polly shrugged. 'The doctor seems to think the bombs and sheltering underground in the damp and cold probably hastened the end. She had an ECG and other tests up at the Chest Hospital, the night it was bleedin' bombed of all times, that showed she had mitral stenosis. The valve that separated the chambers of her heart wasn't opening properly and it made the heart chamber swell, gave her fluid on the lungs an' all. You could see it in the way her ankles used to swell. Poor love couldn't even sleep lying down for the last six months of her life.'

Flossy nodded. 'I see,' she whispered. And she could. Suddenly, everything made perfect sense: Dolly's dramatic decline, bumping into her in hospital that night, the awful pallor of her skin . . . Deep down, she had known all along Dolly was hiding something. There was only one thing that made no sense.

'Why didn't she want anyone at the factory to know?' she asked.

'You have to ask?' Polly replied, raising one eyebrow. 'My niece was the proudest woman I know. She didn't want no one's pity, or folk wrapping her in cotton wool. She'd had a gutful of that growing up. She grew up knowing she would die young, and that has to change a woman, don't it? Dolly wanted to make the most of what time she had left, make her time count, and for Dolly, working and being in the sewing circle was what counted. She never, ever wanted to be – what is it they call it? – a useless mouth.'

Flossy nodded again, and the action broke the floodgates. Hot, desolate tears started to flow down her cheeks and drip onto her bloodstained pinafore. The sudden wave of grief was so savage it took her breath away. How could Dolly no longer be in this world? How? Never again would she see her lovely, compassionate, remarkable, wonderful friend Dolly. Then came another haunting realization: she would never get to the bottom of why Dolly kept her visits to her in the orphanage a secret.

Suddenly, the door to the front parlour swung open and Flossy jumped. An elderly woman dressed head to toe in black and carrying a heavy bag shut the door carefully behind her.

Auntie Polly sat to attention. 'Thanks for coming, Vi, but it's impossible to get a funeral director round 'ere at short notice. They're harder to find than hen's teeth at the moment.'

'They've never been so busy,' said the woman, setting down her bag. 'I've laid Dolly out and prepared her for you. She looks at peace now. I used the lipstick and rouge you gave me, and she's wearing her favourite.' She handed Auntie Polly a small bottle of violet-water scent. 'I know how particular she was over her appearance. My condolences. Dolly was special.'

'Thanks, Vi. My sister will be very grateful to you; we all are,' said Polly, slipping sixpence into her pocket.

Flossy knew Vi was Tavern Street's own 'layer-out', an elderly lady called upon to prepare the street's dead in the absence of a funeral director.

Flossy knew Dolly would have been carefully washed, dressed in a white shroud and stockings with pennies gently placed over her eyes. Heaven was now ready to receive her, but Flossy wasn't ready to see her. In a trance, she made to follow the women, but when she reached the door to the front parlour, she stopped.

'I'm sorry,' she wept. 'I . . . I can't.'

With that, she whirled round and fled from the oppressive gloom of the grief-stricken terrace. Flossy couldn't bear her last abiding memory of Dolly to be cloaked in a shroud, those beautiful blue eyes finally closed forever to the world.

Fourteen

As they had all hoped and prayed, the bombs did cease dropping nightly, which at least meant they could say their final farewells to Dolly Doolaney in peace. Seven days after her death, Bethnal Green stopped still for the funeral of the much-loved tea lady. Peggy watched, awe-inspired at how a battered but proud East End came out in their droves to mark the all-too-short life of a woman who meant something different to each of them. A woman finished off by the bombs, though not in the conventional sense.

It was astonishing how popular Dolly had been, Peggy marvelled, as she stood behind her funeral carriage in Tavern Street. Two of the most beautiful gleaming black horses Peggy had ever seen, harnessed in black leather and silver livery, pulled a black carriage, polished to such a high shine the early summer sun dazzled off the surface. The purple-feathered plumes on the horses' heads ruffled slightly in the morning breeze. You couldn't hear a sound as they set off, apart from the echoing of horses' hooves on the cobbles, and the strangely melodic humming noise the wind made when it rushed past the cables of the barrage balloons hovering overhead.

Dolly was one of Bethnal Green's own. Every person on the street stood still in the silence, simply touching their coat collar or lifting their hat as a sign of respect as the funeral cortège passed by. Even the corner shop at the end of Tavern Street had closed as a mark of mourning. It was quite the spectacle, and Peggy realized that Dolly shone as much in death as she had in life.

Initially, Peggy had been angry when Lucky had confessed that he knew about Dolly's disease. 'How could you keep this from me?' she had blazed, aghast. 'How am I to trust you if you can keep something so huge from me?'

But Lucky had remained unrepentant. 'It wasn't my secret to tell. I made a promise to Dolly.'

In truth, Peggy had understood. Lucky was a man of honour and a man of his word.

At the church, Dolly's last written request was that no one bring flowers, which weren't readily available in any case. Instead, she had asked that every mourner donate an item of food from their rations – a tin of Spam, condensed milk or even a precious egg, whatever they could spare – to the young orphaned girl left to raise her six siblings who had shown up in Trout's that day. It was a lovely touch, and Peggy would have expected nothing less from such a big-hearted woman.

For a tea lady who, in her own words, 'was a bit thick to do much else', she was certainly one of the shrewdest, most resourceful women Peggy had ever come across. By the time her coffin was carried across the church threshold, the boxes by the doors were groaning with enough food to see that orphaned family right for the next six months.

What was it about Dolly that inspired such loyalty and devotion? By the end of the service, when so many had risen to share a cherished memory of Dolly, Peggy knew the answer. Quite simply, she had been a true friend to everyone who had known her. An ally to the forelady, a big-sister figure to Lucky, a surrogate mother to Flossy. And to her? Peggy smiled as she remembered how Dolly had ever so gently brought her down from her pedestal when she had first started at Trout's. Peggy had been breathtakingly rude to her, and despite that, Dolly had encouraged all the women to let her join the sewing circle. Her acceptance in the factory was down to Dolly.

What was it she had said to Flossy that day in the rest centre? *The East End lives collectively*. It was true to say that, in Dolly's case, they mourned collectively too.

'It is with a heavy heart that we now carry on,' said the vicar, as the coffin was lifted to be transported outside for burial. A sepulchral light descended as his softly spoken words sank in. 'For selfishly we grieve for the mortal love we have lost. But love lasts forever, and Dolly Doolaney's spirit lives on in her beloved mother, her sister, her extended family at Trout's, in the sewing circle she founded, in every pair of socks she knitted and every cup of tea she brewed.' A ripple of laughter rang round the congregation. 'And in all who knew and loved her dearly, and whose lives were enriched simply by being on the receiving end of that smile.'

Peggy glanced to her left, where the tears were flowing freely down Flossy's cheeks. In silence, she slid her hand into Flossy's and squeezed it tight, and she kept on holding it all the way back up the aisle as they followed the coffin outside to Dolly's final resting place, under a cherry tree in the corner of a graveyard. The plot backed onto a schoolyard. The school was closed, but in time, when it reopened, the playground would once again be filled with the whoops and cries of playing children. Peggy had a hunch Dolly would love that.

*

Flossy gripped Peggy's hand in her right and Lucky's in her left, and felt so grateful for their support. She looked around the bewildered faces that lined the graveside.

It had been left to her to return to Trout's and break the news. The fallout had been immense. A deep and profound sense of shock and guilt had descended over the whole factory, and even now, seven days on at Dolly's funeral, she didn't think a single person had even begun to come to terms with it, or understand how she could have kept her terrible disease a secret from them all.

Sal and Pat had taken it the hardest. 'How could we not have known?' Sal had sobbed, utterly bereft. 'She did so much for us all. We let her work too hard. This is our fault.'

'Stuff and nonsense,' Vera had snapped. 'No one could tell Dolly Doolaney to slow down. She marched to the beat of her own drum.'

Flossy knew Vera hadn't meant to be unkind, but her grief was overwhelming her. They had even thought about cancelling the party arranged for the following week when their sailors arrived on shore leave, until Archie had inter-jected.

'What, and waste all of Dolly's hard work?' he had admonished. 'I may not have known Dolly as well as I thought I did, but I do know this: her sewing circle must continue as she wished.'

With that, he had pointed to Dolly's finished quilt, with all their names and those of their sailors carefully embroidered within. 'All life's in that cross stitch. You girls better be there to greet your sailors and give 'em that quilt or Dolly'll turn in 'er grave.'

Flossy stared down at the grave now as Dolly made her final journey into the earth. As the coffin was lowered, Archie stepped forward and carefully placed a crocheted blanket the Victory Knitters had made over it, as if he were tucking her in for the night.

'Night-night, sweetheart,' he whispered. 'See you in heaven . . . PG.'

Flossy stayed rooted to the spot as the mourners started to drift away, back to Tavern Street for the memorial tea. She stared at the mound of fresh earth covering the grave and realized that all of Dolly's secrets had been buried with her. Only Dolly knew the real reason for her visits to the orphanage, and she, in her wisdom, had chosen not to reveal it. Flossy's past remained buried and hidden from sight forever.

Peggy touched her lightly on the shoulder and Flossy jumped.

Together they stared at the grave, numb with grief as a light rain started to spatter on the earth.

'She had a hand in all our little triumphs, didn't she?' Peggy murmured, her anguished face contorted against the mizzling rain.

Flossy nodded sadly, wondering what else she had a hand in. 'Come on, let's go.'

Back at Tavern Street for the wake, it was standing room only, as the whole of Trout's and the local neighbourhood stood, or sat on any available surface, plates perched on their laps. Every woman in the area had raided her miserly rations and brought what she could, so Dolly's mum needn't feel the shame of not having a decent spread at her daughter's wake. A good send-off was a mark of pride and Flossy knew Dolly's mother would probably starve for a fortnight to cover the expense of the funeral cortège.

Trays of sandwiches and buns had been piled up next to a piping-hot urn of tea on Dolly's trolley, which Archie had loaned especially for the occasion. The sign *Dolly's Trolley* had been replaced with another: *RIP*.

After an hour, the heat in the packed terrace was stifling and Flossy suddenly felt an aching pain spread up her neck and across her temples. She sought out Dolly's mother and, after paying her condolences, bade her farewells.

The elderly lady suddenly looked quite frail as she fanned herself in the heavy blanket of heat. 'I know I should be grateful to have had my Dolly as long as I did, but it's not the natural way of it, is it? I should never have outlived her.' She sighed deeply. 'Bless you for coming.'

'I thought the world of Dolly, ma'am,' Flossy replied. But as she turned to leave, Dolly's mother caught her by her sleeve.

'Wait, dearie, I nearly forgot.' She rummaged in her knitting bag, stowed away underneath her chair, and pulled out a small brown package. 'I found this addressed to you while I was clearing out Dolly's room. It was in her bedside drawer.'

Outside on the street, Flossy stared unblinking at the package in her hand and realized she was shaking. 'I can't do this alone,' she said out loud, and turning, she headed back inside the terrace and threaded her way through the throng until she found Peggy chatting to the girls.

Peggy took one look at her face and ushered her outside.

'Whatever's the matter?' she asked.

Flossy held up the package. 'It's from Dolly. Will you sit with me while I open it?'

The girls wandered a little way up the street, before sitting down on the kerbside, the warmth of the sun on the cobbles burning their legs. Flossy hardly felt it. Her breath seemed trapped in her throat as she stared, fixated, at the package. The bombs had stopped, yet Flossy felt she was holding something explosive, something that might finally banish the ghosts of her childhood. Whatever it contained, she had a premonition that her life was about to change irrevocably. Flossy had not dared to allow the seed of thought that had taken hold in her head to flourish, but her instincts were screaming. Could Dolly have been more to her than just a friend? Did they share blood? Had she in fact found her real mother, only to have lost her again?

'I need a cigarette,' she whispered.

'But you don't smoke,' said Peggy, smiling at her with a baffled look on her face. 'Come on, just open it.'

Ever so carefully, Flossy eased her thumb along the join of the brown paper and it slid apart in her hands. A painful lump lodged in the back of her throat. Nestled in the folds of the paper was a tiny white wool matinee jacket. A delicate baby's jacket, with a pale pink eyelet trim and a matching pink ribbon bow, it even had two tiny pockets stitched onto the front.

The slight yellowish tinge told Flossy this jacket had been stowed away for years, concealed from light and air. Hardly daring to breath, she lifted it up between thumb and forefinger as delicately as if it were a butterfly's wing. Instinctively, she pressed the soft garment to her cheek, closed her eyes briefly and caught the faintest trace of violet water. A small white envelope fell onto her lap. Spellbound, Flossy carefully placed the matinee jacket on her knee and opened the envelope.

The strangest of sensations overcame her, as if she weren't merely unwrapping packages and letters, but peeling back layers of history.

Quivering with emotion, she unfolded the paper, and suddenly, there was Dolly's voice in her ear, as rich and warm as if she were sitting on the kerb next to her.

To my dearest Flossy,

I know you will be reading this letter after my death. I also know you'll be shocked and hurt that I never told you I was dying, though, Flossy, I know you had your suspicions I was ill. You're as bright as a button; you always was.

Please believe me, if there was any way I could have found it in myself to tell you, I would have. I think the world of you. I always have done, right from when I first met you nineteen years ago, when you was nothing but a little scrap. Yes, that's right. Our paths crossed many years before we met at Trout's. I'm going to tell you a true story that I hope explains what has driven me all these years.

When I was eighteen, I was enjoying a quiet Sunday afternoon off work in Vicky Park. My father was gravely ill in the Chest Hospital and I had just come from visiting him. I'd bought myself a ha'p'orth of broken biscuits and I'd just settled myself down by the boating lake when along comes a young red-headed woman pushing a perambulator. Poor soul, she didn't half look on her downers. She'd tucked her hair under an old black felt cloche hat, but a few curly red locks had escaped from beneath.

Thin as a whippet she was, and clothes hanging off her. Life looked like it had beat her down and she was all hunched over. In fact, she could scarcely meet my eye when she asked if I'd do her a great favour by looking after her baby while she ran a quick errand. I didn't want to. I wanted to be alone with my thoughts, but she pleaded with me in her strong Irish accent, even promised to buy me a chocolate bar for my troubles. She explained how she was recently widowed and had no one else to help her. She was so pitiful that in the end I agreed.

Well, when I looked in the pram, I don't mind telling you I lost my heart, hook, line and sinker. Staring back at me was the most heavenly little creature you ever set eyes on. The baby girl was adorable. All chubby legs and velvet-soft skin, big grey eyes and shiny round red cheeks. She was a treasure. Her mother told me she had given birth not eight weeks before at a maternity home nearby.

And then she turned and left, walked out of there like her heels were on fire, didn't even turn round once.

Looking back, so many people have told me I must have been daft as a brush not to have guessed what would happen next, but her wedding ring led me to believe she was trustworthy . . . that she would return.

Ten minutes turned to an hour, then two. The baby grew cold, hungry and started to wail. I noticed for the first time how dirty her blankets were, and when I felt under them, they were soaked through. The back of her matinee jacket was that damp she was starting to shiver, so I took it off her and headed for home, so that I might fetch her some warm clothing. I'd just reached the gate with the pram when a park policeman stopped me and enquired as to the whereabouts of the baby's mother. I assured him she'd be back before long. He told me I'd been duped, that she was long gone.

I was beside myself when he took the pram handles from me and told me he was taking her to the police station and then a home for foundlings. Foundlings! Such a funny word, I remember thinking at the time.

Then he walked off with the pram, that poor abandoned mite crying until she was red in the face, her little hands squeezed into tight fists. The emotion of that moment has

*never left me. I ran after him, pleaded with him to stop,
but he wouldn't listen to me, just kept on marching in the
direction of the police station. I didn't half cause a scene
– shouted blue murder, told the desk sergeant he had no
right, that baby was left to me to look after – but they
didn't give two hoots for the opinion of an eighteen-year-
old girl, told me I'd do well to mind my manners.*

*As I walked home, I was that stunned I half wondered
if I hadn't just imagined the whole thing, except for the
matinee jacket I was still holding in my hand. At home,
I carefully washed it and prayed to God to forgive me
for not saving that baby.*

*I was told later by the matron of the home that she had
slight curvature of the spine, and they didn't hold out
much hope of finding a family to adopt her. I know you
will have worked out by now, Flossy, that the baby girl
was you. The matinee jacket contained in this package
was the one you were wearing when your mother left
you with me.*

Flossy stifled a scream and instinctively threw the letter
into the gutter as if it were on fire. She heard Peggy's
concerned voice, but it didn't even begin to permeate the
deep layer of shock that had coated her. The truth was so
far removed from what she could ever have imagined. In a
trance, she retrieved the letter, unfolded it and began to
read again, her hands shaking violently.

*I was tormented by not being able to save you, Flossy.
I even dragged my poor mother to the orphanage and*

begged with the matron and her to be able to keep you. They told me that quite aside from my age and being single, it was a ridiculous idea. But it wasn't to me. You see, my condition meant having children of my own was impossible. My heart could never have withstood child-birth. Sounds daft, I know, but I honestly believed that finding you in the park was a sign from the good Lord somehow. That you were the child I would never be able to have.

I can only guess at the dark depths that drove your mother to leave you with me. I know it looks like neglect, but it was in fact the ultimate sacrifice. She would never see you again, poor lady, but at least she knew you would be warm, fed and clothed come nightfall. In time, I came to understand that, but back then, aged eighteen, it was hard for me to grasp.

Shortly after that day in the park, I lost my lovely father. I was broken-hearted and wanted so desperately something, or someone, to call my own. It was around then that my mother and the doctor decided it would be best if I were sterilized, in case I were to accidentally fall. They never said as much, but I could see how worried they were that I might do something rash; I wanted a baby that dearly. I believe the wisdom was that if my womb was removed, it would also somehow remove the longing for a child. It didn't.

After that, I could either let the pain of losing you, my father, my future as a mother drown me or I could

make every second of what was left of my life count.
Bring a little happiness into the lives of others. Despite
this, not getting the opportunity to save you, Flossy, ate
away at me and so I started to send small parcels to
you on your birthday. A second-hand spinning top from
the market, a hand-stitched rag doll, a used copy of
Black Beauty . . . Not much, I know, but they were at
least chosen with love. It also eased my guilt somehow.
I'd made a promise to look after you, and in my mind
I had broken that promise.

I pestered the poor matron of the orphanage to allow
me to visit you. I wore her down, poor woman, and
from time to time, she even allowed me into the
orphanage playroom so I could spend some time with
you.

The last visit came when you were nearly seven,
when there was talk of you being sent overseas for a
new start in life. After that, it was felt my visits
should stop; they were no longer 'appropriate', in
case you formed an attachment to me. But it was too
late, for I had already formed an attachment to you.
I never forgot you after that, Flossy. The parcels
were all I could do for you, but I thought of you
every single day. The only reminder I had that I
had come so close to motherhood was your matinee
jacket, which I kept carefully hidden in my cupboard
at home.

When you walked into the factory a year ago, I felt as
if it were divine intervention. I had you back in my life

*for one very precious year, and I was so proud to see
the beautiful young woman you had become. I was
privileged to see you grow and blossom even more in
that time. Sharing your life this past year, well, it
meant I could die a happy woman.*

*You held a place in my heart that no one else could
occupy, so please, try to find it in yours to forgive me
for not telling you sooner. There is no easy answer to
why I could not tell you this in life, beyond the knowledge that you would have had questions that I couldn't
answer. Maybe there is also a small part of me that
simply won't allow death to have the final word.*

*As for your precious future, I cannot tell you what to
do, but I urge you not to try to find your real mother.
I fear only heartache lies along that path. She did what
she had to do, out of love, not neglect, and you should
remember her in that spirit. The proof of this is
contained within the jacket pocket.*

*I don't presume ever to be remembered as a mother
figure to you, but I loved you like one. Do you
remember what I said to you that day outside the hair
salon?* You're an unpolished diamond. Don't be
afraid to shine. *I have never meant anything so much
in all my life.*

*Please, my dearest Flossy. Fall in love. Have the
children I never had. Live your life to its fullest.*

Yours for eternity,

Dolly x

Flossy stared down at the letter and felt a rush of love so powerful she scarcely felt Peggy's arms wrap round her. Without saying a word, she handed it to Peggy, while she sat motionless, stunned by the revelations of the letter and the enormity of the truth it contained.

By the time Peggy had finished Dolly's letter from beyond the grave, the tears were flowing freely down both their cheeks and they hugged fiercely.

'But why did she suddenly start sending *me* parcels?' asked Peggy, when at last she found her voice.

'Knowing Dolly, I can only imagine that after you were injured, she wanted to help you in any way she could,' replied Flossy. 'She was obviously starting to live on borrowed time by then; the risk of being found out mattered less, I suppose.'

Finally, the mystery of Dolly Doolaney, the tea lady with the heart of gold, was revealed. Her compulsion, the insatiable desire to help others, made sense to Flossy. It's who Dolly was. Every small act of kindness, every parcel, every bundle of sewing, each pair of knitted socks, right down to the cups of tea she lovingly brewed, went some way to appeasing the tearing guilt she felt at not saving Flossy. Dolly wanted so much to make her brief time on earth count.

'All those hours she spent stitching for the sewing circle throughout the Blitz and we urged her to rest. "I'll sleep when I'm dead," she used to say,' murmured Flossy. 'Well, let's hope she's finally at rest now.'

Another thought also occurred to Flossy, and the realization made her shiver despite the hot sun beating down.

'The rag doll she gave me aged nine. She patched it up,

and it was the last thing she ever gave to me when I turned nineteen. She really did never stop thinking of me.'

'I think the fact that she kept the matinee jacket you were wearing when your mother left you, for all those years, rather proves that, doesn't it,' agreed Peggy.

'The jacket pocket!' Flossy exclaimed, drawing back. 'Dolly mentioned something about there being proof in the pocket.'

Slipping her hand into the tiny pocket, she felt nothing inside, except a stab of disappointment . . . until she checked the other pocket. In silent dismay, she pulled out a faded swatch of cream calico fabric. Embroidered round the edges were the prettiest pale blue birds and butterflies in flight, but it was the centre of the swatch to which Flossy's glittering grey eyes were drawn. A heart, darned in red thread with thirteen heart-wrenching words embroidered within.

Go gentle, babe.
I must now depart, but I leave you my heart.

Fifteen

In the seven days since her shocking discovery, Flossy had felt every emotion it was possible to experience for the woman she now regarded as her guardian angel. Regret, heartache, confusion, but the emotion that sang out purest of all was love. She had scarcely slept for analysing every conversation she had had this past year with Dolly, and it all came back to one indisputable fact: Dolly had treated her like a mother would a child. Why, the very last thing she did on earth was to bake Flossy a cake for her birthday, hug her and tell her how proud she was. She might not have been a mother in name, but in her everyday actions, she had more than fulfilled the role.

The contents of the letter had not been the bombshell Flossy had feared, but something altogether more poignant, but then the truth always was stranger than fiction. Flossy intended to fulfil every single one of Dolly's last requests and find the love and family that had so cruelly been denied her. She did not intend to waste so much as a precious drop of her life, but live it in a way that would make Dolly proud.

There was, however, just one request by which Flossy

felt she could never abide. To leave the trail of discovering the identity of her real mother would be impossible. She would sooner cut off a limb than abandon her search now. Dolly had revealed a tantalizing glimpse of the woman who had brought her into this world and, for whatever tragic reason, felt she had no choice but to abandon into the care of a stranger.

Flossy ached to discover the truth and yet all she had to go on was the pitiful keepsake. Why go to the trouble of embroidering such beautifully intricate birds and butterflies but leave so few words to reveal why she had left? Her mother was clearly a skilled needleworker, and with a pang Flossy realized this was where she had inherited her talent with a needle. But what other traits did she share with her? Just who was this woman whose blood flowed through her veins? Endless unanswered questions jostled through her mind. Where did her mother go to after she walked away from Victoria Park? What of her father?

Her mother had told Dolly she was widowed, unless she had been lying, but where would she have got the wedding ring she was wearing? None of it made sense, and until she uncovered the truth, Flossy would never truly feel whole.

In the past week, she had already pounded the bomb-shattered cobbles to visit every mother-and-baby home in the district, clutching her fabric heart and matinee jacket in the hope that someone might recognize it. Not only that but she had visited the local library, trawled the public records and visited an organization that had opened up two years previously, called the Citizens Advice Bureau. The lady at the CAB office, sitting under a huge banner announcing, *We're all in it together*, had been very sympathetic to Flossy's plight, but explained she was far too busy trying to rehouse folk made homeless by the Blitz and told her to come back when the war was over. In growing desperation, Flossy had even placed a small advert in the *East London Advertiser*, but so far nothing.

'You'll be lucky,' the lady at the public records office had told her unhelpfully. 'Half the records in Bethnal Green went up in flames or are buried in bombsites.' The only lead that held out any glimmer of hope had been the last mother-and-baby home she had visited yesterday on her dinner break. The lady on duty had told her she couldn't help, but that if she came back that very evening, their older midwife would be on duty. The lady didn't seem to hold out any hope that she would be of assistance, but Flossy knew she would not rest until every last avenue had been explored.

As the high walls of the factory hove into sight, pride swelled in her heart. It had been nineteen days and nights now since the bombs had stopped and the old building was still standing. A little battle-scarred, its high walls scorched black, a forlorn piece of tarpaulin draped over the hole in the roof, and a tatty Union Jack fluttering from the window, but it was still in one piece. Just. More than could be said for the poor factory a few doors up, which was now nothing but a jagged, twisted pile of bricks, sealed off behind a *Keep out!* sign.

Flossy stopped outside the gates to Trout's. The world turns on tiny things. Had that bomb dropped a split second earlier . . . Had her welfare officer visited that factory to find her employment, instead of Trout's . . .

As she allowed her gaze to travel up the brickwork,

peppered with pieces of shrapnel and jagged with cracks, Flossy squinted into the grimy air. Coincidence? Of course, but Flossy preferred to think that fate might well have had a hand in it.

'You worried it's all gonna come tumbling down?' called out a deep male voice.

Flossy whirled round and her grey eyes lit up.

Coming from the other direction were Lucky and Peggy, with her stick, her loyal fiancé tenderly helping her. They made an unusual couple: he was as broad and strong as she slender and willowy, yet they fitted together like two halves.

'What, Trout's?' Flossy replied. 'Never. I was just thinking, actually, it's a bit of a cliché, but what doesn't kill you makes you stronger.'

'I can't argue with that,' said Peggy, coming to a halt and leaning breathlessly on her stick.

'How is your leg feeling?' Flossy enquired.

'The same really,' she replied. 'But on the plus side, I have so much more feeling now in my hands. The doctor's really pleased with my progress, seems to think all the sewing I'm doing is helping.'

'That's wonderful,' Flossy said. 'Look here, could I beg a favour of you both? I have an appointment at a mother-and-baby home after work. Would you come with me? I'm hopeful it may be the one my mother gave birth in.'

Peggy and Lucky were the only people who knew about Dolly's connection to her and they had decided to keep the truth to themselves for now. The girls had had enough shocks to cope with of late, and besides, where did one even begin to start explaining that?

She saw Peggy shoot Lucky a concerned look.

'Look here, Flossy. Do you really think you ought to? I mean, isn't it best left? What good is it raking over the past? Remember what Dolly said in her letter to you? Besides,' she added, 'the woman left you to the mercy of a complete stranger in the park. What kind of mother would do such a thing?'

'Peggy,' admonished Lucky.

'It's all right, Lucky,' soothed Flossy, knowing Peggy hadn't meant to be unkind.

'I think, Peggy, only a desperate mother,' she replied.

Flossy could have said more, of course. So much more. She could have described the exquisite agony of lying on her cold iron bed at the children's home, night after night, silently sobbing into her starched white pillow, praying each morning that today would be the day that her mother would come and claim her. That there was an empty space in her heart that ached for the love and affection that only a mother could provide. That all she had ever prayed for was to belong to someone, in the way Peggy did.

Instead, she swung open the wrought-iron gate.

'Come on, we better clock in.'

Lucky placed his hand in the small of her back. 'Course we will come with you, Flossy.'

Inside, the factory was subdued and as silent as the grave. In fact, one week on from the funeral, the floor was a sea of black and not one note had been sung. Without the accompaniment of laughter, song and good-natured teasing, even the humming of the machines sounded strangely flat.

Three days ago, news had broken on the wireless that Germany's most famous battleship, the *Bismarck*, had been sunk, a decisive victory for the Allies, and even that hadn't elicited the chorus of cheers it would have under normal circumstances. It was as if Dolly's death had broken the spirit of Trout's.

The morning crawled by, and by tea break, the workers downed tools and sat about quietly drinking their tea and reading letters.

It was Archie who cracked first. 'I can't stand this,' he said, putting his mug down with a thump. 'I can hear myself think. I must be certifiable, but I miss your singing, even your squabbling and your jokes. How long is this going to go on for?'

'Thought you'd be pleased to have a bit of peace and quiet, Mr G?' piped up Sal.

'Not when it's like this,' he replied, standing and rubbing a hand wearily over the crown of his bald head. The piece of shrapnel he had caught on his forearm that first night of the bombings had left a jagged scar, and his pockmarked face was grey with exhaustion, but the foreman still had fight in his voice.

'Look, girls. I know we will never get over losing Dolly. Quite simply, she is irreplaceable. We have been dealt some cruel losses this past eight months, but life *has* to go on. The bombs seem to have stopped, God willing, and we must soldier on.'

He cast his hand about the floor. 'Dolly would never have wanted to see Trout's like this . . . like . . . like some sort of mausoleum. I think the time for respectful silence has passed.'

Vera stepped forward. 'I agree – Dolly would have hated to see us like this.'

'They're right,' sighed Pat, turning to the rest of the

workers. 'All our Doll wanted was to see people happy and smiling.' With that she started to sing the first few bars of a song all the women knew had been a firm favourite of Dolly's.

'You Are My Sunshine' was entirely appropriate, and one by one the women started to join in, the lyrics wrapping them in the golden warmth of nostalgia. There was much comfort and solace to be found in a shared song, and united, their voices drifted out of the open window. With Dolly gone, their sunshine had gone away, but if they sang loudly enough, perhaps, just perhaps, she would hear how much they had all truly loved her.

When the final bell sounded at the end of that emotional day, Flossy was beat. The Scouts had just installed five thousand triple bunks down the Tube, and now that the shelter welfare hall had opened, her home below ground was even more appealing. There mightn't have been nightly bombardments anymore, but it didn't stop Flossy, along with hundreds more, still heading to the sanctuary of the Underground to sleep.

Now that she had a precious shelter ticket for a bunk, she longed to head below ground, perhaps take in a concert in the hall that had been built in the westbound tunnel, before curling up in her cosy bunk with a borrowed book from the shelter library. A wood-panelled library, right there underground! Flossy had scarcely been able to believe it when she had seen it being built. It was such a joy to browse through their volumes, and she had even asked the shelter librarian to reserve a copy of *Black Beauty* when it was returned. A feeling of triumph surfaced inside Flossy. There was absolutely nothing Matron could do about that! She would never abandon the Bible, but now, thanks to the Underground shelter library, Flossy could finally allow her imagination free rein.

'Cooee, earth calling Flossy,' sang Peggy.

'Sorry, I was miles away. What were you saying?' she said.

'I was saying, are you quite sure you won't change your mind?' asked Peggy, as she pinned on her hat.

'You have to ask?' Flossy replied.

Together, the threesome slowly threaded their way through the narrow streets in the direction of the mother-and-baby home.

When at last they reached the large old Victorian home housed a few streets back from the park, Peggy wrinkled her nose. It looked dark and forbidding, its soot-stained window frames sagging and the roof buckling, as if the old house was sinking into the ground under the weight of its secrets.

'Are you sure it hasn't been evacuated? It looks all boarded up. Who in their right mind would want to give birth here?'

'You'd be surprised, Peggy,' Lucky replied. 'Some people have no choice. Babies don't stop being born just because there's a war on, you know.'

In silence they climbed the stone steps and rapped on the tarnished brass knocker.

They waited what to Flossy felt like an age.

'What is this place?' Peggy asked.

'A charitable institution for unmarried mothers having illegitimate children,' Lucky replied. 'I'm not sure who runs it, either the East End Mission or London County Council.

Either way, you come here if you ain't got no place else to turn.'

With that, the door swung open and a lady who looked as old and battle-worn as the building itself peered out from behind the heavy wooden door.

'May I be of assistance?' she asked.

'Er, yes. I spoke with another lady here who said you may be able to help me,' Flossy started, finding herself suddenly tongue-tied. 'I have some, er, questions.'

Without saying a word, the woman held open the door and they all trooped in over the doorstep.

Once inside the darkened hallway, Flossy looked about her. She wasn't sure whether the heavily shuttered and bolted windows were to prevent prying eyes looking in or women getting out. The reception was lit by a solitary low-watt bulb, and the place was sparsely furnished, save for a leaden crucifix hanging on the distempered walls. It was, however, broom-clean, and the parquet flooring smelt of Mansion Polish.

A heavy mahogany stairwell dominated the space, and Flossy felt her eyes travel up the steps. At the top sat a young woman, scarcely older than Flossy, clutching a duster in one hand and a swollen belly in the other. She regarded them suspiciously through the gloom. One look from the elderly midwife and she turned and scurried back up the stairs, out of sight.

'We are keen to observe the privacy of the girls,' said the midwife. 'Please state your business here.'

'Please, ma'am,' said Flossy. 'I am trying to find my mother. I believe she gave birth to me, here. Sometime in May 1922.'

The midwife raised an eyebrow a fraction. 'My dear, do you know how many women have passed through these doors over the course of the past nineteen years?' she replied. 'I really do not think that I can be of any assistance to you. Now, if you'll excuse me, I have duties to tend to.' With that, she gestured to the door.

'We are terribly sorry to have bothered you,' said Peggy, obviously relieved to make her escape from the stultifying atmosphere.

'Please, ma'am,' Flossy blurted, more abruptly than she had intended. This couldn't be it. This was her last hope. 'It's important. You see, she abandoned me and I have to find her. My mother had red hair; she was Irish.'

'I am very sorry to hear that, but I am not in the business of identifying girls who have made mistakes simply through the colour of their hair or their nationality.'

'But that's just it. I don't believe she had made a mistake, nor was she a girl. You see, I believe my mother was widowed. Do you only admit single women?'

A shadow of irritation flashed across the woman's face. 'This particular home mainly admits young unmarried mothers bearing illegitimate offspring. But in exceptional cases, we do admit married women, mainly destitute women. We teach them to care for their babies, carefully monitor their health and well-being, and that of their children, in the hope that we can avoid the child being given up for adoption and put the mother back on the road to respectability.'

The emotion of the previous month surged through Flossy and she was embarrassed to find herself crying. A solitary hot tear slid down her cheek and she looked down at the polished floor in disgrace. The action caused a bolt of pain to slice through her neck. In that moment, a thought came to Flossy. In Dolly's letter, she had remarked that her mother had been hunched over. What if the problems she was experiencing with her neck had been inherited from her mother? What if she too suffered with scoliosis, or whatever the doctor at the children's home had called the neck problems that had cursed her all her life?

'She may have had a problem with her neck that caused her to have a stoop,' she said in desperation.

The midwife regarded her curiously and seemed to be thinking carefully. The impatient look of moments earlier had softened into compassion.

'My dear, upon reflection, I do remember an Irish lady who was admitted that year, in the spring, I think.'

Buoyed by her reaction, Flossy tore her mother's fabric heart and the matinee jacket from her bag. 'I have these too,' she added, breathlessly holding the ageing fabric and the wool garment up to the light so the midwife could see. 'My mother made the heart. She left it tucked inside this jacket pocket. Just in case you re—' Flossy stopped, for the midwife's entire expression had changed. Her gaze remained fixed on the matinee jacket, but her face was wrung with despair.

'It took her weeks to make that,' she said at last, her voice haunted. 'I remember thinking how pretty the pink trim was. I even found her the length of pink ribbon to make the bow. Dear Genevieve.'

'So . . . so you do know her, my mother . . . Please, I beg of you, ma'am, tell me what you know,' Flossy pleaded. 'Genevieve . . .' The name . . . *her mother's name* sounded clunky on her lips.

'Of course I will, but please, my dear, let us retire somewhere more comfortable, to my office, where we might speak with more privacy.'

Seated in a chair opposite the midwife in an even sparser room, flanked by Peggy and Lucky, Flossy felt as if her entire life had been leading up to this moment. She had felt it in her bones when they crossed the threshold, that this was where she had entered the world.

Flossy laid the embroidered heart down on the desk. 'Please don't leave anything out. I need to hear the truth.'

'I can well imagine,' replied the midwife, taking a shaky sip of water. 'Genevieve's story, well . . . it is not an easy one to relay, but I shall try my best. Many years have passed and well, some memories take flight over time . . .' She fluttered her long, bony fingers like tiny birds into the air.

'Please think,' said Flossy with a degree more sharpness than she had intended.

'Flossy, let's remember we are guests here,' urged Lucky, under his breath.

'Forgive me,' said Flossy, feeling humbled as the realization hit her that this elderly lady had helped bring her into the world. 'Please take your time.'

'Genevieve Connor – that was your mother's name – arrived here one fine spring morning in 1922. I remember it well, in fact, as it was the same year they finally pulled down the notorious tenement slums around Brady Street, an admirable intent, as those premises weren't fit for a dog, except it left many, Genevieve included, displaced.'

The midwife shook her head and took another sip of water. 'A shock of vivid red hair she had – you'd never miss her, not even in the blackout. She arrived heavily with child and homeless. Not a penny to her name, poor woman, and her condition exacerbated by a problem with her neck.'

Flossy's body stilled, but her heart was pounding furiously in her chest.

'She was recently widowed, poor soul, about to give birth too and in a terrible state. Imagine losing your husband and your home when you're with child. Could there be a harsher fate?

'If my memory serves me right, I have a feeling he'd been gassed in the first war. Poor man. That war was a disgrace. Have we learned nothing?' she tutted. 'The war that was supposed to end all wars and yet here we are again—'

'But Genevieve . . .' interrupted Flossy gently, desperate to get the midwife back on track.

'My apologies,' she said, shaking herself. 'Yes, Genevieve. She stood out to me as we don't admit that many married women, truth be told, mainly young girls who've got themselves in trouble. She didn't have a farthing to her name. That's why she came to us, threw herself upon our mercy. She had nowhere else to turn. Poor soul was in bits, scared witless, in pain and grieving for her husband.' Her gaze flickered to the crucifix on the wall.

'We looked after her here while she laboured, showed her how to care for a newborn infant; then when the baby was seven or eight weeks old, we had no choice but to discharge her from our care. I knew she was vulnerable and unwell, but that was the longest she could stay. The poor soul, she begged and pleaded with us to stay, but my hands were tied. We have a desperate shortage of beds. We did manage to arrange her a job making matchboxes and a bunk at a homeless-and-hapless lodgings. She would have done anything to avoid the fate of the workhouse.'

'Where?' blurted Flossy, through a storm of tears. She felt Peggy's arm slip through hers, but she was so close now – she had to know the whole truth, no matter how painful. 'Please tell me where this job was, or the address. I have to find her. I mean her no harm, I assure you.'

The midwife's face fell and her hand flew to her heart. 'Oh, my dear. I'm so sorry, really I am, but there is little point . . .'

'But why? Surely it's worth me trying at the very least,' Flossy protested.

'No, you see, it's too late.' The elderly lady's careworn face was shot through with distress. 'Of this I am quite certain. Genevieve died soon after she was discharged. Our efforts amounted to nothing. Phthisis, or "self-neglect", they called it, which is just an archaic way of saying tuberculosis. It was particularly rife in the tenements that year.'

Flossy felt paralysed by the pitiful story, unable to utter so much as a word.

'I do not know the details, my dear,' the midwife continued in a soft voice, 'but that was what was reported to us. Your mother was not in her right mind when she left here. Life had not been kind to her and it broke her, mentally and physically. She loved the bones of the child she bore, that much was obvious, but sometimes love just isn't enough, is it?' she added sadly. 'I wish I could have done more for her, for all the women who pass through these doors, in fact.'

'Is there a grave that I can visit?' Flossy heard herself ask in a tiny voice.

The midwife shook her head. 'I shouldn't think so. She'd have been buried in a pauper's grave.'

Flossy looked upon her mother's embroidered heart, lying on the desk between her and the midwife, and felt her own heart shatter.

Go gentle, babe.
I must now depart, but I leave you my heart.

'She must have known all along she was going to abandon me, even before she left here,' Flossy whispered.

'We can never know what was going through her mind,' replied the midwife. 'But she clearly wanted a better life for you than the one she could provide. She appeared devoted to you, and while you slept, she spent hours knitting this matinee jacket and embroidering. If only I had known . . .'

As she spoke, her long fingers, covered in skin as thin as paper, traced the fine embroidered butterflies and birds. 'Perhaps she hoped you too would fly free?'

Her words crashed down around Flossy like daggers of ice and she gulped deep in her throat.

'Perhaps,' she replied at last. 'Well, I thank you for your time.'

'I'm so sorry to be the one to impart such sad news. Won't you stay a while, let me have the housekeeper fix you a cup of tea?'

Flossy took in the three concerned faces staring at her and suddenly felt waves of panic. She had come here today seeking the truth, the answers she had searched for all her life, but this . . . This was simply too much to bear.

'No . . . no, thank you, ma'am,' she whispered, backing

up towards the door and accidentally colliding with a slightly limp aspidistra perched on a stand, which then smashed down onto the parquet floor. As earth and tangled, exposed roots skidded across the floor of the office, Flossy stifled a sob.

'I'm so sorry,' she whimpered, turning and fleeing from the building. She had to get away, escape from the crushing sense of disappointment that was threatening to engulf her.

Outside, the skies overhead were leaden and grey, matching the torment that tore at her heart, and Flossy pounded along the street. She didn't know where she was going, just that she had to get away as fast as she could. In the space of five minutes, her dreams had crumbled to dust.

Flossy kept on running until she reached the grey waters of the boating lake in nearby Victoria Park and only then did she come skidding to a stop. Sinking down onto a bench, she put her head in her hands and surrendered to her pain.

'Flossy!' rang out a voice. She looked up and through her tears saw Lucky and Peggy. 'Budge up, there's a good girl,' said Lucky.

'You left these at the home,' he said, producing the embroidered heart and baby jacket.

'Keep them. I don't want them,' she replied.

He folded them carefully and placed them back inside his jacket, and together the three of them stared out bleakly at the water's edge.

Flossy broke the silence. 'All my days, because of the parcels, I've clung to the hope that I was illegitimate. I know illegitimacy is considered a sin, but for me, it at least provided me with a reason why she gave me up. Stupid, isn't it? To actually long to be a bastard child, but I believed, rather I dreamed, that my mother couldn't keep me and only gave me away to save a scandal, when in reality she gave me away the first chance she got, and to a perfect stranger too. She was hopeless – either that or I really must have been terribly hard to love after all.'

She sniffed derisively. 'What a fool I am. I should have listened to Dolly and never come here today.'

Flossy shook her head bitterly and closed her eyes against the cutting wind. When at last she opened them again, Lucky had crouched down beside her, and he tenderly took her hands in his. Raindrops streaked his handsome features and Flossy had never seen such compassion etched on a man's face.

'Can you imagine how tormented she must have felt to have abandoned you here?' he said, in a voice of infinite tenderness. 'It must have gone against every instinct in her body. I wonder how long it was before the TB claimed her. Not long, I hope.'

'Lucky's right,' Peggy said, breaking her silence. 'She must have known she was dying and needed to know that at least her daughter would be taken in and fed and clothed. It was the last act of a desperate mother, surely? She must have gone to her grave tortured with guilt.'

Her mother really was dead, buried in an unmarked grave, her fragile remains pressed in together with so many other unfortunate souls, as anonymous in death as she had been in life. An explosion of grief and regret flooded through Flossy and she stood abruptly.

'Well, I can't forgive her either,' Flossy said, her voice as prickly as the barbed wire that edged the park. 'What kind of woman abandons her child? She was a weak and selfish coward. Nature has fashioned our sex for endurance and ingenuity – haven't we ourselves proved that these past eight months? She simply didn't try hard enough.' Flossy spat out the bitter accusation, before turning and walking from the park. This time, Peggy and Lucky let her go.

There was only one person she longed to see now, one man who could help her make sense of this mess, and his boat was docking in just two days' time.

Sixteen

The month of June marched in like a brass band, breathing fresh heart into everyone on the factory floor. The blue skies and dazzling sunshine were certainly putting a bounce in everyone's step, and the women were in a noisy, ebullient mood. Even the fact that it was a bank holiday Monday and they were working, coupled with the announcement on the wireless yesterday, Whit Sunday morning, by the president of the Board of Trade that clothes were now to be rationed – and, with that, yet more coupons – hadn't been enough to put a dent in the women's spirits.

There was almost a carnival atmosphere on the floor that morning as thirty machinists belted out a slightly bawdier version of 'Bless 'Em All'.

Peggy couldn't help but grin to herself as she gazed about the factory floor, the ribald laughter drifting over the humming of the machines and out through the open windows. Nearly every worker under the age of thirty was done up to the nines, with heavy metal rollers anchored under their turbans, and lips freshly coated with crimson lipstick. The smell of Evening in Paris mingled with the scent of Californian Poppy and hung like a blanket over the factory, disguising the slightly fustier smell of Morning in Bethnal Green, Peggy thought with a wry smile.

Could the women's improved mood perhaps be connected to the news that the first dance of summer was taking place at Shoreditch Town Hall the next day, or that a certain ship was docking for shore leave that very afternoon? Peggy had a feeling Dolly, whose presence was still felt in every nook and cranny of Trout's, would very much have approved.

With that, Peggy gazed at Flossy's back from the row of machines in front of her, her slight body rocking back and forth gently as she worked her treadle. She wished she could fathom what Flossy was thinking, but in the two days since her dreadful discovery, she had shut down and flatly refused to discuss the subject every time Peggy had brought it up. Goodness only knew Peggy had been appalled that any woman could leave her child, but after hearing the pitiful story of Flossy's mother, her own heart had gone out to her.

Lucky had warned her to go easy on Flossy, and Peggy could see her emotions were raw, but surely she would have to open up and face the tragic facts of her past at some point? Learning of Flossy's sad start in life had certainly made her more thankful for the unconditional love she received from her own mother, May. Peggy shuddered to think how wretched she had been to her when they had first moved to Bethnal Green just over a year ago. She might still have no news of her father, but she had the love of her mother, and Lucky, and for that, she was truly blessed.

When the machines shut down for mid-morning tea break, Archie strode out onto the floor and recoiled.

'Bleedin' hell, girls, it smells like a tart's boudoir in here,' the foreman sniffed, pretending to stagger and faint.

'Give over, you great lummox,' cackled Pat.

'Them poor sailors don't know what's going to hit 'em,' he chortled.

'Attention please, ladies,' interrupted the forelady, clapping her hands together.

'HMS *Avenge* docks at four this afternoon and Mr Gladstone has kindly said we can all clock off early to meet them, seeing as it's a bank holiday' – a wave of excited chatter washed over the floor – 'provided we finish up the day's quota of bundles,' Vera finished firmly. 'The *East London Advertiser*, the WVS and representatives from the Mayor's Comforts Group will also be there to greet them, and I shall of course be presenting the ship's captain with the quilt we have stitched in honour of Trout's special relationship with HMS *Avenge*.'

'Some people's relationships are more special than others, eh, Floss,' called out Daisy teasingly.

Poor Flossy flushed a high pink. 'Tommy is a special friend, that's all,' she replied, a coy smile playing on her lips.

'But you'll be giving him a little squeeze, won'cha,' Sal winked back. 'You know what they say, Floss – "A hug without a squeeze is like a slice of apple pie without the cheese." You gotta give the man a proper greeting: he's been at sea for Gawd knows how long.'

'I'll be giving my sailor, Ernie, a great big Pat Doggan cuddle,' Pat said with a wicked grin.

'That sounds like a threat, Pat,' chuckled Archie.

'Watch it, you,' Pat bantered back, and jokingly ran her

hands over her ample curves. 'I'll have you know that in my day I was known as Hot Lips, and I still got it. Some men like a mature woman. Inside here, there's a wotcha-call-it? A femme fatale bursting to get out!'

'Just the one, Pat?' quipped Sal, to a roar of laugher.

'I expect all representatives of Trout's to act in a way that befits the good name of the factory,' Vera said stiffly over the laughter. 'Bethnal Green has proved that we can take it; now is our chance to show that we can give.'

'Oh, lighten up, Vera,' sighed Daisy to her fractious big sister. 'Don't we deserve to let our hair down a bit? Bleedin' clothes rationing, it's really got my goat. How's a girl to look 'er best on sixty-six coupons a year? Honestly, I ask you. This war's being fought in the battlefields, in the air and at sea . . . and now in my bloody wardrobe.'

'No swearing on the factory floor, Daisy,' ordered Vera. 'How many times must I tell you?'

Vera looked back down at her clipboard and Daisy pulled a face.

'Personally, I couldn't give a rat's arse,' sniffed Pat. '"Make Do and Mend", I ask yer! That ain't a slogan; it's a way of life in the East End. I was turning collars and patching socks by the age of ten. It's just one more sacrifice.'

A silence descended as Pat's words chimed with every worker. For eight torturous months, they had endured the bombs, and although the raids had stopped and rumour had it Hitler was planning an invasion of Russia, not a woman there didn't live in terror of the bombers' return. The East End was paying a heavy price for this war, and Peggy knew the workers' gallows humour masked a deep fear of what the future held. But that afternoon at least held the promise of sunshine, companionship and the blossoming of new friendships, and that was something to look forward to.

*

The gaggle of women, plus Lucky and Archie, paraded along Commercial Road in the direction of Deptford Docks as gay and chirpy as a flock of starlings. Leather pumps clicked on the cobbles as the group spilt out into the late-afternoon sunshine in a giddy whirl.

Flossy was so nervous she could scarcely speak. Goodness knows how she had done it, but Sal had managed to get her hands on some confiscated Japanese manufacturer's stock of material and had thoughtfully given Flossy a length of beautiful crêpe de Chine, which she had run up into the prettiest dress Flossy had ever owned. The light, silky fabric felt glorious against her bare legs, and the soft teal-green colour of the dress brought out the silver in her eyes. Her freshly combed hair fell in soft waves about her face, and she had been so touched when the members of the Victory Knitters had surprised her that morning by presenting her with a tortoiseshell hairclip, 'just because', which Daisy had carefully clipped in place before they set off.

'You look pretty as a picture, Flossy,' marvelled Peggy as they walked together. 'Ravishing yet demure – how could Tommy resist? You know, you do deserve a little happiness.'

Flossy furiously blinked back the tears that threatened to spill down her freshly powdered cheeks. She knew what

Peggy was hinting at, but she wasn't ready to think about recent events, much less discuss them.

'Please, Peggy, not now,' she whispered. 'I just want to enjoy this afternoon.' And she really did. Nestled in her handbag was Tommy's last letter.

She knew the contents of it by heart already.

Such a prompt response to my letter deserves a hug and two squeezes, and you can expect just that when we meet.

A burst of delight fizzed up inside her at the thought that, very soon, she would meet Tommy for real. If his written words could have this effect on her, just what would meeting her sailor in the flesh do? She knew from the photo he had sent that he was dashing. He was twenty-eight, and his black hair was shot through with flecks of silver, but it had been his startling eyes to which she had found herself drawn. They sparkled with laughter and fun, just as Dolly's had. She couldn't wait to see what colour they were; she had a fancy they were blue, like Dolly's.

Flossy thought back to that fateful evening down the Tube when she had opened his letter and his photograph had fallen out. Just two and a half months ago, and yet so much had happened since it felt like a lifetime! So much revelation. So much sorrow. At least her feelings for Tommy remained reassuringly the same.

The long, busy street was as bomb-shattered as any in the East End, but despite this, it was business as usual, with queues of housewives in headscarves gossiping outside the butcher's and baker's, one hand clamped round a string bag, the other gripping the hand of a small child. Flossy was in two minds how she felt towards the mothers who had refused to have their children evacuated out of London, even at the height of the bombings.

'Irresponsible,' Sal, who had had her two sons sent away during the first wave, had branded them, but in her heart, Flossy held a sneaking admiration for them. She knew from watching them down the Tube shelter that there were many mothers who couldn't countenance being parted from their child under any circumstances, no matter how dangerous. Evacuation, or Operation Pied Piper, was a wartime sacrifice they simply would not, or could not, make. They would rather tear off a limb than send their child to live with a stranger. Pity her own mother had not shared their deep maternal instincts, she thought with a twist of sorrow. Quickly, she squashed down the dark thoughts before they took hold. Today was to be a happy day.

Their route down Commercial Road took the group through the neighbouring borough of Stepney, and all too soon, the girls were assailed by the sound of song, drifting out through the window of a factory. Judging by the bawdy laughter and music, it was unmistakably a garment factory.

A huddle of workers stood outside on the pavement, drawing deeply on their cigarettes, enjoying some nicotine with their fresh air during afternoon tea break, and some precious time away from machining khaki. Flossy recognized some of their faces from the singing competition at the pub, the fateful night before the bombs had started to drop.

Sal's face lit up when she saw them. 'Hello, girls. Good to see you,' she said. 'How you keeping?'

'All right, gal. Well, we got a pulse, and the factory's still standing, so mustn't grumble,' remarked one. 'Gov'nor's got us machining army parachutes now, would you believe? You heard about the Rego, I suppose?'

'Yeah, copped it on the last night of the bombings, didn't it?' remarked Sal. 'Trout's nearly went for a burton an' all. We've got a hole in our roof as big as Pat's gob.'

'Watch it, you,' said Pat, playfully bashing Sal on the bum with her gas-mask box.

'I heard about that . . .' the woman faltered, 'and we heard about Lily and Dolly too.'

A heavy silence fell over the group.

'Yeah, well . . .' sniffed Sal eventually. 'Our losses are no worse than anyone else's, I suppose. I'm sure you've lost girls too.'

The woman nodded and picked a stray bit of tobacco off her lip. 'That we have, Sal. Two young girls and a couple of old-timers in the last big raid, God rest their souls, and too many to mention have been bombed out.'

'Yep, my flat's a bombsite now an' all,' Sal nodded. 'God knows what home my boys will come back to. They'll scarcely recognize the old place . . .' Her voice trailed off. 'I do wish someone would hurry and top that Hitler bastard.'

A bell rang in the distance and the workers wearily mashed out their cigarettes on the kerbside.

'We better let you get back to it, then,' Sal smiled to the Stepney workers. 'But stay safe, and God bless you girls.'

'God bless you too.'

Hugs were exchanged, before Sal threaded her arm through Pat's and they continued in the direction of the docks.

Sal's voice drifted back to Flossy. 'The awful thing is,

whenever you say goodbye to someone, you just never know if it's the last time you'll see them.'

On the quayside at Deptford, the excitement was palpable as the sewing circle mingled with the throngs of crowds and watched as the small flotilla wearily chugged its way up the Thames and into the Port of London.

The minesweeper – a fishing trawler taken over by the admiralty – smelt of oil and was covered in coal dust. As it drew alongside, the boat looked as in need of some tender, loving care as doubtless its crew were. Tommy had never talked of his work or his precise location, but she knew the men of the minesweepers had the most dangerous jobs of all, sweeping the seas to sink any magnetic mines, while under constant threat of enemy bombardment from above.

Tommy had written to say that the vessel was docking before being taken to a dry dock in Chatham for essential maintenance, which gave its small crew one week of precious shore leave. Flossy suspected that as well as seeing his family, he probably longed for a hot bath and a pint, but she hoped there would be enough time for them to get to know one another.

HMS *Avenge* was joined by other sweepers coming into dock, and the squawks of seagulls wheeling overhead through the white cotton-wool clouds mingled with the excited chatter of women and children. The turnout to meet the men was tremendous, and Flossy found herself over-whelmed but gladdened at the patriotic sight.

A Church Lads' Brigade was marching on the quayside, playing drums and bugles. Boy Scouts and Girl Guides, who had so valiantly proved their worth to the community throughout the bombs, were milling about handing out flags and cups of tea. A vendor had even set up selling winkles, whelks and shrimps. It was a deeply satisfying sight. London, like the rest of the country, was struggling to return to normality after the devastation of the bombings. How Dolly would have revelled in this, thought Flossy.

But this was not a day of sadness or reflection, so Flossy painted on a bright smile, nervously smoothed down her dress and watched as Archie and Vera, along with the mayor of Bethnal Green, formally stepped forward to present their quilt to the ship's captain.

'On behalf of all the men of HMS *Avenge*, I would like to personally thank you for all the good things produced for the ship's company. Myself and the twenty-seven men aboard this command have been greatly cheered during the long months at sea by the fruits of your labours,' said the captain over the noise of the crowd. 'I am deeply indebted to the Victory Knitters for the unending morale instilled in my crew through your kind letters and comforts . . .'

But Flossy had stopped listening, because at that moment, the crew themselves started to troop down the gangplank, broad smiles blinking into the dusty afternoon light.

Flossy stood back, waiting patiently as the crowds surged forward and the photographer's flashbulb popped. The sun dazzling off the Thames and the lights of the camera temporarily blinded Flossy, but when her vision cleared, her heart leaped into her mouth. There was a man she recognized from a grainy black-and-white photo. Tommy, her Tommy, and oh my, he was even more handsome in the flesh. The girls in the factory had often talked about how sailors took a great deal of pride over their appearance, and they were right. Tommy looked immaculate in his dark blue bell-bottomed trousers, blue collar over a snowy-white vest and natty blue-topped cap.

He was much taller than she had imagined he would be, but she had been right in one respect. His eyes were pale blue, and they were scanning the crowds intently.

Suddenly, his face lit up into a dimpled smile of recognition as he set down his kit bag and spread his arms wide. With her stomach tumbling, Flossy raised her arm and returned his smile. Should she walk into his arms or . . . ? Gosh, she was nervous.

'H-ello there . . .' she mumbled hesitantly.

Suddenly, her smile froze and her voice trailed away, for with a sickening lurch, it dawned on her . . . She was *not* the one Tommy was smiling at.

Out of the crowd tore a young girl.

'Daddy!' she hollered, flinging herself into Tommy's outstretched arms with such force she nearly knocked him clean off his feet. A bilious dread rose up sharply in Flossy's throat; she stood rooted to the ground and watched in horrified fascination as, a second later, a pretty, flushed-faced young woman joined them. Flossy felt a sob escape her mouth as Tommy threw his arm round her too. The happy family stood embracing in the crowds, clearly oblivious to all but each other.

Searing agony ripped through Flossy's chest.

No, no, no.

'How could you?' she sobbed, before, turning and stumbling, she pushed her way back through the crowd, humiliated tears blurring her vision.

Flossy ran to the only place she could think of. Dolly's grave. Trembling, she sank to her knees on the damp earth.

It was Lucky who found her there later that day, as the sky bruised a deep purple in the settling dusk. Found her sitting hunched over, knees drawn into her chest, surrounded by the scattered pieces of a torn-up photograph.

'He's a bleedin' cad, Flossy, and I ought to box his chops,' he said, as he plonked himself down next to her.

'Oh, please don't, Lucky,' she said, looking up suddenly.

Lucky took one look at her blotchy face and the heartbreak that came off her in waves, and tenderly draped his jacket round her shoulders. 'Very well,' he sighed. 'But if it were anyone but you, I still would have given him a proper clump,' he added.

'It's my fault for trusting a man I had never even met,' Flossy replied. 'I thought . . . No, I really believed he was mine. But he was stringing me along all the time, Lucky.'

With that, Flossy groaned and allowed her head to slump despairingly into her hands.

'I feel so stupid. My name is embroidered next to his on the quilt,' she said, her voice muffled. She turned once more to face Lucky and shivered in the fading light.

'You're a man – tell me, why would he betray me in such a way?'

'I don't know, Floss darlin',' he shrugged. 'You can't have your cake and eat it too, but some men like second helpings, and in some cases, thirds. Remember that toerag Gerald? He had a rag on every bush.'

Flossy rolled her eyes. 'I think this is my problem, Lucky. I expect too much. First Dolly, then my mother, now this . . .

I know now of all times we just have to put a brave face on things, but I really don't know how much more I can bear, Lucky. I just want to belong to someone. Some hope!'

'Now, don't you go talking like that,' said Lucky gruffly, wiping his eyes. 'Next to my Peggy, you're the sweetest girl in all the world and you deserve so much. Dolly we can never bring back, but your mother . . .' His voice trailed off as he searched his mind for the right thing to say. 'I'm not one with the words, but the way I see it is this – what your mother did that day, leaving you in the park with Dolly, some may see it as abandonment, but all she wanted was for you to be warm, safe and fed. She couldn't care for you any longer herself, so she left you with Dolly, the safest, most loving pair of hands in the East End.'

'But she didn't know what kind of woman Dolly was, did she?' Flossy protested. 'She was a perfect stranger to her.'

'Trust me, Floss, when you've lived where your mother did, the Brady Street slums, you quickly develop a sense of who to trust. I'm going to tell you a few home truths now, Flossy Brown, and you might not like it, but when you was growing up, staring out of the windows of that orphanage, you only saw one view of life, not the complete picture.' He shivered, the hairs on his arms standing on end in the chill of the darkening graveyard.

'I've seen sights that would make your hair curl. Some of them slums are the closest you will ever get to hell on earth. Trust me, I know what I'm talking about. I'm from Russia Lane, don't forget, where police only dare go in pairs. You should hear the whistling off the balconies when they walk into the buildings to shut down whatever gambling ring's going on.' He snorted in a way that told Flossy he wasn't joking.

'Tenement blocks riddled with poverty and disease; damp, peeling walls; no running water; families of up to fifteen raised in two rooms; one godforsaken lav on the landing between five families . . . I spent that long in the cleansing station when I was growing up, I started to think it was my second home.' His voice cracked slightly and Flossy listened, transfixed, as Lucky spilt out the sad, unflinching details of his childhood.

'Do you not remember when I told you why I was risking my life night after night? It's for my people. My kind. Some of them vulnerable, the so-called dregs. Your mother was one of them, a victim of her times, not a villain. For most in Bethnal Green, and certainly true of my family, we lived Friday to Friday, earning just enough to keep our heads above water. The true picture of the East End is many thousands working desperately to pay the rent man and put food on the table.

'After my mother died, my father fought tooth and nail to keep a roof over our heads 'cos he knew the alternative. Kids crammed into the poorhouse, sleeping six to a bed, food doled out by the ounce . . . But we survived. Just. We was the lucky ones, but for your mother, well, the dice landed a different way.

'Your father died when she was in the family way with you, and then she fell ill. Can you even imagine? She was a penniless, dying widow with a babe in arms! What hope did she have? So she gave you to a kind-looking lady in the park to try and save you from the other alternative, the workhouse. She made the ultimate sacrifice a mother can make. It's just another kind of love, ain't it?'

Just another kind of love.

Flossy's head spun as she digested his words and gazed up at the sky. At that moment, a white feather drifted down and settled at her feet. Flossy and Lucky watched, captivated, as a breath of wind lifted the feather up and it swirled and twisted through the air before coming to rest lightly on Dolly's grave.

'Looks like someone agrees with me,' said Lucky.

'What do you mean?' asked Flossy.

'When angels are near, feathers appear,' he replied. 'I think it's time to forgive your mother and lay her memory to rest.'

A slow light of understanding dawned in Flossy's soft grey eyes, and for a moment, she was silent with her thoughts.

'I think perhaps you're right,' she said eventually.

'I know I am, Floss,' Lucky smiled, laying a tender kiss on the top of her head. 'You've spent your whole life searching for family. Well, we love you like family. You're like the little sister I never had. You do belong to us, for what it's worth.'

'Thank you, Lucky,' Flossy replied with a grateful smile. 'It's worth ever such a lot.'

'So you'll take this?' he asked, fishing around in his pocket and producing her mother's embroidered heart. 'And try to find it in *your* heart to treasure it? It is a token of love, Flossy.'

Flossy took the piece of fabric and put it back in her

pocket. She wasn't ready to look at it, much less discuss it, but hopefully, in time, she would come to look upon it so.

'Come on, you,' he grinned, getting to his feet and holding out his hand. 'Let's get you home.'

As Flossy walked arm in arm with Lucky out of the darkening graveyard, it struck her that perhaps that was the rub. Her home was a Tube station.

Seventeen

3 JUNE 1941

The next day on dinner break, the Victory Knitters had gathered in the canteen and were busy untangling balls of wool, hearts all of a flutter over the previous day.

'Some of them sailors were ever so handsome, weren't they?' said Kathy. 'I didn't 'alf fancy mine. I even touched his dicky for good luck.'

'I beg your parsnips, young lady,' Sal screeched, as Daisy laughed so hard she choked on her tea.

'You know, Sal, his dicky . . . sailor's collar,' Kathy replied, looked bemused as the rest of the sewing bee fell about. 'It's supposed to bring good fortune.'

'Yes, sorry, Kathy love. I get you,' Sal smiled. 'Mine was a bit of all right too. Not that I'd dare go there, mind, but he was ever such a lovely chap, and it was so good to put a face to a name. You know, see the reason why we've all been working so hard.'

'I'll admit,' said Vera, 'it was very gratifying to meet them, especially the captain. He was at great pains to say what a morale booster the crew found our comforts to be, and the quilt is going on display in the town hall as an example of the fortifying relationships that can be forged between factories and the navy, so the mayor himself personally told me.'

The forelady glowed with pride, and just a hint of smugness. 'Not something London Brothers can lay claim to, I'll wager.'

Behind her back, Daisy rolled her eyes.

'Apparently, there is even some talk of them holding a Navy Warship Week next year during which the community sponsors a ship,' Vera went on, oblivious. 'Our self-denial and endeavours are an inspiration to all. Trout's is quite the big noise.'

'I tell yer what's really inspiring,' piped up Pat. 'My sailor only gave me a carton of fags.' With that, she broke into song. '*You are my sunshine. My double Woodbine. My box of matches. My Craven "A"!*'

'Behave,' laughed Sal, playfully poking Pat with her knitting needle.

'It was a wonderful day, though, weren't it?' agreed Ivy. 'Really took me out of myself.'

Everyone but Flossy murmured their agreement, and Sal clamped her hand over her mouth.

'Flossy, forgive us – how bleedin' tactless of us, blathering on about how wonderful our sailors were and forgetting.' Her mouth twisted into a scowl. 'That Tommy rotter. I could string him up for leading you on like that when he's already married, and with a little 'un in tow too.'

'There's always one bad apple in the tree,' muttered Ivy, sagely.

'What I don't get is how he thought he'd get away with it?' asked Daisy. 'He knew Flossy was going to be there to greet him. Besides, he just didn't strike me as the type to do the double shuffle.'

'Trust me,' snapped Sal, her voice brittle, as she pushed back from the table. 'Some men don't think with their brains. They're led by another useless appendage. Who wants another cuppa?'

'He ought to have it chopped off, in that case,' agreed Pat, forcefully ramming her knitting needle into a ball of wool. 'Yes, please. Be a dear and see if they've got any more biscuits while you're up, Sal.

'To be honest, you've had a lucky escape, ducky,' Pat ploughed on, oblivious to Flossy's discomfort. 'I've seen women taken in by married men before and it ain't pretty. Five minutes' pleasure, nine months' pain and a lifetime of ruin,' she nodded with relish. 'If you want my advice, keep yer hand on yer ha'penny until you've got a ring on yer finger.'

Flossy squirmed and wished the canteen floor would swallow her whole.

'Let's change the subject, shall we?' said Peggy tactfully. 'Who's going to the dance tonight at Shoreditch Town Hall?'

'Ooh, not 'alf,' said Daisy dreamily. 'I've missed the dances so much. They'd have started much earlier in the summer if it weren't for the bombs. I shouldn't think they'll host them in Victoria Park this year, but the summer dances there are the business.'

Daisy stood up and pulled Flossy to her feet, playfully dancing her round the canteen. Flossy giggled uncontrollably, her cares over Tommy quickly pushed to one side, as the beautiful seamstress led her jokingly round the floor.

'Dancing your cares away under the silver moonlight by

the bandstand . . . The quickstep, the waltz and, my favourite, the tango!' she said breathily.

'If you're clever,' interrupted Ivy.

'And don't forget that new dance from America, the jitterbug,' piped up Kathy.

'If you're stupid,' smirked Sal, returning with a small plate of scavenged broken biscuits and setting them down on the tabletop.

'But the fact the dances are coming back,' Kathy replied. 'Do you think it's a good sign, that maybe we're winning the war?'

'I don't think we can even dare to dream, Kathy love,' said Sal.

'All the more reason to go tonight and let our hair down,' said Daisy, finally releasing her grip on Flossy. 'I just want to dance and forget, and then dance some more.'

Vera's face knotted with disapproval. 'I wonder at the wisdom of it. Does it not feel disrespectful to Dolly and Lily's family, not to mention all the women at Trout's who have lost loved ones and homes, if they see you lot out kicking up your heels? Isn't it, well, a bit fast?'

'Do you mind? I ain't no Jezebel,' Daisy protested hotly, but Sal placed a firm hand on her arm to silence her.

'I understand what you're saying, Vera, but we're not dancing to forget Dolly or Lily; we're dancing to forget our cares, and after everything we've been through, don't we deserve to chase our happiness where we can?'

'But still, can't you wait until the war is over and our boys are home?' Vera asked.

'I think when this war is over, it's us women on the Home Front and in the factories who should be getting the medals,'

Sal shot back. 'We're the real heroes, if you ask me. Look at how we've carried on working through the bombs, night after night, clocking on each morning without so much as a whinge, while our lives and our families are torn apart.

'This war has cost me dear,' she said hoarsely. 'My boys and my husband away, and God knows when I'll see them next, and my home destroyed. I have nothing left . . .' Her voice cracked, and Daisy leaped to her side and placed her arms on her shoulders in a gesture of total loyalty. 'Nothing except my friends, and this place, but I refuse to be down-hearted. No one can dare call us women the "gentler sex" any longer. We have proved ourselves to be braver and more resourceful than any man.'

Heads nodded in agreement and Sal scowled, pushing the plate of broken biscuits away. 'We didn't ask for this war, but we sure as hell have taken it on, so if we wanna dance, we should dance.'

*

After dinner break, Peggy caught Lucky before she sat down behind her machine.

'Lucky, got a moment?' she whispered.

'Anything for my beautiful girl,' he replied, wiping his hands on an oily rag.

'I'm worried about Flossy,' she admitted. Lucky had told her how he had found a heartbroken Flossy huddled by Dolly's grave after discovering Tommy's deception, and coming so soon as it had after discovering the truth about her mother, she feared for her friend.

'I've spoken to my mother, and we both think it's a good

idea for Flossy to move in with us permanently. Now the bombs are easing off, she'll have to start thinking about getting proper digs again sooner or later. She can't live underground forever. I just wanted to check that you were happy with that.'

Lucky reached out and smudged the tip of her nose with his old oily rag. 'I think, Miss Peggy Piper, it's an excellent idea. I'm so proud of you and can't wait to make you Mrs Lucky Johnstone.'

Casting a sideways glance to check the forelady wasn't looking, he gathered her in his arms and gave her a long and lingering kiss. But you couldn't hide anything at Trout's.

'Can't you keep yer dirty paws off her for more than a minute?' heckled Sal. The teasing was good-natured. Everyone in the place knew there was no chance of any slap and tickle for the young couple until the wedding ring was firmly in place.

Peggy laughed and felt a sweet rush of delirium. A year ago, she had been too stupid and stubborn to see sense, not even able to accept a jam jar of flowers from the man she adored. But God had granted her a second chance, and she was truly blessed. Now, she was openly in love and she didn't give two hoots who knew it.

*

Flossy watched Lucky and Peggy's lingering kiss and felt her eyes glisten. She truly felt nothing but happiness for her good friend and the love she had found with such a fine chap. But why, oh why did Tommy's betrayal grate her heart?

The women's excited chatter and song competed for airspace over the noise of the machines, but Flossy tuned them out and concentrated on her bundles, so much so that she didn't see Pat's excited face until it was hovering right in front of hers.

She jumped so violently she nearly ran the needle over her finger.

'Pat! You startled me,' Flossy exclaimed, taking her foot off the treadle. 'Whatever is it? We'll have Vera over here in a minute.'

'Never mind that, Floss,' said Pat. 'I think you ought to come here and take a butcher's at this.'

Flossy looked up, startled, to find most of the girls had left their stations and were peering excitedly out of the window.

'What's the meaning of this?' thundered the forelady, marching the length of the factory floor. 'No one gave you permission to stop.'

'But, Mrs Shadwell,' babbled Kathy, gesturing to the street outside, 'it's the sailor what done the dirty on Flossy.' She turned to Flossy. 'He's got some front turning up here after what he did to you.'

'Pipe down, Kathy,' chastised the forelady, flinging the window open and glaring out.

Flossy could make out a deep male voice over the commotion.

'Flossy Brown, I know you're in there. Come to the window.'

In a trance, Flossy moved to the windowsill and peeked out. There, on the street five floors down, stood Tommy. Her heart leaped into her mouth. He looked so forlorn. But then a rush of anger flooded her body. He hadn't looked quite so dejected when his wife and daughter had shown up to greet him.

'Leave me alone!' she yelled.

When Tommy spotted her, his face lit up. 'Flossy!' he cried. 'I was waiting for you. Why didn't you come?'

'Oh, I came all right, but I wasn't the only one waiting. Seems your wife and daughter were waiting too. That's a pretty low blow, isn't it? Pretending your wife had passed.'

For a second, Tommy looked confused; then he shook his head. 'You've got it all wrong, you daft apeth!' he yelled. 'Come on down so I can explain.'

No one on the floor breathed a word, and Flossy resented having her private life turned into such a public spectacle.

'I don't give a tinker's cuss for anything you have to say. Save it for your wife. I'm not coming down,' Flossy replied.

'You heard her,' called down Vera, with a gleam in her eye that, if Flossy didn't know better, told her the forelady was half enjoying herself. 'Now clear off or I'll be contacting your superiors.'

'If you won't come down, then I'm coming up!' he shouted.

'You wouldn't dare,' Flossy shrieked.

'Watch me,' he called back, before turning on his heel and sprinting back up the cobbled street in the direction of the factory door.

Flossy whirled round. 'What shall I do?'

For a solitary moment, there was silence, before all hell broke loose. The women squawked and flapped about in a state of excitement.

'He can't come up here . . . He wouldn't dare . . . He only is . . . As I live and breathe!'

'Gawd, the excitement,' babbled Ivy. 'I gotta go spend a penny. Don't let anything happen before I get back,' and with that, she scurried off all in a lather.

Only Pat stood stock-still in the chaos, rolling up her sleeves. 'I'm gonna knock his block off,' she said cheerfully.

Archie's voice cut through the din. 'For the love of God, will you all calm down? It's like Christmas Eve in a turkey factory in here. Now, will someone please tell me what's going on?'

'Flossy's sailor's taking liberties and he's only on his way . . .' Daisy's voice trailed off, for suddenly, there on the fifth floor of Trout's, looking even more handsome in the flesh in his sailor's-leave tiddly suit with extra-wide trousers, his dark hair streaked with silver, was Tommy.

'I have nothing to say to you, Tommy. Please leave,' Flossy whispered, walking with as much dignity as she could muster back to her machine.

'You heard her,' warned Archie protectively. 'Now on your way.'

'Yeah, you're about as welcome in 'ere as a hole in a lifeboat,' Pat jeered.

'I'm gonna give you precisely ten seconds to sling yer hook,' added Lucky, who had heard the commotion and planted himself next to the foreman.

Tommy looked at Archie and removed his cap. 'I promise you, sir, I didn't come here to cause no trouble.'

'Then what have you come here for, lad?' asked Archie.

The sailor turned to where Flossy was sitting, and placed one hand over his heart. With the other, he pointed to her. 'To tell that girl over there that I love her with all my heart.'

A hush descended over the floor as all eyes turned to Flossy. She felt her lip start to tremble and bit down hard.

'Please, Flossy, I promise you that what I am about to

say is the whole truth, and I need you to believe me,' he implored. 'That wasn't my wife. My wife did pass away.'

'Oh yes,' she mumbled. 'So who was that throwing her arms round you?'

'That was one of my sisters, Irene. Remember I told you about her in my letters? She's been looking after my six-year-old daughter, Betsy, while I've been serving.'

'Your daughter?' screeched Sal, unable to contain herself.

'Oh, I know I should have told you I had a daughter,' Tommy went on, 'but I wanted to wait and tell you in person. I worried you wouldn't want a bar of me if you knew I had a child. But since my wife died, my daughter, Betsy, well, she's the most precious thing in my life. I didn't think I'd ever care for anyone as much as I do her, but then you came along. Your letters have made this war feel bearable. I lived for them at sea. I've memorized each and every single one. I've got them all right here,' he added, patting the jacket pocket over his heart.

'And, well, here's the thing. I love you, Flossy Brown.'

Slowly, he started to walk towards her machine, the women moving out of his way as he passed. When he reached Flossy, he paused. Up close, Flossy could suddenly see for the first time how nervous he was. His large hands trembled as he gripped on to her sewing machine for support.

'What . . . what I wanted to ask you all along was whether you could be a mother to another woman's child. I accept it's a lot to take on, but, well . . . we want you. We need you. Please come to my house after work for tea, meet my little girl and the rest of my family. I know they'll fall in love with you like I have.'

In that moment, it was so quiet you could have heard a

mouse scuttle across the floor. All eyes were on Flossy as she grappled with his words. Instinctively, Flossy's gaze was drawn to Lucky, the man she trusted like a big brother. He smiled and gave her the tiniest nod. If he believed it, then it was good enough for her.

Flossy let out a long, slow sigh and shook her head in frustration at her own stupidity.

'What time would you like me?' she asked, with a tremulous smile.

'Seven p.m. And don't be late,' he replied, with a chuckle, as he scrawled his address on the back of an empty cigarette packet. 'My mum will have been out on her hands and knees all day whitening our front doorstep in your honour.'

'Don't worry,' Flossy said. 'I'll be there this time.'

With that, Tommy reached over the top of her Singer and tenderly took her face in his hands. 'I've been waiting a long time to do this,' he murmured, his pale blue eyes boring into hers.

For a moment, Flossy thought she might faint on the spot, but then, oh my! His kiss was so warm and sweet on her lips. She felt her eyes flicker shut and her body melt to his touch as she surrendered to the moment. As first kisses went, it was magical and Flossy wished it would never end.

With her eyes closed, she couldn't see the women's faces, but their deafening applause and stamping of feet told her they approved of her decision.

When Tommy's lips finally left hers, she blinked and opened her eyes, to see half the floor staring at them doe-eyed.

'Blimey O'Riley! I've come over all peculiar,' Kathy said, fanning herself down with Vera's clipboard.

'Until tonight,' Tommy grinned, replacing his cap. 'And thank you, Flossy, for giving me a second chance.'

As he strode from the floor, Archie clapped him on the shoulder. 'That took guts,' he said approvingly. 'Nice to have a bit of happy news on the floor for a change.'

Five minutes later, Ivy burst through the doors, her face scarlet from racing up five flights.

'I just pissed faster than a Russian racehorse. So what'd I miss?' she wheezed, and the laughter was so loud it carried clean out of the hole in the bomb-shattered roof and over the rooftops of the East End.

When the end-of-shift bell sounded, it was hard to say who was more excited, those going to the dance up at Shoreditch Town Hall or Flossy off to meet Tommy and his family.

'I feel like someone's let a bag of ferrets loose in my tummy,' Flossy gushed to Peggy and Lucky.

'That's a good sign. It means you're in love,' teased Peggy, as she untied her headscarf and shook out her curls.

'Calm down, Peggy,' cautioned Lucky, as he went round oiling the machines. 'It's a bit early for that. Now, Flossy. Peggy and I shan't go to the dance tonight; instead, we are going to chaperone you. This Tommy fella looks like he's on the level, but how much do we really know about him when all is said and done? Besides which, I think your welfare worker from the home would have a fit on the mat if she heard you'd been gallivanting off on your own to sailors' houses.'

'What's it got to do with them?' Peggy asked.

'I am under their supervision until I turn twenty-one and they are supposed to vet any potential suitors,' Flossy interjected. 'So yes, I would like that, thank you, Lucky,' she replied, suddenly feeling shy.

'Well, if Lucky and I are to supervise this date, then I really must insist on dolling you up a little,' said Peggy. 'You know what mothers are like. She'll be judging you the moment you've got a foot over the doorstep. I've got the perfect dress you can borrow, and Mother's got some paint-on hosiery for your legs. It's called Cyclax Stockingless Cream and you'd honestly never know it wasn't—'

'No,' Flossy interrupted. 'No, thank you, Peggy. I appreciate your kind offer, truly I do, but I don't want to be someone I'm not. Tommy and his family must take me as they find me. I'll brush my hair and wash my face, and I have a perfectly good pair of slacks and a nice blouse I can wear, but that's it.'

'Slacks?' Peggy snorted derisively. 'Women in trousers, I ask you. Another downside of the war. I really can't see this fashion for women in trousers catching on, you know.'

'That's as maybe, Peggy, but I don't think pretending to be someone I'm not is the best way to start off a relationship.'

'Couldn't agree more, Floss,' said Lucky, planting a kiss on her cheek and making her blush. 'Now let's get going.'

Tommy's family home was in Poplar, two and a half miles from Bethnal Green, in the direction of the docks. With none of the buses running on their usual routes, as so many roads were closed off and reduced to rubble, it took the trio of friends far longer to get there than they imagined. By the time they paused outside the small terrace, Flossy was flustered.

'Oh, we're late,' she blustered. 'Tommy told me not to

be late and I so wanted to make a good impression, and now his mother will think me rude . . .'

'Calm down, gal,' chuckled Lucky, removing his cap as he knocked firmly on the door.

'Goodness, I thought Bethnal Green had been hit hard,' said Peggy, as she gazed in dismay at the long, narrow street. Huge chunks of the road were boarded off. Tommy's end of the street stood isolated, surrounded by a barren waste-land of rubble, and the grime-covered houses that were still standing looked punch-drunk and seemed to slide tipsily towards the pavement.

'The houses around the docks were worst hit,' frowned Lucky, 'proving there's always someone worse off than your-self . . .' His voice trailed off as the door swung open and a wiry woman who looked to be in her sixties squinted back at them. She wiped her hands on a wrap-over apron and smiled broadly. The smile peeled ten years off her.

'Come in, come in, do. You'll catch your death out there,' she urged, hustling them in over the doorstep, even though it was a perfectly fine summer's evening.

'Which of you pretty girls is the special lady my Tommy's been telling me all about?' she asked.

'Erm, that would be me, ma'am,' said Flossy, stepping forward nervously and wishing she had worn that dress after all.

Tommy's mother stood back in the gloom of the passageway to appraise her. 'Ooh, you're a tonic on the eye,' she grinned. 'My Tommy's told me ever such a lot about you, reckoned it was your letters what kept him going out there. Come and meet the rest of the family.'

Flossy's mouth felt as dry as dust as she was led into a warm, light-filled kitchen.

'You must be special because Mum's agreed to open up the front parlour,' said Tommy, rising from an easy chair and coming to greet them. 'I thought that was a privilege that would be only be granted to the King himself.'

'Get away, you scoundrel,' his mother cackled, lifting a tea towel off the range bar and swiping him with it.

Flossy's heart was in her mouth as she and Tommy locked eyes nervously. Out of his uniform, and wearing a smart suit and pressed shirt, a dazzling white against his dark braces, he looked even more handsome and, for a second, Flossy didn't know where to put herself.

Tommy's smile was soft and tender, though, as he shook hands with Lucky, then placed a gentle hand on Flossy's back and guided her into the heart of the kitchen. 'I'm so pleased you came,' he whispered in her ear.

A fire flickered in the grate, a huge pan of potatoes bubbled on the range, and the spicy aroma of roasting pork filled the room. Tommy had said in his letters he had five sisters, but all crowded into the kitchen, knitting, darning and listening to the wireless, they seemed to number at least twice that. The Bird sisters couldn't hide their curiosity and gazed at her with open, smiling faces. In the corner, in an ancient rocking chair, sat a very elderly woman with a tangle of knitting and a snuff pot on her lap.

'That's Nanny Bird,' said Tommy's mum. 'Mum, say hello to our Tommy's new beau, Flossy!' she hollered.

The woman grunted and looked up, the feathery whiskers on her chin twitching. 'Who you calling bossy?'

'No, Mum, Flossy . . . Oh, never mind . . . Mum's a bit deaf,' she explained.

'She's the only one who's not been much bothered by the bombs,' piped up one of Tommy's sisters. Flossy suddenly recognized her as Irene, the woman she had mistaken for Tommy's wife, and instinctively hung her head in shame.

Tommy cleared his throat nervously. 'Everyone, meet my good friend Flossy Brown, the young lady I told you about.'

Instantly, the room was filled with the sound of chairs being scraped back as the young women leaped to their feet in a babble of cockney voices.

'So you're the one keeping our little Tommy's toes warm,' smiled Irene, reaching her first and throwing her arms round her. 'We've all been worried sick about him, so knowing he has someone as lovely as you keeping his spirits up has been a weight off all our minds.' She squeezed Tommy's cheek playfully. 'He may be all grown up now and in the navy, but Face Ache here will always be our baby brother.'

'Behave, Irene,' Tommy said, blushing.

Flossy giggled and felt herself relax, and soon she was wrapped in a tangle of kisses and hugs as each of the sisters in turn came to greet her. In no time at all, Flossy was flushed as red as Tommy, and her glowing cheeks were covered in lipstick.

'Blimey, give the girl some air, won't you?' said Tommy's mother, batting them away. 'Now, I'm doing sausage, mash and onion gravy for yer tea. The butcher put them by for me when he heard our Tommy was coming home on leave.'

She turned to Lucky and Peggy. 'Will you stay for tea? You'd be more than welcome. I'm sure we can make it stretch to two more.'

'We wouldn't hear of it, Mrs Bird,' Lucky replied. 'You've enough mouths to feed. We just wanted to make sure our Flossy was in safe hands, which I can see now she is. We'd happily take a cup of tea off you, though, before we head off. Don't know about Peggy, but I'm parched.'

'Right you are, young man,' she chuckled. 'In that case, Tommy, take your visitors into the parlour away from this mob, and I'll bring you in a tray of tea and some biscuits in a bit,' she ordered.

Obediently, Flossy, Lucky and Peggy followed Tommy into the front parlour.

Outside, the streets may have been a barren and grey wasteland, but inside, the room was cosy and welcoming. A fire had been lit, and the room was spotless; two side lamps either side of the chaise longue threw out a soft glow.

Flossy's eyes were drawn to the mantel, on which clustered black-and-white images of the family enjoying a holiday on the coast, all guarded over ferociously by two chipped china dogs.

'Mum's pride and joy, them china dogs and photos,' Tommy chuckled, when he followed her gaze. 'My sisters tell me that every time the sirens went, she insisted on packing them up and taking them down the shelter with her.'

'Tell me, Tommy, where did your nan, mum and sisters shelter?' asked Lucky.

'In the crypt of All Saints' Church on the East India Dock Road,' he replied. 'I couldn't believe the scenes when I got home yesterday. Half my neighbourhood has gone. When I left for sea, this street was filled with children playing, horses and carts, a proper village in its own right. Now, my community has been destroyed, my corner shop's gone, as has my local, but I suppose I should count my blessings that my family are safe. All I hold dear is in this house . . .' His voice trailed off and a soppy grin creased his cheeks as he gazed over to where Flossy was sitting. 'Including you.'

Lucky and Peggy exchanged a knowing look as Flossy flushed pink and smiled shyly back.

A gale of giggles drifted in from the other side of the door, and Tommy rolled his eyes and smiled. 'Excuse my sisters,' he said. 'They're over the moon that I'm courting again after my wife. Who needs the jungle telegraph when the Bird sisters get going? They're very curious about you, Flossy.'

Flossy knew she had to ask the question. Being welcomed into the bosom of Tommy's warm and chaotic family life had been wonderful, and his sisters as gay and charming as could be, but there was one special person she was dying to meet.

'And your daughter?' she asked haltingly.

'She's upstairs in her bedroom, playing with her dollies. Mum thought it best I make sure we all feel comfortable with each other before I make the introductions.'

Tommy's face darkened as he gazed into the fire. 'Betsy's been through a lot, and, well, we're very protective of her. First she lost her mum; then I was called up; then she was evacuated out to Wales; and now of course she's returned to London. She doesn't know whether she's coming or going, poor little mite.'

'I can imagine,' Flossy murmured, knowing all too well what it was like to feel displaced. 'I really would love to meet her, Tommy,' she said. 'You two come as a package, after all.'

Tommy turned from the fire to face Flossy. 'I think I would like you to meet her too,' he replied. 'I know this is all happening fast, but, well, time's a luxury these days, and I don't want to waste a second of it.'

With that, he rose and opened the door. 'Mum, would you bring Betsy down?' he called.

Lucky and Peggy stood up too. 'I think we'll go and help your mum with tea,' Peggy said.

While she and Tommy waited, Flossy tried her hardest to contain her emotions, but a thousand thoughts swirled through her mind. Would Betsy like her, or would she think she was trying to take the place of her mother? Would she resent her for taking up her father's leave? She was still turning over the questions in her mind when the tiny figure of a little girl pelted across the kitchen and flung herself into Tommy's outstretched arms.

Flossy choked back a sob of emotion as she watched Betsy nestle into her father's embrace and bury her face into his white shirt. The little girl looked so tiny in his arms.

Tommy closed the parlour door behind them and sat down next to Flossy, stroking Betsy's pale blonde hair. Her hair gleamed like spun gold in the firelight, and pure paternal pride shone from Tommy's face.

'This nice lady is Flossy,' said Tommy. 'Do you want to say hello, sweetheart?'

The little girl shook her head and burrowed deeper into his arms.

'She's shy,' mouthed Tommy, over her head. 'Come on, love,' he coaxed. 'Flossy won't bite.'

Suddenly, Flossy remembered something she had in her bag.

'Betsy, I brought a friend for you,' Flossy said gently, pulling the rag doll Dolly had given her from her bag. 'A very dear friend from my sewing circle gave her to me years ago, and now I'd like you to have her. She's had a few knocks and she needs a little girl who can care for her.'

Wordlessly, Betsy peeked out from under her curtain of blonde hair, her curiosity overcoming her shyness. She was ever such a pretty little thing. A smattering of freckles covered her button nose, and her skin was sun-kissed from days out roaming the Welsh countryside, but her hazel eyes were guarded and watchful, unsure of who to trust. Flossy saw so much of her younger self in her.

'I think her place now is with you,' Flossy said.

A sticky little hand crept out and took the dolly. 'Please, miss, can I call her Dilys?'

'That's a Welsh name, you dafty,' exclaimed Tommy, ruffling her head. 'Why don't you give her a proper East End name?'

'I think Dilys is just perfect,' interjected Flossy quickly. 'And how clever you are, because it means "perfect and true" in Welsh.'

Her mind cast back to the memory of her old friend Lucy. The searing jealousy she had felt all those years ago when Lucy was fostered to begin a new life as Dilys in Wales no longer cut so deep. In its place, another, stronger emotion kindled.

Betsy relaxed at the compliment and wriggled off her father's lap. 'Can you help me make her a sister to play with?' she asked, holding the dolly to her cheek.

'Why, I'd love to,' Flossy replied.

'Now?' Betsy grinned, and Flossy couldn't hide her delight.

'I don't see why not, as long as your father doesn't mind.'

'Go right ahead. I'll just go and see how long tea's going to be,' he said, winking at Flossy.

Betsy and Flossy gazed curiously at one another. Flossy didn't yet know how much the little girl remembered of her mother, how much heartache she felt at then losing her father to sea and being sent away, but she could imagine.

'Are you going to be my new mummy?' the shy little girl asked.

Flossy patted the empty space next to her on the chaise, and cautiously, Betsy sat down next to her and gazed up, huge eyes unblinking in the firelight.

'I'm not sure yet, Betsy,' Flossy answered honestly. 'And I would never try to replace your mother, but I'm terribly fond of your daddy, and I would very much like us to be friends. I'd love to spend some time getting to know you a bit better. I could even visit you after your father goes back to sea. If you'd like, that is?'

Betsy held the dolly to her ear and listened intently. 'Dilys says yes, she would like that.'

'Splendid. You and Dilys can be the newest recruits in our sewing circle,' Flossy replied. And with those simple words, the two settled down to get to know one another.

When Tommy returned, he found the pair deep in conversation.

'Come on, chatterboxes,' he said with a delighted smile. 'Tea's ready. Mum's serving up.'

In the kitchen, Lucky and Peggy drained their mugs of tea and said their goodbyes before discreetly slipping away, leaving Flossy to take her place at the table, alongside Betsy and opposite Tommy. Surrounded by his vibrant family, all piling into plates of steaming-hot sausage and mash, gabbing away ten to the dozen, Flossy felt a peace wash over her.

In the eleven days since Dolly's funeral, Flossy had been

on a rollercoaster of emotions, and she felt as if she had buried not one but two mothers, and been on an earth-shattering journey of discovery. Her brutal start in life was not anywhere close to what she had imagined it had been, and it would still take time to come to terms with being a foundling, but at long last she knew who she was, and where she came from. The truth, no matter how unsavoury, was always preferable to uncertainty. Not that she could blame Dolly for trying to shield her from her heart-wrenching past. She had simply been trying to protect her.

But as for the future? The question that had always burned deep within was, 'To whom do I belong?' Gazing at Tommy now across the warm, crowded kitchen, Flossy realized she knew with a certainty. There were no more nerves or hesitation, just an instinctive feeling that she was in exactly the right place.

Tommy looked back at her through the steam curling off the plates and winked, a gesture that didn't go unnoticed by anyone, judging by the delighted nudges and smiles from the Bird sisters. But no one round that kitchen table felt more rapture than Flossy Brown at the simple gesture, for finally and unmistakably, she had found her place in the world. She had come home.

Flossy caught Tommy's mother's eye and the older woman reached over and patted her hand.

'Tuck in, gal. I baked us a nice big tray of bread-and-butter pudding for our sweet. How's that sound to you, darlin'?'

'Heavenly, Mrs Bird,' Flossy replied with a grateful smile. 'Just heavenly.'

Eighteen

8 JUNE 1941

Over the past six days of Tommy's shore leave, Flossy had fallen head over heels in love with not one but two people. Her handsome sailor was kinder and more tender-hearted than she could have ever dared to dream, but it was his shy daughter, Betsy, to whom she was inexplicably drawn. Perhaps it was because she understood a little of the girl's bewilderment at finding herself without a mother, but Flossy was clear on one thing. She did not want little Betsy to know a moment's fear or unhappiness. Little by little, she could sense the child was coming out of her shell and learning to trust her.

Flossy, Tommy and Betsy – and Dilys – spent as much time together as circumstances permitted, meeting at Tommy's house every evening after work. Tommy also foot-slogged the five-mile round trip from his home to Trout's every dinnertime too, just so he could spend an extra forty-five minutes with Flossy.

For the most part, the trio were happy to sit in Tommy's front parlour, with Flossy teaching Betsy to knit dollies, while Tommy looked on affectionately. With every stitch, the bond between them all deepened. Flossy had been deeply grateful to Peggy and May, and had taken them up on their kind offer to lodge with them, but she had spent that much time with Tommy and Betsy she had scarcely seen them.

On one occasion, when Tommy met up with some of his old pals, he had even allowed her to take Betsy to the picture house. Afterwards, over a sticky bun in a cafe, Flossy had learned that the little girl, in common with most shy people, had a razor-sharp sense of humour and was as bright as a button.

As Betsy had chattered about her life in Wales, Flossy had gazed back at her, drinking in her beauty and innocence. Well, not that innocent, as it transpired. Like most children, Betsy could also be a little mischievous! When Flossy had delivered her home later, she had found an irate Irene waiting for them on the doorstep. Little Betsy had swapped the contents of Nanny Bird's snuff pot with Irene's new face powder. No one had the heart to tell the elderly woman it was Max Factor she had snorted instead of snuff, but it had earned Betsy a clip round the ear. But Flossy hadn't chastised her. She hadn't wanted to quash the little girl's spirit.

When it had come time to say goodbye, Betsy had thrown her arms round Flossy and hugged her fiercely. That hug had been the icing on the cake of what had truly been the best six days of Flossy's life. The only blot on the horizon was that in just twenty-four hours Tommy was to rejoin HMS *Avenge* and sail off to God knows where, and Betsy would be sent back to her billet in Wales.

Sitting behind her machine at work, Flossy forced herself not to dwell on it, but the thought of being parted when the bonds were just starting to establish was agonizing. She needed Tommy and Betsy as much as she sensed they both needed her. War was indeed a cruel mistress, but this parting would be more bittersweet than most.

So lost in her own thoughts was she that she jumped a country mile when Vera tapped her on the shoulder.

'Telephone call for you, Flossy, in Mr Gladstone's office,' said the forelady curtly. 'Look lively.'

'A telephone call? For me? Are you quite sure?' she asked in astonishment.

'Do I look like I am in any doubt whatsoever?' the forelady snapped.

Flossy dared not answer back. Vera had been in a frightful mood all day, since discovering that young Kathy had been just thirteen when she started in the factory. Kathy had since turned fourteen, but this had not improved her mood. She did not like having the wool pulled over her eyes and had insisted on examining every worker's identity card to ensure everything was as it should be.

Inside, the foreman gestured to the shiny black Bakelite phone on his desk. Flossy had only used a telephone a handful of times and it felt large and clunky.

'Flossy Brown speaking,' she said timidly, clutching the receiver in both hands.

'Miss Brown. Audrey Braithwaite here,' boomed back the officious voice of her welfare worker down the crackly line.

Flossy swallowed uneasily. Mrs Braithwaite's heart was in the right place; the problem was, it was rather well concealed, and during her time at the home, Mrs Braithwaite had been more concerned with her moral welfare and sense of servitude than her emotional well-being.

An alarming thought struck her. Had Mrs Braithwaite

heard that she was stepping out with Tommy? She should really have informed her that she was meeting a man, even though nothing untoward had happened.

'Is everything all right, Mrs Braithwaite?' Flossy said, wondering why it was that she felt a strange compulsion to please the people she liked the least.

'Perfectly,' she replied. 'I have been receiving most satisfactory reports from Mrs Shadwell, who assures me you are a credit to the home and your work in the factory is exemplary. Your new landlady, Mrs Piper, has written to tell me you have settled in well to your new lodgings. I shall, of course, be paying the premises a visit to check we are satisfied that they are suitable. In fact, I shall be doing that sooner than I had originally planned, as I need to speak with you on a most urgent matter.

'I shall be in the metropolis tomorrow morning, and Mr Gladstone has already told me he can spare you for one hour, so I suggest we meet at your new lodgings at precisely ten a.m. and I shall explain the nature of my visit then. Good day to you.'

Flossy replaced the phone handle with a clatter.

'Everything all right, Flossy?' Archie enquired.

'I hope so,' she replied, her head in a whirl. 'Thank you for granting me time off to meet with my welfare worker,' she added. 'I promise to make up the time.'

'I know you will, gal,' he said, rubbing thoughtfully at his stubbled chin with a calloused hand. 'You ain't let me down so far. If you need me to speak for you, or if I can do anything at all to help, I'm always here. I must be going soft in my old age, but, well, I feel responsible for you, especially now Dolly's gone—' His gruff voice broke off and in dismay she could see the foreman was struggling not to cry.

'Sorry,' he said hoarsely, 'but Dolly was like family to me. I miss her smile, her singing, even her terrible jokes, but most of all I just miss having her about the place.'

He trumpeted loudly into a handkerchief and straightened up in his seat. 'Don't mind me. I'm just a silly old fool.'

Without saying a word, Flossy walked round to his side of the desk, slid her arm round the foreman's shoulder and squeezed him gently. 'Well, in that case you're a silly old fool that I'm terribly glad to have looking out for me,' she said.

'Bless you, darlin',' he replied, patting her arm with a sad smile. 'Bless you.'

Dolly's death had left deep ripples in all their lives, but it meant the world to have a gentleman as kind as Archie in her life.

The next morning, Flossy was as jumpy as a puppet on a string as she waited for Mrs Braithwaite's visit.

Peggy's mother had kindly rearranged her shifts so she could be with her when the welfare worker arrived, and Tommy had also insisted on being present, something Flossy wasn't entirely sure about.

'Are you sure this is a good idea, you being here, Tommy?' she muttered, shifting uneasily in her chair as they all stared at the ticking clock.

'More than sure,' he insisted. 'You said it yourself, they need to vet potential suitors, and, well, I'm here, ain't I? As of four this afternoon, I'll be back on board HMS *Avenge*, so the timing's perfect.'

'Please don't, Tommy,' she whispered. 'I can't bear to think of you going.'

Tommy reached over, took her hand in his and pressed it lightly to his lips. 'Look, Flossy, the future is certain for no one, but I want to do all I can to ensure *our* future together. That's why I want to meet this woman, assure her I am serious about you.'

'I think Tommy's right,' said May, as she poured boiling water into a teapot to warm through, before popping a red crocheted tea cosy on top. 'You have to show this lady that you wish to be together. Put on a united front.'

'Thanks, Mrs Piper,' smiled Flossy gratefully, as the older lady placed a plate of her good shortbread biscuits on the kitchen table.

'Or, as my grandmother used to say . . .' May remarked with a wistful smile, 'it's time to warm the teapot and follow your dreams.'

On the stroke of ten, there was a swift rap at the door, and May hurried to answer it.

'They always were a stickler for punctuality,' Flossy grinned ruefully to Tommy, as they both rose.

A second later, Mrs Braithwaite swept into the room and immediately started to cast her eye critically about the kitchen of the terrace.

'Sit down, won't you?' gestured May, refusing to be intimidated by the welfare worker. 'I think you'll find my home a most comfortable environment for Flossy.'

'Comfort should not come into it. I'll be the judge of what is suitable for my charge, Mrs Piper,' she replied crisply, neatly removing her coat and gloves as she sat down opposite Flossy. 'She is, after all, my responsibility until she reaches her majority.

'Now, then, Flossy, I'll get straight to the point,' she said, once all the introductions had been made. 'We had a visit recently at the home from a solicitor, executing the last will and testament of a . . .' she paused, unclipping her leather handbag and extracting a letter, which she scrutinized, 'a Miss Doolaney.'

'Dolly!' Flossy exclaimed.

'Correct. As we are acting *in loco parentis* for a minor, all legal correspondence must be seen by ourselves first. It would appear that this Miss Doolaney has been rather generous to you in her will and has left you her sewing machine.'

'Gracious!' Flossy said, remembering the beautiful black Singer with the ornate gold lettering that she had seen in Dolly's home.

'That's not all,' Mrs Braithwaite went on, raising one eyebrow slightly. 'She has also bequeathed to you an endowment policy, the sum of which is a hundred pounds, to be given to you when you turn twenty-one.'

'But that's a small fortune!' declared Flossy. 'How did she have that kind of money?'

'She had it in a post-office account into which she paid weekly sums from the age of twenty-one. I'm somewhat flabbergasted by this generosity. The solicitor will be in touch with you in due course to discuss the execution of this, but you should count yourself very lucky indeed.'

Flossy gulped in incredulity.

'This is a most useful sum of money, which will certainly secure your future,' Mrs Braithwaite went on, but Flossy had stopped listening. Dolly continued to shock and amaze her, even from beyond the grave. Who knew that Dolly was sitting on that kind of money?

'I will of course make a donation to the home,' Flossy said eventually, and the welfare worker smiled for the first time since entering the tiny terraced house. The smile never quite reached her eyes, Flossy noted, but she pressed on. 'But this will come in very handy, because, well, you see, myself and Tommy here, well—' Her voice broke off and she smiled at her beau. 'We've been stepping out, and we very much hope to have a future together.'

The announcement caused precisely the reaction Flossy had anticipated, and for the next hour at least, Mrs Braithwaite trawled over every aspect of poor Tommy's upbringing and prospects as a suitor, jotting down notes in her leather-bound notebook. Tommy answered patiently and politely, with May chipping in to testify as to his character wherever she could.

'I shall need to think on this, and of course we shall have to visit Mr Bird's home, Flossy,' she said, when she had finished her interrogation of Tommy. 'You are a wealthy woman in your own right now, and also somewhat young to consider becoming a mother to someone else's child. I mean to say, what do you know of the suitable way in which to raise a child?'

More than you might think, Flossy thought, but wisely kept it to herself.

'What, for example, does a child need in abundance?' Mrs Braithwaite trilled, looking at her expectantly over the rim of her teacup.

Flossy knew precisely what answer was expected of her.

She had had it drummed into her often enough at the home. Obedience, respect and discipline were the rules that had governed her upbringing, but to hell with the rules. Dolly and the East End's reaction to the bombings had taught her more about compassion in the last year of her life than she had learned in eighteen years from this woman.

Flossy straightened herself and, reaching over, threaded her fingers through Tommy's.

'I think, Mrs Braithwaite, with respect, that what Betsy needs is love, love and more love.'

Flossy returned to work with Mrs Braithwaite's assurances that she would be back for further vetting of Tommy ringing in her ears, but she didn't care. She knew that if Tommy and she could find a way to be together, then they would, no matter what the home made of it. This was 1941, after all, and the conventions of normal life no longer applied.

Tommy had vowed to stop at the factory to say his final goodbyes before he rejoined his crew, and even though he was going back to patrol the oceans – and that was a fact too terrifying for words – she had faith in him. If anyone could find a way back to her and his daughter's side, it was Tommy.

As she walked down Cambridge Heath Road, Flossy took in the hair salon where Dolly had taken her to get her hair set, then further down she passed the town hall, still standing proudly, nothing short of a miracle despite its many near misses.

For a second, she stopped outside the steps and cast her mind back to her meeting there with Dolly in her quest to find the truth about her start in life, which Dolly had, of course, known all along. Flossy shook her head, still shocked at the news of Dolly's generosity. All the while, Flossy had been working so hard delving into the past, while Dolly had quietly been securing her future.

Flossy continued her walk through Bethnal Green and felt the spirit of Dolly everywhere. In the smiles of war-weary housewives, in the queue of grateful punters outside Bethnal Green Museum – now converted to a rest centre and restaurant serving a thousand shilling meals a day – and in the gaggle of Boy Scouts delivering freshly filled sandbags to homes and businesses. Bethnal Green had already been a tightly knit place, but now the bombs had cemented the community to become even more rock solid in the face of fear.

When she neared St John Church, where they had first sheltered in the cavernous crypt, and the Underground opposite, where they had stormed to safety all those months ago, she spotted a less familiar sight. Some of Lucky's lads from the boxing club had cleared out the debris from a nearby bombsite and, using tools borrowed from the fire service, were busy transforming it into an allotment.

'Morning, boys,' she called out. 'What are you going to plant?'

'Potatoes, peas and cabbages, miss,' said the eldest boy, pausing to lean against his pitchfork.

'How enterprising,' Flossy replied.

'Dunno about that, miss,' the boy puffed, wiping his filthy face with an even filthier handkerchief, 'but the job's gotta be done, ain't it? Folk gotta eat.'

Flossy handed him a clean hanky from her pocket and smiled. It was a sight to warm even the hardest of hearts, and it proved to her that, despite being one of the most dangerous places on earth, there was nowhere else she would rather live. Little wonder Dolly had been so reluctant to leave Bethnal Green. The allotment boys' initiative also proved something else. Recovery was possible. Next spring, fresh shoots would grow from the ashes of that bombsite.

'Creating a new world out of the chaos of the old,' Flossy murmured.

'What's that, miss?' enquired the lad, as he spat on the clean hanky and scrubbed at his face.

'Nothing,' she replied with an enigmatic smile. 'Keep up the good work, boys.'

As she turned to continue her walk to Trout's, Flossy realized it was time to apply that motto to her own life, just like the women of Trout's and indeed every garment factory in the East End had.

Eighty tons of missiles and eleven thousand incendiary bombs had dropped on the borough, so Archie reckoned, but her fellow factory workers had not once crumbled under fire. They had simply thumbed their noses at adversity, rolled up their sleeves and got on with it.

By the time Flossy reached Trout's, clocked in and quickly set to work, the women were still getting on with it, while also belting out a rousing chorus of 'We'll Meet Again'.

At 3 p.m., Tommy set his kit bag down on the cobbled street outside Trout's, drew in the biggest breath of his life and called up to the fifth floor of the factory.

Distantly, Flossy heard her name being called over the din of the machines. Her head snapped up, and her foot flew off the treadle. She felt sick with apprehension. It was time. Tommy was leaving again.

Gulping deep in her throat, she put up her hand. 'Please, Mrs Shadwell. Permission to go and say goodbye to Tommy before he rejoins his crew. I'll make sure to stay late and make the time up for that and this morning.'

'I should think so,' replied the forelady. 'Ten minutes, no more.'

'Thank you, Mrs Shadwell,' Flossy gushed, and with that she leaped to her feet and virtually flew down the five concrete flights of steps. Outside, she flung herself into Tommy's outstretched arms.

'Whoa there,' he chuckled, his pale blue eyes shining with amusement. 'You nearly did me an injury.'

'Sorry,' she giggled. 'Although, that mightn't be so bad – at least it'd mean you would have to stay in London.'

Tommy's smile faltered. 'As much as I would love to stay right here by your side, Flossy, I couldn't ever. My crew-mates are relying on me, and my country needs me. We've gotta finish the job.'

'I know,' Flossy sighed, relishing the feel of his broad chest pressed against hers.

'Because you see, Flossy,' he went on, his voice dropping as he took her chin and gently tilted it up, 'I have to do my bit to make England a safer place for you and my little girl. I can't have her growing up under a rule of tyranny. This war has already cast too dark a shadow over her childhood. I'm going to apply to the Soldiers', Sailors' and Airmen's Family Association Fund to get my family rehomed in a safer billet, so Betsy can come home permanently.'

His jaw clenched and a vein twitched in his temple, as

he stared past Flossy to the arc of the sooty skyline. 'Nothing means more to me than giving my daughter a happy and peaceful future,' he choked, his gaze coming back to rest on hers.

'You're a wonderful father,' Flossy replied, 'and Betsy's a really terrific girl. I like her very much.'

'And she you. You've made a big impression on her. It's Flossy this, Flossy that. She's barely stopped chattering about you. It's the brightest I've seen her since her mother passed, and it matters a great deal to me that you and she get along . . .'

Tommy paused and cleared his throat nervously. 'Especially if you're going to be in my life permanently.'

Flossy froze, scarcely daring to breathe. When Tommy sank down to one knee on the cobbles, her hand flew to her mouth.

'I know this is sudden,' he said, taking both her hands in his, 'but who knows when I'll next get the chance? Flossy Brown, will you do me the very great honour of being not just my wife but also a mother to my little girl? I know this sounds soppy, but I think I knew I was in love with you the moment I read your first letter. Your honesty touched me, brought a part of me back to life that I thought had died forever with my wife, and now . . . well, I believe my place is with you.'

When he finished his speech, Tommy's hopeful eyes stared up at her, and for a moment, Flossy was rendered speechless.

'Well?' shouted a distant voice. 'Will yer?'

Flossy's eyes travelled five floors up to see that every window of Trout's had been thrown open and a jumble of hopeful faces were gazing down expectantly at them. Every single machinist in the factory was crowded round or hanging out of a window.

'Yes,' called down Peggy, squeezed in next to Lucky. 'Put the poor chap out of his misery, won't you?'

For a moment, Flossy felt awkward and timid, as the factory held its breath waiting for her reply. Suddenly, she heard Dolly's breathy voice chiming in her ear as clear as a bell. *Don't be afraid to shine.*

'Yes!' she heard herself shout back jubilantly, before turning to look her devoted fiancé in the eye.

'Yes, I will,' she said in a softer voice. 'Nothing would make me happier than being your wife and a mum to little Betsy. I know a thing or two about what it's like to grow up without a mum, and I promise you, Tommy, I will be the very best mother I can.'

And suddenly she was laughing and crying, the words spilling out of her unbidden. 'I want her to get dirty, talk loudly, suck gobstoppers, swing on gas lamps, and, oh, Tommy! I just want her to be seen, and heard, but more than anything, cherished.'

The tears were streaming down Flossy's face as Tommy rose to his feet and gathered her in his arms. Gently, he brushed away her tears with his thumb as he smiled down at her adoringly.

'Go on, then, lad!' hollered the voice of Pat from up above. 'Wotcha you waiting for? Give 'er a kiss.'

And with that, the sailor picked the seamstress clean off her feet. Flossy screamed in delight, until Tommy silenced her with a firm and loving kiss. The applause from the sewing circle was so thunderous a foreman from a neighbouring factory came to see what all the fuss was about.

Flossy still felt as if she was floating as high as the church steeple by the time she and Peggy reached home that evening after work. She could not wait to tell Mrs Piper her news, but when they neared her terrace, they saw that she was already waiting for them on the doorstep, clutching a telegram in her hand and looking pale. Peggy's mother was usually immaculately turned out and composed, but now rivulets of mascara were running down her ashen cheeks, and her hands were trembling as she clutched the door frame.

'Oh, please God, no!' Peggy shrieked, stopping in her tracks and leaning heavily on her stick for support.

'Father . . . ?'

'Yes . . .' May sobbed. 'But, darling, it's good news. He's alive . . . He's alive!' she said again as if she couldn't quite believe it. 'The authorities have freed him and he's coming home.'

Flossy choked back a sob as Peggy fell into her mother's arms and the pair clung to each other. And in a quiet corner of bomb-shattered Bethnal Green, for once, all was exactly as it should be.

Epilogue

On 1 January 1942, twenty-six governments from Allied countries signed the Declaration by United Nations, a new world organization, after America joined forces with Britain following the bombing of Pearl Harbor.

Meanwhile, in Bethnal Green, another, albeit smaller union was about to be made, but this one was to be a declaration of love. It had been seven months since Tommy's romantic proposal outside the factory, and now the day had come to pass.

True to her word, Mrs Braithwaite from the orphanage had returned, time and again, to grill both Flossy and Tommy's mother, before finally giving the home's permission for the pair to wed. A more welcome return had come in the form of Peggy's father from exile.

Mr Piper had said little about his time in the internment camp, preferring instead to focus on his family and aid the war effort on the Home Front, but there was no doubt that his treatment as a German civilian living in Britain served as a lesson in the virtues of tolerance to the Trout's girls. But weddings are about looking forward, not back, and as he stood in the porch outside St John Church, tall and dapper in a smart navy-blue herringbone utility suit, Flossy could see Peggy and her father were determined to put the pain of their separation behind them.

'Rationing may have stopped confetti, but I think Mother Nature's stepping in to help,' Mr Piper chuckled. 'You can always rely on the British weather.'

Soft snowflakes fluttered down from the skies above the churchyard, and they were already settling on the ground, painting the fire-scorched kerbsides a glittering white.

Up on the roof of the Salmon & Ball public house opposite stood a solitary fire-watcher, silhouetted against the pale sky, stoically and silently watching for the enemy.

'A white wedding. How pretty,' murmured Peggy, smiling adoringly up at him. She had been a different person since he had been released; joy and relief exuded from her, and Flossy realized this was the real Peggy.

'Not as pretty as you two,' smiled little Betsy, who looked a picture in her simple white smocked bridesmaid's dress embroidered with pink flowers, her fine blonde hair tied back from her freckled face with a dusky-pink ribbon.

'We have scrubbed up rather well, if I do say so myself,' said Peggy, reaching out to give Flossy's hand a reassuring squeeze.

A double wedding might not have been to everyone's taste, but to the girls, it made perfect sense. From the moment Lucky had formally asked Mr Piper's permission for his daughter's hand in marriage, they had all decided that sharing a wedding was ideal, not just because it helped to make a wartime wedding feel less austere, but because the girls had been through so much together. When Tommy discovered he was to get shore leave over the New Year, they had wasted no time in booking the wedding.

Flossy and Peggy had intended to visit legendary seamstress Hetty Dipple, who everyone in Bethnal Green went to, to have their bridal gowns made, but the Victory Knitters had stepped in and insisted on making the dresses as a wedding gift. And hadn't they ever done the girls proud! Goodness knows how they had done it, but thanks to some parachute silk and a hefty yard of resourcefulness, Flossy and Peggy were about to be spliced in the white dresses of their dreams.

The exquisite flowing gowns certainly made a change from their usual factory attire, and who was to know their veils were actually recycled pre-war petticoats?

Parachute silk was the most coveted material around, and Sal and Pat were staying tight-lipped about where it came from, but Flossy had an inkling that their good factory friends from Stepney, now machining parachutes for the army, might just have had something to do with it. Who knew, but the offcuts of silk had also extended to a pair of beautiful camiknickers, so no nasty passion-killer utility pants for the most important night of Flossy's life!

As East End tradition dictated, the Victory Knitters had sewn a single strand of all their hair into the hem, solidifying the girls' closeness to the factory sewing bee.

Thanks to the girls, Flossy also felt close to another very important influence in her life. She still was not able to think of her mother without feeling so many conflicting emotions. Loss and regret still filled her, but permeating the anger came another, purer emotion. Acceptance. Lucky was right. Who knew what life would have had in store for her had she remained at her destitute mother's side?

How any woman could willingly walk away from her eight-week-old baby with the knowledge she would never return was something that Flossy could not fathom, but standing on the church's doorstep, she knew she *must* forgive her mother. That is why she had finally told the girls about her start in life, and requested they sew her mother's calico heart into the lining of her wedding dress.

The delicate folds of material felt as light as air and silky-soft against her skin, and shivering slightly, Flossy realized her arms were covered in goosebumps. Was it the cold of standing in a snowy porch or the knowledge that her mother was with her in spirit on the most important day of her life?

'I feel like a princess, but golly, am I ever nervous,' she whispered, running a trembling hand round the circumference of her twenty-two-inch waist and exhaling slowly.

'There is nothing to be nervous about,' said Mr Piper. 'When there is love, Flossy, fear cannot exist. It is only the thought of this moment that kept me going during those long months in captivity.'

With that, he held his arm out to each girl as the opening chorus of 'Canon in D' by Johann Pachelbel began to drift back from inside the large church. 'And the fact that I get to walk not just one but two beautiful brides down the aisle doubles my joy. Now, shall we get you girls married?'

'Yes, let's,' replied Peggy, setting aside her stick in the porch and taking her father's arm.

'Are you sure you don't want the stick, darling?' he asked.

'Quite sure,' she replied. 'I vowed that if you made it

home alive, I would do this. Besides, I don't need a stick to hold on to: I've got you.'

The double doors swung open and the girls stepped, blinking nervously, into the church, followed by a very excited six-year-old bridesmaid. The congregation, bathed in candlelight, turned round, faces filled with joy and love.

The walk was slow, but it felt over in a heartbeat to Flossy. She registered nothing, not the emotional tears of the five Bird sisters, the Victory Knitters' beaming smiles, the hulking lads from Lucky's boxing club, desperately trying to hide any sign of emotion but failing, or Audrey Braithwaite from the home, sitting bolt upright in the pew with a stiff upper lip.

Sitting next to Dolly's mother and holding her hand supportively was Archie Gladstone. He blew loudly into his handkerchief as they passed him by, his twinkly blue eyes glistening with tears. 'God bless you, girls,' he mouthed.

It passed as if in a dream, for all Flossy really wanted was to see the look on her fiancé's face. Tommy and Lucky stood proudly by the altar, two strong, fine and upstanding young men, Tommy so handsome in his sailor's uniform, and Lucky dashing in a dark single-breasted, pinstriped suit and braces.

The sailor turned and caught sight of Flossy, his gaze softening, and he instinctively held out his hands to her and Betsy, his pale blue eyes burning with pride from beneath his sailor's cap.

In all her days, Flossy doubted anything would ever quite match the perfect joy of that moment.

Before the vicar commenced the service, he held his hands together in prayer and looked to the ceiling. 'Now, Mr Hitler, if you would be so kind as to allow me to conduct these proceedings with some peace and quiet, I'd be obliged to you.'

A ripple of laughter rang out round the church.

'You tell him, Rev!' hollered back the voice of Pat from the congregation.

There might have been no church bells ringing, on account of the war, but it didn't stop the guests from cheering to the heavens above when 'I do' had been said twice. Flossy Bird walked back up the aisle on her new husband's arm, followed by a beaming Mr and Mrs Johnstone, and two more radiant brides you would be hard pressed to find. No matter that the guests' buttonholes were fashioned out of garden foliage, or the cake waiting back at May's house was a fake, made of cardboard to comply with the Sugar (Restriction of Use) Order 1940. The look of love shining in the eyes of the seamstresses and their sweethearts was real. Optimism and hope for the future abounded. Virtually everything now, or so it seemed, was strictly rationed, except for love.

The moment that Flossy and Peggy married the sailor and the Home Guard hero in a double wedding had already gone down in Trout's history as one of their finest.

As the congregation spilt out into the snowy graveyard, Flossy found herself warmed through with hugs and kisses from the heartland of the East End.

The Victory Knitters were first to congratulate them, descending on the brides like a flock of brightly coloured birds. The girls hadn't let clothes rationing cramp their style and old clothing had been renovated and recycled with amazing ingenuity. In fact, all the guests had breathed new life into something old, or borrowed, which felt appropriate for a wedding, but it was the factory sewing bee who had done it with the most panache.

Vera's younger sister, Daisy, looked ravishing in a fitted hot-pink coat that hugged her curves and contrasted beautifully with her tumbling dark curls.

'Made my coat out of a candlewick bedspread, but don't tell no one,' she whispered breathily in Flossy's ear as she hugged her tightly. Flossy smiled back. Beautiful Daisy had just turned eighteen, and although she hadn't had any responses to her secret letters, Flossy suspected it wouldn't be long before she was snapped up by some lucky chap!

When Daisy moved aside, Sal stepped forward and embraced Flossy in a bone-crunching hug. She couldn't have looked more different to that infamous night when she led the protest on the Savoy Hotel in her factory pinny. Today, she looked more demure in a gay emerald-green suit, its collar trimmed with fur, although Flossy suspected her fighting days weren't over yet.

'That green is gorgeous with your red hair,' said Peggy admiringly.

'Nice, ain't it?' Sal grinned, pushing her tongue through the chip in her front tooth absent-mindedly. 'It's actually a velveteen coat I bought from Petticoat Lane two summers ago. I edged the collar with fur from the epaulettes.'

'Nice to have an excuse to dress up at last,' chipped in young Kathy, who had finally been forgiven by Vera for lying about her age and was looking very trim in a blue rayon crêpe dress with a gingham trim and a fur shrug. 'Made this frock out me nan's old tablecloth,' she announced proudly, twirling round in the snow.

'Well, I think we all look the business,' declared Pat, resplendent in a vast red wool cape, recycled out of a blanket.

'Congratulations, girls,' said Vera, awkwardly stepping forward in a sober grey wool suit and thick lisle stockings, gripping on to her leather handbag like it was a lifebuoy. Poor Vera, thought Flossy. Unlike her sister, out of the factory, the irascible forelady always looked ill at ease and unsure of her place.

'Thanks, Vera. You look lovely. Smashing rig-out,' said Peggy warmly.

''Ere, you wouldn't have said that when we first met you,' screeched Kathy.

'That's true, Kathy,' Peggy laughed. 'I must be a proper East Ender now.'

'Yep, you've certainly changed from the old Miss Snooty Knickers who first walked into Trout's,' Kathy replied, winking to show she was only teasing.

'Jokes aside, though, girls,' interjected Sal, looking round the group fondly, 'I reckon we've all changed this past year, showed the world our true colours.'

'How do you mean, Sal?' Flossy replied thoughtfully.

'I s'pose I just mean that I for one feel stronger. The Blitz showed me what I was capable of. Showed all women what we can truly achieve if we put our minds and our backs into it. Emancipation through bombs, who'd have thought it, eh?'

'E-man-ci-pation?' said Kathy, drawing the word out as she puzzled on it. 'What's that mean, then? Freedom from a man?'

'Something like that, Kath?' Sal smiled, putting her arm

round the young girl's shoulder. 'It means we can go our own way now . . . as man's equal.'

'This talk is all a bit fast for a wedding,' snapped Vera disapprovingly. 'We shan't dominate the brides' time any longer. Come now, girls,' she chivvied.

The girls moved off, and waiting behind them was Dolly's mother. As Peggy walked away discreetly to give them some time alone, Flossy felt her smile falter.

'Mrs Doolaney,' she said haltingly. 'I'm so glad you came.' She hadn't seen Dolly's mother since the wake, and she still looked ravaged by grief, even though she was clearly putting on a brave face. Flossy still didn't know how much she knew about her and Dolly's relationship.

'Congratulations, dearie,' she smiled shakily. 'You know, you were the daughter Dolly never had,' she whispered, and with that, Flossy realized she knew everything. 'And I felt her here today,' Mrs Doolaney added, placing a hand over her heart. 'She would have been so very proud of you.'

'I thought I only had the joy of knowing her for one year, Mrs Doolaney,' Flossy replied, clutching the older woman's hands in hers. 'But in reality she was in my life all along, and that brings me so much comfort now that she's no longer—'

She was interrupted by a triumphant-looking Lucky, standing on the top step of the church, his arm firmly clamped round Peggy's shoulder, every feature on his face radiating love. Dolly had been right: Lucky was utterly uninhibited in his devotion towards Peggy.

'Come on, then, let's be having you!' he boomed, his breath billowing into the frosty air. 'My beautiful wife's getting cold. All back to my mother-in-law's for a good old knees-up.'

'You will come, won't you?' urged Flossy to Mrs Doolaney.

'Thanks, love, but no. I still don't feel up to socializing much. I just wanted to see you get spliced in good heart. It's something I always secretly dreamed of for my Dolly. She would have loved today.'

'I know,' Flossy replied. 'And she will never be forgotten.'

*

Back at May's, the tiny terrace was packed to the rafters with revellers, and despite the cold, faces were already becoming flushed and the talk louder. Peggy took a moment to look around her in astonishment. Their neighbour the irrepressible Kate, whom Peggy had looked down on when she had first arrived in Bethnal Green, had rolled her piano onto the snowy street and was hammering out the tunes, and an impromptu conga line, led by Sal, was already snaking its way past her.

'Smashing do, Peggy,' Kathy grinned, as she congaed past.

'You don't think all this singing will alert the Huns,' said Ivy in a worried voice from behind.

'Nah,' Kathy called back, 'but if we have to go, at least we'll go happy!'

Peggy thought of her treatment of all these decent people when she had first joined Trout's and felt a fierce flash of shame. Thank goodness she had come to her senses. Her shame dissolved a moment later, when she spotted Flossy's rather forbidding-looking welfare worker, Audrey Braith-waite, pinned up against the trestle table by Pat, who had extracted a catering-size tin of Spam from her bag and placed it down on the table with a thud.

'Heavens to Betsy, wherever did you get that?' exclaimed Mrs Braithwaite.

'Ask me no questions and I'll tell you no lies,' Pat replied, tapping the side of her florid nose.

Peggy stifled a giggle; she'd wager the rather dour welfare worker had never been to a wedding quite like this before.

The finger buffet was a sight to behold. Alongside Pat's giant can of tinned meat were plates groaning with freshly baked sausage rolls, ham and tongue, salad and pickles, trifle and jellies, to be washed down with copious amounts of ale. The guests had done them proud and raided their larders and emptied their ration books to produce a feast fit for the King himself. This afternoon at least, they wouldn't go hungry. Little Betsy stood gazing at the spread as if the wonders of the world were spread out before her.

The men stood around somewhat more stiffly than the women, holding glasses of ale and gobbling back the pickled onions, and Peggy smiled as she looked at Lucky and her father, locked deep in conversation. Their voices drifted over to where she was standing.

'Have you heard about these new reforms that economist chap William Beveridge is investigating, Lucky?' her father questioned her husband. 'Churchill's asked him to look into a scheme that would build a safety net for the whole population. Family allowances, free health care and better housing for the poor, maternity leave and funeral grants

. . . Can you imagine if they actually manage to bring these reforms in?' he said passionately.

'I was listening to it being discussed on the wireless, sir,' Lucky replied, nodding sagely. 'And if it really does happen, it will be an incredible step forward. For the poverty in the East End to be wiped out would be beyond anything I could dream of. Decent folk deserve a brighter future. Over forty-three thousand people died in the Blitz, so I heard. So much loss and human suffering, but now the Yanks have joined us, it's sure to bring this war to a swifter end . . .' His voice trailed off as Peggy's mother, clutching a tray of potted meat sandwiches, walked up to them.

'Come, now,' she chided. 'No more talk of politics: today is a day of celebration. This is Flossy and Peggy's happy day.'

'Mrs Piper's right,' chipped in Archie, striding through from the scullery, clutching two dustbin lids in his hand. 'And if I'm not much mistaken, it is also New Year's Day, and tradition dictates we need to see out the old.'

The wedding guests cheered, and both front and back doors of the terrace were flung open, as Archie banged the dustbin lids together, waking Tommy's nan, who had been softly snoring in a chair in the corner, with a start.

'What's he doing?' Peggy shouted over the din to Flossy, who had joined her, clutching Betsy's hand.

'It's the East End way of seeing out the old year and welcoming in the new,' said Flossy.

'Fancy that,' Peggy replied. 'Well, I think we'll all be pleased to see the back of that year.'

Flossy nodded. 'Hear! hear!'

Archie placed down the bin lids and raised his glass in

a toast. 'Before I hand you over to the father of the bride, well, one of 'em, I'd just like to say a few words on Flossy's behalf.'

His voice might have been gruff, but Peggy knew a heart as soft as marshmallow beat inside that round little chest. A hush fell over the guests.

'Flossy joined us over a year and a half ago, and our much-loved and missed Dolly took her under her wing. She was like a little mouse when she started at Trout's, but our Doll saw something in her, and when I look at Flossy now, so beautiful and in love, well—' His voice broke off as he struggled to get his emotions back under control. 'She's a credit to the factory and I'm as proud of you as any father would be, love.'

Peggy had to gulp back tears as Flossy put down her drink and wrapped the rotund little foreman in an enormous hug that made him flush and had him fishing out his hand-kerchief once more.

'To Dolly Doolaney,' said Flossy, raising her glass.

'Dolly Doolaney,' came back a respectful chorus.

As the wedding party continued, Peggy offered up a silent prayer. Her family was reunited and complete, but so many others were suffering, and she prayed like never before that 1942 would see an end to this war. She prayed that machining khaki, rationing, danger and blackouts would fade from the memory, and in its place, bright, pretty things would return. Church bells on a Sunday, silk stockings, bananas, a hot soak in a full bath, planting hollyhocks instead of potatoes . . . She fervently prayed that pleasure and peace would blossom throughout the land one day, that all the joys that had passed into nostalgic memory would return.

But despite this longing, never had she felt so thankful for her lot. Peggy doubted there was anyone in the world happier than she.

*

By 10 p.m., Betsy was beat and Flossy tenderly carried her up the stairs and tucked her into Peggy's bed. She was asleep before her head even hit the pillow.

Carefully, Flossy arranged the quilt that the Victory Knitters had stitched for the sailors of HMS *Avenge* around her so she was snug, before leaning down to kiss her daughter on the forehead, her first act as a mother. The ship's captain had presented them with the quilt as a wedding gift and it was a lovely touch. Smiling wistfully, she traced her fingers in the shape of a heart over Tommy's name, stitched right next to hers. What a lovely memento of the way they met to treasure forever. It had been the perfect day, but as lovely as the ceremony and reception had been, what she was truly looking forward to was her future as Mrs Bird. She couldn't wait to move in now with Tommy's mother, nan, sisters and Betsy in their new lodgings in Hackney, and be a proper mother and wife at last.

As she watched the little girl dream, Flossy made a silent vow. Under her watch, Betsy would never know a minute's loneliness. Childhood was so vitally important and its freedom must be allowed to flourish. Her own had been curtailed by an institution, Dolly's by a protective love . . . Betsy would know nothing but contentment and joy.

Flossy checked the blackout blinds were securely drawn before lighting the tiny gas lamp by Betsy's bedside, casting her sweetly slumbering daughter in a golden glow. She made to leave, but she couldn't resist, and turning back, she kissed her ever so gently once more on the tip of her freckled nose.

'Sleep tight, my darling,' she murmured over the soft hiss of the gaslight.

Flossy tiptoed down the creaky stairs and found her husband standing outside on the pavement in the snow, smoking a cigarette with Peggy and Lucky. The smoky front-parlour windows were blacked out, but Flossy could hear the wedding party still going great guns inside. Someone had brought an accordion along and was playing it with gusto, and the shrieks of laughter and thudding of feet on the ageing wooden boards told Flossy the celebrations would go on for a while yet.

'Here's my beautiful wife,' said Tommy, reaching out to hook his arm round her shoulder. 'Betsy all right?'

Flossy nestled in close to his warm chest. 'Snug as a bug.'

'You're shivering,' he said, taking off his suit jacket and draping it round her.

Together, the newlyweds stared out at the deserted moonlit street, exhausted but happy as they watched the soft snow drift down and settle on the chimney pots.

'It's been the perfect day,' Flossy said at last, breaking the muffled silence. 'Did you see Mrs Braithwaite's face when Pat made her dance to "Knees Up, Mother Brown"?'

'Poor woman,' chuckled Lucky, pulling a giggling Peggy closer into his embrace. 'I thought she'd burst a gasket. Shouldn't think we'll see much of her round these parts now.'

'And what of you, Flossy?' Peggy enquired, twisting to face her. 'Will we see much of you around Trout's?'

'I'm afraid not,' she replied ruefully. 'Little Betsy needs me at home now. It'll be a stretch on only Tommy's wage, but that little girl desperately needs stability, as well as love, after everything she's been through.'

Flossy glanced up at the bedroom window behind which Betsy slept soundly before lowering her voice. 'I often used to wonder why some mothers in the East End refused to have their children evacuated; now I think I understand. I can't possibly send her away again.'

She turned to Tommy with a devoted smile. 'Rather, *we* can't send her away. I need to be the one to greet her at the school gate every day when it opens again, make her tea, help her with her homework and tuck her into bed each night, even if that bed is down the Underground. I want to be a proper mother.'

Flossy felt her heart leap. 'Gosh, doesn't that sound wonderful? Me, a mother!'

'Yes, it does sound rather wonderful. Very well, then, I'll forgive you for leaving,' Peggy acquiesced with a chuckle. 'But do say you'll come back to join in the sewing circle. Dolly would be mortified if you left!'

'Leave the Victory Knitters?' Flossy exclaimed. 'What do you think? Not on your nelly. I haven't just got my own husband's socks to darn. I've got a whole boatload now. Besides, I promised our newest recruit, Betsy, she could join in too.'

'Hopefully I'll be joining you in a life of domesticity soon,' said Peggy with a coy smile. 'Lucky and I are desperate to be parents, and, well, I know it's hardly the right time to be thinking of bringing a child into the world, but we don't want to wait. And now that Lucky's got a new job . . .'

'Have you?' exclaimed Flossy.

Lucky smiled bashfully. 'Yes. I was going to wait until after we got back from our honeymoon in Clacton before I said anything, but the head of the ARP was so impressed with my work throughout the Blitz he's recommended me to the town hall to run a new youth club for the boys from Russia Lane and some of the slums of Bethnal Green. He thinks I'd be the perfect man to supervise them and put them to use repairing bomb-damaged houses and turning the bombsites into allotments to grow food. They've already started it, but they need someone dedicated to it full-time. It'll help the area get back on its feet and keep the lads out of mischief.'

'Why, that's a wonderful idea, Lucky,' said Flossy. 'You're the perfect man for the job. Though I know Archie will be sad to lose you.'

'And I'll miss him, and all the girls at Trout's. But no disrespect, I feel with this new job, I'd really be making something of myself, and helping boys to feel pride in themselves too.'

'No one is prouder of you than me,' said Peggy, planting a big kiss on Lucky's cheek. 'Poor Vera, she won't take kindly to all these empty seats.'

'Don'cha worry about Vera,' said Lucky. 'She's got Archie wrapped round her little finger. He's so sweet on her I reckon he'd sit behind a machine himself if she told him.'

'Archie's sweet on Vera?' exclaimed Peggy. 'Never.'

'You mark my words, those two will end up married one day,' Lucky replied knowingly.

'I'm not sure about that,' Flossy interjected. 'But now that conscription for women has started, I shouldn't think she'll have much trouble staffing the factory. Plus I hear she has a new girl starting in the spring, a country girl by the name of Poppy Percival.'

'Fresh from the country?' remarked Peggy, arching one eyebrow as she cast her mind back to her own rocky start at Trout's. 'That'll be a baptism of fire for her, poor girl. As long as she doesn't impale her finger under the needle.'

'I don't know,' giggled Flossy. 'You're not a proper machinist until . . .'

'. . . you've got your thumb under the needle three times,' both girls chorused together, before doubling over with laugher.

'Come on, everyone,' said Tommy affectionately, opening the front door. 'We best get back inside. We're missing our own wedding here.'

As the snow blanketed the streets, whitewashing the ugly bombsites and craters in a fine white powder, the two young couples stepped back into the warmth.

No sooner had Tommy opened the door than the siren rang out through the moonlit night.

'Moaning Minnie . . .' Tommy groaned. 'I'll go fetch Betsy.'

'Looks like we're going to have to spend our first night as a married couple down the Tube,' Flossy said calmly, her fear long since replaced by resignation.

'Oh well,' remarked Archie cheerfully, as he walked out of the door carrying a plate of sandwiches under a tea towel, followed by a steady stream of wedding guests. 'Hurry up, everyone, and don't forget that accordion. I have a feeling this wedding party is about to get an awful lot bigger.'

And seventy feet below ground, love, life and celebration continued.

Author's Note

Last year, while I was in the process of writing this book, Britain celebrated the seventieth anniversary of Victory in Europe (VE) Day and four months later commemorated the seventy-fifth anniversary of the Blitz. Newspapers, radio and television were full of men and women recalling the momentous day when they learned that the war was finally at an end, and the devastation of the earlier bombings.

It got me thinking about the significance and power of memories and their place in our shared history. I'm not talking about the memories of politicians, celebrities or high-ranking soldiers, whose opinions seem to be the first canvassed on such anniversaries. What I'm interested in is the voice of the working-class woman on the street. After all, it was such women who bore the cold, hard brunt of the war.

During the course of researching *Secrets of the Sewing Bee*, I had the privilege of meeting many astonishing women who were kind enough to share their memories with me of living through the Blitz, funny, feisty firecrackers who inspired the characters of Dolly, Flossy, Peggy, Sal, Daisy and Vera.

These women are hidden in plain sight. I attended

many a tea dance, coffee morning, quiz night and bingo session in the East End of London and was always struck by how unassuming Britain's wartime Blitz survivors are and, in turn, how easy it is to overlook their sacrifices and triumphs.

Whenever I made such a visit, I invariably came away feeling surprised and humbled. *The unassuming silver-haired lady doing her crossword in a comfy chair?* Dug out the bodies of babies from a bombsite with her bare hands. *The sweet elderly lady in a powder-blue twinset tucking into sponge and custard round the communal dining table?* Slept on nearly every station platform on the Central Line for months after her home was blown up. *The woman fretting she may have accidentally taken a pencil home after last week's quiz?* Illegally broke into the Underground to protest against the lack of shelter.

The elderly seem to pale into invisibility as they age, yet the generation that survived the Blitz have the power to shock, move and amaze us each time they open their mouths.

Take my first meeting with Kathy. Nudging ninety and still line-dancing, this sprightly octogenarian told me in detail about her fears on the first night of the Blitz and her raw anguish at seeing the destruction of her community at the hands of the Luftwaffe. After the moving interview, I went to leave, but she called me back.

'I nearly forgot, love,' she said. 'I knitted you something.'

How sweet, I thought, as she took out something in soft white wool from her knitting bag; she's knitted something for my baby son. On closer examination, it turned out to be not a pair of baby booties but a willy-warmer! Kathy and her friend Vera took one look at my shocked face and fell about in raucous howls of laughter.

This always serves to remind me never to judge! Elderly women are rarely the doddery, sweet old ladies we at times perceive them to be. They are funny, fearless, robust and invariably full of incredible gems of wisdom and wit.

Their unique stories go on and on . . . Until they don't. Sadly, occasions like the seventy-fifth anniversary of the Blitz also mark a point where living memory starts to turn into history, and that is why these women's voices need to be heard more than ever. By the next significant anniversary, there will be no more reminiscing. It is so important that we listen.

There are insufficient words to express what a debt of gratitude we owe the women of Britain who saw their Home Front turn into a battlefront. They were called civilians, yet, in truth, they were soldiers.

The Blitz wrought unimaginable destruction but also bred great personal courage, strength, ingenuity and humour. Each of the women I interviewed recalls with astonishing clarity their 'Blitz story', the anecdote their mind automatically reaches for, even seventy-five years after the event. When pieced together, they make fascinating, and at times grimly humorous, reading, as well as proving that no one's war was the same. Here, in their own words, are their Blitz stories. Told without embellishment or sentiment, they are an extraordinary reminder to us all of the sacrifices of an entire generation.

Dolly, 95[*]

'I was a tormenting bugger and always got a kick out of needling my older sister. When the Blitz broke out, I was twenty and bored stiff of being cooped up underground in a stuffy Anderson shelter. I wanted to be out dancing and having fun, thank you very much. So being young and silly, I used to tease my sister something rotten, which drove her and my poor mum mad.

'One night, during a raid, she fumed, "I've had enough of you!" and stormed out to shelter underground at Columbia Buildings. Unfortunately, it was the same night a fifty-kilogram bomb whistled down the ventilation chute and exploded, killing fifty-eight people. Fortunately, my sister survived, but Mum told me in no uncertain terms that had she died, I'd have had her blood on my hands. Needless to say, I kept my mouth shut after that.

'As the war progressed, I got all sorts of jobs, from sewing army uniforms to making tyres for trucks, to filling bombs and bullets with gunpowder. After that, I was too tired to tease my sister.

'Looking back, it's us women who were the true heroes. It's us who deserved the medals. Six years we toiled, while the bombs dropped around us, risking our lives, working and raising families while the Home Front was turned into a war zone. My friend's brother came home on leave during the Blitz. He couldn't believe it. He couldn't wait to go back into the army.'

---

[*]   All ages correct at time of interview

Anne, 87

'I was born in Columbia Buildings, a huge Victorian pile in Bethnal Green, which Angela Burdett, a renowned philanthropist and friend of Charles Dickens, built to ease the East End housing crisis. I loved growing up there. Me and my thirteen siblings used to play with dozens of other kids in a communal play area outside.

'When the Blitz broke out, we used the vast underground public shelter beneath our buildings and the community continued underground. There was great entertainment: singing, piano-playing and so on.

'On the first night of the Blitz, in a million-to-one chance, a bomb went down the ventilation shaft – or, as we called it, the "apple chute" – which led down to the basement shelter, killing and injuring many. We were in the basement next door that night. I don't remember much about it. Noise, confusion, smoke and screams, then my mum rushing me away. My elder brother went to help. He picked up a baby and it literally fell apart in his arms. Such shocking scenes.

'The King came round soon after to visit. He was in his army uniform and I remember thinking how pale he was.

'As the Blitz went on, we all used to discuss it and say things like, "Is the moon out tonight? We'll cop it, I shouldn't wonder." We were very accepting of things and just got on with it.'

Gladys, 83

'An extraordinary thing happened two weeks after the Blitz broke out. I was a child living in Westminster when a great shout went up from outside my block of flats.

'A German Luftwaffe pilot had been shot down in nearby Victoria and had bailed out in his parachute, landing in Kennington.

'That pilot was pursued by a huge crowd of angry women wielding shovels, brushes, sticks and whatever weapons they could grab. They were hell-bent on annihilation.

'One woman reached him and hit him with her saucepan with an angry cry of "That's for my boy at Dunkirk." He got to his feet and tried to run, but his harness was too much for him. Suddenly, an army lorry drew up and half a dozen members of the Home Guard with fixed bayonets jumped out and forced a way through the crowd. They rescued the airman, and the last I saw of him was when, looking very battered, he climbed into the back of the lorry.

'You have to understand how much we hated them. Our anger was very real and very raw. The Germans started it, but we sure as hell finished it.'

Dorothea, deceased

'The Blitz was chilling. I remember pushing my baby along Oxford Street in her pram when the alarms sounded. That was a sound that made your blood run cold. Just for a split second, everyone would stop and look around, to see what everyone *else* is going to do. And then you ran . . . You just hoped you'd reach the safety of a shelter.

'Anyway, as I said, the siren went, I stopped, just for a moment, and there was a man walking towards me, from behind, going in the same direction. I didn't know him, but everyone took concern for everybody in those days. He looked at me with my pram and shouted, "Run and get your kiddies safe. I am right behind—" He didn't finish the sentence, because at that precise moment, a bomb dropped in another street, but the blast sent terrible shock waves right across where we were standing! I heard a bang, a whoosh and a whistling sound, and instinctively ducked as the plate-glass window was blown out of the shop we were opposite. It missed me, went over the top of my pram and sliced the man horizontally in two! For a second, he remained upright in one piece, but as he fell, the two halves of his body separated and then I couldn't look anymore. I just ran all the way home in tears, oblivious to everything around me, and promptly got told off by my mother for not going to shelter!'

Pat, 88

'How I used to love my job as a machinist at the Rego in Curtain Road, Shoreditch. It wasn't just a job; it was a rite of passage. The East End's own finishing school! All the girls singing in great lines, standing around giggling, smoking and plucking each other's eyebrows on tea breaks. You've never seen the like!

'Then the bombs started and everything changed. One

time I was sitting at my workbench machining when the entire front of the building blew off and just slid onto the pavement in a great cloud of dust. We were so shocked we sat staring at the passers-by in the street from behind our machines.

'During the war, you never knew who would be there the next morning. Quite often you'd come in to find empty seats where women had been killed or bombed out. They were very sad times, but despite this, by God we took the war on!'

Gladys, 86

'When the Blitz broke out, I was thirteen. There was no adequate shelter in the East End, so civilians took over the Tubes. What choice did they have? They were getting bombed night after night. Not having a safe place was soul-destroying. No one was trying to break the law; it was simply a case of do or die. Self-preservation, really.

'To begin with, until it was properly fitted out, Bethnal Green Tube was hellish – concrete, bare boards, cold; it was a building site, really, and I was terrified. You had to start filing down the concrete steps from about five p.m., to mark your spot. But at least you couldn't hear the bombs, and the camaraderie was terrific, everyone laughing, joking, eating their dinners and singing. On Sundays, the Salvation Army used to come down and play music up and down the platform.

'We caught everything going down there: scabies, head lice, you name it. You couldn't take proper baths. Occasionally we'd go to York Hall Baths in Bethnal Green and pay sixpence for a wash. You'd have an individual cubicle and shout, "More hot water in number six!" to the lady attendant. Despite this, you were never really clean during the Blitz. As it waged on, we tried more stations, from Liverpool Station right up to Oxford Circus. I must have slept on every platform on the Central Line!'

Dee, 89

'I wouldn't have missed the Blitz for anything. Perhaps because I was young and full of spirit and youthful bravado, but it all felt like a great big adventure to me. I loved the camaraderie, the sense of us against them. I was working as a typist in a City firm at the time but living in the East End.

'At the end of every day, the boss would make us lug our typewriters down to the basement in case they got damaged overnight in a raid! Great big heavy things, they were. I got thoroughly sick of lugging this thing about, especially when I should have been making my way home to the safety of a shelter. I didn't want to get killed because I'd been looking after someone else's office equipment, so one day, I stood up to him and refused. "It's their typewriters, not ours," I told the office girls in a great gesture of defiance. The boss sacked me! That experience taught me to stand up for myself in life.'

Dot, 89

'One shouldn't laugh, but there were some, albeit unintentional, funny moments during the Blitz. I was fourteen and working in a garment factory in Hackney at the time. Every night, I sheltered in a huge basement under a school near my home in Bethnal Green.

'One evening coming home from work, myself and my mum and dad got caught short when the sirens went off, so we dived into the nearest brick street shelter.

'The wail of the siren sounded just as loud inside as it had done on the street. Puzzled, I looked up and my mouth dropped open.

"Here, Mum," I said. "Fat lot of good this shelter is. It's got no roof!"

'Mum put her head in her hands, but it made me laugh.

'The school basement shelter was much safer. Well, it had a roof at least! The shelter warden there was called Jack. Poor chap was so bow-legged he couldn't have caught a pig in a passage. God knows how but he managed to make it up on the school roof each night for fire-watching duties.

'I still remember sitting down in that shelter Christmas 1940, singing "Silent Night" with some visiting curates, with the bombs crashing down all around us, and my friend and I trying to stifle our giggles. Looking back, humour was our best weapon for survival.'

Vi, 78

'The Blitz gave me a passport to a better life. I was only little, so when the bombs started, I was evacuated out to the countryside, away from my two brothers and seamstress mother. It was glorious. I lived with an elderly widower who doted on me. I had my own bedroom overlooking lush green fields, slept on snowy-white sheets, ate fresh food, went to the village school and roamed the countryside. I didn't even mind having to attend church three times on a Sunday.

'Then the war ended and I had to go home. Talk about a shock. Mum did her best, but it was hard for her, as she was a single mother who had to scrape for every penny. Our new home was a filthy, rat-infested hovel behind the Barbican – three rooms in the basement of a bomb-shattered building.

'"Who are those filthy boys?" I asked Mum.

'"Cheeky cow!" she shrieked. "They're your brothers."

'My new bedroom looked out on a rickety iron fire escape into a dark, narrow yard where everyone slung their rubbish. It was all a far cry from my country home.

'Life was a grind, and there was never enough coal for the fire or food for the pot, just scrag-ends of meat that Mum cooked up into a stew. Mum had to go out to work to support us, so me and my brothers would roam the bombsites, getting into mischief.

'One time, we couldn't believe it when we found a big white rabbit in a deserted building. We took him home and named him Jiminy Cricket. I adored that rabbit and for months I fed him every last scrap of food I could find.

'Then at Christmas, he went missing. Turned out, Mum had taken him to the butcher's, where she'd had him slaughtered. She served Jiminy up for Christmas lunch! She hadn't meant to be cruel, just practical, but I sobbed all through Christmas Day. People today don't know the half of it.'

Len, 89

'Do you know who the real heroes of the Blitz were? The mothers of the East End! Night after night they sat there being bombed, but they had no weapons to defend themselves or their children, no rifles with which to fire back or grenades to throw. Nightly they hid from the bombs; then each morning they had to get up and care for children or clock on to work. It was business as usual, see.

'Me, I was just a skinny fourteen-year-old boy, working as an apprentice cabinetmaker on Brick Lane when the bombs started to drop.

'The Blitz was the happiest time of my life. From about six or seven p.m. onwards, you'd hear the drone of the enemy planes, the sirens would start up, and off we'd go. Everyone would muck in together, no matter if you were a millionaire or a skinny cockney kid in tatty trousers like me. Money and status don't matter when you could be dead in the morning. For the first time ever, society was on a level pegging and I felt equal.

'There were hard times, though, of course. A bomb landed near my buildings in Russia Lane and I ended up digging out people I knew from a brick shelter that had been hit. Terrible, it was, seeing the look on the faces of the dead people I pulled out. They weren't safe in that brick shelter: the concrete ceiling had caved in and flattened them. I broke down and cried my eyes out at the sight of them, but the next day, I got on with it. I tell you what, though, I swore after that not to use the street shelters. I took my chances and stayed out in the open, dodging shrapnel.

'Four years later, I turned eighteen, got called up and

went straight into active service in the last year of the war in the Far East. I saw some sights there in the jungles that no man should ever have to witness, but it was the unique camaraderie of the Blitz I shall always choose to remember.'

Glad, 79

'My wonderful mum did an amazing job of hiding her fear from me and my six siblings during the Blitz. She raised seven children in Poplar by the docks, the worst-hit area. Mum did have us evacuated, but she missed us too much, so we came home. She used to calmly usher us all to the nearest street shelter after the sirens went off. God knows how she did it on her own with seven kids!

'I remember her once in the shelters reading us bedtime stories to try and drown out the thump of bombs. When the bombs got louder, her fingers would curl round the spine of the book, gripping it tighter and tighter until her fingers were blood red. That's the only way her nerves betrayed her.'

Kay, 93

'I was eighteen when the Blitz broke out and went from dressmaking to working as a WAAF on ambulance duty, ferrying bomb casualties to hospital.

'One night was particularly bad for fires. Even the fire hoses were burning. We were sent on a job to a point high up above London with sweeping views, and oh my, the scenes! The whole of London was on fire; countless churches and all the spires were blazing! Then the all–clear went. Suddenly, there was a terrific clap of thunder and fingers of lightning lit up the sky. Rain came down in buckets, drenching the fires, and in no time we were soaking and racing back to the ambulances. It felt like divine intervention.

'"Now we'll see what God can do," said a man from the good old Salvation Army to me and my colleague Joan.

'Joan was killed soon after that night. One minute she was working right by my side and we were talking; the next moment I turned around and she was dead on the floor with barely a mark on her. A piece of flying shrapnel had caught her in the neck. The tragedy is, she had only been married a few weeks when her husband, a pilot in the RAF, had been shot down and killed during the Battle of Britain, and now she too was dead. I didn't have time to grieve for her or dwell on the dangers; I just had to get on with things. Seventy-five years on, though, I still think of Joan. I'll never forget her. She was such a beautiful young woman, with turquoise eyes and gorgeous auburn hair, and so full of fun and mischief. We were together right from the start of the war, and I treasured our friendship. After the war ended, I developed a motto which I've lived my life by ever since: "You can't please everybody, so you may as well please yourself."'

Vera, 88

'I was thirteen when the bombs started to drop. My dad wasn't prepared to sit around and wait to be killed. He had a car-hire business, renting out a Daimler, so we used to drive it to Epping Forest each night and sleep in the woods.

'One morning, we returned to find our house was the only one still standing in the street. A parachute bomb had dropped, and God knows how, but ours had survived. It devastated our vibrant neighbourhood, though. Before, our streets were full of kids, playing whip and top or hopscotch, and every doorstep was gleaming. The mothers on that street took such a fierce pride in their homes, and the street was like a village. The community was decimated by the Blitz. I never saw my friends again.

'I visited the street many years later, in the seventies, and was saddened to see it had been turned into a big, faceless, high-rise council estate. The Blitz changed the face of the East End.'

Vera, 86

'Jerry had a ball in the Blitz. On the first night they bombed the docks, Black Saturday, I remember going up to the top of the block of flats I lived in with Mum, Dad, seven siblings, dogs, cats, chicken and ducks. Great columns of smoke were billowing up into the skies from the docks, and a ring of fire surrounded us. I remember feeling absolutely terrified. It was the first time I'd felt fear in my life.

'Mum refused to evacuate me. She wanted me where she could see me, and I didn't want to live with strangers. I worshipped my mum – as long as I was by her side, I knew I would always be protected.

'My sixteen-year-old brother worked as a messenger. He'd finish work in the factories at six; then he'd spend the night cycling round the East End, dodging bombs and delivering messages to fire crews where larger vehicles couldn't get through. I don't think he slept for eight months!

'Everyone who stayed and defended London was a true hero. Apart from the villains, that is. No one talks about them much, but there were certain men in the East End who used to pretend to be wardens and then would go in and plunder from bombsites, taking gold rings from the fingers of dead women. It was disgusting. Not that you dared say anything, mind. You'd end up with a nail through your hand.'

Ray, 81

'I was seven when the Blitz broke out and we used to shelter underground at Bethnal Green Tube. We even spent Christmas seventy feet below ground. Dad put a Christmas tree by the bottom of the escalators, and all the kids sang carols and each received one tiny present.

'The adults tried hard to make it nice, playing the accordion and singing songs, but despite this, I hated living underground. We never got a bunk and it used to reek of Jeyes disinfectant. I can still smell it now in my nostrils.

'They were very frightening times. In the morning, we would emerge blinking into the light and make our way to school, past the freshly smoking houses. No one expected to live until tomorrow.

'People reading this might wonder why my mother never had me evacuated to the safety of the countryside. I must have been five or six when I overheard her talking to a neighbour over the back wall.

'"My Ray stays here," she said. "That way, if we die, we all die together."

'That really stuck in my mind and I never forgot it.'

Pat, 86

'We loved sleeping at Bethnal Green Tube. It was like a little village underground, a sanctuary after the street shelters. You couldn't hear the bombs and we had peace for the first time.

'I used to borrow *Milly-Molly-Mandy* from the library and take free tap-dancing lessons. Us kids all used to hang out together in great packs, roaming for miles up and down the tunnels. It was great exercise, and our parents never worried about us down there.

'I remember watching a wonderful baritone singer in the theatre one night. He sang in Russian and I had never heard anything like it. I was entranced and it sparked a lifelong love of music. Sheltering underground really opened my eyes to another way of life. You never had time to be bored, and I never saw anyone miserable, ever.

'They had electric lighting, which at about eleven p.m. was dimmed and everyone quietened down for the night. There was never any trouble and I slept snug as a bug in a rug.'

Peggy, 86

'It's a miracle I'm alive. My dad worked as an ARP warden, and after seeing the deaths of so many at the Columbia

Buildings tragedy on the first night of the Blitz, he was convinced the shelters weren't safe.

'"We're stopping here," he said, and so for the duration of the Blitz, I slept under the kitchen table with Mum, Dad and my sister.

'We were bombed senseless every night for eight months. Strangely, I don't remember feeling that scared. As long as I had my mum and dad there, I felt I would be all right.'

Emily, 88

'I have never felt such heart-stopping terror in all my life as I did during the Blitz and I'm not ashamed to admit it. Centuries-old houses offered no protection.

'There was no room in our tiny backyard for an Anderson shelter, so we used to share with the family that lived at the back of us. To me, the pulsating throb of the enemy aircraft overhead sounded as if they were saying, "For you . . . For you . . . For you . . ."

'I still feel the heart-gripping fear now if I stop to think about it. I don't care what anyone says, they were terrible, terrible times.'

Sally, 89

'I know I shouldn't say it, but I enjoyed the war years because you met up with people and there was a different kind of freedom. I missed it when it was over!

'The whole community drew together and lived as one, and it brought out the best in people. We thrived in the East End because we are resourceful and stoic. We never stopped to think about it too much. We would never have been able to cope if we had dwelled on our misfortune.

'There were some weird moments, though. One particularly bad night of bombing, I couldn't resist and I stepped out the brick shelter we were in. A bomb dropped nearby and the building opposite literally lifted up in the air and the bricks came apart, vibrated and expanded, like you see in cartoons, before coming back together. It was astonishing. I'd never seen a building jump before.

'I got in such trouble from the warden.

'"Aren't you afraid?" he said.

'"No," I replied, honestly.

I was fifteen or sixteen, and drawn to excitement and adventure. What did I care about personal safety back then? That building is still standing now, and seventy-five years on, I walk past it and wonder how on earth it didn't collapse.'

Babs, 83

'Me, my mum and my sister, Jean, evacuated to Torquay when the Blitz began. We hadn't been there long when we decided to have a walk on the beach. Two planes came out of nowhere and flew down low over the beach.

'"Look, Jean, what are those funny sparks coming out of them?" I said to my sister.

'"They aren't sparks; they're bullets," Mum shouted over the roar of the engines, as she pushed us down onto the sand.

'Turns out they were two German Messerschmitt planes and they were machine-gunning everyone on the beach.

'"Sod that," remarked Mum, as she picked herself up. "We'll be safer off back in the East End." So back to London it was.

'Back in Bethnal Green, I was so proud to have finally been entrusted by Mum with my own front-door key. I felt so grown-up and spent the whole night in the shelter boasting to my mates. I couldn't believe it when I got home and found our front door had only been blown off! Strange times.'

Nell, 90

'I was sixteen when the Blitz broke out and I worked right the way through it. My job was as a seamstress earning twelve shillings a week at a factory in Bethnal Green, sewing the netting into ARP helmets and the lining into sailors' hats.

'I was living in what was then rural countryside in Dagenham. It's astonishing when you think about it. I had to take a blacked-out train into the heart of the bomb-shattered East End, and leave again each night, just as the raiders were returning. I was a sitting duck, really, on the District Line!

'I'm sure my mum worried about me when she packed me off each morning with my corned-beef-and-Daddies-sauce sandwich, but she had no choice. We needed the money.

'Tragically, my mother died just after the Blitz, and as I was the oldest girl, I had no choice but to leave my factory job to care for my younger brothers and sisters. My father was having an affair with another woman by then, and they certainly weren't going to do it.

'It was hard. I missed Mum and my job, and the responsibility fell squarely on my shoulders. No dancing up a storm up West with American GIs for me. Just hard graft and sacrifice.'

Kathy, 88

'It sounds mad, like, but we had a good time during the war. We didn't wait for someone to entertain us; we entertained them! During the raids, we would head down the crypt at St John Church in Bethnal Green and we would have enormous sing-songs. There would always be a fella down there with an accordion and everyone would join in. I never once felt fear.

'Churchill and the King were around the East End lots during the Blitz to raise morale, but I didn't need my morale raising, thank you very much!'

National Service Act

The Blitz officially began on 7 September 1940 and lasted until 11 May 1941. In that time, over a million houses were destroyed and damaged in London, and 43,000 people nationwide were killed. Seven months later, the second National Service Act was passed, introducing conscription for women. All unmarried women and all childless widows between the ages of twenty and thirty could now be set to work for the wider good of the war effort.

Lust, Lies and Law-Breakers – The Secret History of the Blitz Revealed

The Blitz was a time of terror and misery. Almost one hundred thousand people were killed or seriously injured over eight and a half months of brutal enemy action. For those directly affected, the Blitz started and ended there, a period of unremitting darkness.

For others, however, the Blitz was a time of possibilities. Shocked out of their rhythms by fear and necessity, ordinary people pulled together and helped strangers. They spoke to each other for the first time. They found common ground amidst the chaos where none had existed before. And at the same time, they broke rules and exploited each other. They were selfish in ways they could barely have imagined. People behaved very well – and they behaved very badly.

The Blitz, after all, was a time of extremes. Extremes of experience, extremes of behaviour, extremes of reaction. In every possible direction. Take the case of Ida Rodway. Ida was an ordinary law-abiding woman in her late sixties from East London. In early October 1940, she went to fetch her blind husband, Joseph, his morning cup of tea. But as the water boiled, Ida changed her mind. She picked up an axe and a carving knife instead. Returning to her husband, she attacked him with the axe. It quickly broke. So she slit his throat with the knife.

Ida was a devoted wife. Joseph's brother never remembered the couple exchanging a harsh word. But they were as truly victims of the Blitz as anybody killed by an aerial mine or a high-explosive bomb. In September, they had been bombed out of their Hackney home, and after several days in hospital had begun sleeping on Ida's sister's floor. Joseph's mental state was deteriorating and he rarely knew where he was. They were about to lose their labour money and Ida had no idea how or where they were going to live, or what to do about the bombed house that still contained all their possessions. Hopeless, helpless and overwhelmed, she did what she considered to be the kindest thing for her husband. Charged with murder, she was found unfit to plead at the Old Bailey, and committed to Broadmoor where she died a few years later.

This was truly a crime of the Blitz. Yet the extremes of the period had other, more positive, effects. They changed the attitudes and expectations of Britain's citizens. And as expectations altered, the fight against Nazism became intertwined with the fight for a better future. Women, for example, were encouraged to step outside the home, to become independent, to contribute actively to the war effort. Yes, they were paid less than men to do their widely varying work. Yes, they were still required to run the home. And yes, when it was all over, they were expected to step aside and allow the men to replace them. But for the duration, their lives opened up in extraordinary ways.

Sexually, too, attitudes and behaviours shifted. In her diary on 7 September 1940 – the date on which the daytime bombing of London began – nineteen-year-old Joan Wyndham wrote, 'As the opposite of death is life, I think I shall get seduced by Rupert.' As good as her word, she went to bed with her boyfriend. 'If that's really all there is to it, I'd rather have a good smoke,' she told her diary afterwards. But disappointing or not, her experience was not unusual. Many people had love affairs they would not have had before the war. These ranged from isolated experiences to 'wartime marriages', liaisons intended to last for the duration before being dropped – the sexual equivalent, perhaps, of powdered egg.

Many of the freedoms and attitudes that we nowadays take for granted were forged in the Blitz's dark crucible. The country owes a far larger debt to the period than has been acknowledged. This was the time when the vulnerable in society began to be protected, when a sense of collective responsibility began to form, when plans were first laid for a National Health Service and an Education Act offering free secondary education to all. It was the period when a War Aims Cabinet Committee, composed mainly of Conservatives, delivered a paper declaring that economic, social and educational practices would, in future, have to be overhauled in order to secure a reasonable standard of life for the entire population. The Blitz was certainly a time of misery – but it was also a time when attitudes and behaviours changed. And it was a time when the sacrifices made by ordinary British people began to tilt the balance of society in their favour. For better or for worse – depending on one's point of view – we have been living with the consequences ever since.

By Joshua Levine, author of *The Secret History of the Blitz*, Simon & Schuster UK

(30 July 2015)

I really hope you have enjoyed *Secrets of the Sewing Bee*. I'd love to hear your thoughts. If you would like to get in touch with memories, suggestions or simply to say hello, my Facebook site is www.facebook.com/KateThompsonAuthor.

I'm also on Twitter on @katethompson380 or @Singer Secrets, or you can visit www.katethompsonmedia.co.uk, or email katethompson380@hotmail.com.

Acknowledgements

With grateful thanks to:

My inspiring and hard-working agents, Diane Banks and Kate Burke. My super-supportive and lovely editors at Pan Macmillan, Caroline Hogg and Victoria Hughes-Williams, both such a dream to work with, along with all the other talented folk at Macmillan, including Eloise Wood, Natasha Harding and Lauren Welch.

I am by no means an expert on many of the subjects covered in this book, but fortunately others are, and were only to happy to share their expertise and take time to proofread my words:

Author and broadcaster Joshua Levine, for his unfailing enthusiasm in answering my questions on the Blitz.

Alf Morris for showing me where he slept in the Underground as a boy; Derek Spicer, my Bethnal Green tour guide; and Sandra Scotting for pie, mash and East End expertise.

Legendary one-hundred-year-old communist and anti-fascist campaigner Max Levitas from Whitechapel, East London, who brought to life for me with such passion the desperate plight of the working classes during the Blitz, and how he and his fellow communist campaigners helped take over the Savoy shelter during an air raid to protest against the closure of the Tubes. A truly remarkable man. Thank you, Max, and congratulations on reaching a hundred! A more detailed account of this event, lead by communist councillor Phil Piratin is held at the Imperial War Museum in London.

Richard Meunier, archivist and curator at the Royal London Hospital, Barts Hospital Trust Archives, for his help in researching rheumatic heart disease, and Dr John Ford and Dr Chris Evans, medical historians, for answering my many questions.

Terri Coates, consultant midwife on *Call the Midwife*, for being such a stickler for period detail.

Corinne Bradd from *Sew* magazine.

Martine King, archive manager at Barnardo's, for her help in researching children's homes.

Matthew McMurray, archivist at Royal Voluntary Service, for his help in researching the Women's Voluntary Services (WVS).

Emmy Tither, library and archives assistant at the Bishopsgate Institute.

Jennifer Daley, historical researcher, for her expertise on the Second World War.

Malcolm at Tower Hamlets Local History Library & Archives for his unbeatable local knowledge.

Vicky Harrison from St Hilda's East Community Centre in Club Row, East London, and all the other Tower Hamlets organizations who have kindly allowed me to come and gatecrash their community groups.

Further Reading

Books and sources I have found helpful:

Women at the Ready: the Remarkable Story of the Women's Voluntary Services, Patricia and Robert Malcolmson (Little, Brown, 2013)

How We Lived Then: a History of Everyday Life During the Second World War, Norman Longmate (edition used: Arrow Books, 1977)

Journey Through a Small Planet, Emanuel Litvinoff (Michael Joseph, 1972)

Family and Kinship in East London, Michael Young and Peter Willmott (Routledge & Kegan Paul, 1957)

An East End Farewell, Yvette Venables (Simon & Schuster, 2015)

A Working-Class War: Tales from Two Families, Jess Steele (ed.), interviews by Joy Vaughan and Rib Davis (Deptford Forum Publishing, 1995)

Keep Smiling Through: Home Front 1939–45, Susan Briggs (BCA, 1975)

Nella Last's War: the Second World War Diaries of 'Housewife, 49', Richard Broad and Suzie Fleming (Sphere, 1983)

Millions Like Us, Virginia Nicholson (Penguin, 2012)

Women in Green: the Story of the W.V.S. in Wartime, Charles Graves (Heinemann, 1948)

Forgotten Voices of the Blitz and the Battle for Britain, Joshua Levine (Ebury Press, 2007)

Living Through the Blitz, Tom Harrisson (Penguin, 1990)

The Blitz: the British Under Attack, Juliet Gardiner (Harper Collins, 2011)

London's War: the Shelter Drawings of Henry Moore, Julian Andrews (Lund Humphries Publishers, 2002)

'Bethnal Green's Ordeal 1939–45', George F. Vale (Council of London Borough of Bethnal Green, 1945), pamphlet held at Tower Hamlets Local History Library & Archives

Fashion on the Ration: Style in the Second World War, Juliet Summers (Profile Books in association with the Imperial War Museum, 2015)

Knitting America: A Glorious Heritage from Warm Socks to High Art, Susan M. Strawn (Voyager Press, 2011)

If you enjoyed
Secrets of the Sewing Bee,
then you'll love
Secrets of the Singer Girls

Loose lips might sink ships . . .

1942. Sixteen-year-old Poppy Percival arrives at the gates of Trout's clothing factory in Bethnal Green, ready to begin a new life as an East End seamstress. Forced to leave her quiet countryside home, and banished to a war-ravaged London, Poppy harbours a dark secret – one that tore her away from all she knew.

By day, the East End women of Trout's play their part in the war effort, stitching bandages and repairing uniforms for troops on the front line. But Poppy's new friends at the factory are hiding some painful truths. Vera, the salt-of-the-earth forelady, has had a hard life, with scars both visible and concealed. Vera's glamorous younger sister Daisy has romantic notions that could get her into trouble; while Sal, a hardworking mother, worries about the safety of her two evacuated boys for good reason . . .

As the war throws their lives into turmoil, it will also bring the Singer Girls closer than they could ever have imagined.

It's time to relax with your next good book

THEWINDOWSEAT.CO.UK

If you've enjoyed this book, but don't know what to read next, then we can help. The Window Seat is a site that's all about making it easier to discover your next good book. We feature recommendations, behind-the-scenes tales from the world of publishing, creative writing tips, competitions, and, if we're honest, quite a lot of lists based on our favourite reads.

You'll find stories and features by authors including Lucinda Riley, Karen Swan, Diane Chamberlain, Jane Green, Lucy Diamond and many more. We showcase brand-new talent as well as classic favourites, so you'll never be stuck for what to read again.

We'd love to know what you think of the site, our books, and what you'd like us to feature, so do let us know.

 @panmacmillan.com

 facebook.com/panmacmillan

WWW.THEWINDOWSEAT.CO.UK